For all those who take a stand against abuse.

The Doll Maker

By

L. E. Gay

"The hottest places in hell are reserved for those who,

in times of great moral crisis, maintain their neutrality."

- Dante

CHAPTER ONE

The rain was unrelenting. Heavy sheets fell onto the windshield of the small sedan as the wind whipped it back and forth across the glass in a hypnotic, snake-like dance. The wipers beat out a slow and steady rhythm like ancient tribal drums crying out to their gods. As if in response, thunder rolled menacingly in the distance while flashes of lightning illuminated the urban terrain. The rain poured steadily through the beams of the headlights as the car crept along the narrow street. Loose gravel crunched under the weight of the tires. The sound was familiar and strangely comforting.

The trip had been long and Nalia was exhausted, but the adrenaline surging through her body would not allow her to relax. Her knuckles were white against the steering wheel, and her mind was racing at a full sprint from one unconnected thought to the next. Nalia could not remember most of the drive. She could recall bits and pieces, when she concentrated, but she had, for the most part, been on autopilot since leaving the campus several hours ago. Fragments of moving pictures flashed through her mind like the lightning in the night sky – images for which she had no memory, but were somehow a part of her. Anxiety caused her heart to race while her breathing became shallow and ragged. Tears soaked her cheeks like the rain on the windows, but despite the length of the trip, she was no closer to discovering why she was crying. The events of the evening had been truly terrifying, but they were mere ripples on the surface of a very dark lake. Something much larger lurked beneath the waters. There was so much Nalia did not understand. She had so many questions.

Scenes from earlier in the evening played over again in her mind. What went so wrong? Marcus was always such a good friend, kind and caring. She never expected to see him like she had tonight. They met nearly three months ago in one of the common rooms at the college. He attended Nalia's theology study group with some mutual friends. His eyes were the first thing that caught her attention. They were bright green with a certain softness that seemed warm and trusting. Growing up, Nalia had been taught that a person's eyes could tell you everything about them. She never questioned that until tonight.

Over the last few months, Nalia and Marcus often enjoyed each other's company, but always with friends and in a group. Marcus was witty, quipping clever comments with a regularity that drew others in. He was fun and charming, frequently bringing spirited laughter to the crowd. Over time, Marcus became a good friend, gaining Nalia's trust. She felt safe with him in the familiar company of their group. Tonight, however, was different. Tonight there were no other companions, no buffers. For the first time since they met, there was no one else present to divert from awkward moments or knowing glances. It was what they were calling their first "official" date, and despite their familiarity, everything felt new.

Nalia scolded herself for being nervous. "There is no reason for it," she said quietly, re-touching her make-up in the mirror. "You've known him for months." Despite her best efforts, the butterflies in her stomach fluttered on, but there was still a tiny voice in the back of her mind. Apart from the obvious, something had been gnawing at Nalia since the beginning of the evening. There was something unsettling she could not quite put her finger on, like a whisper just beyond clarity.

Marcus picked her up punctually as promised. He wore familiar jeans and a red and navy sports shirt, one step up from his usual V-neck tee. His dark hair was slightly mussed as always, just the way he liked it, and the small tuft of beard under his lip finally looked like more than an oversight. His sunglasses rested on top of his head, and he smelled of Calvin Klein cologne. Marcus was the first white boy Nalia ever dated. She was always drawn to young, African-American men before, not because of their skin tone, but because she seemed to have more culturally in common with them having been raised by a black woman in the heart of New Orleans. Nalia was what folks called a quadroon or three-quarter white. She had light almond skin and dark brown hair. She heard older women say she could pass for white but she had striking facial features that left no doubt to some African heritage. She was slender and athletic, slightly taller than most of her friends and generally high spirited. She and Marcus were very much alike in that respect.

He picked the restaurant. It was a small seafood place on the outskirts of downtown called The Half-Shell. He was decidedly courteous, opening doors and even drawing out Nalia's chair when they reached their table. She poked fun at his "old-school southern manners", but deep down it made her feel special and she liked that.

With its abundance of knotty wood and neon light, The Half-Shell's décor lent itself to popular roadhouse ambiance. It was not exactly what Nalia thought of as a "first date" kind of place, but that mattered little to her. Folks did not come here for the atmosphere; they came for the crabs and the crawfish – all but Nalia who was having the beef. She was not about to order étouffée anywhere but back home. Still, The Half-Shell did have a degree of rustic charm, and besides, she was not expecting anything fancy. Nalia knew Marcus did not come from money and neither did she. While she enjoyed a certain degree of independence afforded her by an adequate college fund, Nalia was leagues away from high society. She came from a family where needs were met, but indulgences were viewed as unnecessary. While her background disqualified her from certain social cliques, Nalia generally had no regrets. She was brought up around plenty of down-to-earth "good people", and the one sitting across the table suited her just fine.

One of Marcus' quick-witted comments made Nalia smile, and she found herself blushing, gazing dreamily into his eyes. She could get lost in those sparkling green pools for days on end, she thought. Was this what was so uncomfortable? Was she falling for Marcus? Was she actually falling for her friend?

After dinner, Marcus drove them to a small club not far from the restaurant. It was the closest thing to a New Orleans jazz club the city had to offer. Mojo's was a dimly lit one room bar with tables in the center and high booths along the walls. At the far end was a small stage where live music, usually jazz, was featured nearly every night. Marcus was acquainted with Mojo's and knew there was something at the club Nalia would appreciate; it stood in the back corner opposite the stage. It was a vintage jukebox that played vinyl forty-fives. The club used it as filler when bands took breaks, and on nights when no live entertainment was booked. It was the only one of its kind Marcus had ever seen outside of the movies, and he knew Nalia would love it. She was a vinyl collector. "Everything sounds better on vinyl, especially jazz," he'd heard her say. "It sounds raw and real, the way it should."

Marcus led Nalia to a booth beside the jukebox so they would be near it when the band left the stage. He was right about Nalia loving the classic piece, but was disappointed by her lack of fascination. "There are a couple of shops down in the Quarter that still have these," she explained. "But it was a nice surprise."

"I've got a better one." Marcus said slyly as he slid from the booth and walked to the bar. As Nalia sipped her cocktail, she could see Marcus chatting with the elderly black barkeep. The gentleman was the owner of the club. He bought and sold old, vinyl albums and jazz memorabilia as a hobby. Marcus spoke with him beforehand and made arrangements for something special. He returned to the booth with a thin square package wrapped in brown paper.

"This is for you," he said, trying to conquer his cocky smirk with an unassuming smile. "The owner has been holding it for me for a couple of weeks. Open it."

Nalia removed the wrapper to reveal a very old vinyl record. It was an original pressing of Duke Ellington's *Great Times!* Her mouth hung open as she looked up at Marcus, leaving her eyes to do the smiling. "Man, this guy is doing everything right," she thought. "I could get used to this." When Marcus' eyes met hers, they were both aware their relationship was on the verge of a new plateau.

Nalia's beaming smile lasted throughout the evening, and when Marcus drove her home, she invited him inside. Her roommate was gone for the night which, while unplanned, was a welcomed absence. Nalia wasted no time in taking the top off her vintage phonograph and sliding Duke Ellington from his jacket. She felt a tingle of excitement when the needle dropped and she heard the soft pop and crackle of the record's edge. God, she loved that sound. "You know, 'In A Blue Summer Garden' is my absolute favorite," she said, biting her lip. As the sounds of the piano poured from the speakers Nalia began to sway back and forth, her hands unknowingly caressing the edges of the record player.

The sensuality of the moment was not lost on Marcus who admired her swaying hips from across the room. When Nalia turned to offer him a beer, she nearly caught his jaw dropping. He hoped she did not notice the slight stammer in his voice when he accepted. Together, they sat on the sofa drinking, listening, and apprehensively avoiding what they both knew was coming. Soon, the mood could no longer be denied, and casual contact conquered temptation. As their bottles grew shallow, so did their reservations.

Then it happened. Something in Nalia's mind turned on like a light switch. It was familiar yet distant, but it was drawing closer and gaining speed. It was dark and unpleasant. Her stomach turned sour in an instant. She began resisting Marcus' advances, but he persisted. She said no, but he didn't listen. She pulled herself from him, but his hand found the hair at the nape of her neck, and he gripped it firmly. His other hand slid up her thigh and pushed up her skirt. Fire danced wildly in his eyes. She could smell his arousal thick on the air with the lingering stench of alcohol. She heard a voice telling her to be still, but it wasn't Marcus'. A vein in the back of her neck seared like a hot ember. As Marcus' wandering hand reached its destination, a floodgate opened in the back of Nalia's mind and terror came flowing forth like a raging river. Flashes of light and shadow, over and over again. She tried to scream but the sound caught in her throat like sand. She could not breathe, she could not speak, she could not move. Gripped with fear, Nalia's vision went dark, and she felt a cold sickening presence wash over her like ice water. Her body went numb, and her mind fell into shadow.

———————

A flash of lightning shattered the night sky as a crack of thunder startled Nalia back to coherence. She was still crying and shaking when she noticed the car was stopped though she could not recall parking it. She didn't know how long she had been there, but the rain was subsiding. Looking out the window, she could make out the wrought iron fence that bordered the back yard. She looked past the tears and through the remnants of the storm to see the old house. As she relinquished her grip on the steering wheel, she noticed a light burning in the kitchen. Though the clock on the dash told her it was three nineteen a.m., she was not surprised to see the welcoming glow in the window. Mama Lucia always had a way of knowing when Nalia was coming home. She had a way of knowing lots of things. Nalia's body finally breathed a sheltered sigh of relief, but her mind raced on. She had so many questions.

As she climbed out of the car, the smell of rain and magnolias filled her senses. It was the smell of home, and it calmed her mind. The tension paining her neck and shoulders gradually began to release. As she ambled up the walk she heard the crickets singing. They seemed to be chanting... *You is home, you is home. Mama Lu gon' put it right.*

The old familiar boards creaked as she stepped up onto the porch. Nalia still remembered each one's unique sound. Through the screen, she could see the back door had been left ajar for her. For living only four hours away, Nalia was suddenly very aware of how infrequently she came home to visit. A wave of guilt flushed her face that she knew Mama Lu would scold her for entertaining.

"Come on in chil', I been waitin' up fo' you," called Mama Lucia from inside the house. Nalia didn't hesitate.

Mama Lu was sitting at the kitchen table with a cold cup of chicory coffee and a small twisted root which she turned over and over in her right hand. She rose and embraced Nalia with the warmest of hugs as the girl she raised from a small child all but collapsed in her arms and began to sob once again. Nalia did not say a word, nor did she need to. Mama Lu held her tight, stroked her rain-soaked hair and let her cry. When Nalia was finally able to lift her head, she tried to speak but Mama Lu touched a finger to her lips. "Hush chil'. Ain't no sense speakin' 'bout not'in tonight. Yo' bed is turned down fo' you. Off you go up dem stairs and take you some rest. We'll talk tomorrow." She turned the root over again in her hand and rubbed it with her thumb. "Me an' ol' Johnny gon' be up a bit longer. We gots a lil' work left to do."

With that, Nalia nodded silently and climbed the stairs, drying her cheeks as she went. Mama Lu sat back down at the table and resumed turning the twisted root over and over in her hand, rubbing it with her thumb as she sang in an old Creole dialect... *Peace gon' come. Peace gon' come. Darkness flee and peace gon' come.*

CHAPTER TWO

The marks were still on the door facing. The house had been painted several times over the years, but the entrance to Nalia's room had not been touched. Mama Lu would never allow it. Nalia let her hand glide gently over the markings. It was always a birthday tradition with Mama Lu to mark Nalia's height with a line on the door frame just after the cake was cut. Memories of birthday parties and colorful hats filled Nalia's mind as she touched each mark. She could still see the camera flashes illuminating balloons, confetti, and streamers as people sang and candles were extinguished by the wishes of an eager, young girl. As Nalia ran her fingers up the jamb, she could envision herself growing up again with each passing line. She wondered how often Mama Lu had done the same.

As her hand reached the top, she noticed different dates written beside the lines that marked ages sixteen and seventeen. She remembered those marks were not drawn on her birthday, but several days later. It was during this time Nalia decided she was too old for silly family celebrations, opting instead to spend her birthdays with her friends. For some reason, tonight, family gatherings did not seem quite so childish. A notion brought on, perhaps, by the absence of marks eighteen, nineteen, and twenty.

She leaned against the wall and allowed her hand to trace back down toward her childhood years, all the way to the lowest number, seven. This was the first birthday Nalia spent with Mama Lu. Below seven, the wall was blank. There were no marks, no dates, and very few memories. Though she still had a vague recollection of her real mother, it was not much more than an idea. In truth, it was a formless image created over time of what she thought her mother must have been like. The actual memories were long gone. She was very young when her mother left, and since she never knew her father, Mama Lu was the only "family" Nalia ever had. She had so many questions.

The door to her room still featured the large glass doorknobs Nalia remembered from her early years. During her childhood, she pretended they were the world's largest diamonds. As she turned the knob and opened the door, Nalia could smell fresh linens and lavender candles. The warm glow of candlelight spilled into the hallway inviting her in, and welcoming her home. The room was exactly the way she left it. Against the far wall was her large four-poster bed made of dark cherry wood. It still had the same lacy pillow shams and ivory duvet. They had been hers before she left for college. They were still hers, she supposed. Her vanity was still in the same place, with its high-back cushioned chair and large oval mirror. On top sat her porcelain jewelry box and polished silver hair brush, as if she just put them there yesterday.

Nalia walked to the vanity and picked up the brush, turning it loosely in her hands. It was a gift for her twelfth birthday from a close friend of Mama Lu, an older woman they called Madame Toulouse. She was a dear, sweet lady who visited often and was quite fond of Nalia. In fact, Madame Toulouse was like a grandmother to her – the only grandmother Nalia had ever known. The brush always had its own special place atop the vanity.

The vanity itself was also a gift that same year. It was hand crafted by Mr. John Barrett, a long time friend and neighbor. Mr. John owned the shoe-shine stand outside Mama Lucia's shop on Decater Street. He worked there in the mornings, mostly for the pleasure of talking with people who enjoyed the nostalgia of getting their shoes shined. As a result, he not only knew nearly everyone in the neighborhood, but he also kept tabs on all the latest "goings on". Mr. John did not like the word gossip. That expression was reserved for the kind of talk carried on by women folk in their beauty parlors and nail salons. Men on the street simply stopped by for a friendly chat.

Mr. John could frequently be found at Mama Lu's shop helping out with this or that, but his real trade was woodworking. He mostly restored and sold antique furniture, but he built many pieces as well. In fact, all the furniture in Nalia's bedroom was crafted by Mr. John.

Nalia remembered lying in bed as a child looking up at the carving on the headboard. The bed was made for her when she was six. Mr. John knew Nalia loved animals so he carved the relief of a circus train into the wood. He positioned the carving just above where the pillows rested so it looked as if the train was riding along the clouds.

The same pattern was carved into the trim on top of the dresser which still stood against the wall opposite the bed. Mr. John trimmed the piece with a carved, raised edge to accommodate Nalia's dolls. He knew she would grow to have a fine doll collection. How could she not? She had been taken to raise by Mama Lu.

Mama Lucia Deminy was known in many parts of the world for her finely detailed, handcrafted dolls. Her work was displayed in churches, cathedrals and basilicas all over the United States and in Italy. She had been commissioned twice by the Vatican – once to craft an image of St. Paul, and again for a replication of St. Mary Magdalene. She was generally considered to be one of the finest porcelain crafters in the world, a silent celebrity here in New Orleans. She had perfected techniques for casting porcelain feather thin, yet hard and strong. Her work, generally religious in nature, centered around the Catholic faith. Her shop sold rosaries, crucifixes and other religious articles, but the draw had always been her dolls. The small boutique was filled with the finest, most touchingly realistic works of porcelain and silk. Each one was handcrafted in painstaking detail. Their faces wore expressions that told grand stories and their eyes were mirrors of humanity. Most, but not all of the dolls in Mama Lucia's shop were cast in the likeness of Catholic saints. Some were even bejeweled with precious metals and gems. Each one was sold with documents of authenticity and carried a very hefty price tag. The most valuable dolls were kept in large, ornate glass cases and removed only for sale. Mama Lucia's dolls were typically not intended to be playthings for young children, but she made a few special ones for Nalia over the years. One of these still stood on top of the dresser.

Nalia carried the silver brush over to the dresser and stared into the eyes of the doll as she had so many times before. This doll had been with her for a very long time. She was tall, nearly two feet, wearing a beautifully tailored red dress and a red velvet hat with white lace. She had dark hair and light brown skin and her eyes were clear, like glass. She wore gold jewelry on her fingers and ears, with a tiny locket around her neck. She was smiling, but there was a small tear in her eye. Her name was Mary, and she was made in the likeness of Nalia's mother.

A friend of Mama Lu and frequent patron of her shop, Margaret Décantrel abandoned Nalia when she was six years old. She brought Nalia to Mama Lu in the dead of night one brisk October evening, and took leave while she slept. Nalia awoke the next morning to find Mama Lu and Mr. John alone at the kitchen table. Her mother was nowhere to be found. Mama Lu explained that there had been some trouble, of what sort she was not sure, and her mother had to leave. She felt it was not safe for Nalia to come along, and left her in the care of Mama Lu. Even though Mama Lu knew in her heart it was unlikely, she consoled the child by saying her mother planned to return for her some day. The years had proven her heart to be right.

Several weeks later, Mama Lu crafted Mary in the stunning likeness of Nalia's mother and presented her with the doll to help assuage her sadness. Mama Lu explained that the tear in the doll's eye was for her mother's grief at leaving Nalia behind. The smile was because she knew Nalia would be happy and safe with Mama Lu. "Mary is here so you will never forget yo' mother chil'…so none of us will ever forget," Mama Lu told her.

The doll became a source of comfort for Nalia, and in later years, a source of anger. Now it was just a reminder of unanswered questions. Her face appeared less vibrant than it had in Nalia's youth. Perhaps Nalia saw her differently now that she had given up hope of her mother's return. "How could she?" she asked herself as the tears began to flow again.

In an attempt to redirect her mind, Nalia turned her back on the doll and crossed the room, admiring the carving of the circus train on the headboard. She smiled when she thought of Mr. John. As early as she could remember, Mr. John was always there to comfort her when she was sad. When she couldn't sleep, he would bring his guitar and sit right on the end of her big bed. He would play and sing his old Creole melodies and soon her eyes would peacefully close. If she closed them now she could almost hear him playing and smell the aroma of his pipe tobacco. He was the closest thing to a father she ever knew. She loved Mr. John, and he loved her back just as much. To hear him talk, one would believe Nalia was his own flesh and blood, the daughter he never had.

She ran her fingers across the raised relief. The animals on the circus train were just as she remembered. The lion and the zebra were tucked safely in their cages. The giraffe poked his head out of the top of his car. The monkey swung playfully from the caboose, and the

14

great smiling snake with the conductor's hat drove the engine. They steamed across the pillows toward the bedside table. Each animal's color had faded over the years but they were still vibrant in Nalia's mind. They helped make the tears go away.

On the night stand, Nalia saw a tall glass of water and a saucer with two aspirin. At the foot of the bed was a large tee-shirt, folded and waiting. Nalia was never one for nightgowns or pajamas, opting always for an oversized tee as her preferred sleepwear. Looking around the room, she could not help but notice all the little things that were done in preparation for her arrival. Mama Lu's attention to detail was even more amazing than her intuition. The fact that Mama Lu knew she was coming was no surprise. What did surprise Nalia was the feeling in the pit of her stomach. She felt like a guest.

It was her own fault, she supposed. That wicked feeling of shame was coming over her again. Maybe she should have come home for more than the occasional holiday, or called more often to keep in touch. This year, she had not even come home for Mardi Gras. Everyone needed to find their independence but Nalia's had come at the price of disconnection. It was a meaningless, self-imposed exile. She tried to put aside the unrelenting feelings of guilt as she observed the room once more. It was obvious Mama Lu still considered this Nalia's home; maybe she should too.

As she placed the brush back on the vanity, Nalia caught a glimpse of herself in the mirror. She hardly recognized her own face. Exhausted and confused, she sat down on the chair and studied her reflection. Her eyes were a mess of mascara and grief. Her face was ashen, save for the blotches of red brought on by the crying. She ran the brush through her hair just enough to remove most of the tangles and the excess moisture. Deciding that was enough, Nalia readied herself for bed.

She removed her wet clothes, deposited them into the woven basket by the door, and slipped into the waiting tee-shirt. The cotton was warm against her still-damp skin. She chased the aspirin with half a glass of water before extinguishing the candles and climbing into bed. As she slid between the fresh linens she thought nothing ever felt so good. It was like crawling inside a toasted marshmallow, warm and inviting. Nalia snuggled herself deep into the covers and hugged the big soft pillows. As she did, her arm brushed against something. She felt beneath the pillow until her hand found the small velvet bag. It was stitched together all around the edges. Nalia did not need to open it; she knew what she would find inside. There would be various herbs, some dried flower petals, certain roots that had been soaked in essential oils, feathers, small stones, and perhaps even a small piece of animal bone. She had seen Mama Lu and Mr. John make these bags many times before, and she knew they were placed beneath pillows for protection. What she didn't know was how much she would need it.

No sooner than sleep overtook her, Nalia's toes began to curl. The muscles in her feet tightened and her knees seemed to draw themselves up to her chest as if they were being chased. Her head moved uncontrollably from side to side, slow at first then faster until finally it came to rest with her chin pressing firmly against her collarbone. Her body went stiff as if trying to flex every muscle all at once. Her heart raced and the veins in her neck began to throb. Then everything went cold, like jumping feet first into a frozen lake, in slow motion. The icy sensation began in her toes then crept up her rigid body. Terror gripped Nalia as she heard the sound of scraping and creaking so loud it pierced her brain like needles. A chilling darkness rose in the distance and from it, the beast, having lain dormant for thirteen years, crawled once again to the foot of her bed. It was fiendish and raw with glowing green eyes. It sank a claw into her calf, ripping the muscle to the bone. Its other claw swung quickly and found her thigh, tearing as it pulled its way up her body. Nalia could not breathe. The beast had come to devour her flesh, and as it inched closer, she could smell its breath strong with gasoline. Frigid air filled her lungs as Nalia finally drew a fleeting ragged breath.

She sat bolt upright in the middle of the four-poster bed. Her scream was heard across the street.

CHAPTER THREE

"Twenty-three minutes", Mr. John calculated, studying his pocket watch. For the past several hours, he sat in the bay door of his workshop watching the house across the road. He was accompanied by an old box guitar and a hand carved maple pipe which currently emitted a sweet smelling smoke that circled his head. A look of worry filled his eyes.

Mr. John was in his late fifties but still fit for his age, the product of a life of hard work. He was a broad shouldered black man with a firm, square jaw and an easy disposition. He was usually in bed long before now, but tonight he couldn't sleep. His heart was breaking for the young girl in the upstairs room across the way. Mama Lu had warned him about tonight, and he knew he could not interfere, so he watched and waited. He rocked slowly back and forth in his great high-backed rocking chair. He built the chair himself and custom fit it with unusually short arm rests which allowed him to comfortably play his guitar. The guitar soothed his mind and he needed that tonight. He had been on edge for two days, ever since Mama Lu told him that Nalia would be coming home. News of Nalia visiting was usually met with celebration, but not this time. Mama Lu warned him that something dark was on the horizon. Mr. John had his share of intuition but he didn't have "the sight" like Mama Lu, so he had learned to heed her warnings. She was usually right, and tonight was no exception. The darkness was no longer on the horizon; it was here.

As soon as he heard the scream, Mr. John knew the nightmares were back. He had noted the time when the light went out in the upper room and again when he heard the shout. Twenty-three minutes was surprisingly fast. The piercing scream released a torrent of harsh memories. The cries of a six-year-old girl were permanently etched into his mind so that he would never be able to forget. Every single night for nearly a year, terror haunted and tortured the child. Mr. John and Mama Lu finally managed to put the nightmares to rest but knew they were not gone forever and were bound to return some day. Defeating the visions was a long-fought, nasty battle, but through it they learned love and patience can work better magic than even the most powerful mojo.

Mr. John watched for the light in the window as he continued to puff on his pipe. His own special blend of perique tobacco, cloves, and mint leaves made a thick aroma that filled his workshop. Lightning flashed in the distant sky. The rain had slowed to a drizzle and the thunder was now barely audible, but the wind still whistled steadily through the trees. Through it all, Mr. John's eyes never left the window.

What was less than a minute seemed to take an eternity, but the light finally flickered on and a faint shadow quickly crossed the room. Mr. John wondered what kind of scene Mama Lu was walking into. How bad would it be tonight? He wanted to go and check on Nalia, to comfort her, but Mama Lu had asked him to keep his distance for tonight. "Patience," he thought, "You gots to trus' her." He kept his eyes trained on the window watching for shadows. Thankfully, he saw no more and that was good. Fewer shadows meant less commotion. The fallout was obviously mild tonight. It wasn't always so.

Mr. John recalled one night when things got particularly nasty. He and Mama Lu were sitting in her parlor as they often did after Nalia went to bed. They were not as anxious as usual due to a declination in the frequency of Nalia's dreams. Several nights of uninterrupted sleep gave them hope the nightmares had taken leave for good. Mr. John sat down beside Mama Lu on the divan. It had been quite a long time since the trouble with Nalia afforded them the opportunity to be close under amorous conditions. Tonight, their minds were on each other. Mr. John reached over and touched Mama Lu's hand with the spark of curiosity she missed so much. But as he leaned in to kiss her, the veil of silence was ripped in two by a shriek that could rival a banshee.

Mr. John made it to the top of the stairs first, but he waited for Mama Lu to open the door. He was never to go in first, Mama Lu had instructed. She was only seconds behind him. She quickly opened the door and darted inside with Mr. John following close behind. He was not prepared for what he saw when Mama Lu turned on the light.

Nalia was not in bed as usual, but instead on the floor in the corner of the room. Her knees were pulled up to her chin. One arm was wrapped tightly around her legs, while the other covered her head as if shielding her body from an unseen attacker. She was so tiny to be so terrified. When she saw the light, she cowered even more. Gazing up at Mama Lu and Mr. John with sheer terror in her eyes, Nalia began to shout, "No! No! No!"

Her feet gripped the floor and her leg muscles tensed. She pushed herself backwards as if trying to break through the wall behind her. With eyes like saucers, Nalia flailed in desperation as the two adults crossed the room. Screaming and crying, she pushed her face hard against the wall and sobbed, "Don't touch me! Don't touch me! Stop it! No!"

Realizing Nalia was still in the dream, Mama Lu cautioned Mr. John to keep his distance. As the child turned her head from side to side, they saw blood flowing down the edge of her face. A large section of hair and small pieces of scalp were missing over her left ear. The shouting persisted as Nalia continued to push herself into the wall. Over and over, with increasing strength, she slammed her body against the hard surface, but soon her heels began to slip. A pool of blood was collecting on the floor. As she turned to the side Mr. John saw the source. There were deep cuts on her right leg, stretching from mid-calf to well above the knee, and they were bleeding heavily. The cuts were not smooth, but jagged, like the skin had been torn away. The four bloody, parallel gashes resembled claw marks.

Suddenly the screaming stopped, but the sobbing continued, "Don't please, don't." Nalia's eyes widened even more unnaturally than before. She was looking straight through Mama Lu, as if in a trance. Her body began to tremble and she slammed both fists down hard on the floor at her sides. With a single, forceful thrust, the back of her head slammed hard into the corner as her eyes rolled into her skull. On impact, her muscles went limp and she slid, slowly down the wall until all but her head rested flat in the pooling blood. Her neck was wrenched in a twisted position with the base of her skull pressed firmly against the wall.

Motionless, the little girl lay there in a helpless pile. Her expression was lifeless, but her eyes said there was a terrified child inside begging for help, unable to speak. She did not appear to be breathing. The horrifying sight sent chills up Mr. John's spine. Then, he saw the tears still pouring down her quivering cheek. "The dead don't cry," he told himself, breathing a sigh of relief.

Finally there was a stifled gasp, like Nalia tried to draw in all the air from the room, but her tiny lungs spat it back out. Mama Lu reached out for her baby's arm. When she did, Nalia sat straight up and screamed once again at the top of her lungs. Then it was over.

It took a few frightened seconds for Nalia to regain coherency but she finally looked up with recognition. Wrapping her arms tightly around Mama Lu's neck, Nalia squeezed hard. Mama Lu held her as Mr. John stroked her hair. "You' bleedin' chil'," said Mama Lu, "What happened?"

"The monster got me," Nalia replied still sobbing quietly through quickened breaths. Mr. John knew the child believed what she was saying, but her tiny fist still clutched a handful of blood-soaked hair. He could also see bits of flesh under the fingernails of her right hand where she had injured her leg. Mama Lu held her tight and rocked back and forth while Mr. John went downstairs for bandages.

————————

Pulling the pipe from his teeth, Mr. John blew a thick plume of fragrant smoke into the air. There were many nights where similar events occurred, but that one was the worst he could recall. The lack of stirring shadows in the upstairs window told him tonight's episode was not nearly so bad. There was no doubt, however, that across the street, a six-year-old girl locked inside Nalia's mind was once again in the arms of her Mama Lu. He stared up at the window wondering what would happen now. Could they make the dreams go away again? What would happen if Nalia found out the truth about who she was?

He placed the pipe in the corner of his mouth and gently plucked the strings of his old guitar as he softly mumbled the song sung on so many nights long ago… *Peace gon' come. Peace gon' come. Darkness flee and peace gon' come.*

CHAPTER FOUR

The first rays of sunlight were long gone by the time the pounding in her head roused Nalia from slumber. She attempted to block out the midmorning rays by covering her head with one of the oversized pillows, but it was no use. The pillow only made her headache worse. Reluctantly, she removed it and slowly cracked open her eyes. As light flooded her pupils, pain seared her forehead. Pressure from all sides closed in like a vice as she tried to sit up. She made it to one elbow but could go no further.

The pain was intense and her vision was still a blur, but she noticed the scent of mint lingering in the air. It was only then she recalled what awakened her. It was not the throbbing pressure in her skull, but the metallic sound of a doorknob clicking in the latch. Her head was still foggy, but it did not take long to realize Mama Lu had been in to check on her and left something on the bedside table. Still battling her heavy eyelids, Nalia looked to the nightstand and saw a thin china cup filled with steaming tea. She leaned over it and breathed deeply, her senses analyzing the aroma. She could smell spearmint, jasmine, and at least one other ingredient she did not recognize. The fragrant steam boosted her will power and she sat up, gathering the sheets around her.

When she reached for the cup, Nalia was surprised by the weakness in her arms. As an avid swimmer, she was not used to finding her body in a weakened state. Then again, her body was not used to experiencing the kind of trauma it endured last night – at least not anymore.

An image from the nightmare flashed across her mind. The memory of the green-eyed beast with the acrid breath turned her stomach. She could sense the child inside her withdraw and cower. Confusion filled her mind. It had been ages since she was plagued by the vile recurring dreams, but last night made it seem as if they had never stopped. Fleeting memories raced through her mind like pages of a magazine being flipped, but not read. The fragmented images moved in and out of focus as she tried in vain to dwell on them, even for a second.

She could recall having the nightmares as a child, but time had softened the edges of reality. Up until now it was as if the experience happened to someone else – like looking through old, black-and-white photos. Last night changed all that. She was no longer on the outside looking in; she was re-living it all in vivid color.

Her fingers fumbled for the cup and finally found the handle. As she carefully sipped the steaming brew, she could taste honey and lemon. She remembered the flavor well. Mama Lu had made this same tea for her many times before. The pressure in her head lessened as she drank, and Nalia was grateful for the relief. Mama Lu was good, she thought. She sat back against the headboard holding the cup with both hands, allowing it to warm her palms while she mentally assessed her body. She ached all over, but some spots were more tender than others. The nape of her neck was especially sore and stiff. She massaged it with the palm of her hand, allowing the heat from the cup to soothe the muscles. She leaned forward and stretched her neck from side to side as she rubbed. The massage helped, but the tea seemed to alleviate the tension more than anything. After consuming a goodly portion, her head felt almost normal.

She set the cup back down on the bedside table and convinced herself to get up. Throwing back the covers, Nalia eased her legs over the side of the mattress. She was alarmed by the dizziness that hit her when she moved and decided to give her mind time to right itself before she attempted to stand. Despite the comfort of the bed, the strain on her muscles had been too much. She placed both hands in the small of her back and stretched. Arching her spine, she swung her shoulders from left to right while twisting her neck in the opposite direction. As she did, she could feel her back and neck crack, easing her headache even more.

Nalia breathed deeply, taking in all the smells of home. As she stood, the vertigo overtook her again. It lasted only a moment, but long enough for Nalia to question her ability to walk. She loathed the feeling of helplessness brought on by her loss of balance.

Finally steady, she picked up the cup containing the last bit of tea and walked carefully across the room to the vanity. She sat down in the cushioned chair and studied her reflection once again. She did not see the same person she saw in her bathroom mirror the previous morning. Yesterday, her mirror showed a strong young woman, bright and energetic, on the verge of being in love. Today she saw a victim.

The tenderness at the base of her neck brought back memories of Marcus. She recalled the force with which he held her down. Nalia considered herself to be a tough woman and did not deal well with feelings of vulnerability. She felt ill. Her breathing quickened as she thought about the young man who had been so kind and caring. She would miss that side of Marcus.

Her sorrow quickly soured as she remembered how he so readily betrayed her trust. In an instant of animal aggression, he destroyed the relationship that had grown so organically over their time together. She now knew what kind of person he was at heart, and there was no changing that. She felt violated physically and emotionally. She recoiled in disgust each time she thought of his advances, but what bothered her most, was her inability to understand her body's reaction. It was as if her mind had begged her body not to fight. She recalled the fear that surged through every inch of her as Marcus forced his hand between her thighs. It was crippling. Nothing had ever immobilized her that way before - had it? Nalia shuddered as her body felt a memory her mind did not possess. Had her mind betrayed her like Marcus?

A reflection in the mirror drew Nalia's attention away from the questions berating her brain. It was a familiar, odd little shape on the windowsill behind her. It was Benjamin.

Nalia's room was still decorated with many of the dolls that shared her childhood. A large wood and glass hutch in the corner housed an extensive collection of porcelain figures, and the great continuous shelf that encircled the top of the room was stacked with more of Mama Lu's creations. The favorites, however, had their own special places. Benjamin's spot was the windowsill. He was the most unique of all the dolls in Nalia's room because he had not been made by Mama Lu and was not really a doll at all. Benjamin was more of a puppet – a kind of marionette without strings. He sat in the window looking out across the lawn, keeping an eye on his creator. Mr. John made Benjamin for Nalia when she was eight years old. It was his attempt to show Mama Lu that he could make dolls for Nalia, as well. Benjamin was hand-carved out of teak: approximately eight inches tall, flexible, and held together with copper wire. He had blue eyes, a red mouth and a small bump for his nose. He was rudimentary in form, not at all the fine quality of Mr. John's furniture, but not bad for a first attempt. Regardless of his simplicity, Nalia loved him dearly, for she loved his maker.

Benjamin was one of the few dolls that had held the honor of sleeping on Nalia's pillow on occasions when she was sick. He kept her company along with the other elite. There was Queen Marie, Nalia's first ever Mama Lu doll, and Myra, who bore a remarkable resemblance to Nalia as a child. Then there was Emily, a ruggedly constructed rag doll sewn by Mama Lu for the express purpose of being toted anywhere, and everywhere. These favored dolls were piled into Nalia's bed during times of weathering colds and flu, when Mama Lu would serve her spicy cure-all chicken gumbo. Together, Mama Lu and Nalia would take turns reading to the dolls, helping the dreary days of illness pass more quickly.

Each of these dolls had its own special place now. In addition to Benjamin on the windowsill, Queen Marie sat atop the headboard, while Myra rested on a small oval shaped stand near the vanity. Mary, the likeness of Nalia's mother, was the overseer of them all from her position atop the dresser. Emily was the only one of the group who no longer resided in the bedroom. When she was there, her place had been on the pillow, but Emily was the one doll Nalia had taken with her to college. She was currently on the bed in her campus apartment. Looking around at these dolls, and the ones on the upper shelf, brought back so many memories.

The figurines in the hutch had their own special memories as well. Each one was made by Mama Lu to commemorate a special occasion such as a birthday or holiday. Although a few slipped her mind, Nalia still remembered the events attached to most of them. Like memories, they were delicate, and as such, well protected in their glass case.

The top of the hutch, however, was home to a different type of doll entirely. Several small rag dolls sat here, different in appearance, by far, from the fine porcelain inside the cabinet. These were rustic, hand-stitched poppets made of burlap and filled with sawdust. They did not wear finely tailored clothes as the other dolls did, but bits of fabric haphazardly pinned to their bodies. Some had small buttons sewn in for eyes while others had faces that were drawn or painted. Some featured bits of wood or leather and some had pieces of jewelry attached.

These were the kind of dolls sold as novelties in the trinket shops and tourist traps off Bourbon Street. They carried the heavy stigma of the voodoo doll, as popularized by Hollywood, but were rarely taken seriously. Visitors to New Orleans would stop in to pick up a voodoo doll as a gag and pretend to torture their boss or their in-laws.

This same type of doll was sold in darkened parlors down on Rampart Street by hoodoo practitioners, with a more serious intent. With the aid of an article from the intended victim (hair, clothing, or even blood), the voodoo doll was used as a torture device to inflict pain upon or to control one's enemies. Instruments such as hat pins and candles were used to affect certain parts of the victim's body. In the right hands they were said to cause headaches, ulcers, broken bones, asphyxiation, and even death. At least, that was the claim.

Mama Lucia's elders came from Haiti where poppets, such as the ones in Nalia's room, had a different meaning entirely. There, it is believed that when a person dies, their soul has a continued existence in the spirit world. Poppets are messengers between the world of the living and the world of the dead. They are made in the image of those who have passed on, often bearing a piece of their clothing or shoes. They are made as a way to honor the dead and commune with them.

Nalia remembered celebrating the Day of the Dead with Mama Lu, Mr. John, and Madame Toulouse. Every year on the second of November, just after All Saints Day, they would gather together for food and festivities. They built altars and said prayers for those loved ones who had passed on. Candles were lit in their memory and poppets were placed on the altars, surrounded by marigolds and tarts made of spun sugar. Small bowls of water were placed before the poppets with hope the spirits of the departed would visit. When they did, their presence would be felt and sometimes heard. It was a time of remembrance, reflection, and celebration. It was a time to honor those who live on in the spirit world.

Nalia had not celebrated the Day of the Dead since moving away. In fact, she had not turned her mind toward the spirit world for quite some time.

As Nalia contemplated her departure from tradition, her attention was caught by a faint blue glow emanating from her bag beside the bed. It was her cell phone, the battery clinging to its last bit of life, announcing there was a voice message.

Mama Lu and Mr. John sat downstairs in the sun-lit kitchen studying their coffee, occasionally glancing up at one another but avoiding eye contact and conversation. The tension mounted with each passing moment.

"We gon' have to tell her dis time Lu," Mr. John finally said with a pleading stare. His eyes begged her to agree and his voice shook with a nervous quiver. His tone was guarded. He tried to hide it, but Mama Lu heard the accusation beneath the surface. She did not speak, but continued to stare at her coffee as if expecting it to answer.

"We gon' have to…"

His sentence was cut short by a scathing look finally fired in his direction. Mr. John twisted in his chair. "Shoulda tol' her the firs' time," he said under his breath, with a pensive bit of boldness.

"We did what we had to do," Mama Lu quipped with a finality that said she wanted no more discussion.

"I still think…"

"She was six years old, John!" Mama Lu interrupted. "She didn' need to know everythin'. We needed to make it go away, and we did. Simple as dat! Poor lil thing didn' need all dem mem'ries fillin' up her mind."

"Well, you made sure she wouldn' remember, now didn' you!" came Mr. John's reply, his anxiety building and his resolve growing stronger.

"Yes I did! An' I do it again if I have to. Don't act like you was innocent in all dis John. You had jus' as much a part in dis as I did. We done dis together, or has you forgotten?"

26

"But dat was den, Mama!" said Mr. John in a hushed shout as he slapped his hand down on the table. "We gon' have to tell her dis time," he pleaded, lowering his tone.

Mama Lu fought the tears hard, but lost out to one that escaped and trailed down her cheek. "Do you realize what dat's gon' do to dat girl John?" she said, wiping the tear away and fending off more. "What dat's gon' do to us?" Mama Lu sat in thought for a few moments. She considered the repercussions of telling Nalia about her past. How would she react? Surely the nightmares would get worse, violent even. What would she do when she found out what Mama Lu and Mr. John had done? Would she understand? Could she? After all, everything they did was for her protection. There were dangerous people involved. There was no guarantee they would have come looking for her, but there was no reason to believe they would not. But times were different now, thought Mama Lu. It was doubtful those people were still interested in Nalia. It had been so long, and so much had changed. Key players were long gone; they made sure of that.

Surely the physical threat was minimized, but the emotional risk was still very much present. What would happen when Nalia found out she wasn't who she thought she was? What kind of resentment would she hold for what they had done? Would she hate them?

Then there was the other matter: the one they had to keep guarded. It was the one secret Nalia could never know about – that no one could ever know about.

"Just how do you suggest we explain all dis, John?" Mama Lu asked in an exhausted whisper.

"We got to give dem mem'ries back."

"But we can't control it, John! We start doin' dat and there ain't no telling what's gon' come rushin' back to haunt dat girl. We can't let everythin' out, John. Dat's jus' cruelty, and I won't have it," said Mama Lu with as much authority as she could muster.

"Cruelty didn't stop you befo'," Mr. John replied looking at the floor.

Mama Lu's eyes burned with rage as she pointed a finger in John's face. "Dat woman deserved what she got, John! Still does!" she shouted unapologetically. "Dis is Nalia we talkin' 'bout. We can't put dat girl back through the hell she went through befo'."

"Then it ain't never gon' go away," said Mr. John. "You can't put somethin' livin' into a cage and not 'spect it to try and get free. It might lie still and quit tryin' for a while, but its gon' want out again. Dat's wha's happenin' now, and if we don' deal wit' it proper dis time, it ain't never gon' end."

Mama Lu thought about what it would be like for Nalia to re-live the most traumatic events of her life, events so horrifying they had been blocked out, or essentially erased. How would her mind react to the forgotten life hiding in the shadows? What toll would it take on her body? Then there was the process of giving the memories back to consider. It was not like they could just explain what happened; Nalia would never believe it. That was the nature of the magic that took the memories from her in the first place. No, she would have to be shown, and that meant re-living the emotions. It would be most unpleasant, indeed.

"The shock could kill her, John." Mama Lu said quietly with a rare tone of vulnerability. She had given up the fight and the tears were flowing freely now.

"We not gon' let dat happen," Mr. John reassured as he reached for her hand. "We got to undo dis, Mama."

As he looked into her eyes, movement in the background caught his attention, and a chill went through his body. Nalia was standing at the top of the stairs.

CHAPTER FIVE

Mr. John froze. Every muscle in his body stiffened with panic. He was undeniably aware his face bore the expression of a cornered animal, but he was powerless to change it. Every thought escaped his consciousness, save one – what had Nalia heard?

Having no idea when she appeared on the staircase, the thought that Nalia could have been standing there for the entire conversation paralyzed him. Would he and Mama Lucia now be forced to unravel the twisted knots tied into their lives by years of secrecy? It wasn't supposed to happen this way, he thought - not like this, not now. This house of cards had to be disassembled layer by layer, not leveled with a single push.

John tried to speak but could not form words. He tried to warn Mama Lu that Nalia was in the room but could only manage a dumbstruck stare. Mama Lu was puzzled by John's frozen gaze, but quickly recognized something was amiss. Anxiety mounted inside her as she spun around in her chair. Her fear was realized as her eyes met Nalia's. Her mouth hung slightly open and a thousand thoughts raced though her head all at once. Explanations, excuses, diversions, and even lies swarmed her brain like angry bees. What could she say to regain control of the situation if Nalia had overheard too much?

Mama Lu watched as Nalia slowly descended the staircase, still wearing the over-sized tee-shirt she slept in. For a moment, Mama Lu read Nalia's cautious steps as apprehension, but soon realized her slow pace was, instead, caused by distraction. Nalia's left hand was raised covering one ear and a faint blue glow illuminated her right cheek.

With a scowl she pulled the phone's earpiece from the side of her head and slammed it into her other hand. As she wrapped the wire around her phone in frustration she looked up to see the stunned faces of Mama Lu and Mr. John. Their blank stares took her by surprise. "What? Do I look that terrible?" she asked.

Relieved by Nalia's apparent inattention, Mr. John's distressed expression melted into a smile. More than a year had passed since his aging eyes beheld the face of the young woman he would forever call his baby girl. Her hair was still tussled from sleep and he could tell her eyes had still not fully embraced the morning, but to him, she was just as pretty as ever.

As he sat in his familiar chair watching Nalia descend the stairs, Mr. John smiled in remembrance of the many mornings spent in the very same spot when she was a child. He wondered how many times he had watched her come down for breakfast while he sipped his morning coffee with Mama Lu. No matter how she aged, he thought, he would always see her as that wide-eyed little girl.

Mr. John still held a picture in his mind of a young Nalia bouncing down the stairs clutching her rag doll, Emily. The little doll had her own chair beside Nalia where she would pretend to share juice and French toast. They would laugh and tell stories of what the day held in store. Those were good days, he thought, when Nalia always started her day smiling.

Not every day, however, began with such joy. There were other times when Nalia would come down the stairs sullenly, with Mary held tightly against her chest. Mary was never a "good day" doll. If Nalia came to breakfast holding Mary, it meant she had been thinking of her mother and wondering why she had been left behind. She often asked Mama Lu why her mother did not want her anymore. Surely a child must be awful if her mother chose to abandon her.

Such mornings were spent with Mama Lu and Mr. John reassuring Nalia she had done nothing wrong. They promised her she was wonderful, beautiful, and amazing in every way; her mother's departure was certainly not her fault. The world was a strange place to live sometimes, they would tell her, and things did not always make sense or work out as planned. They taught Nalia to look for the good in every situation, for even the face of adversity had another cheek. Though her mother had been forced to leave, Nalia could not have been left with anyone who loved her more than Mama Lu and Mr. John.

"Even if you search over the whole world," they would say "You'll never find nobody to love you more than us."

After those long comforting talks, many hugs and kisses, and a hot breakfast of beignets and milk, Nalia would feel better. Then Mama Lu would carry Mary back upstairs and put her back in her place atop the dresser. She would come back down with Emily, and Nalia would tote the little rag doll along until the next day of self doubt, when it would start all over.

Today, Nalia carried no doll, only her phone and a heavy air of aggravation. Remembering her question, Mr. John responded, "You look beautiful, baby girl. Yo' pretty as a peach ripe for pickin'. Jus' like the day I firs' laid eyes on you."

Nalia blushed and smiled sweetly back at John. Her eyes lit up like rays of morning sunshine, and her frustration seemed to dissolve. "You always know just what to say," she said with a wink.

She approached the back of Mama Lu's chair, wrapped her arms around her from behind and kissed her gently on the temple. "Mornin' Mama," she said with all the love and admiration of a tiny child. She squeezed hard and Mama Lu smiled with contentment, all the tension leaving her muscles. "Thanks for the tea," she said, "Any coffee left to chase it?"

"In the pot, darlin'. I made extra," replied Mama Lu.

Mr. John jumped to his feet. "You go 'head and sit down here, sweetie," he said, "I'll pour you a cup." He gave her a fatherly hug as they met. "Sho' is good to see you, dumplin'," he said.

As she hugged him back, Nalia thought of how much she missed him and how her time here in this place, with this family, was far too sparse. As she released her embrace, Mr. John held on a bit longer, just to let her know how precious she was and how much she was truly missed. When he finally let go, he placed his hands on her shoulders and held her at arms length. With a wide smile of adoration, his eyes tried to catch up from a year's worth of absence all at once. Nalia continued to blush as John finally allowed her to pass. He focused his attention back to the coffee as she sat down across the table from Mama Lu.

"You still take cream and sugar?" John asked.

"Black," came the surprising response.

Mr. John paused for a moment, confused. It was like losing his place half-way through a page and having to re-read. He finished pouring the chicory brew and set the steaming cup down on the table in front of Nalia, who was avoiding eye contact.

Mama Lucia was studying Nalia closely, examining every bit of skin she could see for marks and bruises. She focused on the ones around Nalia's neck just below the jaw-line.

"How bad did he hurt you?" she asked.

"I'm alright, Mama," Nalia replied, palming her cup with both hands in an attempt to assuage the shaking.

"Dat's not what I asked, chil'."

Nalia sat in silence for a moment. "Bad enough..." she finally said, tightening her lips, "Bad enough that I freaked out, for some reason." She paused, wondering whether or not to continue but the room's thick silence influenced her. "Then I blacked out..." she went on, tears beginning to form, "I don't remember much about what happened after that – just that I couldn't stop crying until I got here."

A mixture of sorrow and hatred overcame Mr. John. He tightened his grip on his coffee cup as he fought back tears. He watched Mama Lu slip her hand into the pocket of her robe and knew she was rubbing the twisted bit of root she kept there. Choking back emotion, he muttered "You jus' tell us who done it, baby girl. Me and yo' Mama Lu, we fix 'em up right!"

"He's nobody, Mr. John. Not anymore," Nalia responded shaking her head. "I know you're upset and I appreciate your concern, but I don't want y'all *fixin'* nobody for me. I can take care of it."

"Nobody hurts my baby and gets away wit' it," interrupted Mama Lu, fuming.

Nalia raised her eyebrows as she ran her fingers around the rim of her cup. "I didn't say he was gon' get away with it, I said I didn't want you to 'fix' him. He'll get what's comin' to him, you can be sure of that. It's like Madame Toulouse always says – all that you do gon' come back to you."

"Oh, I can make sure it comes back to him!" snapped Mama Lucia, striking a hand down on the table. Her eyes were aflame with rage.

32

"I know you can, Mama," Nalia replied, her frustration rising, "But that comes back on you. Besides, he ain't the worst of it right now." The end of her sentence trailed off as she stared at her coffee once again. Mama Lu and Mr. John kept quite, waiting anxiously for what would come next. Finally Nalia broke the silence. "I think I might be goin' crazy Mama," she said with a frightened edge to her voice. She inhaled deeply through her nose, attempting to stave off the threatening tears. "I'm hearing voices in my head…last night there was something gnawing at the back of my mind like it was trying to send me a message. I didn't just think it, I heard it. It was cold, and dark, and…evil. Then…" She put down the coffee and sat back in her chair, folding her arms in front of her. She bit her bottom lip and rolled her eyes toward the ceiling. "When he touched me, my body freaked out…"

Mr. John suddenly felt very uncomfortable, and it wasn't hard to tell Nalia was too. "Sounds like I need to run on, and let you two talk in private," he said, trying to politely excuse himself.

"No, it's okay Papa." (He loved it when she called him that.) "You stay," said Nalia, drying her eyes and gathering her strength. "I'm not ready to talk about all this just yet," she said. With a deep breath she attempted to regain her composure. "I've got to go anyway. I left my phone charger at school," Nalia explained, "I've got to go buy a new one. My battery is dead and I've got this voice mail I need to figure out."

"Figure out?" questioned Lucia.

"Yeah, someone left it last night from an unknown number. I tried to make it out but there was too much static. I could hear someone talking, but I couldn't quite make out what they said. Then my battery died."

Mr. John and Mama Lu fired a look of relief at one another, both now fairly certain Nalia did not overhear their conversation.

"I need to call Julia, anyway. She'll be wondering where I am," Nalia continued. She noticed the puzzled faces of the others. "My roommate," she explained, "I want to let her know I'll be here for a few days." Suddenly, she considered the presumptuousness of her comment as she was overcome by the unfamiliar feeling of being a guest, once again. "If that's alright with you, Mama?" she added to remedy her possible faux pas. Her voice was filled with question, even though she had little doubt.

"You stay here as long as you like, chil'" came the expected response from Mama Lu, who sounded affronted. "Dis is, and always will be yo' home, girl. Don't you ever let me hear you ask permission to stay here no mo'. Understand?" Realizing her tone was a bit harsh, Mama Lu continued, "And don't you worry none about dat school givin' you no trouble, neither. I know the girls ol' Dean Crawford runs 'round wit' when he come to town for Mardi Gras. He knows I talk to his wife too. He ain't gon' give you no trouble, b'lieve me."

Nalia tried to hide the grin that was forming on her face, but when she noticed Mr. John fighting the same battle, she couldn't help but laugh. Mama Lu laughed too.

Nalia excused herself from their company and headed for the stairs. On her way, she placed a hand gently on Mama Lu's face and kissed her on the cheek. "Thanks Mama," she whispered, "Can we talk when I get back?"

"Come by the shop, baby," said Mama Lucia, "I got some work to do there today."

"On Sunday?" questioned Nalia sarcastically. "I see some things never change," she added disappearing up the stairs.

John watched until she was out of sight, then sat back down quietly, across from Mama Lu. "You min' tellin' me how you can see days into folks' future and past, but you can't see dat girl come down the steps behind yo' head?" he scolded with wide-eyed accusation, as the gravity of the situation once again draped itself over them like a heavy coat. They lowered their voices and leaned in to speak.

"If we gon' do dis, we start tonight," said Lucia. "Dat girl is hurtin', John, and there ain't no sense draggin' it out." She took the twisted root out of her pocket and rubbed it nervously between her fingers.

"Agreed," said John, "I got everythin' we gon' need in my stores over at the shop."

"You go gather it up, and don't you tell a soul, you hear?"

John nodded.

34

"I mean it John, not a soul. You make sure all the protections are in place," Mama Lu said, nervously rubbing the root. "We can't let nothin' happen to dat girl."

"We won't, Mama. We won't."

Mama Lu shuddered as she raised a single finger. "When these dreams come back, and the mem'ries start fadin' into 'em, they aint gon' be shadows and monsters no mo'. She gon' see 'em for what they really was." She stared intently into Mr. John's eyes. "You best be ready for some sleepless nights."

Their conversation was interrupted by a knock at the back door. Startled, Mama Lu looked up. Through the screen, she could make out the figure of an elderly woman wearing an emerald green dress and matching hat. The hat was trimmed in black lace and tulle creating a partial veil over one eye, with a large peacock feather draped down the back. The woman wore black opera gloves and held a tortoise-shell quellazaire in one hand. Mama Lu recognized her silhouette at first glace; it was the unmistakable image of Madame Toulouse.

Lucia rose quickly, tucking the root back into her robe. As she opened the door, Madame Toulouse greeted her with a wide smile.

"Mambo Lucia," she said, her smooth voice purring like a kitten, "How lovely to see you." As she stepped over the threshold, she offered her cheek to Mama Lu and was obliged with a cursory kiss hello. She sauntered into the kitchen where John politely rose from his chair. "Hello Doc, how ya sleepin'?" she asked, not expecting an answer. "Not too much, I imagine, with all that was going on here last night. I figure stoppin' by right about now, I'm sure to be interruptin' a thrilling conversation." She paused for a reply, but stunned silence hung thick in the air. Turning her attention back to Lucia, she continued. "Take y' hand out of your pocket, Lu. I'm sure you've all but rubbed a hole in ol' Johnny the Conqueror by now," she said. "Hell, I felt the tension clear 'cross town."

Mama Lucia gripped the root in her pocket and held it tight.

"You know that ol' root ain't good for nothin' but attractin' men no-how, don't you?" said Madame Toulouse with a taunting grin.

"Works different fo' me," replied Lucia sheepishly, "Johnny's always brought me luck…and protection."

Madame Toulouse rolled her eyes and turned toward John with a pleasant smile. "Doc, now might be a good time to take that leave you was thinkin' 'bout earlier," she said placing the tortoise-shell cigarette holder between her teeth. "Not that I don't love you, John. You know I do," she explained, "It's just that Lucia and I have some matters to discuss in private. You know, woman to woman. You understand don't you?"

John nodded so low his gesture could have been mistaken for a bow. He set his cup down on the counter and quietly departed for home.

Madame Toulouse turned her back to Mama Lu offering her shawl. "I'll take some tea, dear. Peppermint, with honey and cream," she purred as Mama Lu removed the shawl and hung it on the coat rack near the door.

As Lucia prepared the teapot, Madame Toulouse removed her gloves. Laying them on the table, she seated herself in the chair previously occupied by Mr. John. She leaned against the straight back of the chair, crossed her legs and folded her arms, tightly clinging to the cigarette holder.

"Now then, Mambo Lucia," she said, her smile withering into a firm gaze, "Let's discuss these plans o' yours."

CHAPTER SIX

Madame Toulouse carried herself with all the sophistication of an aristocrat. Her wardrobe was tastefully elegant and her appearance was always impeccable. She kept her silver hair tucked neatly under the hat of the day, and she rarely wore the same one twice. Her posture was perfect, especially for a woman of her age, and she walked as if gracing the red carpet. Her long gloves and theatre-length cigarette holder were reminiscent of Audrey Hepburn, although the cigarette at the tip remained unlit. Madame Toulouse gave up smoking years ago, but still enjoyed the mystique and charm of the quellazaire. The large jewels worn around her neck and on her ears said she was no stranger to money, while her confident air suggested a lack of paranoia. It was well known that she had an affinity for playing the horses down at Fair Grounds and an uncanny knack for winning. She was generally a pleasant woman, but had the stern temperament of a Catholic school teacher when times called for it. Now was one of those times. Serious matters called for a serious tone and that's exactly what Mama Lucia was getting from Madame Toulouse just now.

"I'm not here to say 'I told you so', Lucia," she said, "But for your own growth, you need to acknowledge dis is all comin' back to you, from years ago." A well-spoken black woman of French-Haitian descent, Madame Toulouse's accent was a bit less Creole than most. "Just like a spinning wheel, everything you do gon' come back around to you."

Mama Lu hung her head. She knew everything Toulouse said was true. It was a reality she learned all too late in life. The early period of Lucia's craft, unfortunately, was not governed by the wisdom she had acquired over time. Years of practicing without restriction had returned to haunt her on many occasions. While she made no apology for her actions, she came to realize exercising discretion often afforded one a certain measure of protection later on. She learned it was possible to harness vengeance for the purpose of self-preservation. Still, sometimes justice needed to be dealt, regardless of the consequences. The events of Nalia's youth fell into this category.

"I done made my mistakes, and I'm payin' fo' 'em," said Mama Lu with tearing eyes as she placed peppermint leaves in a ceramic steeping-pot, "But why does dat baby have to pay for what I done?"

Madame Toulouse softened her demeanor. She placed the cigarette holder on the table beside her gloves, uncrossed her legs and leaned forward. Folding her hands together on the table in front of her, she assumed a much more approachable posture. "We pass it on, Lucia," she replied with understanding eyes, "Most often to the ones we love. That's just the nature of things, darlin'. We can only take comfort in the fact that what we learn from our mistakes, we teach those who reap what we sow."

Lucia placed a kettle of water on the stove and lit the burner, then sat down across from her mentor. She stared at the table for a moment, looking up only when Madame Toulouse took her hands. The old woman's failing eyes held all the wisdom of her age. "You have learned so much over the years, Lucia...grown so strong," she said. "You've overcome the impulsiveness of your youth. I've watched you learn patience through wisdom, and wisdom through patience."

"Nalia already understands so many more truths than I ever did," Mama Lucia replied.

"Take comfort in that, Mambo. Peace will come."

"But what she's gon' have to suffer ain't right. It ain't fair!"

Madame Toulouse squeezed Lucia's hands, adding weight to her words. "You may not see it as fair, Mambo, but it is right. That girl has a right to know her past, however unpleasant it may be. It was not your right to take it from her. Now you must both endure the consequences. We can only hope it makes her stronger in the end."

"Will she be?" asked Mama Lu, "Can you see it?"

"Lucia, you know I can never see the outcome, for the outcome can always change. I can see only the possibilities." Madame Toulouse placed her hands on top of Mama Lu's, then gently let go as she sat back in her chair. Her expression became troubled. "I have to be honest though, Lu. I see a lot of possibility for disaster here. This tree casts a mighty big shadow, and its roots run deep. It's not gon' fall easily, and when it does come crashin' down, it's gon' bring much devastation. The ground where it once stood will never be the same. But in that, we find hope. You see, once that tree is uprooted and the soil is tended, then new trees can be planted – healthy trees. Ones that will grow taller and stronger than any that stood before. So handle this carefully, Mambo; handle it right."

Lucia rubbed her hands together nervously. "It starts tonight," she said.

"Well no wonder Johnny's 'bout wore out," replied Madame Toulouse. "Tea is ready, darlin'."

Mama Lu looked around at the stove, but saw no steam. Seconds later the kettle began to whistle. She looked back to see Madame Toulouse wearing a confident smile as she retrieved her cigarette holder for good form. She folded her arms in front of her again and returned to her stern disposition. "Now," she said, "On to other business."

As Madame Toulouse spoke, Mama Lu poured the boiling water over the tea leaves in the steeping-pot. She set it on the table with a cup and saucer, a small pitcher of cream, and a glass jar of wildflower honey with a wooden drizzle stick.

"You've no doubt heard about the activities of your Madame Luciénne?" Toulouse continued with a tone of displeasure and an urgent look in her eyes.

"Yes, I heard," replied Lucia, returning to her seat, "I know about the rituals."

"Has she contacted you yet?"

"Not yet."

"She will, Mambo, and soon. Make no mistake about that!" said Toulouse. She gripped the handle of the steeping-pot and poured, holding the lid in place with her other hand. Steam rose from the spout as the fragrant brew filled the cup. She inhaled deeply allowing the thick aroma of peppermint to fill her lungs. "She needs you, or at least believes she does," she continued. "She's gon' want you at that first ritual."

"What does she want from me?" asked Lucia sitting back in her chair to mirror her mentor's posture. "I resigned my position years ago 'cause of Nalia."

Madame Toulouse kept her silence as she poured cream from the pitcher. Then, holding the drizzle stick above her cup, she permitted a healthy amount of the thick amber honey to sweeten her steaming drink. When she decided the mixture was right, she stirred it slowly with a small spoon from the table, purposefully delaying her response. Finally, she looked up into Lucia's restless eyes and answered with a grave tone, "Transference of the power."

"Dat don' make no sense," said Mama Lucia, rolling her eyes in disgust. "I resigned, she took over, end of story. People know dat!"

"But there was no rite of transference, like there was when I passed it to you," explained Toulouse. "Many believe, as well they should, that the power still lies with you."

"She can never receive it!" snapped Lucia. "She works alone, refuses the council of elders, and don' respect her heritage! The power will never truly rest with someone like her."

Madame Toulouse leaned in sipping her tea. "Don't you see?" she asked, "With her it's not about the power, it's about the money. She knows too many people still choose you over her for their healings and dealings. She figures a formal rite of passage will change all that. It's commerce, Lu, plain an' simple. Up until now, her whole practice has been a farce. A lot of folks know that, but if she gets you to bow down in this sham of a ritual she's cookin' up, then all them people gon' believe it's real, jus' based on appearance."

Anger filled her eyes. She set her cup down on the table and pointed a finger at Mama Lu. "It's greed-driven folks like her that have corrupted our religion into the state it's in today. She should never have been allowed to take over! Refusin' the council of elders? Hmph! Our institution is passed on from teacher to student, mother to daughter. It's kept in family lines, so it stays pure. There is a natural order to things, Mambo, and that woman don' care nothing for it."

"I don't intend to give her any power," noted Mama Lu.

"She's already powerful, Lucia. Can't you see that? You don't need magic to be influential when it's all business. You jus' have to know the dirt on the right folks, and Luciénne's got the dirt on everybody. You, of all people, ought to know that fact."

Mama Lu looked away in shame, anger piercing her spine. Would the sins of her past never cease to haunt her, she wondered? She sat in silence as Madame Toulouse continued to sip her tea.

"All I'm sayin' is," continued Toulouse, "Give Luciénne a wide berth. Your focus needs to be on Nalia. You don't need Luciénne's antics clouding your head, especially with the police gettin' involved, like I hear rumored."

"Since when did the New Orleans police care what goes on down in the secret places?" asked Lucia.

Madame Toulouse raised one eyebrow and looked down her nose as if she knew the best bit of gossip in the sewing circle. "Since the Reverend Hammond from over at Mt. Sinai Baptist climbed into bed with Congressman Stockholm, that's when!" She sipped her tea with a knowing glare. "Stockholm is up for re-election," she added, "So when he got wind of the rituals startin' up again from his buddy, the good Reverend, he decided it would make a grand publicity show for the both of 'em." She twisted uneasily in her seat, too disgusted to sit still. "If you ask me, Luciénne is behind the whole thing. The only bad press is no press," she said. "Regardless, this is about to turn into one first-class, holy, political mess; one neither you, nor I, need to be involved in. Understood?"

"Understood," Mama Lu replied obediently, avoiding eye contact.

Satisfied, Madame Toulouse stirred her tea and crossed her legs again. "That's what I wanted to hear, but don't be naïve, Lucia. That woman's gon' tempt you, threaten you, and try every trick she knows to get you there for that ritual."

"She can't touch me." Lucia said firmly, looking up and staring across the table.

Madame Toulouse kept silent but sat back, sipping her tea and studying Mama Lucia's expression. She never saw the outcome, thought Mama Lu, only the possibilities.

The firm expression on Madame Toulouse's face suddenly turned cheerful when she saw Nalia descending the stairs. She wore a shiny, black silk shirt with charcoal grey jeans. She was putting on earrings as she came down the steps. Her eyes lit up when she saw Madame Toulouse.

"Madame T.!" she said, running to hug the only grandmother she'd ever known. "I should have known you'd show up here today," she said sheepishly, tucking her hair behind her ear.

"You know I'm not gon' miss seein' my baby when she comes to town. Turn around and let me look at you."

Blushing, Nalia twirled for Madame Toulouse as she had a hundred times before. The elderly woman's eyes sparkled with grandmotherly affection as she remembered the child who blossomed into the stunning young woman standing before her. "You look thin, baby. What's the matter? All that studying left you no time to eat?"

"Good grades don't make themselves, Madame T."

Toulouse beamed, enchanted by the memories of youth.

Nalia pulled a chair from the table and started to sit, but Madame Toulouse raised her hand in protest. "Now don't think just 'cause I'm here, you got to sit down and gab with this ol' woman," she said, "That's what I got Lucia for." She gave a wink to Mama Lu, then turned her attention back to Nalia. "I understand you gon' be in town for a few days, so we'll have plenty o' time to catch up. You go on and do what needs doin'. I tell you this though, those phone chargers get expensive when you have to keep buyin' 'em. Next time make sure you pack it 'fore you travel."

"How did you…?" Nalia started to ask, before remembering who she was talking to. "Nevermind," she finished, shaking her head.

Nalia appreciated the pleasantries but knew that Madame Toulouse's gracious dismissal was a courteous way of saying she wished to continue her obviously serious conversation with Mama Lu, uninterrupted. She kissed each of the ladies on the cheek and politely excused herself.

As the back door closed behind Nalia, Madame Toulouse's expression went from pleasure back to business in a heartbeat. "So it's settled then," she said, "You'll steer clear of Luciénne, and you and John will begin your work tonight. I'll be putting up protections for you, so be strong Mambo. It's all for the best." Madame Toulouse took one last sip of tea before putting her gloves back on. Rising from her chair, she pointed her cigarette holder toward the window. "That'll be my ride," she said, "My stole please?" As if on cue, a taxi appeared on the street outside.

Mama Lu fetched the wrap from the hat rack and lovingly draped it around her mentor's shoulders. She kissed her on each cheek and opened the back door.

Madame Toulouse was halfway across the threshold when she turned around. "One other thing, Lucia," she said with a charming nod, "You and John should learn to keep your voices down when you're discussing your secrets." She lowered her head as if looking over spectacles. "If I hadn't left Nalia that garbled voice mail last night, you two would have a lot of explainin' to do right about now," she said with a wink. "Au revoir, darlin'," she added, chuckling quietly as she turned away.

Mama Lu's jaw hung open as she watched the elderly lady stroll down the walk to the waiting taxi. Madame Toulouse never ceased to amaze.

CHAPTER SEVEN

The temperature was approaching the upper eighties and the afternoon's abundant sunshine had done a respectable job of drying the rain-soaked ground. The concrete was mostly dry along the street and sidewalk now, except in front of Mama Lu's shop. The source of the puddles was not last night's storm, but a hose Mr. John was using to water the large ferns that hung from the second floor gallery.

The building was a large two-story red-brick structure on Decatur Street that housed three businesses. Mama Lu's shop was located in the building's center space. Each space featured a downstairs shop and an upper room, with a wide gallery outside spanning the length of the second floor. Supported by sturdy posts, the gallery protruded over the sidewalk below with large ferns hanging in two rows, one on each level. The building featured a decorative wrought-iron roofline with a matching railing that ran along the gallery, typical of the Spanish architecture dominating the French Quarter. The hanging ferns made for a shaded, cozy walkway that complemented the store's entrances and Mr. John's shoe-shine stand.

The shops beside Mama Lu's each had a large display window while hers featured two, one on either side of the doorway. The merchant on her right was an antique dealer whose shop was called Glorious Finds. It had been in the same spot for nearly as long as Mama Lu. The space on the left had been home to a number of businesses over the years and was currently occupied by a high-end boutique called Toujours.

Mr. John's station was located between Mama Lu's shop and the antique store. He had two high-backed wooden chairs with leather seats elevated on a concrete platform with brass footrests. A small, locked storage space behind the chairs held various pastes, waxes, brushes and polishing cloths. Mr. John was generally not open for business on Sunday, so his presence today was atypical. However, matters being as they were, he felt the need to be near Mama Lu. A few customers had already visited the stand even though it was closed. Business had a way of finding Mr. John, even if he wasn't shining

44

shoes. Truth be told, most of Mr. John's customers didn't want their shoes shined at all. Tourists enjoyed his quaint little station for its nostalgia, but locals knew the shoe-shine stand as the place to find "the doctor".

Mr. John didn't much care for the name, but that's what they called him. While, on some level, he found the reference flattering, his humility would never allow him to attach himself to the history associated with the name "Doctor John". Known as the "original healer" of New Orleans, "Doctor" John Bayou made quite a name for himself in the early 1800's. The popular witch doctor was even said to have taught much of his craft to famed Voodoo Queen Marie Laveau.

In contrast, Mr. John was a simple man, and preferred to keep his reputation quiet. He did not assume the level of skill associated with his nickname, even though he was known for making powerfully effective gris-gris. His customers swore by them. Unlike the many hoodoo practitioners in the city, Mr. John's merchandise was widely known as the real thing. Locals paid hefty prices for his potions and gris-gris bags, without complaint. His remedies worked – and worked well. For serious problems or ailments, folks knew to see the doctor "down on Decatur St., out front o' Mama Lu's".

Mr. John finished watering the ferns. They hadn't really needed it with last night's rain; he did it more out of desire to occupy his mind than their need for hydration. His thoughts were already on nightfall. Before joining Mama Lu at the store, he spent some time in his workshop gathering all the appropriate materials for the evening. Everything was in place with nothing left to do but wait - a task that seemed to be getting the best of him. Many tiny eyes watched from behind the large windows of the storefront as he rolled the hose and let it drain into the street.

In each of the windows was a grand display of fine porcelain dolls. They were various sizes, both male and female, all beautifully adorned with finely tailored clothing of silk and velvet. Most were religious in nature but some replicated more historical figures. A few were simple china dolls, but all were fine quality pieces, each uniquely detailed and remarkably realistic. The displays were lit from the front near the bottom edge of the window, like footlights on a stage. Looking through the window was like sitting in the audience for a grand theatrical production, the actors suspended in time.

Passersby had a habit of stopping in front of the windows, marveling at the dolls' realistic expressions. Mama Lu's displays were known to cause large, pedestrian traffic jams on the sidewalk in front of the store. All the attention suited Mr. John just fine whose shoe-shine stand benefited greatly from the ambling crowds.

He carried the hose to the doorstep and reached for the brass handle. The door to the shop was made of thick cherry wood, stained dark and trimmed in gold. It had a glass pane in the center with an arched top and a frosted border. Suspended above the door was a large wooden sign with beveled edges. It hung on two thick chains between a set of natural gas lanterns, perpendicular to the doorway so it could be easily seen from the sidewalk. Old English gold-leaf lettering simply read:

The Doll Maker.

Today, as every Sunday, a blue and white plastic "CLOSED" sign hung in the glass panel on the door, suspended from a thin gold chain.

Mr. John opened the door and went inside carrying the hose. As he did, the small bells over the threshold tinkled, announcing his entry.

"Don't you be trackin' up my floor, John Barrett!" came a shout from the back room.

Mr. John grumbled and continued through the shop. He walked carefully around the large circular displays that stood tall in the middle of the room. If a Christmas tree could be made out of dolls, he had often said, that's what it would look like. Mama Lu had threatened in jest to decorate one of the four displays with lights and tinsel for the holidays one year, in response to his many comments. The "doll trees" were filled with fancifully displayed dolls like the ones in the windows, only not as pricey. Less costly dolls were placed here because they could be reached more easily. They had a tendency to be handled more often, and sometimes broken.

46

The most elaborate and by far most expensive dolls in the shop were kept in locked glass cases along the side walls. One case featured likenesses of many well known Catholic saints displayed among rosaries and crucifixes. Most of them were clad in extravagant robes lined with gold and jewels. Mama Lu even commissioned a local jeweler to create authentic miniature jewelry for many of the pieces, out of twenty-four karat gold and diamonds. Over the last few years, the struggling economy made the sale of these dolls fewer and farther between. But Mama Lu still managed enough volume to keep her business stronger than most shops in the Quarter. She certainly did not see a need to diminish her inventory; the display cases were always full.

In the center of the case on the left wall was a very large doll, over three feet high and dressed in blue. The doll had bronze skin with a reddish hue and wore a full skirt that reached to her feet. She wore solid gold, hoop earrings and numerous oversized gold bracelets. She had a scarf around her head and a red sash around her waist, each tied with seven knots. She was the likeness of Marie Laveau, and she had been in the shop ever since Mama Lu opened the doors. She was not for sale.

Mr. John passed the case where she stood and continued on to the workroom where Mama Lu was heating up the kiln. The back room was large – nearly twice the size of the shop in front, and the kiln made it warm and dry. A large wooden work table with a Formica top stood in the center of the room with several canvas dropcloths spread out on it. On the table sat several molds and a number of figurines waiting to be fired. A variety of doll parts lay beside them. Tiny feet, hands, arms, torsos, and heads were all arranged like little porcelain skeletons. The entire area was covered with a thin layer of powder and dust. The table had a shelf underneath filled with boxes of various sizes containing many years worth of collected supplies – the type of clutter that gets stored in case it's ever needed but never is. Above the table hung the first of two braided air hoses that dropped down from the ceiling and ran to a small compressor in the back beneath the stairs. The second air hose ran to a smaller L-shaped table behind the large one, off to the right. This table held paints, glazes, and airbrush nozzles.

All in all, the workroom looked like any other that one might find in the back of an art gallery or studio – the dusty room where the dirty work behind the masterpiece takes place. There was one feature, however, that made Mama Lu's workroom different. Above the paint station and along the side wall were large wooden shelves that held a peculiar collection of bizarre poppets. Like the ones that sat atop the hutch in Nalia's bedroom, the poppets were constructed mostly of burlap and filled with sawdust. They were memories. Each one represented a relative or friend who was close to Mama Lu and had passed on to the spirit world. Much love and care was put into the making and maintaining of these rustic little dolls.

Mama Lu often worked alone in her shop on Sundays. Sometimes, when she chose to put off her work, she would simply spend time among the poppets. She would dust them and straighten their simple clothing. Sometimes she would just hold the bits of fabric between her fingers and remember the individual to whom they had belonged. She often said that if you listened with your heart, and if they allowed it, you could hear the poppets speak. The voices of the departed could be heard through their poppets, and sometimes it was good to talk with the dead. Keeping the poppets displayed in the workroom reminded Mama Lu to practice her art with love, history and tradition.

In the middle of the shelf over the painting table, near the back, stood two very different dolls. Both males, they stood about two feet high, more closely resembling Mary than the smaller poppets around them. Mama Lu called them "the twins". They were clothed identically, both wearing black suits with white dress shirts underneath. They were fair-skinned with salt and pepper hair and similar features. The dolls were exactly the same, except for their expressions. The twin on the left had a very solemn face and kept his hands folded in front of him. Were it not for his eyes, which were wide open, he would look as if he were ready for his own funeral. The other twin's appearance was altogether chilling, and folks found him most disturbing. His arms were stretched out to the sides and twisted into an almost unnatural position. His mouth was wide open as if screaming. The expression on his face was pure agony and the look in his eyes was one of panic.

A fine layer of dust and powder rested on the twins' shoulders, indicating they had been there for a long time, neglected of the love and attention shown to the poppets.

The last area of the shop was separated from the workroom by a thin wooden partition with a thick plastic curtain at one end. In this

48

section were three sewing machines, various hand tools and lots of fabric. It was referred to as the sewing room, and it was the place where the dolls were fitted with clothing and completed. The sewing room was set apart from the workshop in order to keep the fabrics free of the dust and powder that collected there. Once dolls entered the sewing room, they were sent on to display, or shipped off to their destination.

In the corner of the workshop opposite the sewing room stood the kiln. Mama Lu was setting the temperature and preparing several pieces for firing. Mr. John walked past her to the storage area beneath the stairs to put away the hose. He returned with a worried look and sat down on a stool at the large table. "I can't stand the waitin', Lu," he said looking at the floor.

"Well you gon' have to find somethin' else to occupy yo' mind, John, because yo' hangin' 'round here is makin' me crazy," Mama Lu replied.

"You can't blame dat on me, woman. You was crazy long befo' I met you."

Mama Lu stood up with a hand on her hip. "You workin' my last nerve John Barrett. I'm warnin' you! You best leave while you still got legs." She looked at him threateningly, then allowed her expression to melt into a smile. She softened her voice and spoke with a more sobering tone. "You really do need to make yo'self scarce befo' Nalia gets here, hon. So she feels more comf'table talkin'."

Their conversation was interrupted by the tinkling of the bells above the front door. "Too late," said Mr. John, "I'll jus' slip out the back door." He took Mama Lu's hand and gave it a quick squeeze for support, then turned to exit. His departure was interrupted by a shrill voice from the front room.

"Lucia?"

Mr. John looked back at Mama Lu so quickly he nearly snapped his own neck. They stared intently at each other, both immediately recognizing the voice. It was Madame Luciénne.

"Stay here," Mama Lu whispered to John. She walked to the front taking off her shop apron and throwing it on the table in frustration as she went. She opened the door to the front room and flipped on the light switch. As the florescent overhead bulbs flickered to life, the figure that had been silhouetted against the glass came into sharp relief.

Madame Vivian Luciénne lifted her head with a slight tilt and peered out from underneath a black, wide-brimmed sun hat decorated with white tulle. The sheer fabric was pulled tightly around the band then formed into a large bow at the rear before cascading halfway down her back. She managed a sly smile from under the wide brim and addressed Mama Lu. "I thought I'd find you here."

Mama Lu couldn't help but be disappointed. The woman standing before her had changed so much over the years. As a young lady, she was apprenticed to Mama Lu – taken in off the streets out of pity and given the chance for a fresh start. Initially, she wanted nothing more than a job and a chance, but over time, Vivian showed promise and honestly sought enlightenment. Mama Lu began to groom her in the arts as a candidate for succession, but the voices from Vivian's past proved too strong to overcome. Without confidence in herself, her hope withered. Nalia had been the final straw, and the young apprentice who showed such promise spiraled out of control. She removed herself from the oversight of Mama Lu and refused to be directed by any elder, which was taboo among traditional Haitian lines. Without proper council and guidance, Vivian Luciénne quickly soured into a pretentious swindler, corrupted by greed and power. She proudly took to calling herself "Madame", a title traditionally reserved for the eldest and wisest of their faith.

Mama Lu found it sad and disgusting. As she looked at Madame Luciénne now, she could only imagine that if evil could take the human form of a slender black woman, this is exactly how it would appear.

Madame Luciénne wore a black, silk dress well-tailored to her trim figure, with a neckline that plunged to a low revealing V. It was trimmed in white and drawn tight around her waist with a blood-red sash that matched her lipstick. She was a well proportioned woman of striking good looks, the kind that turned the heads of both men and women. Her jet black hair was styled in a short coif and shined like the midnight sky. Her appearance was insanely important to her. She more than thrived on the attention it brought her – she craved it like a drug.

She walked toward Mama Lu with a casual saunter and deposited her black, beaded clutch on the glass-topped counter. She struck a powerful pose, one hand on her hip, the other stretched out over the counter-top. Her French-tipped nails clicked hard against the glass.

She wore plenty of shimmering gold jewelry, but judging from the strong scent of her cheap perfume, Mama Lu presumed it was as fake as her smile.

"It's a scorcher out there, Lu. Looks like we're in for one hell of a summer, wouldn't you say?" said the self-proclaimed Madame. "How ya been darlin'?" she added with the toothy grin of a satisfied cat.

Mama Lu was at a loss for words. On the few occasions when she and Vivian Luciénne had spoken since their parting of ways, she found herself in much the same situation. What could she say to a woman who stirred such feelings of anger and disappointment? "What do you want Vivian?" was all she could finally manage with an exhausted sigh, disgust evident in her eyes.

"Well," said Madame Luciénne, her smile melting into a snake-like expression, "So much for pleasantries." She turned up her nose and flared her nostrils, "Since you know I'm not here for Sunday brunch, I'll cut to the chase." Her Creole accent was mixed with a thick southern drawl, "St. John's Eve is gon' mark a new era in our culture. A revival of old ways and ancient traditions. We gon' be re-establishin' the ceremonies on the sacred grounds down by Lake Pontchartrain."

"What do you know of sacred?" interrupted Mama Lu with an accusatory glare.

Madame Luciénne's mouth hung open wide. She lifted a hand to her bosom and gasped.

"Why Mambo Lucia, I am appalled," she said, "You of all people ought to know what a deep appreciation I have for ceremony and tradition."

"No! I know you have an appreciation fo' yo'self and fo' money, Vivian, and they have clouded yo' judgment where any matters of tradition are concerned," said Mama Lu. "But who am I to tell you? You certainly don' need advice from someone like me. You don' need the council of anyone, do you?" she added. "Dat's a tradition you was quick to cast aside."

"Practicing alone does not mean I am without council. I look to the masters who have gone on before," Madame Luciénne responded, as if reading from a script. Her sly smile returned as she lifted her eyes skyward and fluttered her lashes. "I read their will in the twinkling of the stars."

Mama Lu couldn't believe what she was hearing. "You might sell dat load of crap to yo' simple-minded clientele, Vivian, but surely you know better than to think I'm gon' buy it," she replied, rolling her eyes. Shaking her head, she asked, "Why are you doin' dis?"

Discontent darkened Madame Luciénne's face. "I look around dis city and I am disgusted to my very core at the level of simplicity that our religion has been reduced to by over-the-top commercialism," she said. "We was once a thrivin' power in dis city, Lu, but not no more. Now our Voodoo has become nothin' more than a novelty, and it hurts my soul to think of its future if we don't take action now. St. John's Eve gon' be a new beginning – you mark my words! It's gon' start our return to a powerful drivin' force in dis town. We gon' run dis city again, Lu, an' I'm gon' be queen!" Madame Luciénne straightened herself, standing tall and arrogant, nostrils flaring. There was a look of superiority in her eyes, but Mama Lu could still see a hint of fear. Looking down her nose with a sneer, Madame Luciénne continued, "Which brings us to the reason for my visit."

"You don' fight commercialism with drama, Viv," replied Mama Lu before she could go on. "Dat's jus' throwin' gas on the fire." She stiffened herself to match Madame Luciénne's posture. "I know what you're drivin' at, but it ain't gon' happen. I will not be a part of yo' lil' theatrical production."

Her anger swelling, Madame Luciénne traced circles on the glass-topped counter with her fingertips. With her tongue in her cheek, she thought for a moment. She needed Mama Lu but she was not about to beg. In fact, pride prevented her from even extending the courtesy of an invitation. "The ceremony on St. John's Eve *will* feature the rite of transference," she insisted. "You *will* publicly relinquish the power to me, and you *will* acknowledge me as queen." She nodded to the doll of Marie Laveau in the glass case on the wall. "Officially!" she added with a snap.

Mama Lu took a step forward. "Yo' big hat must be impairing yo' hearin', Vivian, 'cause I b'lieve I made myself clear," she replied. "You don't care nothin' for the purity of our religion. You just want to see it revered so you can pad yo' pocketbook. I will not participate in dis charade of yo' 'rise to power'. Dat would only serve to increase yo' ability to blackmail and extort folks, and I'll have no part of it."

"It was not a request, Lu! You will be there!" shouted Madame Luciénne, her voice slightly cracking with rage, "One way or another!"

"You don' scare me, Vivian. You got no power over me," said Mama Lu staring straight into the eyes of her adversary.

Madame Luciénne kept silent but her eyes roared like fire. She glared at Mama Lu, ready to explode.

In the back room, Mr. John was listening at the door. He waited anxiously for the silence to be broken, but it hung in the air like a heavy cloud.

The two women held their gaze like predators locked in a standoff, each waiting for the other to show the slightest sign of weakness. Madame Luciénne scrambled to imagine the most effective form of coercion, and when she was satisfied, a sinister smile slipped onto her face. "Well," she said, "We'll see about that." She paused for effect as she pretended to change the subject. "I hear yo' dearest daughter is in town. I may have to pay her a visit, I would jus' love to catch up," she said with a smirk. "She ever find out what really happened to her mother? I'm sure she'd *kill* for that information."

Every ounce of hatred in Mama Lu's body surged forth from her mouth like a flood. "You ever breathe a word to Nalia about what happened to her mother and you'll meet the same fate she did," she spewed, rage coursing through her veins.

Mr. John jumped in disbelief.

Madame Luciénne fought hard against the fear welling up in the back of her throat. She knew the true nature of the power held by Mama Lu; she had witnessed it first-hand. She was downright terrified of being on the receiving end of the wrath of a high-priestess, but if she let it show, her threat was meaningless. She had just begun to stammer when she was saved by the tinkling of the bells above the entryway. "Well, speak of the devil," said Madame Luciénne as Nalia entered the store looking as if she was interrupting a Papal prayer. "Nalia Deminy, it has been ages!" gushed Madame Luciénne. Knowing Mama Lu would never continue their conversation in the company of her daughter, she was filled with a new, brash confidence. "Yo' Mama Lu and I were jus' talkin' 'bout you. My, oh my, how you have grown." She looked Nalia up and down with a more-than-friendly admiration. As Nalia walked to the counter, Madame Luciénne studied her curves with interest.

Nalia managed an uncomfortable *hello*, but Madame Luciénne did not hear it for all the devilish ideas screaming in her head. She cut her eyes at Mama Lu and gave a wicked smile as she circled Nalia like a vulture. "Lucia you didn't tell me yo' baby had grown into such a fine young woman. Chil' I can remember when you was jus' a lil' thang, no higher than a toad-stool," she said addressing Nalia. "Now look at you. All grown up, and ever so pretty. *Mm mmm!* I bet all the boys are jus' dyin' to get their hands on you."

A stinging memory of Marcus shot through Nalia's body as Madame Luciénne positioned herself behind her. Staring at Mama Lu over Nalia's shoulder, Madame Luciénne looked like hell's darkest demon. "It's not nice to keep secrets, Lucia," she hissed with a twisted smile. "You should have told me how lovely yo' daughter turned out to be."

Having her fill, Mama Lu spoke to Nalia in the calmest voice she could manage. "Why don't you go on in the back, baby. Check the temperature of the kiln for me," she said, still glaring straight at Madame Luciénne, "And watch out for Mr. John. Yo' liable to hit him with the door if you ain't careful."

On the other side of the door, Mr. John jumped like he'd been shot. He began to nervously tidy up the tables, although he wasn't sure why.

Nalia walked silently around the counter as the two women continued to stare each other down. When she disappeared, Madame Luciénne donned a sinful grin. "Well, you know I'd just love to stay for afternoon tea, Lu, but I really must be going," she purred.

Mama Lu's eyes were steeled with unwavering resolve. "I think that would be best," she said, "and you heed my words, Vivian."

"It's 'Madame Luciénne'," she corrected.

54

"No. It's not 'Madame', it's not 'Mambo'. It's not anything," said Mama Lu firmly.

With that, Madame Luciénne snatched her clutch from the countertop and scowled. Her hat whipped around like a shield as she turned to leave. She straightened herself and stood tall as she exited the shop with her head held high and haughty.

Mama Lu breathed an exhausted sigh of relief as Madame Luciénne disappeared from sight. With the source of her anxiety gone, she remembered the words of her mentor, Madame Toulouse – "Your focus needs to be on Nalia." She gathered her composure, turned off the lights, and retreated to the workroom.

CHAPTER EIGHT

"What was that about?" cried Nalia, as Mama Lu entered the room.

Mama Lu wasn't sure if she was referring to the obvious altercation or the inappropriate advances. Choosing to address the altercation, she replied, "Notin' for you to worry yo'self 'bout, chil'. Dat's between me and Vivian. I'll handle dat."

"Well when you handle it, let her know I'm not into chicks," replied Nalia. "Even if I was, I wouldn't be interested in some skank who's a decade older than me and smells like a cheap hooker."

Nalia, Mama Lu, and Mr. John all stared at each other for a moment. When the humor of Nalia's comment sank in, they all began to giggle. "Dat perfume o' hers was a little strong, wasn't it?" said Mama Lu.

"A li'l strong?" coughed Mr. John. "I could smell it all the way back here."

The three of them continued to laugh and carry on like they had not done in a long while, and for a moment, Mama Lu forgot all about the argument with Madame Luciénne. She did not think about the terrifying screams that disrupted the quiet of the previous evening. She was not pained by the possibilities of what could happen when Nalia's world came crashing down around her. She was not anxious or worried. For a moment, she simply laughed and talked with the young woman whom she had called her daughter for the last fourteen years. For a moment, her soul was smiling.

Mr. John's face bore a peaceful and pleasant expression as he watched the two of them carry on. Although he knew his departure would undoubtedly bring an end to the light hearted conversation in favor of more serious discussion, he felt it was better to excuse himself. Important matters needed to be addressed, he thought, and his presence was hindering progress. He retrieved his pipe from his shirt pocket, said his goodbyes, and left by way of the back door.

His departure was followed by a brief moment of silence when Nalia allowed the regret of the past two years to get the best of her. She stared at the table where Mr. John had been leaning and began to silently weep. "I miss you guys," she said finally, with tears gently falling down her flushed cheeks.

Mama Lu pulled a stool up beside her, sat down and took her hands. "Don' you start regrettin' the decisions you made," she said looking into Nalia's tear-filled eyes. "You can't hang 'round here wit' us fo'ever. Everybody got to move on, chil, in they own time."

"I don't regret moving away, Mama," Nalia replied. "But there are different degrees of absence, and when I say I've been gone a long time, I don't mean geographically." Wiping the tears from her eyes proved to be an exercise in futility, as they continued to pour. She tried to regain her composure but did not have much luck. "I just feel like I'm focusing so much on my future that I'm losing my grip on the present." She looked up at the poppets on the shelves. "And the past," she added.

For an instant, Mama Lu reflected on her own past, remembering a time when she too had realized the importance of family and heritage. She turned her eyes toward the dolls on the shelves and recalled the ones she loved so dearly. "If we look to the past and honor those who have gone befo' by keeping dem close to our hearts, they will guide our steps in the present and lead us to a joyful future," she said. She looked back at Nalia and helped to wipe away the tears.

"Is that why you spend so much time here with the poppets?" asked Nalia.

"They bring me comfort, chil'," she explained "they bring peace and wisdom."

Nalia nodded in acceptance but found it difficult to speak through the tears and the swelling lump in the back of her throat. "Except those two," she finally managed, choking on emotion and pointing to the twins. "Those two always creeped me out," she chuckled, wiping her nose on a nearby shop towel.

Mama Lu looked up at the twins, then back at Nalia with a silent smile.

"Why do you keep them up there?" Nalia asked. "They're so strange."

Mama Lu hesitated, choosing her words carefully. "Every doll up there is a memory, chil'," she explained, shifting nervously on her stool. "And every one, a reminder. Some o' dem are reminders fo' everyone, some are jus' fo' me." She looked back at the two large dolls in solemn reflection. "The twins are a reminder jus' fo' me."

Nalia understood there were some things Mama Lu kept private, even from her. She knew there were things in Mama Lu's past that were not pleasant. She had heard Mama Lucia's name associated with rumors of hexes, curses, and powerful gris-gris. She knew her Mama Lu was once a greatly feared woman in the city of New Orleans, but people often feared what they did not understand. Nalia understood her Mama Lu's practice was nothing to be feared. The woman who sat with her, drying her tears, was the kindest woman she ever knew.

"Come on, chil'. I need to show you somethin'," said Mama Lu rising from her seat and walking toward the front room.

Nalia followed, her eyes still fixed on the strange twin dolls. "They look older than I remember," she said. "Did you give them grey hair?"

"Dat's just the dust and the powder, chil'," Mama Lu called back.

When Nalia entered the front room she found Mama Lu standing in front of the display case that held the large doll of Marie Laveau. The setting sun flooded the otherwise darkened store with light through the large picture windows. It generated an intriguing display of light and shadow that danced over the dolls. Nalia walked over to Mama Lu who seemed as though she was in some sort of trance. She stood beside her Mama and looked at the doll.

"Do you remember dis doll?" asked Mama Lu.

Nalia was puzzled by the strange question. As long as she could remember, the likeness of Marie Laveau stood in the same place – in this very cabinet. How could she *not* remember this doll? "Of course I do, Mama," she replied.

"But do you remember the first time you saw dis doll?" Mama Lu asked again, already knowing the answer. There was no way Nalia could possibly remember the first time she saw Marie Laveau. She was only six years old, so recalling such an event would be a stretch even for someone whose memory was not magically altered.

Nalia thought for a moment. She struggled to remember the first time she ever saw the doll. Surely it was the first time she visited Mama Lu's store, she thought, but the memory was not there. She looked up, puzzled, but Mama Lu offered no assistance; her gaze was still fixed on the doll.

"No," Nalia finally answered, "I don't." She was still trying to connect her thoughts. Confusion was clouding her mind and she felt as if she were trying to make pieces from two different puzzles fit together into a single image. The feeling made her strangely lightheaded. "I just remember her always being here," she said.

Nalia thought of the small doll that sat on her headboard, the one she called Queen Marie. "I know my Queen Marie looks just like her, only smaller, and I know that's the first doll you ever gave me." Nalia found herself even more puzzled. "But I only know that because you told me. I don't remember when you gave her to me."

"There is much about yo' past dat you can't remember," said Mama Lu, still staring at the doll in the glass case. "The memories are there in yo' mind, but you can't see 'em. They're hidden from you. They're the voices dat call out to you, and I 'spect they are the reason you reacted so violently to dat young man last night. Yo' body has memories dat your mind don't, and yo' mind is trying to reconcile dat."

Nalia did not understand. She was confused and slightly frightened.

Mama Lu finally broke her gaze and turned her head toward Nalia. When Nalia saw her face, she was taken aback. Mama Lu's eyes burned like fire, and in the darkened room, they seemed to glow. Nalia felt an unusual tightening in her chest, like something inside her was being drawn toward Mama Lu. It was as if an invisible hand reached inside her chest, took hold of her very soul, and tried to extract it through her rib cage. She felt pressure, but no pain. In fact, the stronger it pulled, the more comfortable she became – like an unexpected visit from an old friend. She felt a cold draft, though there were no open doors or windows. Even if there were, it was June in New Orleans.

She tried to call out to Mama Lu but found she could not speak. She could form the thoughts in her mind, but her mouth would not respond to her brain.

Slowly the edges of her vision grew dark, like passing backwards through a tunnel. As the darkness closed in, Mama Lu's eyes grew brighter until they were all she could see. Two lonely stars in a coal-black sky.

"You ain't gon' understand what I am 'bout to tell you." The words came from Mama Lu but seemed to echo in Nalia's head like she was standing at one end of a large, empty room. "It ain't fo' you to understand, only to hear and remember. There are parts of yo' past dat are locked away inside yo' mind, blocked out so they can't be retrieved without help. Dem memories was hidden from you fo' yo' own protection, but now they gots to be revealed for the same reason."

The voice reverberated inside Nalia's head. Each echo seemed to grow louder, never fading - like rubber balls released in a steel room, one after another, until a hundred balls bounced from wall to wall, never touching and never stopping.

"Listen carefully and remember," the echoing voice continued, "Queen Marie is the key to unlockin' yo' past. Tonight, as you dream, look fo' Queen Marie. When you find her, follow her. She will lead you to me. Give her to me, that I may speak."

Slowly the light faded back in, a small dot at first, in the center of Nalia's vision. Then the dot grew wider until she could just make out Mama Lu's face. Her eyes were still glowing, and her lips did not move when she spoke. "Remember," said the voice, "look for Queen Marie."

Suddenly, Nalia felt the tension in her chest release and thought she would fall backwards. Mama Lu's face returned to its normal appearance and Nalia's vision slowly began to clear. She was instantly aware that she had no recollection of the past several minutes. A wave of heat fell over her body and she became nauseated and weak. Mama Lu stepped over to steady her as Nalia felt her body grow faint. She collapsed into Mama Lu's arms but quickly came to. Mama Lu held her until she regained her balance.

"I don't feel well," said Nalia.

Dream-speak always affected the target in exactly the same way, thought Mama Lu, but at least the effects did not last long. "You'll be fine in jus' a few minutes," she said. "Let's sit you down."

She guided Nalia to the stool behind the counter. As the dizziness faded, Nalia became curious. "What just happened? Did I black out again?" she asked.

"You fainted, darlin'," lied Mama Lu. "Yo' body's been through a lot and it's weak. You need to eat, chil'. Sit here while I lock up and we'll get you home. I'll cook you up some gumbo that'll have you right in no time."

"But don't you still have pieces to fire?" Nalia asked, remembering the kiln and the porcelain pieces that were laid out on the table in the back.

"Everythin' I came here to do has already been done," Mama Lu replied.

When she was assured of Nalia's stability, she walked around the counter and across the shop to the front door. She turned the bolt and checked the handle to be sure it was locked.

"Mama?" asked Nalia with childlike wonder, "Have you seen Queen Marie? Is she still in my bedroom?"

Mama Lu turned around with a sweet smile. "I believe she is, chil'," she said, "I believe she is."

CHAPTER NINE

Chuck's Cash Express was located near the docks just off South Front Street. It was a small brick building that had been around for nearly twenty years. It was frequented by dock workers seeking to cash paychecks and acquire payday loans when money was tight. It began as an upstanding business, founded by an honest man named Charles Leonetti. A retired shipyard worker, Leonetti opened his business to lend a hand to the dock workers he labored alongside for so many years. He was well-known and well-liked. His business flourished for several years until he was killed during a robbery, leaving the business to his then twenty-eight-year-old son.

Tony Leonetti had a much different approach to business than his father did, and kept a much shadier clientele. The business that once served to aid local union workers, now ventured into gambling, loan sharking, drugs and organized crime – all under the guise of Charles' legitimate practice.

Until recently, Tony Leonetti had always been a large man. His size was attributed to many years spent consuming generous portions of pasta made by his Italian mother. Mama Leonetti was well known for her cooking, especially her sauces. She cooked for the homeless outreach program at St. Anthony's until her death in January. The elderly Italian woman remained blissfully unaware, even to her dying day, of her son's involvement in the gambling and drug circles of New Orleans. In her eyes, Tony was just as saintly as his father, carrying on the family business.

Tony took her death hard and turned to heroin for comfort, spiraling into depression and enslaving himself to his business associates. His status dropped from a controlling partner to a user and a puppet.

Five months later and one-hundred-twenty pounds lighter, he was finally getting a handle on his addiction. He didn't have an epiphany or acknowledge his problem in some twelve-step program. He simply came to the stark realization of how much his habit was destroying his profit margin – your product makes no money when you shoot it into your veins.

Today, Tony was outside his building, smoking a cigarette and kneeling beside his Harley. He was studying the long, deep scratch on the side of his gas tank. It was just above the logo, through the middle of his custom demon-wing paint job. He was plotting revenge when he noticed a familiar black Lincoln pull into his small, empty lot. The back door opened and Tony watched as a black stiletto heel hit the concrete and a large, wide-brimmed hat tipped its way out of the vehicle.

Tony stood and took a long drag from his cigarette as he watched Madame Luciénne saunter toward the building. He carefully studied every curve of her body as she walked.

Madame Luciénne could feel his eyes on her and she liked it. A surge of excitement came over her, putting an exaggerated swagger in her hips. The pleasure she took in knowing the kind of power her appearance held over Tony fueled her stride all the more. As long as Tony kept his attention on her body, he would be easy to control, she thought, and that's exactly what she needed.

"Madame Luciénne," said Tony in the slickest tone he could manage, "To what do I owe dis pleasure?"

"What makes you think I'm here on pleasure?" she responded with a tempting smile. "Can't a girl stop by to talk a little business?"

"Business, pleasure – it's all the same to me, darlin'," replied Tony, fixing his eyes on her breasts.

Madame Luciénne pointed to the scratch on the side of the bike. "Who'd you piss off dis time?" she asked.

"Oh dis? Dis is notin'. Jus' some punk kids from up the block who obviously don't know who I am," Tony replied. "I'll fix 'em."

Madame Luciénne cared nothing about the bike or Tony's neighborhood problems, but small talk afforded her the opportunity to scour the area for anyone who might be watching. "Let's step inside where we can have a little privacy. Shall we?" she said. She held her beaded clutch close to her chest and caressed Tony's face with the palm of her hand as she passed him on her way to the door.

A chill ran down Tony's spine as he took one last drag from his spent cigarette and tossed the butt on the ground. He ran a hand through his short, greasy black hair in a vain attempt to neaten his coif and followed Madame Luciénne inside.

She walked around the high counter, straight to the tiny room in the back and sat in a small armchair across from Tony's desk.

The office was dirty. From where Madame Luciénne sat she could count seven used Styrofoam coffee cups, four empty beer bottles, and half a dozen crumpled fast food wrappers. A small fan sat on the desk in the corner circulating the smell of stale cigarette smoke, burned coffee, and sweat. There were stacks of papers and unopened mail next to the computer with a loaded 9mm magazine serving as a paperweight. The computer's screensaver cycled through photos of topless women with pouting lips, straddling motorcycles, while its speakers played old *Pantera*.

Aesthetically, the stylish Madame Luciénne looked quite out of place, but she was not at all bothered by her surroundings; she had been in Tony's office many times. Despite her appearance, Madame Luciénne was not above getting her hands dirty when it was necessary. The teenage years she spent on the street taught her plenty about survival. She knew all too well how to lie, cheat, steal, and use others to get what she wanted. Nothing in this world comes cheap, and no one gives two cents about you, *but* you – just one lesson Madame Luciénne learned the hard way. She repeated that lesson in her mind at times like these, when she found herself sitting in a familiar nest of filth where the walls felt like a cage and the voices would whisper again: *You'll never be good enough! You'll never amount to anything! Why can't you be more like your brother? If you were prettier, your daddy wouldn't have run off and taken him away! No one gives two-cents about you...* "*But* you," Madame Luciénne said almost audibly as she drew a stiffening breath and steeled her mind.

Tony flipped the sign on the front door to "CLOSED" and drew the thin, metal blinds. He stepped around the counter and into the cramped office where Madame Luciénne waited. As he brushed by her chair and squeezed around the desk, Tony retrieved a small wastebasket to quickly clear the area of spent food and beverage containers. He bumped the computer's mouse, ending the cycle of pornographic photos, and turned down the blaring music. When he

64

was finally satisfied, Tony sat down at his desk across from Madame Luciénne. "Now," he said, "What can I do for you?"

Madame Luciénne sat back in her chair and crossed her legs to the side making sure Tony could see plenty of thigh. She looked at him seductively and bit her lip as if in thought. Tony began to sweat and reached for the crumpled pack of cigarettes in his shirt pocket. He fumbled one out of the pack and placed it between his lips before offering the pack across the desk.

Madame Luciénne didn't really care for a smoke but knew she could use the cigarette as a prop to enhance her flirting. Knowing he would enjoy watching her smoke, she took the last cigarette from the crinkled pack and allowed Tony to light it for her. Leaning across the desk, she offered a generous showing of cleavage. She wrapped her lips around the filter and took a long drag as the flame from Tony's Zippo danced across her high cheekbones. When the cigarette was lit, she sat back in the chair, leaned her long neck back and exhaled straight into the air.

"How are your communication skills?" she asked, after a lengthy pause. Tony held a blank stare. He had never been accused of being the sharpest knife in the drawer, and Madame Luciénne could tell he was not following. "I need a message sent," she explained with a heavy sigh. "Can you handle that?"

She watched as comprehension struck Tony hard in the face. "Oh," he said sitting back and lighting his own cigarette, "O' course I can handle dat. I got guys who can handle anything." He gestured widely with his lit Camel. "For the right price o' course." Placing the cigarette back in his mouth, he rummaged through the lap drawer of his desk. He retrieved a pen and a small note pad and pushed them across the table. "What kinda message are we talkin'?"

Madame Luciénne was familiar with the procedure as she had dealt with Tony on a number of occasions. Tony never talked about this kind of business out loud, it was bad luck. Besides, writing down the details greatly reduced the margin for misinterpretation.

Madame Luciénne set her cigarette down on the edge of Tony's ashtray and leaned over the desk. While she wrote, Tony shifted in his chair to better align himself with the gap in the fabric as the V-shaped front of her dress fell slightly agape. When she finished, she pushed the pad back across the desk to Tony and retrieved her cigarette for another drag.

Tony took one look at the page and swelled with confidence. "Dis is it?" he asked. "Piece o' cake, babe. Dis ain't even a challenge." He held his cigarette with his mouth again and reclaimed the pen. When he pushed the pad back across the table it contained a figure for the requested job.

Madame Luciénne leaned in again and looked at the figure. Raising a single eyebrow, she glanced up from the page. "Pricey," she said, blowing smoke across the desk. "Times getting' tough 'round here?"

"Notin's free in dis world, darlin', especially when you want a job done right."

Madame Luciénne had reservations about Tony doing anything *right*, but he never failed to *complete* a job, one way or another.

"That'll do," she continued, "But I have some specific instructions." She picked up the pen and jotted down her requests. As she made the list, she casually raised her other hand to her chest and allowed her fingers to gently trace the plunging neck-line of her dress. She hooked her fingertips on the fabric tugging slightly as she ran them up and down the seam. She pulled off the display as effortless, but Madame Luciénne knew exactly what she was doing.

Tony was enjoying the show, but he was aware of her tactics. He could see now that she wasn't wearing a bra, which told him she planned her little charade long before her arrival. He knew that meant there was sure to be a catch, but for now he would let her believe he was captivated. He retrieved the pad when she finished and read the instructions. "No problem," he said, a little apprehensive. "Just write down the address and consider it done."

This is where it got tricky, thought Madame Luciénne, as she considered what extra incentive she might need to give. She took the pad and sat back. She placed it in her lap and shifted in the chair allowing her skirt to rise up before crossing her legs once more. Her thigh was now exposed nearly up to her hip. She jotted down the address and glanced up to make sure Tony was watching the show.

He was watching, but suspicion suppressed his enjoyment. He knew if the bomb was going to drop, this was bound to be it. When he saw the address on the paper, he knew he was right. All manner of pleasantry faded from his expression. His brow furrowed and his forehead began to sweat as he took a moment to consider the request. "That figure just tripled," he said, crushing out his cigarette and leaning in with his elbows on the desk.

Madame Luciénne did not speak but stared at him in disbelief. Tony kept his silence as well. The look in his eyes said, "Yeah, you heard me right." They stared at each other, both waiting to see who would hold out the longest.

The uncomfortable silence got the best of Tony first. "Look, I know whose place dat is, a'right? My guys ain't goin' near there for any less than dat, if I can convince 'em to do it at all." He nervously wiped the sweat from his forehead into his greasy hair. "I'm cuttin' you a deal here. Dis is gonna be no profit for me on dis," he said. "I'm doin' you a favor!"

Madame Luciénne sat in silence, thinking. This was going to prove harder than she expected. She took one last hit from her cigarette and snuffed it beside Tony's in the ashtray, then rose from her chair and kicked off her shoes. She traced the edge of the desk with her fingertips as she slowly walked around it. With a seductive look in her eyes, she stepped in front of Tony, placing one leg on either side of him. Never breaking her gaze, she untied the red silk sash that bound her dress around the waist. With a sensual smile she let it fall to the floor. The absence of the sash allowed her dress to fall loosely in front, the V plunging to near non-existence. Locking her eyes with his, she placed her palms on the desk behind her and lifted herself onto it. Leaning forward she grabbed Tony's hands and pulled him from his chair. She drew him close and placed his hand inside the opening of her dress against her waist.

Heat rose inside Tony as his fingers caressed her warm, smooth skin. He knew what she was doing. His mind considered resisting but his body would not allow it.

Her feet slipped behind his knees and she slid his hand up her side until it cupped her bare breast. "Just how much convincing do you think *you'll* need?" she asked, whispering in his ear.

"You know how I operate, Madame," Tony said with a sly grin. "There's always room to negotiate."

CHAPTER TEN

One by one, the street lamps flickered to life as a blanket of darkness fell over New Orleans. The neighborhood was quiet as Mr. John sat in his rocking chair in the bay door of his woodshop. The smoke from his pipe circled overhead as he studied the lights in the house across the street. Over the years, he had become somewhat of an expert at discerning motion, gauging light and shadow, predicting movement. He could usually tell what was going on in Mama Lu's house just by glancing in that direction. So far tonight, the only action was in the kitchen, so he waited and watched.

The workshop behind him had been rearranged. The large workbench and woodworking tools that usually occupied the center of the room were moved to the side and to the back. The wide empty area in the center was swept clear of sawdust in anticipation of the evening's activities. Other preparations left the air thick with the smell of boiled chicken and black-eyed peas. The lingering scents mingled with the sweet-smelling pipe smoke to create a familiar aroma that helped Mr. John to center his spirit.

The workbench against the wall was draped in white linen, forming a makeshift altar with pictures depicting various saints of the Catholic faith hung above it. In the center was St. Raphael, the patron saint of healing. On either side were pictures of St. Michael and St. Anthony, the saints of protection and of lost things.

On top of the cloth stood two large unlit candles, each in a wide, shallow bowl. They were eight inches high and three inches wide, each wrapped seven times around with cotton cord tied in seven knots. The candle on the right was blue and stood in a bowl of sugar. The one on the left was pale yellow and encircled by a line of black pepper. Their purpose was to provide protection and ward off enemies – flesh and spirit.

In front of the candles sat a glass bowl filled with clear water encircled by nine silver coins. The coins were very old and not of any recognizable currency; they were there to call for the aid of helpful spirits. On one side of the bowl lay four dark amber vials containing oily liquids. On the other side was a large bundle of leaves called cinquefoil, arranged into five separate strands and bound together like a feather duster. Each strand was woven from smaller stems, each containing five leaves and bound together with silk thread. The strands were bound to each other near the base with copper wire, giving the appearance of a large hand. The thin, copper wire wove up and wrapped around the first, third, and fourth fingers of the hand for the purpose of enhancing luck, wisdom, and power.

On the floor in front of the altar, on a small block of wood, stood an ornate djembé. The sides of the tribal drum featured brightly colored lines and symbols, carved and painted between the cord that stretched the worn leather head taut against the bearing edge. The drum looked as if it had been well used. The markings on its side were scraped and its head was discolored from repeated striking. The red silk neck strap was nearly threadbare around the edges from years of use.

From a small speaker in the back of the shop, a recording of tribal drums droned low, barely audile. Mr. John's guitar sat in the corner untouched. He would not be playing it tonight. His mind was focused, and his eyes were firmly fixed on Mama Lu's house.

In his mind, Mr. John could picture Mama Lu in her kitchen, stirring a small pot of chicken gumbo. He watched her make it many times when Nalia first came to stay there. Mr. John remembered it well. The nightmares haunting Nalia grew so traumatic, trying to conquer them through ritual alone proved difficult to the point of failure. Over time, they determined that more drastic measures must be used. Mr. John assisted Mama Lu by providing certain "ingredients" known to soften the mind, allowing a person's will to yield without conflict. Mama Lu would add these ingredients to Nalia's gumbo. When consumed, they allowed the rituals to effortlessly remove the memories from Nalia's mind. It was an arduous cycle of trial and error, but with love, patience, and lots of attention, the battle was finally won.

Tonight the cycle needed to be reversed, and the memories returned. It would be the beginning of a long and difficult journey. Earlier in the evening, Mr. John left the proper herbs in a ceramic jar in Mama Lu's kitchen as instructed; there was no doubt in his mind she was cooking with them now. He smoked his pipe and rocked while he watched the light in the kitchen burn for several hours.

As Mr. John studied the light and shadows, he quietly listened to the recording of the drums. He could feel the tribal rhythm in his blood, and though the sound was faint in his ears, it pounded loudly in his veins. His heart beat in tempo as he became one with the cadence. His mind was sharp, like a woodland creature suddenly alerted to the presence of a human.

Finally, the kitchen light went out, and moments later a single candle burned in Nalia's bedroom window. Mr. John knew it was time.

Placing the pipe between his teeth, he picked up a large glass jar from beneath the small table beside his chair. The jar was filled to the top with a dark red powder. Mr. John stood and carefully carried the jar to the edge of the wide doorway. There, he tipped and shook the jar, steadily spilling its contents onto the concrete slab. Slowly, he walked, pouring the red powdery substance in an arc from one corner of the bay door to the other. Brick dust was good for warding off evil and protecting against other forms of magic. Mr. John always poured a solid line of it just beyond his doorway before the start of a ritual to keep the rites pure of any outside influence. Stepping back, he knelt and examined the arc for consistency. He puffed his pipe and squinted, carefully checking for flaws or gaps in the line. Satisfied, he placed the jar on the ground and closed the overhead door. He would not cross the line until sunrise.

He placed the palm of his hand over the pipe and drew in a strong breath, creating a vacuum. The tobacco extinguished immediately, and he laid the pipe down on the table beside his chair.

Unbuttoning his shirt as he walked, Mr. John made his way toward the open kitchen door at the back of his workshop. As he passed the altar on the workbench, the two candles spontaneously flickered to life, first the blue one, then the yellow. Retrieving a box of salt from the kitchen counter, he gently poured a line across the threshold of the door, examining it for continuity just like the brick dust. When the protective barrier was sufficient, he closed the door to the kitchen and turned off the workroom's overhead lights, leaving only the candles to illuminate the shop. Peeling the shirt from his shoulders, Mr. John revealed a collection of tattoos spanning his back and chest. Images depicting gods and goddesses from Haitian and African religions intermingled with pictures of Roman Catholic saints in a mosaic of colored ink that enveloped his body.

Around Mr. John's neck hung two charms, one long and one short. The shorter of the two was a rugged, black leather cord with a small cone-shaped bone hanging in the center. The cord was knotted three times on either side then once more in the back.

The longer necklace, made only hours before, consisted of three small chicken bones hanging from a thin piece of black thread. Mr. John reached behind his head and gripped the thread with both hands as he approached the altar. Snapping the thread, he released the bones and placed them into the bowl of clear water.

Slowly and methodically he picked up the vials of oil. Opening them one by one, he poured their contents into the bowl. The colored oils floated on top of the water like moving pictures. Mr. John watched them, examining their movements as the various colors danced around the bones.

He held the five-finger grass in his hands and waved it high over the flames of the candles, then in a circular motion over the bowl of water and oil. As he circled the bound leaves over the bowl, a dance of light and shadow engulfed his body exchanging blows like a battle between good and evil. The oils began to swirl on top of the water in a hypnotic vortex. Mr. John rolled his head back and forth on his neck in a circular motion. He dipped the five-finger grass in the oil and anointed his head and shoulders, the rhythm of the drums pounding stronger in his veins.

Mr. John dropped to his knees before the altar and surveyed the red, silk strap of the djembé with his fingertips. Lifting it over one shoulder, he placed the strap around his neck and slung the drum onto his back. His head fell backward with his face toward the sky and slowly rotated until his chin came to rest against his chest. His eyes rolled back into his head as he sat for a moment in meditation.

As his mind slipped seamlessly into the spirit world, Mr. John traced his hands along the floor in large arcs, eventually sliding them beneath the white cloth to retrieve a rough, wooden box. The candles on the altar began to burn brighter when he pulled the box from underneath. It was black with copper-plated corners, a silver latch, and several small holes in the top. Fastened through the latch was a rosary. Mr. John flipped the latch to release the rosary then quickly secured it back in place. As he held the rosary in front of the altar, he began to chant softly.

Loa… Loa… come b'tween.

Sing you to Bondye. Sing you of me.

His words were a prayer to the saints of old: "intercede for me, sing of me to the good god." Over and over he chanted as the candlelight swelled into tiny beacons of radiant white light. As he continued, his head became dizzy and his mind grew numb to the physical realm. The white light seemed to permeate his body, making it light as a feather as if he was spinning and floating in the air. Mr. John felt euphoria, like standing in the presence of angels, and though he continued for nearly half an hour, time stood still in his mind. As he brought his chanting to an end, his body grew heavy but the dizziness lingered like the end of a carousel ride. Several cleansing breaths helped bring his mind back to his body.

When his bearings returned, Mr. John reverently placed the rosary around his neck and swung the djembé over to his hip. He rose and slowly thumped the leather head of the drum with his palms and fingers. He moved to the center of the room and began to spin in a circle, completely focused on Nalia. Louder and faster he pounded and danced in rhythm, channeling all the protective energy he could conjure.

Mama Lu stood at her kitchen counter, gently stirring the tea. She and Nalia had just spent the evening talking and dining on her famous cure-all chicken gumbo and now, Nalia was upstairs readying herself for bed. The tea was steeped using chamomile, spearmint, and the herbs left in the jar by Mr. John. After all, Mama Lu thought, Nalia was a grown woman now. There was no longer a need to slip the potion into her food. She could simply brew it into a hot tea, the proper way.

She sweetened it with honey and added a slice of lemon to mask the bitter taste of the herbs, then placed it on the tray next to the stove.

The moment had a sense of finality as well as beginning; it was the dawning of a new reality and with it, new fear. Mama Lu considered pouring the infusion down the sink and not going through with the plan, but she knew it would be a useless effort. An age of security was passing away and nothing could stop that now. It began last night when the beast reared its ugly head again.

She breathed deeply and lifted the tray. Nervously, she climbed the stairs to the upper floor and walked down the hall, pushing herself with every step. As she passed the bathroom, she could smell the fragrance of Nalia's lavender bath oil rising on the steam from under the door. "Soothing," she thought, "Dat's good." She continued on to Nalia's door, carrying the small tray with the tea, two aspirin, and a blue taper candle.

She set the tray down on the bedside table and carried the candle over to the window. Drawing back the sheer curtain, she placed the candle next to Benjamin – a signal for Mr. John. Through the window, she could see the glow from his workshop across the street. She watched as he sprinkled the line of brick dust across the threshold and rolled down the overhead door.

Years spent knowing this night would come did nothing to prepare Mama Lu for the reality of its arrival. She looked across the room to the top of the carved headboard, where sat the doll called Queen Marie. "It's up to you now," she said, "I'll be waitin'."

Mama Lu hung her head and stared intently at the floor. She pulled Johnny, the twisted root, from the pocket of her dress and began to rub it nervously. Leaning against the wall beside the window, she talked quietly to herself in an attempt to calm her growing anxiety. "Don' make no sense bein' nervous now. Wha's done is done," she said. "You gots to be strong now, yo' baby needs you."

For a long while, Mama Lu waited in the bedroom, mentally preparing herself for the task ahead. Her eyes danced a dizzying path from Queen Marie to the twisted root, then out the window to the closed door of Mr. John's workshop. Her body was already weary with the weight of her heart. Though she could not hear it, the rhythm of

Mr. John's drum began to pulse in her veins. When she felt the pounding cadence, she knew the doctor was at work and it gave her strength.

She took a deep breath and tucked Johnny the Conqueror back into her pocket. As she walked to the door she saw Mary, the likeness of Nalia's mother, standing tall on the dresser. Memories of the woman who abandoned her child exploded in her mind. Hatred filled her eyes. "You did dis!" she spat at the doll. "You and yo' greed!"

She left the room quickly, trying hard to regain some semblance of self-control. The bathroom door opened just before she passed and Nalia emerged wearing her big tee-shirt and drying her hair with a towel. Mama Lu gave her a hug and told her goodnight. "I left some tea for you on the table. It'll help you sleep," she said.

"Thank you, Mama," replied Nalia. "I have a feeling I'll need it."

Mama Lu turned to watch her walk down the hall and into her bedroom. Instinctively she reached for the root in her pocket and gripped it tight. "Sweet dreams, baby," she whispered as she heard the door click shut.

She continued down the stairs and through the kitchen, nervously rubbing the root, all the while feeling the pulse of the drum grow stronger beneath her skin. She walked past the parlor toward the front of the house, stopping in the entry hall to face a large set of richly stained folding doors. She opened the doors to reveal a long closet filled with hanging clothes. Pushing all the garments to one side, Mama Lu stepped inside the closet and closed the folding doors behind her. The pounding in her blood grew more intense. In the darkness she felt along the back wall until her hands found two small knobs. Pushing them gently in either direction, she opened a smaller set of folding doors. As she stepped into the secret room beyond the closet, two candles flamed brilliantly to life, revealing a large desk with many tiny drawers. On top of the desk was an altar similar to that of Mr. John's. Above it hung a large painting of Marie Laveau with drawings of saints tacked to the wall around it. The top shelf was lined with porcelain likenesses of Catholic saints and several very old burlap poppets.

Mama Lu closed the second set of folding doors behind her and sat down on a small stool facing the desk. Reaching into the pocket of her dress, she retrieved Johnny the Conqueror once again and held the twisted root close to her heart as she rubbed. When her mind was at peace, she placed Johnny on the altar in front of her and began to chant.

Loa... Loa... come b'tween.

Sing you to Bondye. Sing you of me.

She rocked back and forth as she stared into the flame of the candles.

Somewhere far across town, the elderly Madame Toulouse stared into the flames of an identical set of candles. The rhythm of the drum pounded in unison through their veins.

CHAPTER ELEVEN

Nalia was sleeping soundly when the icy chill grabbed the base of her spine. The fact that she had fallen asleep at all was surprising. Her body succumbed to exhaustion but her mind would not surrender. At the very thought of sleep, terror consumed her, the nightmare playing like a tape in her head. The beast's glowing green eyes flashed over and over in her mind and her legs still tingled with the memory of its claws. She fought to keep her eyes open, but her body's fatigue and Mama Lu's chamomile tea eventually won the battle.

Now her much-needed rest was interrupted as the bitter cold slowly crept up her back. She could sense the darkness rising across the room. The beast was coming; it was a certainty. Her mind fought to gain control. "Wake up!" it demanded of her body, "Wake up!" The blackness grew colder and darker than ever before. Then, in the air – the emergent smell of gasoline. Nalia panicked. "Wake up!"

Something in her mind snapped and Nalia sat straight up in bed. Her breathing was hindered, and her pulse was racing like a locomotive. Her lungs screamed out for oxygen as she scrambled to draw a decent breath. She gripped the sheets, white-knuckled with fear. Finally, when she felt she could hold out no longer, her throat opened and her starving lungs filled with air. She breathed deeply, over and over again, as if rescued from a raging sea seconds before drowning. Her heart rate steadily decreased and she felt the tension leave her body.

The room was quiet and dark, save for the single candle burning on the windowsill. Hadn't she blown it out before bed? Confused, Nalia studied the room. The clock read 12:01, but that couldn't be right. Her last glance before falling asleep told her the time was 11:52. Surely she had slept more than nine minutes.

She noticed a faint floral fragrance lingering in the air. Carnations, perhaps? She wasn't sure. The aroma was so faint she had trouble discerning whether she actually smelled it at all. Nothing had clarity.

Even the low rhythmic thump in her ears was indistinct. It was too steady to be thunder. Was someone beating a drum? Did she truly even hear it, or was it her imagination? Though the sound was barely audible, it was not distant. It was definitely near but muffled, like she was listening underwater. Her head was swimming in confusion.

The entire bedroom seemed slightly awry. The porcelain figures were in the hutch, but the poppets were missing from the top. Mary stood on the dresser in her usual spot, but Benjamin was moved. He was sitting on the oval table near the vanity in Myra's place, and Myra was on the windowsill. Had Mama Lu rearranged the dolls while Nalia slept? In that brief nine minutes?

At least Emily was on the pillow where she belonged. Wait! Hadn't Emily been left in the apartment on campus? How did she get here?

Nalia become fearful. Anxiety crept into her muscles again causing them to stiffen. Her eyes darted around the room, trying to identify anything else that might be out of place. When they found the headboard, she realized Queen Marie was missing. Where was she?

"Look for Queen Marie," a voice echoed in her mind. She felt strangely nauseated, but impassioned to find her doll. "Perhaps she fell," Nalia thought. She checked the pillows and threw back the covers. She looked in the crevice between the mattress and the headboard. Not there. She climbed out of bed and looked beneath it, searching near the wall and behind the nightstand to no avail.

Aggravated and confused, she burned with a desire to set things right. She walked straight to the vanity, plucked Benjamin from the oval table and carried him to the windowsill. As she set him down in his rightful place, she saw the first rays of morning's light peeking over the trees. She looked back at the clock which still read 12:01. "The clock has stopped," she determined. She sighed with relief as she picked up Myra and toted her back toward the vanity. While returning the doll to the oval table, a twinkle of light caught Nalia's attention in the mirror. It was then she noticed her bedroom door was slightly ajar, and a thin beam of light was squeezing through.

She walked to the door and carefully peeked through the crack. Rays of sunlight flooded into the seemingly empty hallway through the window at the end, giving it the amber glow of early morning.

"Look for Queen Marie," the voice said again. Nalia instinctively looked back to the spot on the headboard, but the doll was still missing. She opened the bedroom door slowly and quietly, just enough to get a better look into the hallway. It was indeed empty, as expected, but something was wrong. It was more than empty; it was like a vacuum. The air was stagnant and no sound could be heard, as if someone had suddenly muted life's volume.

She looked toward the window. It was open, but the sheer curtains hung motionless and straight. In the other direction, the staircase was dark, but propped against the railing near the top of the steps was Queen Marie in her blue dress and gold hoop earrings. "There you are," Nalia thought, "How did you get out here?"

"Follow her," echoed the voice. Nalia was startled when she realized the voice she was hearing was her own. Staring at the doll, she tiptoed out of the bedroom into the hall. Her footsteps made no sound as she moved down the corridor toward the stairs.

As she passed the bathroom, the door suddenly slammed shut as if caught by a rushing wind. The deafening sound shattered the silence and the echoes that followed were terrifying. Nalia jumped and pressed her back against the opposite wall, her heart beating frantically. She was suddenly overcome with the sensation of a thousand eyes watching her, but a quick glance down the hallway proved she was still alone.

With trepidation she continued toward the staircase. To her surprise, Queen Marie was no longer there. Curious, she hurried over to investigate. The staircase was still dark, but she could see a thin beam of sunlight shining through the kitchen below. At the foot of the stairs, she could barely make out the blue dress of the elusive doll.

"Follow her," said her own voice again. Uneasiness came over Nalia as confusion clouded her mind but for some reason, perhaps because it was her own, she trusted the voice enough to keep going. Hesitant and cautious, she descended the stairs.

As she neared the bottom, she could see into the kitchen. She stopped and studied it for movement, but as far as she could tell, no one was there. Where was Mama Lu? There was no rustling of newspaper and no smell of coffee. As she reached the bottom step,

Nalia crouched to pick up the doll, but Queen Marie had vanished again.

Nalia wasn't sure she liked this game. In what world had she awakened? Had she really awakened at all? Everything seemed so real. She stepped into the kitchen, examining every detail for authenticity. Visually, everything was as it should be, from the wallpaper with the cornflower-blue diamonds to the tiny pig-shaped salt and pepper shakers on the counter. However, everything here was also silent and still.

Then, slowly and unnaturally, the back door crept open, as if pulled by an unseen hand. Fear quickened Nalia's pulse as she peered through the open doorway out into the yard. Everything was motionless outside as well. There was no breeze blowing the leaves in the trees, no sound of the bird's morning songs – nothing.

She stepped over the threshold for a better look. There was no traffic. There were no bicycles and no neighbors. Across the narrow street, she could see the back of Mr. John's house and his workshop, but it was closed up, devoid of activity. Looking back into the kitchen, she saw the clock on the stove read 12:01. Now she was unsure what to think. "Has time stopped?" she asked herself.

Seconds later she found her answer. As she stepped further onto the porch, she saw it just above her head. It was a hummingbird with tiny feathers of blue and gold hovering in mid air – its wings dead still.

Nalia was now quite certain she was dreaming. Her fear turned to fascination as she approached the hummingbird for a closer look. She pondered the obscurity of walking through a single moment frozen in time. If the dream lasted, she thought, she could walk through the entire city and observe all that was happening everywhere, all at once. Was this how it felt to be God?

Carefully, she examined the bird. She could see each feather on its outstretched wings. As she studied the gold pattern on its breast, she noticed the tiny creature seemed to be breathing. Its tiny chest puffed sporadically in and out. It appeared to be in distress.

Concerned, Nalia reached up to touch it. As her fingertips drew near, the hummingbird moved its head and looked directly at Nalia. It looked angry. Perhaps it had been a mistake to breach its territory. An instant later, its wings roared to life and the bird flew off over the house, and away.

Nalia was startled by the sudden motion, then downright frightened when the back door slammed shut behind her. She tried to open it, but it would not budge. The knob would not even turn. Her hands slipped around it like someone was holding it fast from the other side. Nalia instinctively became self-conscious when she realized she was trapped outside wearing nothing but a tee-shirt, but soon rationalized the notion by insisting this was only a dream.

Giving up on the door, Nalia turned back toward the yard. It alarmed her to find the world's color fading from view. She blinked and rubbed her eyes but nothing helped. She saw everything in shades of grey and bronze, like watching an old movie filtered in sepia tone. Then, all at once, there was motion. Clouds racing furiously across the sky sent large, moving patterns of light and shadow dancing frantically across the ground. Confused and frightened, Nalia looked around for any sign of the doll she was supposed to follow, but Queen Marie was nowhere in sight.

With panic mounting, a strange awareness caught Nalia's attention. She noticed music playing. What's more, she realized it had been playing all along – the only sound in the peculiar silence. It was faint and far off. She listened carefully trying to identify the instruments. Horns, she concluded, in the distance, with some sort of percussion. It was coming from the east.

Nalia hurried down the sidewalk to the wrought-iron gate, trying to more accurately discern the location of the instruments. As she stepped into the street, she saw a glimmer of reflected light. The sun was shining on something gold, moving in the distance three to four blocks down.

Nalia walked toward it, but the sound faded. It was getting away. She walked faster, finally breaking into a jog. As she ran, she felt the sensation of gliding and noticed she could not feel the ground under her feet. She stopped running, but even though her legs were motionless, she continued to move forward. The neighborhood around her whipped by faster and faster until it became a blur, the music growing progressively louder.

Then abruptly, everything stopped and Nalia found herself at a cross street. Looking to the left she saw a jazz band, marching in bright blue military-style jackets and hats, their brass horns gleaming in the morning sun. They brought the only color to the sepia-toned backdrop. The band followed eight tall men walking in step, two by two. The group moved at a casual pace, as if in a parade, but they were alone on the street – the only sign of life.

Nalia quickly followed them, trying to catch up. Why were they here? Where were they going? She recognized the tune they played as the old hymn, "Just a Closer Walk with Thee". Across the back row she could see the percussion section: two snares with a bass drum in the middle. They had gold cuffs on their sleeves and decorative, gold ropes draped across the shoulders of their jackets. Each snare drummer used one stick and one jazz brush to create a slow, maraca-like sound with a driving *pop* for the tempo.

Nalia caught up with the percussionists and walked alongside, but their attention remained focused dead ahead. She called out to them but they did not respond. They marched and played as if she were not even there.

In the next row was a sousaphone, flanked by two saxophones, stepping in sync. The front row featured a trombone in the center with a trumpet on either side. The horn players made synchronized up-and-down and side-to-side movements with their instruments as they played. Leading the group, a single clarinet player marched to and fro across the front line. He occasionally turned to face the band, marching backward and staying in step all the while. They were a lively looking group, Nalia thought, to be playing such slow and somber music.

In front of the band, the eight men walked in two straight lines. They were broad shouldered, black men with oddly similar features. They were dressed identically in dark tuxedos with tails. Their steps were so synchronized they resembled a machine, and their expressions conveyed no more humanity. As Nalia drew nearer she could see they all wore white carnations in their lapels, tied with bright blue and gold ribbons. They hid their eyes behind gold, mirrored sunglasses. Their lines were perfectly straight and Nalia could now see why. They were carrying a long, shiny, black box between them.

Clarity struck her like a hammer; this was a funeral band. Ahead in the distance she could see the gates of St. Louis Cemetery Number One. In addition to the music of the band, she could now hear the footsteps of the pallbearers growing in intensity. Something told Nalia she shouldn't be here. She wanted to run away but her spirit felt trapped, and once again she found it increasingly difficult to breathe.

"Follow her," the voice in her head reverberated louder. Nalia looked up to see Queen Marie sitting atop the white stone at the iron gates of the cemetery. The voice in her head and the presence of the doll calmed her anxiety, urging her onward.

She stepped to the side, allowing the procession to pass through the gates and suddenly her mind was spinning, like a child watching the sky from a merry-go-round. Dizziness overtook her. She felt as if she was going to fall, but she couldn't tell which way was down. The world spun out of control. Her body became as light as a feather and darkness veiled her eyes.

Moments later, her feet grew heavy and she felt them slam against the ground. The world around her was once again motionless and still devoid of color. She found herself standing in the middle of the cemetery beside a stark-white tomb three spaces high and covered in markings – "XXX". The band was standing in tight formation a short distance away among the many other crypts. Nalia could still hear their music, a slow, beautiful, smooth jazz version of "When the Saints Go Marchin' In", but the musicians were now frozen in time, like dolls in Mama Lu's display. As she walked closer, she marveled at the positions of the musician's lips and jaws. The trumpeter's cheeks bulged as if they'd been blowing a lengthy note when time decided to stop.

Beyond the band, the pallbearers stood facing each other with their hands folded together in front of them. More static than Palace Guards, they stared through their mirrored glasses. Their two rows formed a human corridor leading to the casket, which Nalia could see was now open. Fearful yet curious, she felt compelled to investigate.

As she walked between the pallbearers she stretched out her hand and considered touching one to see if he would react, but remembered the hummingbird, and thought better of it. She felt a lump rise in her throat when she noticed they all wore identical gold watches – each one read 12:01.

Slowly, she made her way toward the casket, each step a prayer she would not find it holding someone she knew. She wanted to close her eyes as she approached, but her curiosity was too insistent. When she felt she was close enough, she lifted her head to look inside. A vice-like grip tightened around her chest and she froze, dead-still staring at her own body lying cold on the satin cushions. She stood slack-jawed gazing at her corpse in disbelief. What was this? Was she not dreaming after all? Was she dead?

A scream boiled in the back of her throat but before it could erupt, the world came roaring back to life. Shades of green poured back into the foliage beyond the white cemetery wall, and the sky returned to a brilliant blue. One of the trumpeters blew a spirited solo riff and the band sprang back into action. The pallbearers clapped and danced as the musicians broke out into a hearty, up-tempo version of "Second Line".

The group turned and began a lively march back in the direction of the gates. Their steps were snappy and their expressions jovial. The clarinet player leapt from side to side, turning and spinning as he marched with high, exaggerated steps.

Nalia stood watching in shock, wanting to cry. She shouted in anger, "What's wrong with you people? This is a funeral!" They carried on, oblivious to her presence. "This is *my* funeral!" The words were sobering. "This is my funeral," she whispered to herself. "I'm dead."

She felt faint and dizzy. Her knees grew weak and she found herself on the verge of collapse. Instinctively, she grabbed at the casket for stability. She was shocked back to coherency when her arm slipped inside and her fingertips touched her own cold, dead flesh.

She jumped and screamed, turning her back to the coffin. She couldn't bring herself to look at it again. She watched the band as they wound their way through the dilapidated crypts of the cemetery and past the white tomb with the X's. To Nalia's amazement, she saw someone sitting on top of the structure. It was a woman. Her back was turned, but Nalia could see she wore a bright blue dress and gold hoop earrings.

"Follow her," said the voice again, and Nalia obeyed. She walked toward the tomb, focused on the woman in blue. "Queen Marie?" she thought. Could it be? As she stepped closer she wondered if she was about to come face to face with a living, breathing, life-sized version of her doll. It was silly, she thought, but possible in this bizarre place.

The inscription on the tomb read "Paris" and "Glapion", but a bronze plaque on the corner said it was the reputed burial place of Marie Laveau. If Nalia had really passed into the spirit world, was this the spirit of the famed Voodoo Queen of New Orleans sitting atop her tomb? She crept around the corner and stared up into the face of the mysterious figure. The woman was smiling as bright as the sun. It was Mama Lu.

Nalia's heart leapt and her anxiety faded away instantly; the sight of her Mama Lu brought great relief. Now, she felt safe. She spoke to Mama Lu but got no response, save for the beaming smile. Looking into her eyes, Nalia could tell she wanted to say something, but could not. It was then Nalia noticed Queen Marie sitting there on the ground. She jumped back with fright when she saw just behind the doll, coiled next to the tomb, was an enormous white python. It raised its head and stared at Nalia, powerful and majestic in its appearance. It made no attempt to strike, but instead, slowly lifted its head toward Mama Lu.

Mama Lu looked down at Nalia from on top of the tomb with a calm reassurance. "Give her to me, that I may speak," the voice echoed in Nalia's head. Mama Lu simply smiled.

Nalia looked back at the great, ivory reptile. It made no threatening movements, so Nalia cautiously inched forward. She stretched out her hand slowly, constantly watching the serpent for the slightest motion. The snake remained perfectly still as if granting permission. Before she knew it, Nalia had the doll in her grasp and was lifting it steadily away from the watchful python. When she was convinced of her safety, Nalia stood on her tiptoes and lifted the doll high into the waiting hands of her still-beaming Mama Lu.

Once the doll was in her grasp, Mama Lu threw back her head and took in a deep, satisfying breath of air. She savored it and held it in, as if the breath of life was touching her body for the very first time. As she exhaled, she laughed heartily. Her slow, deep cackle echoed throughout the cemetery, reverberating off the abundance of stone and concrete. Finally, she looked down at Nalia and smiled. Her eyes sparkled with the joy of a mother gazing at her newborn baby. Her blissful expression comforted Nalia. After all she had been through, she needed it.

Her sense of safety was shaken, however, by the sensation of movement near her feet. The giant snake was uncoiling itself. Slowly it slithered, its head bobbing up and down against the tomb. Little by little it unwound itself and stretched out the length of the slab. Its muscles writhed rhythmically as it began to circle the stone structure on which Mama Lu was perched. Nalia watched its movements in awe as it made its way around, then disappeared on the back side of the tomb. When it was gone, she raised her eyes to the top of the crypt, but Mama Lu was no longer there.

"Precious, precious chil'," came a startling voice from behind her. Nalia whipped around to see Mama Lu leaning against a nearby brick mausoleum. She held Queen Marie and wore the sweetest of smiles. Her face beamed with joy, but Nalia sensed worry in her eyes. "You has done well," said Mama Lu.

Nalia took a deep breath. She walked toward Mama Lu, wrapped her arms around her and held her tight for a very long time, like a scared little child. Mama Lu did not say a word, but simply held Nalia close, waiting for her to feel comfortable enough to ask the many questions she was sure to have.

When Nalia's spirit was calm, she spoke.

"Mama?" she asked, still locked in the embrace, "Where are we?"

"Why, we in New Orleans, chil'. St. Louis Cemetery Number One," Mama Lu replied jovially. "Don' you recognize it, darlin'? Did you bump yo' head?"

Nalia was confused by Mama Lu's casual response. Surely she could see the circumstances surrounding their situation were, at the very least, atypical. Couldn't she?

"Mama?" she asked again with cautious restraint, stammering. The question she wanted to ask proved so difficult she had trouble forming the words. She was quite certain she did not want to hear the answer, but she had to know. Before she could talk herself out of it, she blurted it out. "Am I dead?"

Mama Lu shook her head and laughed so hard Nalia was sure she felt the ground shake. She held Nalia at arms length and smiled. "Now I know we in a cemetery, chil', but don' you think if you was dead, you'd be part of it, not up walkin' 'round in it?"

Mama Lu's response did nothing to assuage Nalia's confusion. Nothing made sense. "Then am I dreaming?" she asked.

"Not exactly, but then again, you ain't exactly awake neither."

Nalia still did not understand. She couldn't conceive how she could be awake and asleep at the same time. Was she sleepwalking? She looked around at the deserted cemetery with its marble, brick and concrete tombs. She glanced over the inscriptions on the stones trying to discern what was real, what felt like truth. Her gaze was drawn to the casket sitting alone in the distance. "If I'm not dead," she asked, "Then who is in that coffin?"

Sadness filled Mama Lu's eyes as she hung her head. She was visibly shaken and struggling to speak. "Dat chil'," she finally articulated, "Is a young woman by the name o' Nalia Deminy."

Nalia's heart skipped a beat as her confusion reached an exponential level. "But I'm Nalia Deminy," she said, "Deminy is my name."

"No," replied Mama Lu, "Deminy is *my* name. It's the name I gave to you when I took you to raise."

"Well yeah, I know, but it's my name too," replied Nalia. "I haven't gone by Décantrel since before I can remember."

Mama Lu did not look up and did not speak. She stared at Queen Marie, fumbling nervously with her clothing. She straightened the doll's dress over and over. Nalia finally broke the silence. "Mama?" she asked apprehensively.

"I can't explain to you why I done what I done, baby," replied Mama Lu with tears in her eyes. "You gon' have to see it fo' yo'self. You may hate me fo' what I done, but you need to know, I done it fo' y'own good. I done it to protect you."

Seeing her Mama Lu in such distress broke Nalia's heart. She wanted to comfort her and tell her everything would be alright, but a sting of betrayal loomed over the unanswered questions in her mind. "What are you sayin', Mama? What did you do?"

Mama Lu caught a deep breath of courage and looked Nalia straight in the eyes. "You were never Nalia Décantrel. I told you dat to help hide you away. I changed yo' name to keep you alive."

Nalia's mouth hung open. She could not believe what she was hearing. With a single statement her entire existence was shaken to its foundation, and the possibility that her whole life was a lie began to dawn on her. The forgotten fears of a six-year-old child entrenched her mind before she could defend it, leaving Nalia confused and uncomfortable. Chills crawled across her skin like spiders as she listened.

"Décantrel was yo' mother's maiden name, but didn't nobody know dat 'round here and she didn't have no family left to speak of," continued Mama Lu. "Your real name is Nalia Barronne. Dat was yo' father's name."

Nalia was shocked. She had no memory of her father. She had been told her mother was a single parent; her father left before she was born. How on earth could she share his name? This information had her completely baffled and growing angry. She had enough trouble discerning reality from fiction as it was, here in this strange world. Now she was being asked to entertain a different identity inside an altered reality. Enough was enough. A thousand questions flooded her mind, demanding explanation. Was this true? Was it real? Was *any* of this real? Mama Lu was the only one who had the answers, but where would she begin?

Sensing the barrage of questions on the horizon, Mama Lu continued, "I can't explain all these things to you, chil'. Bad as I wants to, I can't tell you what the truth is. I can't explain to you what is real and what ain't. I can only show you the mem'ries I took from you."

Nalia didn't understand what Mama Lu meant, but she was nonetheless offended. "Took from me?" she questioned.

"Fo' yo' own protection, chil', I had to hide dem mem'ries from you." She could see Nalia's anger breaking though the confusion, and attempted to counter it with further explanation. "You gon' have a series o' dreams, similar to dis, but these new dreams is gon' be mem'ries. Yo' mem'ries."

Nalia struggled to grasp the concept of what she was hearing. "I'm going to dream my own memories?" she asked.

"Not just yo' own, but mine too. Wha's more, you gon' see Mr. John's and Madame Toulouse's 'cause we all connected, you see, by the drum."

Nalia was suddenly aware of the still beating drum. It had been there all along, she realized: in the rhythm of the band, the steps of the pallbearers, even the movement of the snake. It pulsed inside her body like a heartbeat.

"Everyone is here to help you, chil'," Mama Lu continued. "You gon' see images dat belong to us all. You gon' see whatever the magic needs you to see fo' you to know the truth. Dat's the way it works."

"Magic? Truth? What truth?" asked Nalia, finding truth to be a foreign concept, considering the circumstances.

"The truth about yo' past, baby; the tragic truth dat was hidden from you," Mama Lu explained with sad eyes. "But I have to warn you, seein' dem mem'ries ain't gon' be easy. In fact, its gon' get downright nasty. Dat's why I'm tellin' you we all here to help you, baby."

She reached for Nalia's hand, but Nalia pulled it away in anger. She felt betrayed. How could you hide someone's entire past from them with lies and call it ok? Her life had been molded to Mama Lu's will because she thought it was better that way. "How was that fair?" she thought, "Who was she to play God?" Nalia didn't know how to react. She looked at Mama Lu with disapproval, her face twisted as if she smelled something sour. "You're here for me?" she asked in disgust. "You lied to me my whole life and now you're here for me? What am I supposed to say? Oh, it's fine that I'm not the person I thought I was *my whole life!* I'll just be someone else now! Who would you like for me to be this time? Just thought I'd ask, you know, since you're *here for me!*"

Mama Lu began to cry. She knew on some level she deserved this, but hearing such harsh words come from Nalia's lips was heartbreaking. It was like witnessing the death of a sickly relative: no matter how much you prepare for the inevitable, nothing lessens the sting. Still, she knew what she did was right. It saved her daughter, and ultimately that was all that mattered. "I've always been here fo' you, baby," she said softly through the tears. "I lied to you 'cause I had to, to keep you safe. But through it all, I've *always* been here fo' you. I love you."

Nalia turned away. She felt justified in her anger and she wanted to stay that way, but Mama Lu's tears stirred her compassion. As badly as she hurt, as betrayed as she felt, she couldn't stand to see her Mama Lu hurting, too. After all, she thought, this was the kindest woman she had ever known. This was the woman who took her in when her own mother left her behind, the woman she'd known as Mama since she was six years old. These truths were written on her heart. They could not be denied, regardless of her past before them. Mama Lu abandoned all else to devote herself to raising a child who was not her own, and now she stood before her, making no demands. She did not infer a single thing was owed to her, nor did she expect anything to be given. She simply stood there, offering truth and asking forgiveness. For that, Nalia thought, despite all her wrong, she deserved a chance.

"I know you love me, Mama," Nalia said, "So if you say you're here for me, then I guess I have to trust you."

Mama Lu breathed a shallow sigh of relief. She knew this was only the first, small step on a very long journey, but at least it was a step in the right direction.

"But I want some answers," continued Nalia in a tone abandoned of all warmth and understanding. "You can start by telling me about my father."

All the color left Mama Lu's cheeks. "Chil' if I tell you about yo' father, then I only tell you *my* truth," she replied. "You must find *yo'* truth. There are many things dat you must learn, but you can't walk before you crawl. You gots to be shown dem mem'ries as you knew 'em befo', otherwise they become altered again. It's all up to yo' mind and the magic."

Nalia was baffled once again. She wanted answers, not riddles. Still, her heart said "trust", and she trusted her heart. The drum droned on inside her mind and somewhere in its rhythm she heard the still, small voice of Madame Toulouse. "Patience, my baby. Everything in its time. Trust yo' Mama. Peace gon' come."

Just as Nalia was finally able to calm her racing thoughts, she felt a rustling beside her leg. She looked down and jumped in shock. The white serpent had returned and was slowly making its way past her toward Mama Lu. Its scaly body moved across the ground in large arcs like a great ivory river. It circled around Mama Lu, then back toward Nalia, crossing itself in a large figure eight. Nalia stared at Mama Lu, afraid to move or speak. Noticing her frightened expression, Mama Lu spoke with a calm soothing tone. "Don' be frightened, chil'. Zombi ain't here to harm nobody; he's here to channel the power."

"Is this your snake, Mama?" Nalia asked in utter confusion, not remembering her Mama Lu to have ever owned a snake.

Mama Lu chuckled in response. "No, chil'. Zombi belonged to Marie Laveau 'bout two hundred years ago. He still hangs 'round here sometimes."

Fairly certain she heard correctly, Nalia struggled to comprehend the puzzling statement. "And, where exactly is *here*?" she asked, looking around at the surreal setting.

"*Here* is New Orleans, baby," said Mama Lu. "Jus' a little different than you know it. You see, we are on what you call a different plane than what is normal to you. See, New Orleans is here; its going on all around us right now. You jus' can't see it 'cause we're on another level, not unlike the spirit world. Yo' body stays on one level but yo' mind, yo' spirit, can travel between 'em if you know how to let it."

Nalia could only stare. Two days ago her primary concerns were the affections of a young man and her English exam. Today, she was standing next to a two hundred year old python in a cemetery, in the middle of New Orleans, on a "different plane" discussing quantum physics with what was apparently the spirit of her Mama Lu. Her brain was spent.

Suddenly, there was a loud rushing sound in the air, like static between stations on a radio dial. Mama Lu looked to the sky in panic. "Somethin's wrong," she said. The clouds accelerated, swirling like a storm. The great snake vanished and Nalia felt something inside her shift. Without warning, great pain overtook her body, like she was being ripped in half. She felt opposing forces pulling at her, dragging her in two different directions: one toward the ground, the other toward the sky. Color faded from the world around her like water down a storm drain as the sound of static became deafening. Nalia covered her ears with the palms of her hands, pressing hard against her head. The pain centralized in her gut as she doubled over and fell to the ground. The clouds circled faster and darker overhead until all the world went black.

In the dark there was nothing but emptiness. The noise hushed and the pain retreated. Nalia saw nothing, heard nothing, and felt nothing.

Moments later, the cold sensation of hard earth returned to her increasingly aching body. Slowly, feeling returned to her limbs as the ground softened beneath her, becoming like cotton. Nalia breathed deeply and took in the rich aroma of chamomile and spearmint. She did not open her eyes, but could sense she was home. She felt the warmth of her duvet around her and breathed a long awaited sigh of relief. Anxiety released its hold on her body as she cradled her pillow tightly. When she rolled over in her bed and stretched, her arm brushed against her familiar plush rag doll, Emily. She pulled her close and held her like a child, taking in the moment.

Then her eyes sprang open. "Why is Emily here?" she thought. She was supposed to be back in her apartment. How…? To her horror, she could smell the faintest stench of gasoline.

Her body stiffened in panic. White-knuckled, she gripped Emily and held tight as the beast surfaced over the foot of her bed. Its green eyes were bloodshot and hungry and its hot breath rolled over her feet like a heavy fog. In the distance she could see the darkness rising taller than ever before, arrogant and haughty. Nalia pushed her feet into the mattress and kicked, propelling her body toward the headboard, as if she expected it to provide shelter. The bitter cold sensation gathered in her throat, closing off air to her lungs. Stronger and faster she kicked, but to no avail; the beast gained ground.

Pain seared Nalia's flesh as the beast tore its claws into her thighs, first one then the other. Nalia could feel her flesh ripping as it dragged her down toward the foot of the bed. A single claw found its way under her shirt and dug deep into her stomach. She could sense it savoring the feel of her flesh. The smell of the beast's gasoline-soaked breath hung thick in the air. Nalia's lungs cried out in desperation as her throat finally opened, allowing a rush of air into her body.

Adrenaline surged, tightening her every muscle as she forced out a piercing scream that was heard throughout the neighborhood.

———————

The sound stopped the beating of the drum. Panic ripped Mr. John away from his meditation and he raced to the bay door. Throwing it open he fell to his knees, studying the arc of brick dust. It was perfect. No flaws. What went wrong? This was too soon. He watched with angst as the light came on in Nalia's bedroom and a frantic shadow rushed across the window. Anxiety seized his body like a cold fist tightening its grip. His mind was full of questions and his heart raced like a rabbit. Helplessly, he watched and waited.

———————

Mama Lu held Nalia close, cradling her head against her shoulder. She rocked back and forth, stroking her hair just as she had when Nalia was a child. Nalia curled into a ball as tightly as she could, her body still shaking uncontrollably.

Something wasn't right, thought Mama Lu. The nightmare returned too quickly, as if it forced its way in. There was supposed to be a natural order to things, and this was not it. The visions should have preceded the nightmare. This was backwards.

As Nalia's body trembled in Mama Lu's arms, she sobbed and whimpered like a beaten animal. Her breathing was labored and sporadic. She bit her lip hard, but even the taste of blood did not pull her out of her trance-like shell.

Mama Lu continued to rock as she cursed under her breath. She questioned every decision made in the last twenty-four hours. How could she put her baby through this? She briefly considered calling the whole thing off, but knew it was much too late for that. It was already started and must be endured to the end. Guilt pricked her heart, but she knew this was not her fault. She was simply cleaning up the aftermath of someone else's destruction, and she had been doing it for years. She turned her head and glared in disgust at the doll on top of the dresser as she held her daughter close.

The clock read 12:02.

CHAPTER TWELVE

The spark of the cigarette lighter illuminated the blackness of the car's interior. The streetlights in the alley behind the building had been shot out using a silenced .22 caliber pistol. The black Lincoln sat parked in the resulting darkness.

Madame Luciénne pulled a syringe from the small pocket inside her beaded clutch and used the plunger to stir the mixture of powder and water in the spoon. In the flickering glow of the Zippo, she could see the sweat beading up on Tony's forehead as he held the spoon over the flame and watched the mixture turn clear.

"I still can't believe I let you talk me into dis," Tony said with a nervous twitch. "You're gonna get me killed, here."

"Relax," purred Madame Luciénne, "You've got not'in to worry 'bout. She ain't the big, bad, Voodoo priestess she used to be. She got no power anymore. Hasn't had fo' years, now."

The drug began to bubble slowly in the center of the spoon. Tony's eyes grew wide with excitement as he began to move the flame slowly, back and forth.

"Well, if she can still do even half a what she could back in the day, then you got me in deep…"

"Those are just stories," Madame Luciénne interrupted, "Made up and exaggerated over the years. I know. I've known her for a long time." The heroin was now cooking evenly, emitting the slightest smell of vinegar. "She could never really do all those things you hear about."

Tony removed the Zippo from beneath the spoon and held it over the mixture so they could see. "I know the Verelli brothers had a beef wit' her years ago, and ain't nobody seen or heard from dem since," he argued. "I know dat for a fact. Not only dat, but I heard about dem creepy voodoo dolls she keeps, and about things she's done to people wit' 'em – unnatural things."

Madame Luciénne dropped a tiny piece of cotton into the mixture and drew the drug through it into the syringe. She watched the hunger consume Tony's eyes as she handed it to him. "I'm tellin' you, she's harmless."

Extinguishing the lighter, Tony took the syringe and held it like a long, lost friend. "Just this once," he thought. Madame Luciénne flipped on the dome light long enough for him to slip the needle into his arm, then quickly turned it off again, scanning the alley nervously to be sure they were not seen.

Tony didn't need a blood return to know he had found the vein; this was like coming home. As his body embraced the drug, a rush of anxiety released like he was opening a pressure valve. A warm sensation took over, and his eyes rolled back as his vision narrowed. A sly smile was all he could see in the darkness. He felt Madame Luciénne's hand on his. She guided his fingers down and cupped them around the cold, solid wood of a Louisville Slugger.

"Do it," she whispered as she reached across him and opened the car door.

Tony stumbled over the empty whiskey bottle at his feet, out of the vehicle and into the alley. Madame Luciénne could barely make out his silhouette in the shadows as he disappeared around the front of the building. Moments later, the night was ripped apart by the piercing sound of shattered glass.

It was a good thing, thought Madame Luciénne, that she would have little use for Tony after this evening. She had a feeling she just signed his death warrant.

CHAPTER THIRTEEN

In the quiet parlor of her large, old house, Madame Toulouse sat before her altar, gnawed by the unmistakable feeling that something was amiss. The room was dark now and the smoke from the lifeless candles hung dauntingly around her head. Even before the candles mysteriously flickered out, Madame Toulouse knew the stability of the bond was compromised. The once strong and steady flow of energy became sporadic, meaning it was dangerously unprotected.

Madame Toulouse rarely entertained anxiety, but this new development was troubling. Her wondrous gift of inner sight allowed her to easily see events of the future and the past, but whatever disrupted the bond also dimmed her psychic vision.

Frustrated, she resigned herself to exploring alternate methods of divination. She felt like a racecar driver riding a bicycle as she gathered the appropriate articles. She retrieved a shallow bowl, a small amber vial, and a black silk satchel from a nearby armoire and placed them in the center of the altar. She then hurried off to the kitchen, returning with a bottle of water and a book of matches. As she struck a match against the side of the box, she wondered how long it had been since she lit an altar candle by hand. She couldn't remember.

When her two candles were once again burning brightly, she opened the satchel and emptied its contents into the shallow bowl. A set of small stones with rudimentary markings clinked against the ceramic surface, accompanied by several small, bleached bones. Opening the bottle of water, Madame Toulouse poured it over the items in the bowl until they were covered. She then pulled the stopper from the amber vial of oil and waved it under her nose, inhaling and analyzing its vapor. Convinced that its content was adequate, she tipped the vial over the water and carefully poured a short, steady stream into the bowl. She watched closely as the dark oil pooled on the surface of the water hovering just above the runes and the bones like a gathering storm cloud.

Madame Toulouse leaned in low over the bowl, studying the shapes made by the pooling oil, waiting for a recognizable pattern to materialize. Then, without warning, the pool exploded into a thousand tiny beads that scattered across the surface of the water. The beads of oil raced from the center of the bowl to its edge, clinging there like frightened children.

Madame Toulouse gasped, drawing away so quickly she nearly toppled her chair backward. From a saucer beneath one of the candles, she pinched a healthy portion of sugar with her fingertips and cast it into the bowl of oil and water. She dipped her finger into the mixture and marked X's hurriedly across the front of the altar. With her wet fingers, Madame Toulouse extinguished the flames and quickly left the room. She used the telephone on her kitchen wall to call for a cab. She would need to gather her belongings and an appropriate hat for a hurried trip to Mama Lu's.

Across town, Mama Lu sat on the edge of Nalia's bed, still stroking her daughter's tousled hair. Nearly an hour had passed since Nalia was violently awakened by the nightmare. She'd spent that time cradled in the comforting arms of her Mama Lu. Only once since the screaming had Nalia spoken. Just before she drifted back off to sleep, Mama Lu heard her softly whisper one word – Barronne.

Mama Lu was still puzzled by what went wrong as she laid Nalia's exhausted body back down on the bed and covered her snugly with the duvet. Nothing had ever broken the bond before. The energy was always strong, especially when Mr. John and Madame Toulouse both provided protection. Their barriers had never been penetrated. Mama Lu felt vulnerable.

She rose and walked to the window. Drawing back the curtain, she could see Mr. John sitting on the edge of his rocking chair across the narrow road, waiting anxiously for a sign. When he saw Mama Lu in the window, Mr. John rose and stood in the open bay door just inside his arc of brick dust. He held his pipe and stared at the window until

Mama Lu nodded to him reassuringly, letting him know Nalia was alright and sleeping once again.

Mr. John tilted his head and furrowed his brow with an inquisitive look. Mama Lu knew he was also wondering what went wrong. Their many years of familiarity yielded exemplary non-verbal skills. She shook her head in response and then waved him over.

This was unheard of, thought Mr. John, smudging through the red line with his foot. Never before had he felt like such a failure. A swarm of questions surfaced in his mind. Was this his fault? What had he done wrong? Something crossed the barriers. Something foreign got in and he felt responsible. If anything happened to Nalia, he would never forgive himself. He closed the bay door behind him, stepped over the useless line, and made his way across the street with his pipe in his teeth and his hands stuffed deep into his pockets.

The bedroom was lit by a single candle Mama Lu left burning on the vanity. Nalia's slumbering body curled into a ball as she clutched her pillow tightly with the duvet drawn snugly around her chin. Her spirit demanded rest.

As she drifted into a deep sleep, her mind wandered into a vast field beside a wide lake. She could smell the wildflowers blossoming in the tall grass as she stood near the water's edge allowing the dew to moisten her bare feet. Slowly, she walked along the shoreline watching the rising sun glisten off the rippling water as dragonflies kissed the surface. In the distance stood a large white gazebo with a pointed roof and shimmering, gold wind chimes.

The octagonal structure was open on two sides, with steps inviting her in. The other six panels featured a wide hand rail and were covered with latticework from the rail down to the deck. Nalia heard the wind chimes calling her name like a soft voice summoning her spirit. The gazebo was beautifully made, and against the vivid green of the field, it offered the allure of complete tranquility. Nalia felt confident her soul would find rest in the shade of its thatched roof. She quickened her pace, running across the field as carefree as a child on a playground. As

Nalia approached the gazebo, the sun grew higher and brighter, shining on the blinding white-washed wood. She could still smell the fresh paint as she stepped up onto the deck marveling at the crisscrossed patterns of light and shadow cast by the morning sun through the lattice. Inside the railed panels were wide benches with bright red cushions that formed a large sitting area. On the middle cushion, on the side nearest the lake, sat a small familiar doll dressed in blue with gold hoop earrings, smiling as if waiting for Nalia to arrive. The doll's earrings sparkled in the sunlight like a surreal message in Morse code summoning Nalia across the rough, wood-planked flooring to sit on the cushion beside Queen Marie. As Nalia picked up the doll and held her close, the gleaming earrings reflected the full brilliance of the blinding sun and the world faded away into blackness around the glare.

When her eyes recovered and Nalia was finally able to focus, the gazebo looked different. All eight sides were now fully enclosed by latticework from top to bottom and a bright white light shone through the tiny checkered openings so nothing could be seen beyond the latticed walls. In the center of the floor was a large hole with a thin iron handrail which followed a winding staircase down into the earth below the gazebo. Surprisingly, Nalia was not frightened by the odd turn of events, but welcomed it as a peaceful transition. The tranquility of the gazebo enveloped her like a warm blanket. It made events which would normally be viewed as bizarre seem welcoming and comfortable, like she'd been here before.

Gripping Queen Marie tightly, Nalia made her way over to the top of the steps, placed her hand on the cool, metal railing and peered into the opening. The winding stairs led to a small, dark room where a thin beam of light stretched across the floor. Nalia's curiosity swelled as she slowly descended the cold, iron steps. The darkness limited her vision, making her steps unsteady and her mind wary. She felt relieved when her foot struck against the smooth hardwood floor below.

Nalia could see the thin beam of light was coming from a doorway, slightly ajar, on the far side of the room. Shadows occasionally broke the beam, indicating movement just beyond the door. She could hear indistinct noises coming from the other side. Cautiously, she crossed the dark room, but oddly, did not seem to get any closer to the doorway. The more she walked, the farther the door seemed to be – like it was running away. Confused, Nalia looked back toward the stairs to find the room was much larger than she originally anticipated, as if it was growing. In the distance, she could see rays of sunlight, illuminating the winding, iron staircase from above. Calculating the distance in her head she perceived herself to be about halfway across the room, but when she turned back around, she nearly ran into the previously elusive door. Nalia felt a strange paranoia, like it snuck up on her from behind.

Clinging tightly to Queen Marie, she leaned close to the opening. As the sounds beyond the door became clearer, Nalia could make out the muffled noises of traffic and the distinct mutterings of a familiar voice. Gently, she opened the door to reveal the storefront of Mama Lu's shop. On the far side of the store she could see her Mama Lu fumbling with the dressings of a large doll in the glass case beside the replication of Marie Laveau. Mama Lu was mumbling to herself and humming a low tune Nalia recognized but couldn't quite place.

"Mama Lu," Nalia said, advancing through the doorway. Mama Lu did not respond, but continued straightening the doll's garments as if she heard nothing at all. When she was finished, she closed the glass case and walked quickly behind the counter, through the other door and into the workroom.

Confused and disoriented, Nalia turned to the door behind her, looking for the darkened room with the sun-lit staircase. Instead she found the sewing room, right where it should be, with its large stores of fabric on the shelves against the wall, and its strong smell of hot glue.

Suddenly, the bells above the front door tinkled to life, startling Nalia. Turning around, she saw a well-dressed woman entering the shop with a young girl following close behind. She was tall and slender – a light-skinned black woman wearing a bright red dress and a matching hat. Her dress was cinched at the waist with a wide ivory belt. Her face was heavily painted and her fingers were adorned with many gold rings, the largest of which was on the ring finger of her left hand. It featured three gold bands ornamented with a cluster of small stones and one very large diamond, at least a half carat, set in the center. Around her neck she wore a perfect set of polished pearls that matched her earrings. The woman also sported a wide cuff bracelet encrusted with gems, and on her left lapel, a heart-shaped diamond broach. She was a striking young woman with strong features and a distinct air of elegance.

The young girl behind her, however, wore a plain, simple red dress and appeared slightly awkward and shy. She was fair-skinned but noticeably not white. She had straight, shoulder-length dark hair curled into bouncy spirals, and looked to be about five or six years of age. Though her eyes widened at the vast display of dolls, she appeared to have a strong discipline for keeping her hands to herself.

Just then, the workroom door opened and Mama Lu peered out. "Sorry Miss, but we ain't open fo' business today," she said to the woman standing by the door.

"I beg your pardon, Ma'am," the woman responded in a thick southern drawl. "I saw the sign on the door, but the gentleman outside told me it would be alright if I was to come in just for a look around. I don't mean to impose, and I certainly won't expect to be buying anything today, you being closed for business and all. I just couldn't help admiring the beautiful dolls you have on display here."

Mama Lu stepped out of the workroom. Looking through the display window she could barely see Mr. John tipping his hat. She would have to have a word with that man about the meaning of the word "closed", she thought.

Noticing Mama Lu's obvious irritation, the woman continued, "If it's a bother, I'll be glad to come back another day."

Mama Lu noticed the young girl walking carefully between the tree-like displays with her hands folded tightly in front of her. The girl gave a nervous look in the woman's direction to make sure she wasn't being watched before gently extending a hand to feel the fabric of a dress worn by one of the dolls on the bottom tier. Barely disturbing the doll at all, she brushed her fingers gently against the hem of the delicate garment. Mama Lu was moved to quiet curiosity, and couldn't help but smile when she saw the care with which the little girl handled the doll.

"Don't be silly," Mama Lu said to the woman at the door, "You already here. Take yo' time an' have a look 'round." Mama Lu slipped behind the counter and removed her apron.

Relieved, the woman smiled and walked across the shop to the counter, extending a hand to Mama Lu. "Margaret Barronne," she said "but most folks call me Mary."

Mama Lu shook her hand. Noticing the woman's rings, she understood why Mr. John let her in. The woman's wealth was obvious and it would surely have been unwise to turn away a potential customer of such stature. Perhaps that talk with Mr. John could wait, she thought, as she saw him winking through the window.

The woman's grand display of baubles caused Mama Lu to wonder if she was somehow associated with any of the various local businesses that bore the name Barronne. Feeling that asking the woman outright could be viewed as inappropriate, Mama Lu opted for a more subtle form of interrogation.

"Lucia Deminy. Pleased to meet you," she said. "Pardon me fo' askin', but Barronne sounds like an Italian name. You don't look Italian, and that accent tells me you ain't from 'round here, so where you from, Mrs. Barronne?"

"I moved here about six years ago from Atlanta. My husband is from New Orleans but he has a business there, and that's how we met. He brought me back here when we married." The little girl joined the woman at the counter. "This is my daughter, Nalia," she said resting a hand gently on the girl's shoulder.

Still watching the events from the sewing room door, Nalia drew a rapid breath as the realization of what was happening hit her. The scene unfolding before her eyes was a forgotten memory from her past. As she watched the little girl, Nalia tried to come to terms with the fact that she was viewing herself as a child, but more fascinating, by far, was the fact that she was now looking upon the face of her mother. Her throat grew dry and her heart rate quickened. She could see the woman's features were remarkably similar to those of her doll, Mary, which stood on top of her dresser. For a brief moment her mind drifted to Mama Lu's skill and craftsmanship as she realized the doll was nearly identical. Without thinking the word spilled from her lips, "Mother?"

The woman did not answer. She gave no indication she'd heard anything at all. As she continued to talk with Mama Lu, Nalia stepped over to the counter. For the first time she could remember, her eyes beheld the woman who gave her life. It was as if the woman had walked out of a fairytale storybook, a fictional character suddenly brought to life.

Nalia moved behind the counter, near Mama Lu, and stared into the woman's eyes. She could see the resemblance in her mother's cheek bones and in her lips. She wanted to reach out and touch her, but could not bring herself to do it for fear her hand would pass right through as if one of them were a ghost. The trouble would be deciding which one. Still, Nalia longed to embrace the woman, as somewhere inside her stirred the longing of a six-year-old girl. Yet, at the same time, anger climbed up her spine, demanding answers to years of questions. "Why did you leave me?" she thought, wanting to scream it at the top of her lungs. To her surprise, a tear dropped onto her cheek. She wiped it away quickly as if embarrassed, then leaned back against the wall to watch the scene unfold.

"I suspected you was from Georgia," said Mama Lu to the woman in red. "It's hard to hide an accent like dat."

"That obvious, huh?" asked the woman, chuckling and blushing through her heavy makeup. "I've lived here for six years now and I still stick out like a cat in the hen-house. I've tried to lose it, but it just sticks with me."

"Honey, don' you dare try an' lose dat accent," replied Mama Lu. "Dat's part of what makes you who you are. Don' never try an' be somebody you ain't. You jus' be yo'self wit' no apologies."

The woman gave a quick glance to the rings on her fingers before a sheepish expression washed over her face. "I did have some people from around here though," she said quickly in an attempt to avoid the awkward self-reflection. "My maiden name is Décantrel. My grandmother once told me we had some family that lived over this way, back around the 1800's. They're all gone now, of course."

"Well, wit' a name like dat I'd say it was likely. Décantrels got some history here 'round dat time. Did yo' grandmamma say who they was?"

"I'm sure she did, but I don't remember any names. She passed away about ten years ago, and she was the only family I ever had. She's actually the reason I stopped in here. One of the dolls in your display window reminds me of her."

"Well don' let me keep you from lookin' 'round darlin'," said Mama Lu. "You didn't stop in here to gab wit' me."

The woman thanked Mama Lu and proceeded to browse the shop. As she wandered, Mama Lu noticed the young girl standing in front of the glass case, staring up at the Marie Laveau doll with sad eyes. Mama Lu waited until her mother was on the far side of the shop, then silently stepped from behind the counter and walked over to the case. "You like dat doll, chil'?" she asked quietly.

"She's very pretty," said the young girl, nervously twisting back and forth. "I like her because she has skin like mine."

"Ah, you mean quadroon," said Mama Lu.

"What's quad-drune?" the child asked.

"Means one o' her parents was mixed."

The little girl's gaze dropped from the doll to the floor and her posture slumped to reflect her withdrawn demeanor.

"Aw, wha's wrong, chil'?" asked Mama Lu. The little girl kept silent with her head hung in shame. Mama Lu sensed a deep sadness in her spirit; something was stirring well below the surface. "It's ok chil', you can tell me. What is it?"

"That's what they call me at school – mixed," the child finally offered. "I get picked on a lot 'cause my skin is different."

"Picked on?" Mama Lu asked in surprise. "Beautiful girl like you, get picked on? Dat's jus' silly lil' children, don' know what they talkin' 'bout," she said dismissively. "So what if you dif'rent? Jus' imagine how borin' dis ol' world would be if everybody looked the same. Yo' beautiful jus' the way you are, chil'."

The little girl looked up from the floor and into Mama Lu's eyes. Mama Lu met her gaze with a wide, comforting smile. "Da color o' yo' skin don' define who you are, baby. Jus' 'cause other folks look a lil' diff'rent than you, don' make them no better than you, understand?"

Seeing the little girl's head droop once again, Mama Lu put a hand gently under her chin and raised her head until she could see the tears welling up in her eyes.

"Let me tell you a story," Mama Lu continued. She pointed to the doll of Marie Laveau behind the glass. "Do you know who dis is? Dis woman had skin jus' the same color as yours and they called her mixed too, but you know what? She was one of the mos' powerful women ever lived in dis whole city. So much in fact, dat they called her the Queen o' New Orleans."

Mama Lu winked as the young girl's mouth dropped open and her eyes widened with wonder.

"Where is her crown?" the little girl asked in a near whisper.

"Oh, she didn't need no crown, chil'," replied Mama Lu straightening to a very serious posture. "When everybody know you the queen, there ain't no sense in wearin' one. There wasn't a livin' soul in the city o' New Orleans what didn't know Marie Laveau."

The little girl smiled. Behind the counter, against the wall, Nalia smiled with her.

The child looked back at the large doll with a newfound admiration as her tiny chest swelled with pride. Something changed at that moment and a bond was formed between the child and Mama Lu. The seeds of self-confidence and self-respect were sown.

The young girl looked back at Mama Lu with wide eyes and a shy smile. "Can I have this doll?" she asked.

Mama Lu chuckled at the simplicity and innocence of the child's request. "Oh chil'," she responded, "Marie is my doll, and she's very special to me. Dis doll been wit' me fo' a long time now. I couldn't even think 'bout partin' wit' her. But I tell you dis, you have yo' mama bring you back another day real soon, and I'll see what I can do 'bout findin' you a doll dat'll be jus' as special fo' you."

"Really?" asked the little girl with excitement.

"You bet," replied Mama Lu.

With that, the young girl beamed and ran off to tell her mother the news as Mama Lu slipped back behind the counter.

The bells above the door tinkled and Nalia looked up to find Mr. John entering the shop. She noticed his face had fewer lines, and his upper body reflected a bit more youth.

"You through gossipin' wit' ol' man Leonetti?" asked Mama Lu.

"Gossip?" Mr. John said, sounding affronted. "Ain't no gossip goin' on out there, woman. Jus' two grown men catching up the events o' the neighborhood, dat's all."

"Um hmm, like I said…," replied Mama Lu.

"You gon' be lockin' up sometime dis century? 'Cause I'm yo' ride, if you ain't already forgot," said Mr. John with his eyebrows raised.

"I ain't never depended on no man fo' notin' in all my life, and I ain't about to start today," quipped Mama Lu. "So you go on, if you need to. I can catch the St. Charles line. I'll get home jus' fine by myself, you understand?"

Mr. John grumbled.

Margaret Barronne heard the conversation. Not realizing the tension was mocked, she decided it was time to go. She returned to the counter to thank her host. "As I said before, I don't want to trouble you when you're not open for business, but there are several pieces here that I'm interested in purchasing." She looked down at the little girl, whose appearance had reverted to sheepish and withdrawn. "And Nalia tells me you have something special in store for her."

The little girl looked up at Mama Lu with a shy smile, twisting and wringing her hands in a very submissive state of excitement.

"I do," replied Mama Lu, returning the little girl's grin.

"I'll be back later in the week," said the woman. "Thank you again for allowing us to come in on a Sunday."

"Do we have to leave, mommy?" the young girl pleaded in a desperate whisper.

The woman shot her a look that communicated a very deep level of displeasure and the little girl hushed immediately.

"Yes Nalia, we have to meet your daddy at Café Du Monde," replied Margaret sharply. Young Nalia dropped her head in disappointment, but Mama Lu caught her eye and gave her a quick wink. Margaret grabbed her daughter less than gently by the hand and led her out of the shop where her driver was waiting beside a long silver Cadillac.

Nalia stood against the wall behind the counter watching her mother walk out. She wondered if she would see her again, or if this was the only glimpse she would ever have of the woman who walked out of her life so many years ago.

Mama Lu stared straight at the front door. Mr. John recognized the troubled look in her eyes. "What's wrong Lu?" he asked.

"I don' know yet, John," she replied still staring. "Somethin' 'bout dat lil' girl is special. There's a sadness got a hold o' her spirit with a death grip. I could sense it befo' she even walked in here. Somethin' ain't right, and I don' like it."

"Well you know who dat is, don' you?" asked Mr. John. "Dat's Michael Barronne's wife. Why you think I let her in here? Dat woman's got mo' money than she know what to do wit'."

"You talkin' 'bout Michael Barronne as in the 'Le Barronne Hotel'?" asked Mama Lu.

"And the Barronne Shipyard," Mr. John added. "He got other hotels too, jus' not 'round here."

"Apparently one in Atlanta," said Mama Lu.

"They gots money all over the south," continued Mr. John.

"Mob money," interrupted Mama Lu, "But dat's not wha's makin' my skin crawl. It's bigger than dat, and its got somethin' to do wit' dat lil' girl." Mama Lu paused for a moment, deep in thought. Mr. John knew better than to break the silence.

"Ol' man Leonetti used to work down at dat shipyard," she finally continued. "I know he still got ties down there. You talk to him and see what he can find out 'bout dat lil' girl."

Mr. John nodded his agreement as he leaned against the counter and removed his pipe from the pocket of his shirt. He placed the stem between his teeth and struck a match. Nalia watched the flame grow brighter, and as the world around it faded into darkness, she felt her head become dizzy.

Soon the familiar comfort of her warm bedding surrounded her body and Nalia knew she was home. The serenity, however, was short-lived as the acrid smell of the demon's breath grew thick upon the air and the chilling sensation froze Nalia's body once again.

CHAPTER FOURTEEN

The sun was not yet cresting the horizon, but its rays were already flooding New Orleans with the day's first light. The neighborhood was still quiet. The early morning noise of school buses ceased a few weeks earlier and would not be heard again for at least two months. Songbirds, high in the trees, began their morning serenade – the only evidence cheerfulness still existed in the world.

Mr. John's head hung low over his coffee cup as the golden light of morning spilled through the sheer ivory curtains of the kitchen window. He breathed deeply, hoping the aroma of the chicory blend would give him enough energy to lift the cup to his lips. So far it was not working. His body, mind, and spirit were spent. It was a long, nail-biting night, full of worry and fear. Mr. John couldn't decide which was worse: the screaming or the waiting.

Mr. John and Madame Toulouse spent most of the night in the parlor, with Mama Lu joining them when she could, during the brief periods of serenity between the outbursts. Throughout the night, Nalia cycled through a disturbing pattern of sleep and terror, never actually reaching a fully awakened state of consciousness.

Mama Lu spent most of the evening in Nalia's room, tightly holding her daughter's trembling body. Several times she wondered if she were embracing a twenty-year-old young woman or a six-year-old little girl. In the end, it was not important. All that mattered was comforting her daughter, letting her know she was not alone and above all else, she was loved.

Mama Lu saw no need to fight back her tears. They continually flowed down her face like a faucet left dripping in the night. She had so many questions of her own. Had this been the right decision? The right time? Then, of course, there was the question they all wanted answered: what had upset the balance?

Madame Toulouse asked herself that same question a thousand times and each time became more agitated by her inability to see the answer. She could only assume there were powerful forces at work. Whoever was using Voodoo against them was strong enough to break the bond of three seasoned elders. Madame Toulouse felt greatly disadvantaged at the thought of facing such a worthy adversary without the use of her inner sight. It made her nervous, and though she would never admit it, slightly fearful. She shuddered when she considered the possibilities. It wasn't as if this mystery enemy was vying for business or territory or even notoriety. This wasn't a battle for money or power. Nalia's very life was at stake here. If Madame Toulouse and the others were unable to regain control of the situation, Nalia's mind could be permanently damaged – if her body survived the trauma at all.

As Madame Toulouse pondered who could possibly have gained enough knowledge and power to break their bond, her first thought went to Luciénne. She dismissed the notion almost immediately, scolding herself for entertaining a thought so ludicrous. "Madame" Luciénne, as she called herself, was little more than a bully. She had politicians and city officials in her pocket by means of blackmail and whatever connections she kept with the local mob, but beyond that, she was no real threat. She had no real power. Madame Toulouse would be surprised if Luciénne retained any knowledge at all of the mystic truths she'd learned under the guidance of Mama Lu. She certainly had not retained any respect for tradition, nor any reverence for her elders or for the spirits of Voodoo. No, it surely could not be Luciénne.

"But what if Luciénne had enlisted the help of someone else?" thought Madame Toulouse. After all, she was planning on reinstating ceremonies sacred to practitioners everywhere, and that meant activating an underground network of Voodoos far and wide. Had Luciénne located someone strong enough to break their bond? Madame Toulouse dismissed that notion as well. Any Houngan or Mambo worth their salt would know better than to align themselves with someone they had not thoroughly investigated. Even the slightest inquiry into the practices of "Madame" Luciénne would reveal unsavory habits that would turn the stomach of anyone with enough real power to achieve such a feat as penetrating a circle cast by three of today's most powerful Voodoos.

Madame Toulouse sat across the kitchen table from Mr. John, her mind cycling through the possibilities as she watched him try to keep his nose from falling into his coffee cup. He was fighting a losing battle, she thought. She held great admiration for Mr. John, though she rarely told him so, for the sake of his own humility. It was one the qualities she admired most about him. Despite the hard time she usually gave Mr. John, she knew he was cut from a dying breed of good, honest men who placed the welfare of others above their own. The man never met a stranger and he treated everyone as an equal, regardless of their stature or standing. Of course, that was until someone wronged Papa Bear's cub. Then his gnashing teeth and formidable claws were admirably bared and ready to fight. He and Mama Lu shared that passion.

Madame Toulouse watched, slightly amused, at the way Mr. John's head continually bobbed up and down on his neck as he fought to stay awake. She stifled a chuckle as she watched his eyes droop, then his head fall just enough to jar him back to consciousness only to repeat the cycle again and again in a ridiculous contest between body and will.

"John, why don't you go back into the parlor an' lie down on the divan?" asked Madame Toulouse. "You not doin' yo'self or nobody else any good in here. Besides, pretty soon you either gon' burn your nose or drown yo'self."

Her words startled Mr. John back to coherence, and he was able to lift his cup to drink. He pulled it away quickly as the steaming brew scorched his lips. Hoping the incident had gone unnoticed he cut a quick glance at Madame Toulouse only to find her watching and smiling. He was glad, however, that she chose grace over sarcasm and kept quiet.

"I'll be jus' fine," he said. "As long as dat baby's okay and we keep brewin' dis coffee."

Unlike Mr. John, Madame Toulouse showed little sign of fatigue. Though the night proved long and arduous, she sat properly at the table with her hands folded neatly beside her coffee mug. Tea was her preferred beverage choice for the early morning, but today she opted for a stronger concoction. Her dress was a deep red with a matching ruffle-trimmed jacket, and her head was mostly covered by a felt cloche with a gold buckle on the band. Were it not for her less than perfect hairdo, which could be seen peeking out from under her hat, the casual observer would be none the wiser as to her lack of rest. But Mr. John and Mama Lu, the two people who knew her best, recognized the worry that plagued her mind. Her elbow-length opera gloves were noticeably missing as was her jewelry, and though she brought her tortoise-shell cigarette holder, it remained tucked away in her bag. Departure from even one of these norms signaled distraction. The combination meant distress.

Conversely, grief was readily apparent in Mr. John. He looked careworn, full of angst and worry. John was always an easy read for Madame Toulouse. He wore his cares on his sleeve, seeing little point in the hiding of emotion. This morning, his face was drawn into a scowl of anguish, concerned for the safety of the girl upstairs. He widened his eyes and raised his brow as he sipped his coffee, allowing the steaming liquid to soothe his body and his mind. But the more relaxed he allowed himself to be, the more he lost the battle to stay awake. Realizing his weakness, he rose from his chair and began to pace back and forth across the kitchen.

A thump on the back porch announced the arrival of the morning paper. Desperate for a stimulating activity, Mr. John walked outside to retrieve it. He could smell the morning dew on the magnolias in the yard. The temperature was already climbing as the first sounds of the morning bustle reached his ears. The opening and shutting of the neighbors screen doors and the first hums of traffic signaled the start of another Louisiana Monday. Humanity around him rushed on, while Mr. John's world stood still as he anxiously awaited news of Nalia's condition. Life wasn't always fair, he thought.

Walking back inside, Mr. John saw Mama Lu descending the stairs in her robe. "How is she?" he asked hurriedly as she entered the kitchen.

"Back down again," Mama Lu replied. "We'll see how long it lasts dis time. Maybe she gon' rest better now dat it's daylight. When she was younger, the sun always helped drive away the darkness, you remember?"

"How could I not?" asked Mr. John.

Mama Lu crossed the kitchen and sat down at the table facing Madame Toulouse, while Mr. John took the liberty of pouring her a cup of coffee. Her fatigue was evident in her slumping posture. As much as Mama Lu hated to admit it, she was not as young as she used to be, and her body was feeling the toll of the sleepless nights.

"You look like hell, Lu," Madame Toulouse said without apology.

Mama Lu looked up with a sarcastic smile. She wanted desperately to retort but couldn't bring herself to disrespect her elder. "Well, I have a feelin' I'm gon' look worse before I look better," she replied.

"Wrong!" quipped Madame Toulouse. "We gon' get hold o' this situation, and quick. First and foremost, we can't let nothin' happen to that chil', but that ain't the end of it. We all know there's somethin' bigger goin' on here."

Mr. John exchanged a look of concern with Mama Lu as he set her cup down on the table.

"If we got some hoodoo workin' against us, then we all in a fix," continued Madame Toulouse. "Not only are they strong enough to break down the walls, but they also know what we're doin' and when. That puts us all in jeopardy and makes Nalia's situation much more delicate."

Mama Lu reached nervously into the pocket of her robe.

"We gon' need a lot more help than ol' Johnny can give us, Lucia," said Madame Toulouse, the gravity of the situation evident on her brow. "We got to find out who's involved here. Any ideas?"

"Luciénne's got to be behind dis," offered Mr. John.

Madame Toulouse recoiled in dismissal. "Luciénne couldn't hex the mites off a titmouse," she said. "Ain't no way this is her work."

"She's pullin' the strings though," added Mama Lu with a sobering edge in her voice. "She may not have the power to be pullin' off dis kind o' work, but you can best believe she's got her hand in the pot somehow. Dis is about me, an' dat ceremony she's plannin'. She all but told me she was gon' pull somethin' to force my hand, but how she knew what we was doin' last night and who's helpin' her is wha's got me stumped."

"She knew Nalia was here?" asked Madame Toulouse.

"Seen her at the shop yesterday afternoon," replied Mama Lu. "But she knew befo' dat. Somehow, she already knew."

114

"Dat don' surprise me," said Mr. John, leaning against the counter. "Word gets 'round dis town faster'n a hawk on a field mouse."

"But how did she know we were buildin' the bond last night?" asked Madame Toulouse. "Who else knew?"

Mama Lu and Madame Toulouse glared knives at Mr. John who jumped away from the counter like he'd been shot. "What?" he asked, affronted. "Don' y'all be lookin' dis way, I didn't tell a soul!" Both ladies raised an eyebrow in disbelief as Mr. John continued. "Why y'all always point the finger at me when you think somebody been runnin' they mouth?"

"Because you jus' told us how fast word gets 'round dis town," replied Mama Lu.

"And we know yo' the main reason it does," added Madame Toulouse.

"Well not dis time," said Mr. John defensively. "I didn't tell nobody. I didn't want to take no chances wit' my baby girl. Besides…"

Before he could continue, the conversation was interrupted by footsteps on the porch followed by a forceful knock on the back door.

Having the best view through the screen, Madame Toulouse leaned over just enough to make out the uniform and badge of a patrolman. "Lucia," she said, "You might want to get this."

Mr. John walked to the window. Pushing aside the curtain, he could see a police motorcycle pulled up to the curb outside the fence. Mama Lu stood and adjusted her robe before walking to the door. She did not open the screen, but stared through it at the officer on the other side. He was a short, white man of average build, looking to be in his mid to late twenties. His posture was confident, but not authoritative enough to suggest experience. A rookie, still a bit green, decided Mama Lu.

"Lucia Deminy?" he said taking off his sunglasses.

"Yes?" Mama Lu replied with a worried inflection. Police officers didn't just show up on one's doorstep this early in the morning unless something was seriously wrong.

"Sorry to disturb you so early ma'am, but Captain Beauchamp said I should come right over. Said to tell you he would've come himself, but couldn't get away from the station."

Mama Lu listened intently as Mr. John moved to the door behind her. She felt a lump of anxiety gather in her throat as Mr. John placed a consoling hand on her shoulder.

"Captain says, knowing you as well as he does, he's sure you would want to know right away," the officer continued.

"Yes, I know the Cap'n well," said Mama Lu in growing frustration. "What is it dat I want to know 'bout right away?"

"Well, you own the doll shop down on Decatur Street, is that right?"

"Yes, yes," said Mama Lu losing her patience.

"It appears your store was broken into last night, ma'am."

Mama Lu gasped and covered her chest with her hand. Mr. John helped steady her as she briefly lost her balance. Madame Toulouse hung her head in silent reflection.

"I don't have all the details, ma'am, but the Captain said with the nature of the crime, you might want to go down and check the place out pretty quickly," said the policeman.

"The nature of the crime?" questioned Mama Lu.

"Like I said ma'am, I don't have the details."

Mama Lu thanked the officer. As he rode away on his patrol bike, she looked back at Madame Toulouse and Mr. John who both wore expressions of serious concern. *The Doll Maker* had never been burglarized before. People knew better, or at least they used to. Mama Lu had known Captain Beauchamp for a very long time and so had Mr. John. He knew about their Voodoo practices and had been a customer of Mr. John's for years. If *he* said to get down there quickly, something was wrong on a whole different level.

"You two go," said Madame Toulouse, "I'll stay here wit' Nalia."

As Mama Lu hurried up the stairs to change, Madame Toulouse grabbed Mr. John by the wrist and looked him straight in the eye as she spoke with a stern voice.

116

"When you get there, check the upper room."

CHAPTER FIFTEEN

Having burned throughout the night, the candle on the vanity was getting low. Madame Toulouse extinguished it with a quick breath as she took a seat on the high-back cushioned chair. The morning sun shone through the window bathing Nalia's bedroom in an amber hue. Nalia lay sleeping on the bed, her head gently resting on the clouds below the circus train.

From the corner of her eye, Madame Toulouse caught her reflection in the large oval mirror. Her face was long and burdened with worry. She could see the lack of sleep beginning to take its toll in the form of dark circles under her eyes, along with several lines she did not remember seeing yesterday. She adjusted her hat and fussed with the small tuft of hair that would not behave, grateful she would not be appearing in public today.

Being in Nalia's bedroom brought back fond memories. Madame Toulouse recalled sitting in the very same chair, many years ago, staring at a much younger reflection. She noticed the polished silver hair brush sitting on the vanity in the place Nalia always kept it. She remembered the day she presented it to her. It was Nalia's twelfth birthday, and Madame Toulouse wanted to get her something special. The child had been through so much, and was growing up so fast. She knew Nalia was never given nice things as a child, a pity considering the wealth she came from. Madame Toulouse wanted to give her a gift that was simple and elegant, fit for the young lady she was becoming. She wanted Nalia to have something that would make her feel like a princess every day.

She was browsing an antique store down in the Quarter when she found the rare, ornamented, polished silver brush. It could not have been more perfect, she thought. When Nalia opened the gift, she held the brush close to her heart as if she'd never seen anything so beautiful in all her life. She could still envision the joy on the young girl's face.

Myra, the doll on the small oval table beside the vanity, was the startling likeness of that young girl. As Madame Toulouse looked from the doll to Nalia's sleeping form, she could picture her growing up again, becoming the woman she was today. She wondered how much more time they would have to share, as a dreadful feeling chilled her bones.

With Madame Toulouse watching over her, Nalia drifted into peaceful sleep. As her mind relaxed, she dreamed of the wind gently brushing her face as she held tight to the wide, polished handrail of a grand old riverboat. Mist rose from the water, kissing her skin as she stood alone on the upper tier of the front deck. Nalia could feel the strength of the vessel's great paddle wheel biting into the current, propelling it down the river. Its two tall smokestacks reached high into the air and its steam whistle blew loudly, echoing off the buildings in the distance along the banks of the Mississippi.

The handrail was supported by a decorative white-washed iron railing draped with semi-circular, red-and-white striped flags. Nalia felt the rough wooden deck boards underneath her feet as she stood in the wind, absorbing the sight and sounds of the river. She closed her eyes and breathed deeply, drawing in the serenity of the moment. While the gentle waves lapped against the hull, Nalia could hear a jazz ensemble playing in the distance. She had just identified the tune as "High Society Rag" when she heard a small voice somewhere behind her head, whispering her name.

The cabin behind her was lined with etched glass windows and a large wooden door with a frosted glass pane. On either side of the door were long wooden benches with red leather cushions. Nalia turned to face the cabin searching for the source of the whisper. She did not see anyone there, but did notice a small doll standing on the back of one of the seats with its back turned. It was Queen Marie, staring into the window above the bench. Nalia wondered what or who was inside the cabin, but condensation prevented her from seeing through the glass. She walked across the deck and knelt on the bench beside the doll. As she placed her nose close to the cool glass pane, Nalia could see light and movement in the room beyond but was unable to make out the images. She rubbed the window with the palm of her hand trying to improve her view, but the glass was fogged on the inside as well. She turned to Queen Marie as if expecting answers. "What am I supposed to see in there?" she asked the doll in a whisper. The end of her sentence echoed across the water as if she'd screamed it at the top of her lungs. The reverberation shook the windows and a bright white light appeared beyond the glass and began to grow. As it intensified, a wide beam of light stretched across the surface of the deck from the crack under the wooden door.

The steam whistle startled Nalia as it blew once again, and she could almost make out her name in its scooping tone. Her stomach lurched as she felt the riverboat calling to her, inviting her inside the cabin. Nalia picked up Queen Marie and held her close as she made her way to the door. The light was beaming through the frosted glass pane, but Nalia could see no better here than she could through the window. Nervous, but not fearful, she placed her hand on the brass handle and slowly pushed the door open. Briefly blinded by a burst of white light, Nalia stood still, waiting for her eyes to regain focus. Large, red blotches in her vision were still dissipating when she realized she was entering the front door of *The Doll Maker*.

All the lights were on and several shoppers were browsing through the displays. The clerk, a striking young black woman, sat at the register on a stool behind the counter. She had short, jet black hair and wore a low cut blouse. With her head resting lazily in the palm of her hand, she flipped a bent paper clip back and forth across the counter. After a moment of study, Nalia was all but certain she was looking at a very young Madame Luciénne. As if confirming her suspicion, Mama Lucia's voice echoed from the sewing room. "Vivian?" she shouted.

Startled, young Vivian Luciénne jumped, then walked around the counter toward the sewing room. Curiously, Nalia followed her through the displays. As Vivian opened the door, Nalia could see into the sewing room where Mama Lu sat on a stool at a small table. She was working with a male doll dressed in long, white and gold vestments and a red stole with tiny crosses embroidered on either side. She wore a pair of glasses fitted with a loupe and a light, which indicated to Nalia she was working either with gems or with very fine stitching. Mama Lu swiveled around to face Vivian and flipped up the loupe. "These two are ready for display," she said, indicating two small female figures at the end of the table. "Put dis first one in case number three. Dat other one can go on the middle display tree, but don' put it on the bottom shelf."

120

Vivian entered the sewing room with Nalia on her heels as Mama Lu flipped the loupe back down over her eye and continued concentrating on the white-robed doll. When Vivian picked up the two smaller dolls and left the room, Nalia moved closer to Mama Lu. She peeked over her shoulder, still apprehensive about touching anyone or anything. Nalia watched as Mama Lu attempted to attach a tiny gold chain with several small diamonds to the neckline of the doll's chasuble. The doll looked like a priest, and Nalia assumed it was representative of a saint, but she wasn't sure which one. Its chasuble was embroidered down the front with a repeating pattern of decorative ovals and flowers with a depiction of the Virgin Mary just under the collar. The doll was exquisitely detailed.

As Nalia watched the steadiness of Mama Lu's hand, she marveled at her patience. Reflecting on her childhood years, she remembered Mama Lu always being even-tempered and kind. Now, as Nalia observed her attaching the miniature chain to the doll's garment with the tiniest of needles and hair-thin metallic fiber, there was no doubt how Mama Lu's patience had been honed.

Though Nalia had considered Mama Lu's patience and precision on many other occasions, today she noticed something for the first time. Looking around the sewing room, she realized there were no partially completed dolls. Searching her memory, she could not recall a time when there had been. On occasion, a doll might be set aside until the arrival of a specific fabric, or a custom piece of jewelry, but never more than a day or two. Upon the arrival of the proper materials the doll would be completed immediately and put out for display. There was never a doll that sat partially finished on a shelf, or a project that was not seen through to completion. Mama Lu always finished what she started. "Diligence," thought Nalia, "patience and diligence."

Behind her, the door to the sewing room opened again, and Vivian poked her head through. "I need the keys to case number three," she said. "And there's a woman out here asking for you."

"Who is it?" Mama Lu asked without looking up from her work.

"Says her name is Mary Barronne," replied Vivian. "Says she was in 'bout a week and a half ago, on a Sunday?"

Nalia watched as recognition struck Mama Lu's face. "Yeah," she said to Vivian, tossing her a set of keys from the pocket of her apron. "Lil' girl wit' her?"

"Um hmm," replied Vivian, catching the key ring with one hand.

"Tell her I'll be right out."

She finished stitching the last two loops of thin metallic cord, attaching the gold chain to the doll's robe, then set her loupe-fitted spectacles down on the table. She affixed the doll to its short wire stand before rising and removing her apron.

On the floor, beside a sewing machine on the opposite wall, was a brown wicker basket - the kind one might take on a picnic or see in a calendar featuring playful kittens with colorful balls of yarn. Mama Lu knelt beside the basket and opened it up. From inside, she extracted a small doll wearing a blue dress with gold hoop earrings and many tiny bracelets. Nalia drew a quick breath of excitement as she watched Mama Lu fuss with the doll's clothing to make certain it was perfect. She recognized the doll as Queen Marie, but marveled at its pristine condition; it looked like a shiny new penny. The surface of Queen Marie's porcelain face was without blemish. A freshly airbrushed rosy glow graced her cheeks and her features were crisp and flawless. The blue tignon on her head was tied in seven tiny knots, as was the red sash around her waist. She was a small, but exact, duplicate of the larger replication of Marie Laveau kept in the shop's glass case. She was perfect for a little girl to hold in her arms.

When Mama Lu was satisfied with the doll's appearance, she carried it over to the workstation. From underneath the table she retrieved a flat grey chipboard box and folded it to its appropriate shape. She then pulled several sheets of white tissue paper from a bin on the wall and placed them gently inside the container, leaving just enough hanging over to cover the doll once it was placed inside. When the package was complete, she closed the box and secured it with a length of coarse brown twine, tying it in an easy-to-open bow. Mama Lu breathed a quick sigh of satisfaction and carried the box through the door to the storefront. Nalia followed in anticipation.

Margaret Barronne stood next to the counter, looking as if she'd just stepped off the pages of a spring catalog. She wore a breezy, off-the-shoulder, purple sun dress with a print of bright yellow flowers. A white, soft brim, cotton sun hat with a wide purple band sat gently tilted atop her head and a white silk scarf loosely hugged her neck. Her eyes were hidden behind a vintage pair of Armani sunglasses. Her fingers were heavily ornamented with jewelry and her face was generously painted, as usual.

Behind her, with hands folded sheepishly together and her head lowered like a frightened puppy, stood her daughter Nalia. The little girl wore a navy school jumper with a plain white, long-sleeved mock turtleneck underneath. She was twisting nervously, shifting weight from one foot to the other, her mind in a different world.

Mama Lu entered the room, placed the chipboard box onto the counter, and greeted Margaret with a smile. The little girl, still preoccupied with her shoelaces, did not notice her entrance. "Hello, Nalia," said Mama Lu, turning her attention toward the child and grinning.

Nalia looked up in surprise and returned the greeting with a wide smile and a relieved sigh, as if a weight had been lifted from her little shoulders. Her eyes widened, but she kept quiet.

"Had you given up hope on me?" asked Margaret in a sugar-coated southern drawl. Mama Lu looked puzzled. "Things got so crazy last week I wasn't able to make it in like I told you I would. Thought you might be wondering if I was really coming back."

"Oh," answered Mama Lu, "I had no doubt you'd be back in eventually." She gave a quick wink to the little girl, who beamed with excitement. "How can we help you today, Mrs. Barronne?" Mama Lu asked with a pleasant smile.

"Mary," said the woman, taking off her sunglasses and hanging them on the neckline of her dress. "Please, call me Mary." Mama Lu nodded as the woman continued. "Mostly I came in to have another look around. Don't get me wrong, there are several dolls I'll be taking home today, but I could just spend all day browsing and admiring your work. Your pieces are simply captivating. It's like walking through a gallery." She looked around making a wide sweeping gesture with her hand. "Excuse me for embellishing, but there's more beauty in your little shop here, Lucia, than I've found in all of New Orleans, and that's saying something."

Mama Lu did not blush. She was used to her work being complimented. Although Margaret Barronne's fascination seemed sincere, her flattering comments reeked of an attempt to gain favor. Mama Lu never allowed the adulation of others to swell her ego or influence her opinion.

"Do you do all the work yourself?" asked Margaret.

"I have others who help me wit' the assembly sometimes, but I do all the firin' and the paintin'. All the faces and the details are done by me."

"And the jewelry?"

"No, I have a fella does the jewelry special fo' me. Mos' of it has to be made so small, you know. He's really good with the delicate work. He got a few pieces on consignment down in dat last case on the right if yo' interested. Right down there next to the rosaries."

"I'll bet with the right purchases, these pieces could really appreciate over time," said Margaret with an inquisitive gleam in her eye.

"I've had a few folks tell me dat," replied Mama Lu. "But I try not to focus too much on the investin' side of my work. I tried dat once and the dolls I made jus' didn't seem to have any life to 'em. Since then I jus' focus on makin' the dolls best I can and let whatever will be, be."

"Well that's got to be what makes them so exquisite," said Margaret. "You really are a master of your craft."

Feeling a bit awkward with Margaret's embellishing comments, Mama Lu gracefully dismissed the conversation. "Well, feel free to look around. Let me know if I can help you wit' anythin'."

Margaret smiled contently and left her daughter standing by the counter while she perused the shop. The little girl looked up at Mama Lu with eyes full of questions but did not speak. Seeing the young girl's restraint, Mama Lu looked over the counter and smiled. "And is there somthin' I can help you wit', ma'am?" she asked with her hand on the chipboard box. The little girl looked around nervously for her mother.

Seeing that Margaret was preoccupied, the little girl shyly turned back to Mama Lu and nodded her head.

"Well, what is it I can do fo' you, chil'?" Mama Lu asked.

"I'm not s'posed to ask," said the girl quietly.

"Oh, I see. 'Cause somebody thinks dat would be impolite, huh?" said Mama Lu cutting a quick eye to the girl's mother. Young Nalia nodded enthusiastically in response as Mama Lu stifled a laugh. "Well then, I bet if you was allowed to ask, you'd want to know if I remembered yo' doll, huh?"

The little girl nodded again, her petite body trembling with excitement.

Mama Lu slid the box across the counter and placed both hands on top. "I'll bet you'd want to know if I had a doll fo' you in dis box right here," she said, rolling her eyes playfully.

Unable to contain her excitement any longer, the little girl burst forth with joy. "Oh really, really? Do you really?"

Mama Lu grinned as she mimicked the girl's tight-lipped silence, raising her eyebrows and nodding her head.

"Is it for me? Is it really for me?" begged the little girl.

Mama Lu nodded again. The little girl drew a healthy breath of joyous disbelief as her chest swelled to bursting. She wrung her hands nervously as if afraid to reach up and take the box. Her eyes became so big, Mama Lu wondered if the child had ever been given a gift before.

"Well go on chil', it's yo's to have," said Mama Lu reassuringly.

The little girl gently reached up to the counter and took the box with both hands. She held it close to her chest and stared at it like she was holding a newborn kitten. "Can I open it?" she asked as if it were the most important event of her life.

"Why yes, darlin'," said Mama Lu.

The little girl was shaking with excitement as she set the box on the floor and gently tugged on the twine to loosen the bow. Opening the lid, she folded back the tissue paper to reveal the beautiful new doll. The girl could not speak, but carefully lifted the doll from its wrapping and held it up in admiration. Without a word she walked over to the glass case where the large Marie Laveau doll stood. Mama Lu stepped from behind the counter and followed her.

The little girl stood in front of the case holding up the doll, comparing every detail to its larger version behind the glass. She gazed up at Mama Lu with tears of joy flooding her eyes. "She's perfect," she said. "Just like the big one."

"Only, you can take dis one home wit' you," said Mama Lu. "Do you remember dis doll's name?"

"Marie La…" said the little girl, trying hard to recall. "La…"

"Laveau," said Mama Lu, "Da Queen o' New Orleans."

The little girl held her doll tightly. "I'm going to call her Queen Marie," she said, wiping the tears from her eyes.

As she dried her wet hand on the front of her shirt, the collar was tugged down enough for Mama Lu to notice what looked like bruising around the child's neck. Mama Lu stiffened with anxiety as the little girl thanked her repeatedly, hugging her doll. Mama Lu looked up and located the child's mother, who was still perusing the displays. Anger swelled as a thousand questions fired off in Mama Lu's head. Distressed, she cried out to Mr. John in her mind. Glancing through the display window, she knew he heard as he turned to meet her gaze. The two locked eyes for a moment, staring intently through the glass as Mr. John gave an understanding nod.

Mama Lu looked back at the young girl who was still clutching Queen Marie and swaying from side to side. "You don' get hot in dem long sleeves, baby girl?" she asked. The girl stopped swaying and stood motionless, like she'd been caught sneaking a cookie. Shyly, she shrugged her shoulders.

Realizing her question upset the girl, Mama Lu knelt beside her. "You know what I think dat doll needs?" she asked in a calming tone as Mr. John entered the shop and approached the case. "A pillow," finished Mama Lu. She looked at Mr. John as the little girl held the doll tightly and backed away. "It's alright, Nalia," Mama Lu explained, "Dis is my friend, John Barrett. You can call him Mr. John. Sometimes he makes little pillows for my dolls, so they have someplace to rest their head and they don' get broken."

Mama Lu turned to Mr. John with a knowing look. "Mr. John, do you happen to have a small velvet pillow dat would help protect dis little thing?" she asked with a raised brow.

Mr. John understood. "Oh, I think I got jus' the thing she needs right outside," he replied. "I'll be right back." He smiled at the little girl and dismissed himself back to his shoe-shine stand.

"Mr. John gon' get you all fixed up chil'," said Mama Lu. The little girl smiled again as her mother walked back to the register.

"Well Lucia, I just can't make up my mind," said Margaret. "There are so many wonderful pieces here, but I'm going to start with the two I simply cannot pass up. I've picked out one for myself, and one for the church."

Mama Lu stood, instinctively stepping between Margaret and the little girl. With a forced smile she said, "Wonderful. You jus' show Vivian which ones you want and she gon' take care of it." Mama Lu motioned for Vivian to take over as Mr. John walked back through the door carrying a small velvet bag sewn up around all the edges.

Feeling slightly put off, Margaret wandered back through the displays with Vivian, while Mr. John handed the pouch to the little girl. "There you go, young lady," he said.

"Now if you're allowed," said Mama Lu, "You can put dat pillow right next to yours and Queen Marie can sleep beside you every night."

The little girl thanked Mr. John politely. She held the pillow and the doll close, waiting quietly for her mother. Mr. John picked up the empty chipboard box from the floor as Vivian returned to the counter with the two dolls Margaret picked out. She winked at Mama Lu when she passed, indicating a good sale. The dolls were not the most expensive in the store, but they were definitely not priced for the average shopper. One was a tall, bejeweled china doll that wore a long black evening gown with a fur stole draped around her shoulders. She was decorated with miniature pearls, tiny diamonds set in gold, and bits of black onyx with a thirty-two hundred dollar price tag. The other was a replication of Saint Peter with a jeweled robe and a rosary made of tiny, beaded gemstones. Its price was twenty-eight hundred.

"I'll get some boxes for those," said Mr. John as Vivian ran the woman's credit card. He hurried off to the sewing room, making a mental note that he was in the wrong business.

Margaret finally looked down and noticed her daughter was holding the new doll. "Oh, I see you kept your word to Nalia," she said to Mama Lu.

"Of course," she replied.

"I didn't ask, Momma," interjected the little girl emphatically.

Margaret gave a questioning look to Nalia, causing her to shy away. Obviously irked, Margaret turned back to Mama Lu. "How much for that one?" she asked.

"Ain't no charge fo' dat one," replied Mama Lu looking down at the little girl. "Dat one is a gift." The child smiled wide once again, clutching the doll and twisting in place with enthusiasm. "Dat is, if it's alright wit' yo' momma," added Mama Lu eyeing the girl's mother for permission.

"Now surely I can pay you something for your time." insisted the woman, visibly uncomfortable.

"If you pay me, then it's no longer a gift, now is it?" said Mama Lu, making eye contact with the child and giving her a quick wink, "And dat takes away the blessing."

Margaret Barronne paused briefly, noticing the exchange of looks between Mama Lu and her daughter, who tried her best to return the wink but only managed a strangely contorted squint. "Well, I suppose I can't argue with that." she said. Young Nalia squeezed the doll tightly, overjoyed at her mother's decision.

Vivian finished the transaction and boxed the purchases carefully while Mama Lu made inquisitive small talk with Margaret, gathering and mentally cataloging all the information she could. When everything was boxed and bagged, Margaret and Nalia thanked Mama Lu and promised to return soon before leaving the shop.

"Don't forget about her pillow," said Mama Lu to the young child as she left.

"Oh I won't," she replied, bouncing after her mother to the car outside.

Mama Lu and Mr. John watched them drive away as Vivian looked on from behind the register. "Somebody mistreatin' dat baby, ain't they?" asked Mr. John.

"Yes they is," replied Mama Lu. "I bet if you pulled up them long sleeves she got on, you'd see plenty o' proof all up and down her little arms. She had some bruisin' on her neck too, I seen it. Ain't no tellin' wha's goin' on in dat household, but we gon' find out, I tell you dat."

"Old man Leonetti say he ain't found nobody yet what even knew Michael Barronne had a daughter, or a wife fo' dat matter. When I told him she was black he understood why," informed Mr. John. "He still diggin' though. He ain't through yet."

"Well you tell him to step it up," said Mama Lu. "I want to know all I can 'bout dat lil' girl. I'm 'bout to put a stop to dis."

In the corner of the shop, near the door to the workroom, Nalia stood with tear-stained cheeks watching the memory of her forgotten past as if she had stepped unnoticed onto a stage where it played out in the spotlight. She was clutching Queen Marie tightly. She felt alone and confused. Even though she longed for her mother over the years, she always knew, deep down, she was better off with Mama Lu. However, finding out for certain was heartbreakingly painful. She closed her eyes and let the scene fade away as she felt the softness of her bed returning to envelop her body. Somewhere in her half-awake dreamlike state, Nalia's body stirred in restless anticipation of something unseen and dreadful. Her body tried to awaken her mind, but it was too late. The beast was at the foot of her bed.

Nalia clutched Queen Marie so tightly she nearly ripped the doll in half. She wanted to scream but could not push the sound from her lips. She could feel the beast's heavy breath at her feet, as she kicked and scrambled to get away. The icy cold sensation gripped her body as the beast tore a claw through her flesh. A voice inside her head echoed like a terrifying spectral presence. "Don't fight," said the voice. "It won't hurt if you don't fight." Nalia opened her eyes to see the green glow of the beast's eyes drawing nearer. "Don't fight."

Across the room, the ever-present darkness rose tall. Its formless shape began to solidify, rolling like a dark fog. It hovered over the beast, as if controlling it. The fog churned like thick smoke from an oil fire until it reached nearly to the ceiling and took on the outline of a human. Nalia sat terrified as, all at once, two bright beams of white light appeared like eye sockets where the figure's head took shape.

"Get on with it," said a sinister voice from out of the darkness as the beast below threw another claw in a sweeping arc that caught Nalia's shoulder. She felt the weight of the beast against her as it slithered up her helpless body.

———————

Nalia sat straight up in bed with a jolt, soaked in a cold sweat. A look of utter terror twisted her face but she was unable to make a sound. She sat, catatonic, as Madame Toulouse rushed to her side.

CHAPTER SIXTEEN

By the time Mr. John and Mama Lu arrived on Decatur Street, the sun was up and glistening off the dew-coated ferns that hung in front of the building. It also shimmered off the broken glass that lined the sidewalk. Yellow caution tape stretched from the brass handle of the front door out to the posts that supported the second floor gallery, then back to the base of Mr. John's shoe-shine stand.

A tall, black patrolman stood just inside the line of tape with one hand on his belt and the other resting on the grip of his Glock 21. The large window behind him was completely shattered, and the dolls in its display box were covered with shards of broken glass.

Mama Lu's heart sank when she approached the entrance. She never expected anything like this to happen at her shop. There was a time, not long ago, when even the thought of a crime against Lucia Deminy sent chills down the spine of any would-be perpetrator. While folks far and wide loved and respected Mama Lu, they feared her even more. Mambo Lucia Deminy was well known as a powerful Voodoo priestess. Rumors and legends of her influence and wrath were widely circulated. The locals all knew the tales of ritualistic practices after hours at *The Doll Maker*. Stories abounded of dark magic, spells, hexes, and gris-gris powerful enough to strike someone ill, blind, or even dead. Rumors were told of folks being hoodooed into doing unnatural things, their minds under the control of the great Mambo. The windows of the upper room often glowed with strange lights while mystic rituals were performed that claimed the souls of adversaries. Afterwards, the Voodoos could be seen on the second floor gallery drinking blood from human skulls.

There was little truth to any of the far-fetched stories that circulated about Mama Lu, but they provided great protection for her store and also helped bring in additional revenue. Buying merchandise from *The Doll Maker* was surely a good way to avoid the wrath of Mambo Lucia.

Though the tales still surfaced from time to time, it had been years since Mama Lu did anything to encourage them. The broken glass currently crunching under her feet signified the end of an era. Perhaps it was time to entertain the thought of more conventional means of security. Though she still retained all the power and knowledge she ever had, Mama Lu felt respect for her craft was dwindling. Voodoo was becoming less appreciated, and its practitioners less revered. Perhaps Madame Luciénne had a point, in that regard.

Mr. John approached the officer, whom he knew as one of his long-standing customers, and began to acquire information about the break-in while Mama Lu broke the caution tape and opened the front door. To her surprise, the scene before her was not wrought with the amount of destruction she had envisioned. The display trees were, for the most part, still intact. Only a few dolls on the lower tiers were knocked over. The display in the broken window was disheveled and covered in shattered glass but the dolls all appeared to be present. The cases on the right-hand wall were untouched and the bejeweled dolls behind the glass were still in their places. "So many stones here for the takin'," thought Mama Lu. What had the burglar been after?

As Mama Lu examined the display box near the busted window, she noticed a blood-stained strip of denim caught on the jagged edge of a large piece of glass. "Oh, so you left somethin' behind fo' me," she thought. After glancing at the officer to make sure he was conveniently preoccupied with Mr. John, she quickly retrieved the patch of fabric. An old, familiar tinge of preeminence stirred deep within her soul as she slipped the ragged bit of denim into her pocket.

Mindful of the glass-covered floor, Mama Lu stepped cautiously around the center display. As she reached the counter, she could see the register was still present and apparently untouched; this puzzled her even more. She was making her way to the light switches, when she nearly tripped on a rounded, solid object lying beside the counter. Looking down, Mama Lu discovered a baseball bat amid another scattered array of broken glass. What she saw next shook her to her very core.

The jagged shards that surrounded the bat came from the glass case that lined the left wall of the shop, near the counter. Mama Lu looked up to see the broken case where the large replication of Marie Laveau was kept. The doll's porcelain head was shattered into a thousand tiny pieces. Her jewelry and adornments littered the bottom of the case in small piles around her feet. Her garments were torn and her large hoop earrings lay on the ground, bent and broken. Mama Lu's jaw dropped open. She felt a heaviness in her chest as she leaned against the counter and wept.

Outside, Mr. John learned the police were alerted to the burglary by EMTs responding to a distress call just a block away. Tony Leonetti was found crawling along the sidewalk, screaming in pain with cuts on his arms, legs and torso. His hands and face were covered with strange burns, and he claimed he could not see. He was taken to Medical Center Hospital where he was treated for his wounds, then released to the custody of New Orleans P.D. According to the officer, he was probably in a holding cell downtown. Mr. John thanked the patrolman, then went inside to help Mama Lu assess the damage. He found her still crying beside the register. As he wrapped his arm around her, he noticed the source of her sorrow.

The doll of Marie Laveau was the oldest in the shop. Mama Lu crafted the doll just before she opened the doors and Mr. John knew it held a special place in her heart. It was an icon in her store – a symbol of the shop and of Mama Lu herself. Mr. John suspected it also carried some sort of connection to the spirit world. He often found Mama Lu speaking to the doll in the same way she spoke to the poppets in the workroom. Though she never told him so, Mr. John knew Mama Lu communicated with spirits of the departed through the doll. Sometimes he wondered if she spoke to the spirit of Marie Laveau herself. Whatever its meaning or connection, Mr. John could see that Mama Lu was devastated by the loss of the doll. He had rarely seen her so shaken with sorrow.

For a long time he held her close. He could feel her grief resonating in his own body as an overwhelming sensation of helplessness overtook him. Nalia, Luciénne, the lack of sleep, and now this – it was all too much. The weight of despair was tremendously heavy.

Then, Mr. John felt a spark of anger ignite in Mama Lu. She pushed him away and looked him straight in the eye, raising a shaking finger to his face. He saw a fire in her eyes he had not seen in years: an angry passion for vengeance. "Luciénne is behind dis, John," she said trembling with fury. "Dis is a message. She trying to get me to cave in an' join dat ritual. Well, dat evil bitch has overstepped her bounds dis time, John. Dis is war!"

For the next several moments, Mama Lu stormed around the store, talking to herself and occasionally breaking into short bursts of chanting. Avoiding her path, Mr. John retrieved a broom and dustpan from behind the counter as Mama Lu took a mental inventory of the shop. "There's not a thing missing, John! Not a thing!" she shouted. "Dis was all about dat doll. Oh, wait 'til I get my hands on dat woman!"

She continued to pace and shout as Mr. John swept the broken glass into piles, keeping a close watch on the activity outside. When two other officers arrived, Mr. John stopped Mama Lu and spoke to her quietly. "You needs to calm yo'self down, Lu," he said in a grave tone. "Go outside, talk to the police. Tell 'em what they needs to know, and *only* what they needs to know. I'm gon' make sure everythin' is secure upstairs."

Mama Lu hated being told what to do, but she knew Mr. John was right. She gathered her composure and walked outside while John slipped into the workroom. As far as he could tell, the intruder did not make it this far, but he had to be sure. The stairs were against the far wall in a narrow recess with peeling wallpaper. The light bulb was burned out, so the stairwell grew darker as Mr. John ascended. When he reached the landing, he felt for the solid wood door on the left. Fumbling in his pocket, Mr. John eventually produced an old set of keys. The faint beam of light spilling in from the bottom of the stairwell was barely enough for him to identify which key was which, but he eventually fitted three separate keys into three different deadbolt locks and turned them accordingly. When the last bolt was released, he turned the knob and pushed on the heavy old door.

As it creaked open, Mr. John could smell the dust – his first confirmation nothing was disturbed. Sure the locks on the door were intact, but when one was dealing with Voodoo, locks meant very little. Mr. John had known safe rooms to be breached with no locks being disturbed and no doorknobs being turned. Certain mystics were rumored to travel like vapor.

134

Mr. John flipped the light switch on the wall and a single, low-wattage bulb sparked to life. It dangled from a bare strip of wire on an open socket in the center of the room directly over a large, round table made of oak. On the far side stood two stacks of empty, wooden crates with wide boards stretched between them. The boards were heavily coated with melted wax and the dust-covered stumps of long-dead candles. On the wall above the crates hung a large painting of a nude woman silhouetted by the light of a bonfire, lifting a large snake over her head. Around it were several smaller drawings of various Catholic saints, along with a painting of a blue-robed black woman praying for a man in a darkened jail cell. The woman held a rosary in one hand and three Guinea peppers in the other. The man behind bars was depicted as being plagued by grotesque demons.

The other walls of the room were heavily marked with various runes and symbols that seemed to glow in the dim light. Some were large and drawn with spray paint. Others were smaller, written in ink. Some sections of wall were completely covered by long phrases written in a strange language.

In one of the room's darkened corners, a length of rusted chain lay piled on the floor in a heap. In another, a small table held ritual items such as rosaries, crucifixes, and a large knife with a long double-edged blade. Near the table stood a large set of well-worn conga drums.

Mr. John entered the room reverently and walked to the edge of the table. The wood was stained blood red, heavy in the center then lighter around the edge. The hardwood floor was also stained a deep red in a wide, circular pattern just beyond the reach of the table's edge.

Mr. John stretched out his hand, touching the table with his fingertips. He closed his eyes and drew a long cleansing breath through his nose. Holding it in, he listened carefully to the silence, waiting for the room to speak. He felt the room's energy surround him and pass through him, whispering stories of the past. Satisfied, he released the breath through his mouth and walked back to the door. No magic had breached this room, he was sure of it.

CHAPTER SEVENTEEN

The coffee was good – strong, but good. Madame Toulouse was unsure of how it would turn out, but after giving it a cursory sip, she found she was quite pleased with the results. It had been a long time since she brewed a full pot of coffee. Having lived alone for so many years now, she was quite accustomed to her single-cup coffee maker, and even more familiar with Café Du Monde.

If it were not for her fervent need for caffeine, she would not be brewing coffee at all. She could not remember the last time she consumed more than a single cup of coffee in a day's time, especially in the morning hours. Madame Toulouse preferred to take her coffee in the evening as an after-dinner beverage. She enjoyed sipping it slowly, savoring its flavor and robust aroma. Today she was simply downing cup after cup for the sole purpose of keeping her eyes open.

The mug warmed her hands and the steaming brew soothed her throat as she took inventory of her fleeting faculties. Though her mind wandered, she made a hearty attempt to enjoy the earthy flavor of the full-bodied coffee. She used the chicory blend Mama Lu and Mr. John were so fond of. She hoped Nalia would enjoy the flavor as well.

She would never forget the look of terror in Nalia's eyes when she awakened a short time ago. Frightened stiff and unable to speak, Nalia sat up with blankness in her eyes as if her body was devoid of its soul. Madame Toulouse rushed to her side, sat on the edge of her bed, and held her ice-cold hands while she trembled. Nalia did not acknowledge her presence, but stared straight ahead with eyes like glass. Her expression reflected nothing – no emotion, no connection, no life. If Madame Toulouse had not been able to feel her faint pulse and see her shallow breathing, she would not have known Nalia was alive at all. She held her hands tightly, chanting over her and offering prayers to Saint Jude.

After what seemed like an eternity of staring blankly across the room, Nalia's eyes welled with tears. Slowly they spilled onto her cheeks, one after another in a steady downward stream. Then Nalia began to speak. Her voice a faint whisper, she spoke with increasing haste. "No. Please, no. Don't, not again. No, please." Over and over she spoke, faster and faster, hushing herself when she became more than barely audible. Then, suddenly and violently, she pulled her hands away from Madame Toulouse, pressing them firmly against the sides of her head and pulling her knees up to her chest. Rocking back and forth, she continued to stare into oblivion while whispering instructions. "Don't look in his eyes. Don't look. Just keep still. It'll be over soon. Don't move. Don't fight. For God's sake, don't fight."

Knowing where Nalia's mind was, Madame Toulouse made no attempt to touch her. She watched helplessly as Nalia trembled and wept until her fragile form finally collapsed on the bed.

Moments later, Nalia opened her eyes with a disoriented expression. For a brief moment she did not recognize Madame Toulouse or her surroundings. A look of panic overtook her, but clarity struck just before she screamed. Realizing where she was, Nalia collapsed into the arms of her Madame T., weeping and desperately trying to sort fact from fiction.

The moment played over and over in Madame Toulouse's mind as she sipped her hot coffee. Only the sound of footsteps on the stairs jarred her from her trance. She lifted her weary eyes to see Nalia descending the staircase. Madame Toulouse took note that Nalia was not the picture of perkiness she normally presented. She wore a plain white V-neck tee, with a pair of ripped and faded jeans. Her hair was less than stylishly tousled and pushed back by dark sunglasses. Her face was still a bit ashen with minimal makeup, and when she heaved her purse onto the floor beside the coat rack, her expression reflected the aches of a restless night. Nalia's stiff, sore muscles yielded sluggish movements as she made her way to the kitchen table. Every muscle in her body screamed as if she had done too much running or swum too many laps in the pool. She grimaced as she sat down in the chair and breathed a sigh of relief when her body was finally motionless. She propped her elbows gently on the table with her head in her hands as if she never wanted to move again.

"You take it black now, don't you?" said Madame Toulouse.

Nalia looked up, confused, as if Madame Toulouse were speaking Chinese. "What's that?" she asked.

"Your coffee, darlin'. You take it black, right?"

"Oh," replied Nalia, coming to her senses. "Yes, I do, Madame T. I'm so sorry, my head is in a fog."

"Thus the coffee, my dear," Madame Toulouse responded with a sweet smile. She left Nalia to her thoughts while she searched the cupboard for an oversized mug. She was counting on the awkward silence to spur Nalia into conversation. No such luck. "So we do this the hard way," thought Madame Toulouse.

"Yo' awfully quiet this mornin'," she baited, as she set the steaming cup down in front of Nalia.

"I guess crazy people tend to be that way," Nalia replied placing her fingers through the handle of the cup. "That way people don't know they're crazy."

Bingo.

"What on earth are you sayin', chil'?" asked Madame Toulouse, pulling out the opposite chair and sitting down gingerly. "What makes you think yo' crazy?"

Nalia shied away, shifting her eyes from one side to the other as she chose her words. She ran her index finger back and forth along the lip of her cup, watching the steam rise. Finally, she looked up. "Do sane people wake up screaming and crying, insisting their dreams are real?"

Madame Toulouse was pleased. This was right where she wanted the conversation to go. It was critically important for her to gather all the information she could about Nalia's condition. The reintegration of someone's memory was delicate business. It could be a lengthy process that blurred the lines between reality and fantasy. If one were not careful to be perpetually aware of the effects of the process at each stage, the subject's mind could splinter into a permanent state of altered reality. With Nalia's situation, the visions were already causing physical symptoms such as shortness of breath, anxiety, elevated heart rate, and dissociative flashbacks. There was also the potential for outbursts of violence and self-harm, adding to the concern for her physical well-being.

138

With all these factors playing such key roles, it was vital for Madame Toulouse to ascertain what stage of the process Nalia was currently experiencing and then monitor her progress as the process unfolded. Without the use of her inner sight, conversation and the accurate interpretation of non-verbals were the only tools available. This conversation was a very good first step.

Madame Toulouse refrained from showing any emotion other than sympathy as she stared into Nalia's eyes. "Oh baby, I know this is difficult for you, but yo' not crazy. Sometimes our dreams are reflections of reality, but sometimes they jus' dreams. Wha's got you so wound up?" she prodded. Question after question fired through her mind.

Were the memories returning? How much had she learned?

"I don't know," replied Nalia. "If these are just dreams, then why do they feel so real? Why am I freaking out so badly over them?"

Had the guide been clear? Was Nalia aware these were memories and not just dreams? What did she know? What did she believe?

"Tell yo' Madame T. 'bout 'em, baby," said Madame Toulouse, careful to contain her anxiety.

Nalia was apprehensive. Her eyes began to scan the room again. Madame Toulouse could feel the table shaking as Nalia's leg began to twitch. Her index finger resumed its path around the coffee mug, and she cleared her throat before she spoke. "I don't know," she said. "It's the same old recurring nightmare: monsters under the bed and all that nonsense. It's stupid, really." She rubbed her eyes with the palms of her hands, trying to clear her head. "It just seems so real," she concluded.

What else? What about the memories? What does she remember so far?

"Is it jus' the nightmare, baby? Or is somethin' else botherin' you?" Madame Toulouse cooed. "Sometimes it helps to talk about it." She gave Nalia a look that said she knew more than she was letting on. Her reticent expression and barrage of questions seemed unusual to Nalia. Madame Toulouse was usually forthcoming with what she knew – proud of it even.

Nalia looked up from her coffee. Her hand stopped circling the cup. "Just weird dreams about dolls and stuff," she allowed in a guarded tone.

She knows I'm prying. What else can I get?

"What dolls, baby? Yo' dolls?"

Nalia's eyes grew suspicious. She wondered why Madame Toulouse seemed to be interrogating her. What she was digging for? Nalia lifted her coffee cup while she watched Madame Toulouse's reaction. "I had a dream about Queen Marie."

So the guide is in place. What has she shown you?

"Oh, I always loved that doll," said Madame Toulouse, trying to keep her poker face through the thick tension. "What did you dream about?"

Something clicked. Nalia broke her stare. Her eyes went back to her cup and her tone became reserved. "I can't really remember," she said, taking a sip of her coffee. "Wow! Madame T. you make a stout cup of Joe. I may need that cream and sugar after all."

Gone.

Nalia rose with a grimace and walked to the counter as Madame Toulouse's heart sank in her chest. The moment had passed, and she knew she would get no more information from Nalia. More importantly, she could tell Nalia was hiding something, but she wasn't sure why. Madame Toulouse desperately wanted to believe Nalia was not forthcoming with details about the dream because of embarrassment, awkwardness, or even fear she was losing her mind. However, her gut told her differently. Something darker was behind Nalia's reservation. Madame Toulouse could feel it.

Nalia opened the cupboard and removed a large, travel mug with a lid. Madame Toulouse watched out of the corner of her eye, as Nalia transferred her coffee into the other cup, then added a bit of sugar and a healthy amount of cream. She knew Nalia was about to make an escape.

As Nalia screwed the lid on the cup, Madame Toulouse could stand the tension no longer. "You goin' somewhere, baby?" she asked, desperately clinging to the hope of extracting anything useful.

140

"Yeah, I think I'll go down to the Quarter. I need to walk for a while. Stretch my muscles. Clear my head."

One last attempt.

"I should have known you'd have plenty of other things to do than sit and visit wit' this ol' woman," said Madame Toulouse with a wide, sugar-coated smile, hoping guilt would sway Nalia into sitting back down.

"I love you, Madame T.," Nalia said, kissing her on the cheek. "But I've got to get out for a while." With that, she grabbed her cup and her purse and exited through the back door.

As Nalia strode down the sidewalk, her mind shifted into overdrive. Visions from the dreams played over and over in her mind. These were not simply dreams as Madame Toulouse suggested. She remembered the vision of Mama Lu at the white tomb and the explanation of the returning memories. There was no denying these dreams were indeed visions from her past. Mere dreams did not come with such a demanding sense of reality, or such an undeniable feeling of déjà vu. She definitely lived through these moments before, and that meant the vision of Mama Lu was telling the truth.

Madame Toulouse wasn't fooling anyone. The woman was prying for something, but Nalia didn't know what. What information did her past hold? Nalia did not know the answer, but she knew where to look. She would not be visiting the Quarter at all. She needed internet access. She was going straight to the City Archives at the New Orleans Public Library to find out everything she could about Michael Barronne.

———————

It was just after noon when Mama Lu and Mr. John returned from the shop. When Mama Lu saw Nalia's car was missing, she began to fret. With each step up the walk, she rationalized scenarios in her mind. Madame Toulouse had everything under control, she thought. Maybe Nalia drove Madame Toulouse home, or perhaps they went out for a bite to eat. She prayed Nalia was in a fit state to drive after last night's restless ordeal.

Despite Mama Lu's best efforts to reassure herself that all was well, hope vanished when she approached the screen door. Something was definitely amiss. The screen was shut, but the back door was ajar. Surely Nalia and Madame T. would have locked up when they left, considered Mama Lu. Had someone broken into her home, too? Were they still inside?

Quietly, she expressed her concerns to Mr. John and they proceeded cautiously through the door. The house was still, and the smell of burned coffee filled the kitchen. Mama Lu saw the pot was nearly boiled dry. Mr. John started to speak but Mama Lu held a finger to her lips. As they slipped quietly through the kitchen, Mr. John picked up a rolling pin and held it like a club.

Vigilantly, the pair drew near the parlor. The room was dark, save for a scarce bit of light spilling in from the hallway. Mama Lu and Mr. John peered into the room and waited for their eyes to adjust. In the far corner, a motionless figure sat in Mama Lu's high-back, Victorian style chair. Mr. John gripped his rolling pin as Mama Lu reached for a nearby lamp with trembling hands. As the bulb flickered to life, its glow revealed the figure to be Madame Toulouse. Mr. John and Mama Lu breathed a sigh of relief until they noticed Madame Toulouse was still not moving. She sat straight up in the chair with her hands folded on her lap. Her eyes were open wide and she stared lifelessly across the room. Terrified, Mama Lu hurried over with Mr. John close behind. Madame Toulouse remained motionless as they knelt on either side of her. Mama Lu leaned in closely, looking for signs that Madame Toulouse was breathing. It was only then she and Mr. John heard the faint sound of snoring.

Mama Lu looked at Mr. John in disbelief. "She asleep, John," she whispered. Slack-jawed, Mr. John leaned in closer to Madame Toulouse, examining her wide eyes. He lifted his hand close to her face and moved it up and down. No response.

Madame Toulouse snored once again. Bewildered, Mr. John looked back at Mama Lu. "How she sleep wit' her eyes wide open like dat?" he asked.

Mama Lu shrugged.

"You gon' wake her up?" asked Mr. John.

Mama Lu's eyes widened as big as her elderly mentor's. "I ain't wakin' her up," she said. "You wake her up."

Mr. John looked as if he'd been asked to hold a live grenade. He shook his head vigorously back and forth.

"Well, one of us got to do it," said Mama Lu.

"Well it ain't gon' be me," replied Mr. John. "You do it. She likes you."

"Madame T.," whispered Mama Lu.

Mr. John jumped up quickly. "Wait a minute, woman. I don' want to be dis close when she comes to." He backed up several feet, giving the two ladies a wide berth.

"You big chicken," said Mama Lu, shaking her head. Mr. John nodded in agreement. With her cowardly friend safely out of the way, Mama Lu leaned in close to Madame Toulouse's ear and spoke in a hushed, but natural voice. "Madame T."

"Jellybeans!" cried Madame Toulouse, jumping six inches and gripping the arms of the chair with both hands. Her eyes bulged as she scanned the room in a confused panic. Though her body continued to tremble with fatigue, it took only seconds for her bearings to return. When Madame Toulouse realized where she was and what had happened, embarrassment reddened her cheeks. Mama Lu was so exhausted she could not contain her laughter. Mr. John made a mental note to check the racing schedule for any horse named "Jellybeans".

"Lucia, you can't do dat," said Madame Toulouse, catching her breath. "I'm old, Lu. I got a weak heart. I could have palpitations."

Mama Lu's laughter proved contagious as Mr. John began to shake, but Madame Toulouse did not look amused. Seeing her solemn expression, the two of them tried to stifle their giggling, but every time they attempted to keep a straight face, their laughter erupted with renewed enthusiasm.

"Oh go 'head an' laugh, both of you. Get it all over wit'," scolded Madame Toulouse, fatigue permitting her Creole accent to shine through. "You wouldn't be laughin' if you had give me a heart attack an' I fell over dead on dis floor." She sat up straight and turned her head. "Hmph, the two o' you prob'ly would. Leave me breathin' my last right here in yo' parlor while the two o' you jus' whooped it up. You'd laugh me all the way to my grave, now wouldn' you?"

Mama Lu and Mr. John once again tried to regain their composure by avoiding eye contact and holding their breath, but one small snort of air from Mr. John's nose was all it took for them to burst into another round of howling.

Having her fill, Madame Toulouse decided to put a stop to their carrying on. "Soon as you get through laughin' all over yo'selves, I'll tell you where Nalia's run off to."

The sobering comment served its purpose well and gave Mama Lu and Mr. John the wherewithal to silence their laughter. "Where is she?" asked Mama Lu.

"Don' know," replied Madame Toulouse. "Said she was goin' down to the Quarter, but I believe dat 'bout as much as I believe it's gon' rain champagne dis evenin'. She was hidin' somethin'. Got real evasive when I asked about her dreams."

"You think the mem'ries done come back?" asked Mr. John, "Even though the bond was broken?"

"Oh, they definitely comin' back," answered Madame Toulouse. "She didn't tell me too much, but I could see it in her eyes. She's rememberin' a whole lot more than she'll admit to."

"Wha's she seen?" asked Mama Lu.

"Can't say fo' sure. She told me about Queen Marie so we know the guide is in place, and I reckon she trusts it, too. Somethin' tells me she knows dat these ain't jus' dreams, and I'm willin' to bet dat she already seen her mother."

"What about the nightmare?" asked Mama Lu, her voice shaking.

Madame Toulouse looked Mama Lu in the eye and took her hand. "Hard to tell, Lu. She was re-livin' it when she woke up, but I couldn't tell if the vision was fully manifestin' itself or not."

"Re-livin' it?" asked Mr. John

"She was completely dissociated when she woke up. Her body was here, but her mind was somewhere else entirely. Y'all got to understand wha's goin' on wit' dat girl is threefold. Her mind is workin' separate from her body and her spirit."

Mama Lu and Mr. John listened intently.

"As these visions unfold," explained Madame Toulouse, "Her mind is re-learnin' her past, intellectually – like it's on the outside lookin' in. Her spirit, on the other hand, is re-livin' it all from the inside out, you see? All the pain an' the heartbreak dat goes along with these mem'ries is bein' felt by her spirit, and her body is reactin' to it. It's jus' along for the ride, and takin' a beatin' all the way."

Mama Lu and Mr. John pondered the concept. They could see where Madame Toulouse was right, and they knew it was tearing Nalia apart.

"It's very important we know what she's rememberin' and when," continued Madame Toulouse, "So we can deal wit' it outright. Dat means we got to get her talkin', and dat ain't gon' be easy. Right now she's tight-lipped as a monk at midnight mass. She's fragile, and so is our bond of protection. If we got somebody workin' against us, we can't protect her like we need to." She looked at Mr. John. "Had the room been breached?"

"No," Mr. John replied adamantly.

"You sure of it?"

"Sure as I saw the sunrise dis mornin'," Mr. John went on. "Wasn't nothin' upset at all, 'ccpt fo' dat doll of Marie Laveau."

Madame Toulouse gasped. "What?"

"Broken to pieces with a baseball bat," said Mama Lu. "Tony Leonetti. But he ain't done dis on his own. I tell y'all both, Luciénne put him up to dis. When I get my hands on dat woman, I'm gon'…"

"Dis is good news, Mambo," interrupted Madame Toulouse spiritedly. Her comment was met with looks that questioned her sanity. "Don't you see?" she continued. "Dat means Luciénne ain't found no big bad Voodoo man dat's broken our circle," she said mocking a savvy strut. "The bond was broken when they broke dat doll."

Mama Lu and Mr. John looked confused.

"Lucia, I had you make dat doll fo' yo' transference of power ceremony," Madame Toulouse explained. "It was present at the ritual when I transferred power over to you. While the doll ain't got no power of its own, it's been so closely linked to our Voodoo over the years dat it's become a conduit fo' the energy dat binds the three of us. When dat doll was broken, it disrupted the flow of dat energy."

Mama Lu and Mr. John nodded in agreement. While Mama Lu was still not happy, she understood how this would make the battle much easier.

"We can't replace dat doll, Lucia, or what it meant to you," Madame Toulouse said, consoling Mama Lu. "But we can rebuild the bond to protect Nalia, and dat's wha's important. We'll jus' have to do it a lil' different now, dat's all."

Madame Toulouse looked from Mr. John to Mama Lu as she took their hands. "As the kids say today, Mambo," she said, "We gon' have to get ol' school."

CHAPTER EIGHTEEN

Evening settled on the city of New Orleans as the hearty smell of down-home, Creole cooking emanated from Mama Lu's kitchen. It started with the earthy scent of fresh cut celery and matured into an irresistibly sweet-smelling aroma with the addition of each ingredient. Mama Lu diced onions and bell peppers, adding them to the celery in a hot skillet with olive oil and chili powder. She made sure the vegetables were softened and caramelized before pouring in crushed tomatoes and salt to form the base of her Creole dish. The mixture simmered slowly on the stovetop, steadily puckering gentle kisses to beckon Nalia home. Mama Lu had not seen or heard from her all day.

Nalia's cell phone was turned off, and that meant she did not want to be found. Mama Lu did not question her mentor's notion about Nalia's evasive behavior. She knew Nalia must have countless questions in her mind and didn't blame her for wanting to keep them private, but that didn't make her absence any less troubling.

As she added pepper sauce to the reducing vegetables, Mama Lu wondered where Nalia actually went. Witnessing visions from her past, it would not be surprising for Nalia to seek out places from her childhood: her school, the hotel, maybe even her old home. Neither would it surprise Mama Lu to find Nalia walking among the crypts of St. Louis Cemetery. She tried to convince herself that Nalia was on a harmless trip to one of these places, trying to substantiate images from the dreams and pull them into reality, but she knew better. Her gut told her Nalia had seen visions of her mother and quite possibly her father. She wondered if Nalia's mind retained the name she uttered in her half-awake state of consciousness, "Barronne". If so, trying to keep Nalia from looking into her past would be like trying to snatch a bone from a pit-bull. Wherever Nalia was, she was hurt and confused. Mama Lu knew that for a fact. She could feel Nalia's pain in her own soul.

Two tablespoons of Worchester sauce.

Mama Lu went over the recipe in her mind. The house was quiet now. Madame Toulouse took a cab home and Mr. John, while insisting he should stay, was asked to leave. Mama Lu knew he would push himself to the point of collapse if she did not force him to go home and rest. She knew some time alone was best for everyone, but the silence of her old house only added to the anxiety, which did little to alleviate her fatigue. The few hours of sleep her body had forced upon her left her only slightly rested, far from vibrant and alert.

At least she would not have to deal with the demands of the shop. After assessing the damage to the store, and considering the physical and mental strain of Nalia's situation, Mama Lu decided to close down for the week. With no pressing orders at hand, she determined business could wait. Mr. John chose to join her on hiatus, locking up his shoe shine booth with a small CLOSED sign on a chain that stretched across the chairs.

A bit more salt and some white pepper. The shrimp would be added when Nalia got home. Until then, simmer and stir.

When *would* Nalia be home? Mama Lu briefly wondered if she would return at all. Given the stressful and fearful state of affairs, she would not be surprised if Nalia was on her way back to school. After all, Nalia hadn't really left anything in her duffle upstairs she couldn't live without. Why not just escape back to campus and run away from it all?

"Answers," Mama Lu told herself. Nalia still needed answers – that's why. "The answers are here," she thought, "and dat's wha's gon' hold her here." Yes, Nalia would definitely be returning, and from the sensation Mama Lu suddenly felt in the pit of her stomach, she would arrive quickly.

No sooner than she removed the prepared shrimp from the refrigerator, Mama Lu noticed the headlights of Nalia's car pulling up to the curb outside. As she added the shrimp to the simmering sauce, she breathed a sigh of relief. Now that Nalia was home, Mama Lu could cease her instinctive motherly worrying. Regardless of the turmoil going on in Nalia's mind, at least now Mama Lu knew that she was physically safe from harm, and some sense of control could be maintained. She wondered just how the evening would play out as she covered the pan and set the egg timer for four minutes.

Mama Lu heard the car door slam shut and moments later, Nalia entered the kitchen through the back door.

"I was beginning to worry 'bout you, baby," said Mama Lu in a lighthearted tone. She intentionally kept her back turned, nervously fumbling with utensils on the stovetop. Nalia did not respond, but Mama Lu heard her purse hit the floor beside the coat rack. "You must be starvin', chil'," she continued. "I'm gon' plate you up some shrimp creole, been simmerin' all afternoon."

As Mama Lu spooned a helping of rice onto a nearby plate, the silence grew maddening. She toyed with the rice and the spoon as long as she could, avoiding conversation. Finally, unable to tolerate the quiet any longer, she turned to find Nalia standing beside the kitchen table with her arms folded across her chest. Her posture reflected the bitter end of the afternoon's soaring downhill slide to the edge of madness. In a single afternoon Nalia had cycled through denial, doubt, confusion, anger, and betrayal. Ultimately, her expression settled on disappointment as she stood, slowly shaking her head from side to side. "So you think you can just cook up a good ol' Creole dinner and everything's supposed to be okay?" Nalia asked with contempt.

Mama Lu didn't know what to say. Her mouth went dry as her mind began to search for options. Without adequate knowledge of the vision's revelation, there was no way to tell exactly where this was going, but she knew it was nowhere pleasant.

"When where you planning on telling me about my father?" Nalia continued. "Or was that something you were just going to keep hidden for the *rest* of my life?"

Ding.

The egg timer echoed through the silent room. Feeling as though her heart had just been ripped from her chest, Mama Lu turned back around and set the plate of rice down on the counter. With her head hanging low, she turned off the burner under the shrimp and waited for the words to come. All afternoon her mind explored the possibilities of how this night would unfold. She had considered this type of attack, but dismissed it as unlikely. Looking back now, she realized that was just wishful thinking. Mama Lu leaned onto the counter with both hands, closed her eyes, and took a deep breath. Her chest heaved with nervous anticipation.

Though Mama Lu was visibly shaken, Nalia did not relent. "Michael Barronne," she said curtly. "Apparently, a pretty wealthy businessman. Quite a different story than the one I grew up with. You remember, the one about my father leaving my mother before I was born?" Nalia shifted her weight to one foot and held a cocky expression as the sarcasm continued to roll off her tongue. "You know, it's funny, I've always had a picture in my mind of a single mom, struggling to raise her only child alone after the worthless father took off and left them. Eventually, she becomes so overwhelmed with the burden she has to leave the child to be raised by someone else. It's almost the whole 'baby in a basket left on the steps of the church' story." Nalia's expression turned to disgust as she stared a burning hole into the back of Mama Lu's head. "Never once did I picture a family – mother, father, and child. A *wealthy* family that owned a shipyard and a hotel – one of the finer hotels in New Orleans, mind you. Chateau Élégante? Formerly the La Barronne? A hotel *my* family should have left to their daughter. A hotel which should have been *my* inheritance. A hotel which should still bear *my* family name!"

Mama Lu was shocked and angered. She was offended by Nalia's frivolous use of the word "family" to describe her relationship to her birth parents. Mama Lu, Mr. John and Madame Toulouse were the only *real* family Nalia had ever known. Nalia was aware of that, Mama Lu told herself. This was just the anger talking, but it still cut like knives.

"You know, I bet I could step out onto the back porch, throw a stick, and hit a dozen lawyers who would love to dig into this little story and help me reclaim what's rightfully mine," Nalia said, raising an eyebrow and straightening herself into a haughty pose. A thousand mental images fueled her resolve – exaggerated comparisons to classmates with more money, better clothes, newer cars, and the latest gadgets. She seethed over hours spent in the library pouring over dusty volumes of encyclopedias and sharing campus computers, while her "friends" reclined in their dorms with their iMacs and smartphones.

"There's just one, little problem," Nalia went on, growing more venomous. "Of all the records I pored over today, there was one I couldn't seem to find, no matter where I looked. A pretty important one, actually – missing. Somehow I have a feeling you know which one I'm talking about."

Mama Lu knew exactly what she was referring to. "Birth Certificate," she said under her breath.

"My Birth Certificate," Nalia continued with triumphant arrogance. "I bet it took some real doing to make sure that document vanished. Or did it? With all your connections it probably wasn't difficult at all."

Mama Lu turned her head and cut her eyes at Nalia, angered by the accusation, however valid it might be.

"No record at all that I was ever born to Michael and Margaret Barronne," Nalia went on. "Funny how that document is conveniently missing, but I'm sure there has got to be a record of my relationship with them somewhere: a tax record, doctor's chart, school enrollment form, church baptismal record. You couldn't have hidden everything. I'll find something, and when I do, I'll also find one of those eager lawyers – a good one. I intend to get back what belongs to me."

A chill went straight up Mama Lu's spine. It frightened her to see Nalia so consumed with greed. "Dat sounds like yo' mother talkin'," she said.

"Well I wouldn't know, would I? How could I possibly remember my mother?" Nalia snapped with thick sarcasm, flaring her nostrils in revulsion.

Mama Lu didn't know whether to cry or lash out in anger. She took a deep breath and paused to remember the words of Madame Toulouse: "It's very important we know what she's rememberin' and when." Mama Lu told herself to remember Nalia was somewhere between finding out who her parents were and discovering the nastiness of their nature. She obviously did not see the whole picture, so of course it was natural for her to be angry, to feel betrayed and victimized. Knowing only half the story gave way to misplaced aggression. Nalia was on the fence and fragile. At this stage, it was normal for her to be consumed with curiosity about the father she did not remember, while also being enraged by the fact secrets were kept from her. It was obvious Nalia had only seen enough to know *about* her father, not to truly know him. Mama Lu understood Nalia's anger and longing, but she also resented the implication that her protective measures were maliciously orchestrated. She took another deep breath to calm the fury building inside her. Mama Lu inhaled slowly through her nose and released the air through her mouth as Nalia silently awaited a response.

Finally Mama Lu turned around and looked Nalia square in the eye. "Time is a tricky thing, chil'," she said in the calmest tone she could manage. "There are things in dis world dat you may think you understand, but time will tell you different. Time will tell you the truth. Be cautious wit' what you say and what you do until time reveals the true nature of what you seen."

Nalia turned up her nose. "What kind of philosophical crap is that?" she fired back. "You lie to me my whole life, and then you say time will help me understand? Time has done nothing but help you twist my life around your design."

"My design was the best thing for you," snapped Mama Lu, her rage resurrecting itself. "My design kept you out o' harms way. My design is the main reason you standin' here today young lady, so put some caution in dat tone o' yours!"

"Or what?" snarled Nalia. "Am I going to disappear like my dad?"

Mama Lu was shocked into silence.

"That's right," Nalia continued, "I read all about it. Missing for nearly two weeks without a trace, then they pull his body out of the river down by Audubon Park. Shot twice in the back of the head with his hands and feet still bound. The coroner's report said his tongue was removed."

Mama Lu dropped her gaze to the floor. She never felt remorse for Michael Barronne before and she didn't today, but she hated for Nalia to find out about his murder in this manner.

"I know all the stories about you, Mama," Nalia went on. "I've heard and dismissed all the rumors over the years because I trusted you." She began to shake, and her voice cracked a little as a tear defied her anger and dropped onto her cheek. "Now I want more than anything for you to assure me you had nothing to do with my father's death. But after all this, I'm not sure I can even trust you to tell me the truth."

Mama Lu was cut to the quick. Having no part in Michael Barronne's death did not mean she hadn't wished for it. The man was a nasty piece of work. If Nalia knew "the truth" about how despicable he was, she would not be presenting these accusations. Yet, here she was defending the memory of a man who tore her world to pieces while attacking the woman who put it all back together. Mama Lu was reaching her limit. "You can believe what you want to," she said, with unwavering resolve. "I didn't have notin' to do wit' yo daddy's death. I didn't have to. You'll see dat fo' yo'self."

"When the rest of my memory comes back?" Nalia fired. "The memory you took from me? What was I, some kind of experiment? Was I just a lab rat for you?"

That was it. Mama Lu could stand no more. The anger growing inside her could not be bridled. "Lab rat?" she shouted. "Is dat how you feel I treated you all dem years? I've never once regretted takin' you in, Nalia, an' I don't now, but you on thin ice." The look in Mama Lu's eyes was a mixture of fury and pain, tension and tears. "Lab rat?" she continued. "I treated you like you was my own since you was six years old. I done shown you more love and attention than yo' own mother and father ever thought about. So I'm not gon' stand here and be questioned 'bout the way I raised you or the means I took to protect you."

Mama Lu stood steady as a rock. A line was crossed and the look on her face told Nalia to tread lightly on this new ground. Though it slowed the impassioned barrage of accusations, there was still a tinge of animosity in Nalia's voice when she spoke. "Protect me from what?" she asked.

Mama Lu could tell one of Nalia's walls was breaking down. She took another deep breath and softened her tone. "You don' know all dat was goin' on at dat time. You don' know 'bout the people who was wantin' to harm you, and yo' momma. Same people dat done what they done to yo' daddy. I done what I had to do – to hide you away so they couldn't get to you."

"What people? Are you saying you know who killed my father?" Nalia asked.

Another wall down.

Mama Lu could see Nalia's anger giving way to curiosity. She knew Nalia was not really angry with her; it went much deeper. Nalia was lashing out because she was angry about the unknown. Answers were the key to de-escalation. Mama Lu knew if she could give Nalia enough information to calm her down, she could get her talking about the visions. Of course, a little hex wouldn't hurt either, she thought.

"There are some things I can tell you, chil', and some things I can't." said Mama Lu in a slow, soothing tone. "Bad as I wants to, I can't tell you what the truth is."

The words echoed in Nalia's head. She remembered hearing them before. As Mama Lu turned and removed the lid from the steaming skillet, a vision flashed through Nalia's mind – an image of Mama Lu sitting atop a stark-white tomb.

"I can only tell you *my* truth," Mama Lu went on, "You must find *yo'* truth." She dished another plate of rice and spooned the shrimp creole over both. The smell of the still-bubbling sauce filled the kitchen. As Nalia breathed in its hearty aroma, her racing nerves began to brake. She could not hear Mama Lu's quiet chanting.

Nalia felt slightly light-headed and decided it would be a good idea to sit down just as Mama Lu carried her dinner to the table. Mama Lu looked directly into Nalia's eyes and spoke with a velvety voice. "I need you to understand, chil', there are certain things I can't reveal. You got to see yo' mem'ries as you knew 'em befo', not tainted by my bias. Now I *can* tell you dat yo' daddy was dealin' wit' some dangerous folk. I don't know what name they go by now, but back then we called 'em the mob."

"I know that," said Nalia trying to clear her head of confusion. "I saw that in a dream…a memory. Are you saying the mob killed my dad?"

"Who do you think took over dat hotel, baby? The shipyard, too," replied Mama Lu. "Now if you wants to know more about yo' father and what happened to him, I'll be glad to help you. I'll even go down and look up some o' dem records wit' you. But you gon' have to trust dat I got yo' best interest at heart."

With her defenses withering and her stomach rumbling, Nalia could not resist the tempting dish any longer. She hoped the food would ease the lingering dizziness as she picked up her fork and began to eat.

Mama Lu continued, "Nalia, you know I love you, and I would never do nothin' to bring you no harm. Everything I done, I done to protect you."

Nalia believed what she heard and peace swept through her body like a gentle wind. Mama Lu continued to chant in her mind and suddenly sensed she was not alone in her effort. She could feel the presence of another, chanting with her.

Nalia continued to enjoy the meal, still trying to assuage the light-headed feeling that had her slightly off balance. There was no denying Mama Lu's cooking was delicious, but it was not helping her to regain focus. Nalia thought she saw Mama Lu's eyes begin to glow as the image of the tomb flashed in her mind again – the mid-day sun glistening through the gold hoop earrings, and the bright blue dress blowing in the gentle breeze. "Everyone is here to help you, chil'," a distant voice resounded in Nalia's head. "Patience, my baby. Everything in its time. Trust yo' Mama. Peace gon' come."

Suddenly, Nalia snapped back to coherence and found herself falling into a half eaten plate of shrimp creole. She came to just in time to avoid the dish as her head dropped gently onto the table. As she lay there staring at the side of the plate, she was strangely overcome by a warm feeling of trust for the woman sitting with her. Her hostility faded away. Then, for a moment, the world went dark as the muffled echo of a distant chant rang through her head.

When Nalia came to, Mama Lu was cradling her, helping her to sit up.

"What happened?" asked Nalia. "Did I faint again?"

"More like went to sleep, chil'," said Mama Lu. "You jus' laid yo' head over and went out fo' a minute. You gots to be exhausted, baby. You need to go upstairs, take yo'self a nice hot relaxin' bath, and get yo'self off to bed."

A sudden chill rushed through Nalia's body. "I don't want to go to sleep," she replied. "The nightmares are getting worse. It's like they are becoming more real. Sometimes I can't tell if I'm awake or asleep." As fear crept into Nalia's exhausted mind, she began to weep. Mama Lu wrapped her arms around the frightened shell of the young woman she called her daughter. "I'm scared, Mama," Nalia said in a childlike voice.

"There, there, baby girl," said Mama Lu. "I'm gon' be right here wit' you. Yo' not alone, you understand? Everyone is here to help you."

The vision swept through Nalia's mind again, further clouding her assessment of reality. The sense of déjà vu was so profound it blurred the line between past and present. Nalia was confused and disoriented.

"I'm gon' make you some tea to help you sleep," said Mama Lu reassuringly. "Maybe dem nightmares will leave you be dis evenin'."

When Nalia felt strong enough to stand, Mama Lu helped her to the foot of the stairs. From there Nalia assured her she was alright and could manage on her own. As Nalia made her way upstairs, Mama Lu listened carefully to her movements. When she heard water running in the bathtub, she went to the phone, dialed Madame Toulouse, and updated her on the situation. Madame Toulouse, in turn, informed Mama Lu of the strong calling she felt to join in the chant which helped to calm Nalia's spirit. Her inner sight was returning. Madame Toulouse briefly revisited the instructions she left with Mama Lu and Mr. John before her departure earlier that afternoon – a return to ancient traditions and a pure form of ritual. She instructed Mama Lu to make haste with the preparations.

"And I'm gon' give John a call jus' to make sure he don't forget nothin'," said Madame Toulouse as she hung up the phone.

With all points covered, Mama Lu proceeded with her plan. She steeped Nalia's tea as before with the herbs provided by Mr. John. As she added lemon and honey to mask the taste, she was struck with a thought. Opening the cupboard, Mama Lu pushed aside various containers of seasoning until she reached a collection of small amber vials hidden away in the back. One by one she pulled them out, checking their hand-written labels for a specific marking. Finally, she found it – belladonna.

"We gon' put a stop to all dis family research," said Mama Lu uncapping the vial. "Least 'til you done seen all you need to see." She tilted the dark vial and spilled a few grains of the crushed herb into Nalia's tea. "Gon' make sure you have a nice long sleep. By time you wake up, you ain't gon' want nothin' to do wit' the name Barronne, I tell you dat." Mama Lu stirred the steaming brew until the drug was dissolved. "Oh yeah, you gon' sleep now, young lady," she said. "You gon' sleep good indeed."

CHAPTER NINETEEN

Mr. John was slightly offended by the implication he might fail to remember Madame Toulouse's instructions. Then again, he thought, he did tend to forget things from time to time. That considered, he convinced himself to put his feelings aside and concentrate on the matter at hand.

When a single candle appeared in Nalia's window and the brick dust was dispensed, Mr. John lit the candles on his altar and removed the shirt from his tattooed back. Tonight's ritual would be a return to ancient rites, older and purer than any the elders had practiced before.

Hundreds of years ago, slaves and free blacks brought African Voodoo traditions with them to Haiti where they were intermingled with Catholicism and clan traditionalism. Eventually they evolved into a less than pure, yet, still effective form of the older religion. This was the melting pot of magic which Madame Toulouse, Mama Lu and Mr. John practiced. Over the years, the trio invoked it to many good works. Tonight, however, they would revert their practices to the purest known form of worship in order to re-establish the bond which was broken when their conduit was destroyed. Tonight their energy would flow through its rightful agent – the serpent.

Mr. John reached beneath his altar to retrieve the large wooden box with copper-plated corners. He removed the rosary from its silver latch and placed it on the altar beside the candles. He took a deep breath and slowly opened the vented lid. Reaching inside, he grabbed hold of an aged ball python. Coil by coil, Mr. John lifted the serpent from its box and placed it gently around his neck. The snake's name was Draco. It was black and copper, just over four feet long, and had lived with Mr. John for a very long time.

In ancient rituals, the serpent would be brought before a bonfire by the high priest. The spirits of Voodoo would then enter the snake. The snake served as an instrument by which the spirits passed into the Queen, or Mambo, who received them as she danced before a gathering of followers. In time, the spirits possessed all those present, leading them to one collective consciousness. Vigorous dancing and trancelike worship followed until the spirits of Voodoo were appeased. The requests of the Mambo would then be granted.

Tonight was not a public gathering. It was a private ceremony in which the high priest would present the serpent before his altar in hopes the spirits of Voodoo would smile upon him. If so, they would be channeled into the waiting Queen who was making her own petition across the street as their elder watched over them through her inner eye.

With the great snake draped over his shoulders, Mr. John knelt before his alter. After performing the proper rites, he began to beat a slow and steady rhythm on his ancient drum.

Across town, Madame Toulouse sat in a red, silk robe on a cushioned chair before her altar. Bathed in candlelight, she stared at her reflection in an ancient piece of smoky glass etched with runes and symbols. As she gave the proper ritual tools their due attention, her blood began to pulse with the rhythm of the ancient drum. She felt the energy swelling in her body stronger than it had in years. Mr. John carried out her instructions perfectly; she could tell. She reached for the red, silk sash around her waist and untied it, allowing her robe to drape over the back of her chair. She then wrapped the sash around her nude torso and tied it in seven identical knots.

As the energy of the spirits consumed her, she felt her inner sight growing strong once again. She looked into the glass and watched the world around her dissolve into darkness until she could see only the reflection of her eyes. Madame Toulouse sat staring into her own soul as the rhythm of the drum pulsed louder and stronger in her veins. She closed her eyes, but the reflection in the glass continued to stare back. She could still see it in her mind. Gradually the image began to change, rippling like water across the glass until the eyes were no longer hers, but Nalia's. Madame Toulouse could see her sitting in a darkened bedroom lit by a single candle. Slowly, Nalia sipped hot tea from a thin china cup as her eyelids grew heavy with fatigue. Beside her head, the snake with the conductor's hat, in the engine of the carved circus train, seemed to be watching her, smiling.

Madame Toulouse watched with her inner eye as the image shifted, and she observed Mama Lu sitting in her hidden room behind the closet at the large desk with many tiny drawers. She was positioned identically to Madame Toulouse, wearing only a red, silk sash tied in seven perfect knots around her waist. Her body was drenched in the warm glow of the tall candles on her altar. Madame Toulouse watched while all the appropriate offerings were made, and when Mama Lu's eyes rolled into her head, she knew the spirits were taking over her body. Soon they would possess Madame Toulouse and Mr. John as well, and it would be time for the Queen to make her petition. Protection and safety would follow.

Peace gon' come. Peace gon' come. Darkness flee and peace gon' come.

The belladonna worked quickly, causing Nalia to fall into a deep, restful sleep, and soon she found herself walking down a dirt path lined with evenly planted oak trees on either side. Their heavy branches stretched across the pathway forming a tranquil canopy of foliage – a perfect picture of early spring. The morning sun shimmered down through the leaves, creating a pattern of light and shadow that danced wildly on the lush grass below. Looking closely, Nalia could see groups of bumblebees gathered over sporadic patches of blooming clover. They hovered, suspended in time with their wings aloft and motionless.

Nalia got the familiar feeling she was walking through a snapshot. The only indication to the contrary was a low rhythmic pounding in the distance steadily growing louder. As the thumping became more audible, Nalia recognized it – hoof beats. She looked around at the road behind her and in front, but still found no evidence of motion. She peered around the trees as the hoof beats drew closer but saw nothing. Soon, she heard the distinctive sound of pebbles being crushed under rolling wheels and the unmistakable neighing of a large horse. The noises were close. Nalia became frightened as the phantom hoof beats grew louder and louder. Her muscles tightened. She shut her eyes and covered her ears. Just as she felt she would be overtaken, the clamor stopped and all was quiet.

The air stood stagnant while the maddening sound of silence expunged all audible signs of life. It took a moment for the tension to leave Nalia's body, but when her nerves finally settled, she released the air held captive by her lungs and slowly opened her eyes. It was then she felt the horse's forceful snort on the back of her neck, just inches away. Nalia jumped as if shocked by a cattle prod. She turned to find an antique carriage pulled by an enormous black stallion. The great beast's lustrous mane draped down its muscular neck as it stood proud, staring down the narrow oak-lined road. Heavy blinders kept the graceful creature steady while it unearthed clumps of dirt with its front hooves.

The coach was beautiful, tall and black, polished to a mirror-like finish and trimmed with gold striping. Its large, spoked wheels stood almost as tall as Nalia. The coach featured a high, open passenger compartment with red, leather seats and brass railings.

Up front, on the tall driver's bench a strapping black man sat holding the stallion's reins and a long buggy whip. He wore a black coat with tails, a tall, leather coachman's hat, and mirrored sunglasses identical to the pallbearers of St. Louis Cemetery. His expression was static; he stared straight ahead like his equine companion.

Both horse and driver kept still as Nalia circled the carriage. Beneath the open half-door, she found a polished brass stepladder extended, bidding her welcome. On the passenger's bench, behind the coachman, sat Queen Marie in her bright blue dress and her gold hoop earrings. Nalia was not the least bit surprised. In fact, she rather expected it. Gripping the brass railing, she hoisted herself into the carriage, sat down on the rear bench, and pulled Queen Marie into her lap so they both looked down the narrow road.

"I'm all yours," Nalia said to the coachman, not really expecting a response. The driver obliged her with silence and snapped the whip. The coach accelerated at a steady pace until Nalia could feel the rhythmic bumping of the dirt road below. She held tight to Queen Marie and wondered where the carriage would take her as the hoof beats pounded in her head once again.

Before long, the tree-lined road began to wind, eventually coming to a covered bridge. It was a large, old structure made of rough, knotty wood. The sides were fully enclosed except for a row of small openings that ran along the roofline.

The oversized wheels of the carriage rolled over the bridge's rough wooden slats producing a hypnotic vibration. The combination of shuddering movement, complex geometric lines, and the strobing of light and shadow lulled Nalia into a shallow trance as the world faded away into the darkness of the bridge's canopy.

With a blurred sense of time, Nalia was unable to determine if she was inside the bridge for several minutes or several hours, but as darkness surrendered to the sunlight of the other side, the carriage's ride smoothed to a steady roll. The wheels of the coach generated a low hum as they glided over the flat pavement Nalia recognized as Decatur Street. Though the landmarks were familiar, the scene was not. Nalia had never witnessed Decatur Street so very empty and lifeless. There was not a soul in sight as far as she could see, but as the carriage passed the oddly empty patio of Café Du Monde, Nalia caught the distinctive smell of fresh beignets and coffee. A voice echoed inside her head, "We are on what you call a different plane." Nalia could not pinpoint exactly where the notion came from, but she briefly wondered if smells could travel from plane to plane. She contemplated the gravity of the thought as the carriage hummed southward, finally pulling to the curb outside *The Doll Maker.*

The street was completely still except for the cadenced swaying of the wooden sign suspended from the heavy chains above the doorway. It whooshed back and forth, echoing the rhythm of the horse's hooves as the driver brought the carriage to a halt.

The windows were dark and the shop appeared empty. Nalia could scarcely make out the outline of the dolls in the display. Then, through the smoky glass, Nalia saw tiny twinkling lights darting to and fro in a fanciful exhibition, like fairies dancing on the air. Drawn to their hypnotic display, Nalia knew where she needed to go.

With Queen Marie in hand, she placed a foot onto the polished brass rung of the stepladder and stepped from the coach onto the empty sidewalk. She glanced up at the coachman, thinking it would have been nice of him to at least tip his hat before he pulled away.

Instead he sat stock-still, quietly staring into the distance through his mirrored glasses.

"Thanks for the ride," Nalia offered under her breath while walking to the door of the shop. As she gripped the handle and pushed, a burst of blinding white light flashed from the open doorway. Nalia's vision went red and splotchy. When her focus returned, she found herself standing inside the shop, face-to-face with Margaret Barronne.

"Fabulous," said Margaret enthusiastically. "Absolutely exquisite. I've got to have it."

Nalia almost dropped Queen Marie as she stood frozen with her mouth agape. It took several stunned moments for her to realize Margaret was referring to the china doll she was holding up between them. Nalia was so close she could smell Margaret's expensive perfume. The woman held herself with an air of superiority, overly adorned with fashionable clothes and sparkling accessories. "Can she see me?" thought Nalia, immediately dismissing the notion as she continued to watch Margaret examine the bejeweled doll. The woman's eyes danced with light as they reflected the brilliance of the diamonds on its wide necklace. For the first time since the visions began, Nalia felt the harsh sting of truth – the undeniable notion that even if her mother could see her, she would not care at all.

"Momma, Momma!" cried a young excited voice behind Margaret. "Guess what?"

Nalia stepped aside to see a little girl – the younger embodiment of herself – bouncing merrily toward her mother. The child could hardly contain her excitement. Margaret's eyes rolled into her head as she sighed with frustration at the sound of young Nalia's voice.

"What is it, Nalia?" she asked. "Can't you see I'm busy?"

The young girl's voice became low and sheepish. "Mama Lu wants to know if I can go into the back and help with the dolls? Can I Momma, please?"

Visibly aggravated, Margaret turned around and snapped at her daughter. "What?" It was then she realized Mama Lu was watching from across the shop. Her tone changed quickly, sliding into an overly-sweet timbre. "What did you say, darling?"

The little girl repeated her question while Margaret held eye contact with Mama Lu.

"She'll be fine, Mrs. Barronne," Mama Lu called out. "I ain't got the kiln fired up jus' now. I was jus' gon' show her the sewin' room, anyhow."

"How exciting," dripped Margaret. "Just as long as she's no bother."

"No bother at all," Mama Lu called back. "I'm lookin' fo'ward to it."

"All right then," Margaret replied with some hesitation.

The girl turned and started back toward Mama Lu, but Margaret caught her by the arm and swung her around, hard. Gripping her tightly, Margaret knelt down and whispered under her breath, "If you break anything, young lady, so help me…"

The girl's eyes resembled those of a scared puppy as Margaret released her grip. Cautiously, the child turned away from her mother and walked toward Mama Lu. The closer she got, the more she began to bounce and skip. By the time she reached the counter, she was jumping for joy and Mama Lu, although a bit more reserved, was jumping with her.

Margaret stood up, watching her daughter carry on with Mama Lu. A scowl crept across her face and her nostrils flared. Behind her, still standing just inside the front door with her arms folded across her chest, Nalia donned a scowl of her own. Fully aware she was watching a real event from her past, Nalia took notice of every subtlety she observed, particularly the plain school jumper and the ragged, dingy-white sweater worn by the young girl. The child's simple attire was a stark contrast to the lavish garments worn by her mother. It made Nalia wonder – if things had turned out differently for her, would she have ever enjoyed her parent's wealth anyway? "I'll get control of that hotel just to spite you," Nalia thought as she stepped around Margaret and made her way to the sewing room where Mama Lu took the child.

As Nalia opened the door, she saw the younger figure of herself, wide-eyed with wonder over the many bolts of fine fabric and the group of unfinished dolls in line for assembly. Mama Lu was currently working on a series of four dolls, all identical in form but attired differently. From the look of the outfits set before them, it appeared Mama Lu was fashioning them according to the seasons. There was a thick fur coat with gloves for the winter doll and a brightly colored Easter dress for the spring. The summer doll would feature a light, floral sun dress while the autumn doll awaited an earth-toned pant-suit with a waist-coat. Each doll stood on its own stand with its clothing displayed in front of it, almost as if Mama Lu left them waiting for the child to arrive. There was even a small plate of cookies and a box of juice sitting next to the table.

From the doorway, Nalia watched Mama Lu instruct the child how to handle each doll and which article of clothing to put where. The young girl listened carefully and did exactly as instructed, beaming with joy all the while. She and Mama Lu dressed each doll, playing with them and making silly voices as they worked. Mama Lu was gentle and patient, even stroking the child's hair at one point when the autumn doll's coat presented some difficulty.

"Take yo' time," said Mama Lu. "Ain't no need to rush. Tell you what, let's break for a cookie den come back to it."

Young Nalia agreed enthusiastically as she put down the doll. Mama Lu handed her the juice box, and in her excitement, Nalia squeezed. Red juice erupted from the straw like a volcano splashing on the front of Nalia's sweater.

"Oh no!" she said with tears filling her eyes. "Momma's going to be mad!" She looked up at Mama Lu in desperation.

"It's alright, chil'," Mama Lu reassured her. "I got a sink right in back. Take dat ol' sweater off and Mama Lu'll see if she can't wash dat stain out right quick."

The girl nodded and reached for her buttons, then hesitated. She looked up at Mama Lu, unsure of herself, not wanting to proceed.

"It's alright," said Mama Lu, "I'll have dat sweater good as new in no time."

As Nalia slowly peeled the sweater off her arms, Mama Lu saw the bruising hidden by her sleeves. She caught herself gasping in time to stifle it so as not to make the child self-conscious. Mama Lu played it off as if she had not noticed, smiling as she quickly took the sweater from Nalia.

"You wait here, baby. Mama Lu be right back," she said, sweating from anxiety. She walked quickly to the sink at the rear of the shop and began to scrub the stain off the front of the sweater, a fusion of sadness and anger churning inside her. If Margaret was already beating this child, Mama Lu was not about to let a stained sweater add fuel to the fire. The mild soap solution she used did a good job, and the chanting didn't hurt either. She focused her attention on Mr. John and cried out for him in her mind.

With the stain mostly gone, Mama Lu rung out the sweater and took it to the large wooden work table where she hung it over a doll stand. She retrieved a small heater from the paint table and turned the blower onto the damp garment. All the while, Mama Lu's anger escalated and her mind raced with questions. Who was abusing this precious child? Was it her mother? If so, did her father know? Or was her father the culprit?

Mama Lu needed information. This kind of situation was delicate. If not handled correctly, it meant more danger for the child, and that was not an option. She wanted answers, and she wanted them fast. As Mama Lu re-entered the sewing room through the thick plastic curtains, she found young Nalia once again struggling with the autumn doll's coat. She watched as Nalia finally got the garment to fit the way it was fashioned. This is how a young girl's childhood should be spent, thought Mama Lu. Not dodging the outbursts of an aggressor. Mama Lu put on the happiest face she could manage and walked over to the little girl.

"I got it," Nalia said triumphantly, "Does it look right?"

"It's jus' perfect, chil'," said Mama Lu placing her arm gently around Nalia's shoulder and kissing her on the forehead. "And dat sweater o' yours will be dry in 'bout five minutes. Dat ol' stain came right out."

Nalia looked up at Mama Lu with wide eyes. "My momma's not going to find out, is she?"

"Oh, I think I can keep yo' momma busy 'til it's done," responded Mama Lu, walking to the door. Peeking out, she saw Mr. John chatting with Margaret near the front of the store. "Oh yeah," said Mama Lu, pleased. "She gon' be busy fo' a while."

Nalia and Mama Lu played with the dolls for a few moments longer, unaware they were being watched by the teary-eyed, older embodiment of the little girl. She noticed the kindness and patience Mama Lu showed when interacting with the child. She was already treating Nalia like her own.

After several minutes, Mama Lu retrieved the dry sweater from the workroom and helped Nalia put it back on to cover her bruises. When the sweater was buttoned, the child wrapped her arms around Mama Lu and squeezed her tightly for several moments, thanking her profusely.

When the little girl was ready, Mama Lu walked her back out to the front of the shop where they found a weary-looking Margaret still listening to Mr. John ramble on about the smell of masking tape.

Relieved to see Mama Lu, Margaret politely excused herself and made her way to the counter where Vivian sat at the register, filing her nails and popping her gum. Still holding the widest smile she could fake, Mama Lu reluctantly ushered Nalia over to her mother.

"Did you find yo'self a new doll?" she asked Margaret through teeth so tight she could bite the head off a tenpenny nail.

"Momma, I got to dress four of the dolls!" Nalia interjected excitedly.

Margaret did not acknowledge the girl, but kept her attention focused on the doll she handed over to Vivian. "I did," she said to Mama Lu. "This little gem is going to be the centerpiece of the table in my foyer. I want people to be captivated by her elegance as soon as they enter my home."

"I did a good job dressing them too, Momma. Mama Lu told me so," Nalia said again, to the deaf ears of her mother.

Mama Lu was sick to her stomach. She wondered why she bothered with the sweater at all, feeling Margaret would not have paid the child enough attention to even notice the stain. It was all she could do not to slap the woman across the face. Instead, she turned her attention to the doll.

"Let me see dat one, Vivian," she said holding out her hands as Vivian ran Margaret's credit card. "Oh, I remember dis one. She been here fo' 'bout a year now. Made her jus' after Mayor Marchande's wife passed. Dat's who she looks like, you know. I was gon' give her to Mayor Marchande on account o' he was such a good friend of Mr. John and all. But Mr. John told me he wouldn't have it." Mama Lu leaned in close, reducing her volume to a healthy whisper. "Turns out Mayor Marchande wasn't too fond of his wife, and neither was his girlfriend, if you know what I mean. Anyhow, dat doll's been sittin' here ever since, jus' waitin' fo' the right buyer." While Mama Lu was jabbering on, she slipped the nail of her pinky finger into the back of the doll's olive-green, silk dress and began to rip the seam. By the time she finished her monologue, she had acquired a firm hold so when she offered the doll back to Vivian, she was easily able to pull the dress apart right down the center.

"Oh dear!" she gasped, "Curse my clumsy hands. Musta caught it on my ring."

Margaret Barronne turned up her nose like she smelled rotten fish. Her eyes went wide as saucers.

"Oh Margaret, I'm so sorry," Mama Lu went on. "Don't you worry, I'm gon' fix her right up. I'll even give you a break on the price fo' yo' trouble. I can have her ready by tomorrow if you wants to stop back by. Or I can have her run out to you if you'll jus' jot down yo' address."

Realizing she was presenting a scowl of displeasure, Margaret quickly adopted her usual fake grin. "Oh nonsense, Lucia. I'll just drop back by tomorrow. Around this same time?"

"Dat'll be jus' fine," said Mama Lu with a smile. "I'll have her ready fo' you."

The two women exchanged an awkward glare – like two pots, both about to boil. Margaret gathered her composure and took Nalia firmly by the hand before making her exit. When the door closed, Mr. John turned to Mama Lu. "What was all dat nonsense 'bout Mayor Marchande? You jus' cast dat doll two weeks ago. I remember, I put it out on the shelf fo' you."

Mama Lu held her tongue and her smile until Margaret's car drove away, then turned to Mr. John and exploded with a burning rage. "You got twenty-fo' hours! You hear me?" she said forcefully as Mr. John jumped back. "You gon' find me out wha's goin' on wit' dat baby girl or I'm gon string you up by yo' jewels." The look on her face indicated she was not joking at all.

"Hold on jus' one minute, woman!" Mr. John stammered. "You ain't 'bout to string nobody up by they… nothin'. Wha's wrong wit' you?"

"John, dat girl got bruises all up and down her lil' arms, and I ain't talking about no accident, neither. She got em all 'round her wrists and up by her lil' elbows. They done turned all different colors – like she got bruises on top o' bruises. I'm tellin' you, John, I want to know who's doin' it, and I want to know quick. I can't let dis go on no longer, John. You got twenty-fo' hours."

"Might not need dat long," said Mr. John as the bells above the front door chimed to life. "Wha'cha got fo' me, ol'man?"

"I got your 'old man' for you right here, dat's what I got," replied old man Leonetti in his thick Italian accent.

Charles Leonetti was a feisty, elderly gentleman. His ancestors emigrated from Sicily to New Orleans during the early 1800's as shipbuilders and since then, a steady line of family had called the city home. He entered the shop wearing a textured, white Guayabera shirt opened at the collar exposing a tuft of white chest hair and a thick, gold chain with a St. Christopher medal. Though the thought of leaving New Orleans never crossed his mind, Leonetti looked as if he could be seamlessly transplanted into any well-to-do retirement village in Southern Florida. His thinning dark hair held its color for many years but recently gave up the fight, surrendering to a distinguished shade of silver. He had smoked many a cigar sitting at Mr. John's shoeshine stand over the years. The two went back a long way. Over time, they established a trust, bonding them like family, so when Mr. John asked for a favor, Charles Leonetti did his best to oblige. He stopped by now to report on one such favor.

"You got some news fo' me?" Mr. John asked, leaning casually against the counter and winking at Mama Lu.

"Yeah, I found out a few things," replied Leonetti. "We all friends here?" he asked, gesturing toward Vivian.

"Yeah, Viv's alright." said Mr. John, making introductions.

"No disrespect to you Mama Lu," continued Leonetti. "I just like to make sure. You know, when there's sensitive information involved."

"We all know what you getting' at, Charlie," said Mama Lu. "Just flip dat sign around and tell us what you done found out."

Old man Leonetti gave a quick glance out the window, flipped the OPEN sign to CLOSED, locked the bolt, and cleared his throat. "Alright, here's what I got," he said, shuffling to the counter. "Turns out all dis time I been sniffin' around the wrong places. I'm askin' around the shipyard for personal info on Michael Barronne, and don't nobody know nothin'. The guys a real recluse, you know? But then I think – dis guys got mob ties, right? Everybody knows dat. So I figure I got to start sniffin' a little closer to the Verellis. Long story short, I go down to Arthur's Pub and I find a couple of good-for-nothin' scumbags that are runnin' with my good-for-nothin' son. I get a few drinks in 'em an they start tellin' me dat dis guy Barronne, he don't want nobody knowin' about his family, see? On account of his wife is black, and dat don't sit well wit' his redneck, good ol' boy business partners dat are backin' his hotels."

"Half black," corrected Mama Lu.

"To these guys, dat's even worse," said Leonetti, with a look that conveyed his disgust. "Anyway, turns out dat Barronne presents himself as dis real upstandin' guy, right? But behind closed doors he's dis ragin' alcoholic wit' a quick temper and a short fuse."

"Dat man's a loose cannon," said Mama Lu exchanging a knowing look with Mr. John. She was already forming a mental picture of what Nalia's home life must be like.

"Now get dis," Leonetti went on. "I also found out dat Barronne's been goin' off the deep end lately. Couple of weeks ago, he shows up at the shipyard 'cause there's some kind of dispute between the union rep and one of his dock foremen. Anyways, Barronne gets into it wit' his foreman – ends up bustin' dis guy's head open wit' one of dem aluminum clipboards. Well, somethin' ain't right for the guy to just snap like dat, right? So I buy these guys a few more drinks and I find out that Barronne's business is in trouble – I mean big trouble. The guy's got a gamblin' problem, see? He likes to play the ponies, only he ain't exactly Lucky Louie, know what I'm sayin'? Anyway, word is the Verelli brothers got him over a barrel for a few million."

Mama Lu, Mr. John and Vivian all stood slack-jawed as Leonetti raised his eyebrows.

"I know, right?" he continued. "Dis guy is stressed out like you wouldn't believe. I mean, these are the Verellis we're talkin' about, right? Those guys'll cut your throat in a heartbeat. Wit' dat kinda pressure – the drinkin', the money, and the mob – dis guy is beyond 'loose cannon', he's a friggin' time bomb, capice?"

"How 'bout dat lil' girl?" asked Mama Lu. "You find out anything 'bout his daughter?"

Leonetti pulled a folded handkerchief from his pocket and dabbed the sweat from his neck. "Dat's where everybody gets real tight-lipped. Most people don't even know the guy's got a daughter. But I heard some talk – real hush-hush stuff. I don't know nothing for certain, but I hear he's workin' some kind of deal wit' the Verellis, and it's got something to do wit' dat little girl. Dat's all I got."

"Dat's all I need," said Mama Lu. "You a good man, Chuck Leonetti. You may have jus' helped save dat lil' girl's life. You a good, good man."

"Yeah? Well don't go spreadin' dat around," replied Leonetti. "I got a reputation to uphold."

No sooner than Leonetti finished speaking, Nalia heard the hoof beats once again. Glancing through the window, she could see the carriage pulling up to the curb outside. Nalia did not want to go, she wanted to see more. She wanted to stay here in the safety of the shop. She turned toward the counter hoping to hear more of the conversation. To her surprise, Mama Lu and the others stood motionless and silent, mouths open in mid-sentence with hands raised in unfinished gestures – like someone pressed *pause* on life.

The horse whinnied and snorted, calling Nalia's attention back to the carriage. The coachman sat patiently still, his hands ready at the reins. As Nalia moved toward the doorway, the sun's setting glow blanketed the windows in amber light that seemed to move and grow in intensity. Soon, bright light flooded into the store as if the sun were back-tracking its path across the sky. Dazzling rays of sunshine hit the floor at the front of the shop and quickly worked their way toward the back, casting long shadows of anything in their path. The light became blinding as Nalia reached for the door handle, and then a sound like a mighty rushing wind overtook her. Suddenly, the blinding light burst through the door jamb, ripping the door from its hinges and pulling it violently into the wind-blown street.

Nalia watched as the horse turned its head toward her. It stood menacingly unaffected as debris from the street whirled about in the fierce wind. Its jet-black eyes were cold and lifeless like a shark's. Nalia tried to look away but she could not; her gaze was drawn to the blackness. She became dizzy and the world grew dark. Her body went numb as she felt it spinning and falling. Unable to catch herself, she waited for the impact of the ground. It did not come.

Instead, the strong smell of gasoline jarred her to her senses. Like the vicious odor of smelling salts, the rancid fumes caused Nalia to jump.

The beast was upon her. With a massive claw, it gripped her wrists and held them over her head as its nostrils flared, breathing heavily onto the side of her neck. Its teeth were bared and it snarled in a laughter-like cacophony of twisted satisfaction. Its grotesque head loomed over Nalia's face like a cloud as she tried in vain to look away from its gaze. She found herself drawn into the mesmerizing eyes of the beast. They were not glowing as usual, but instead glistening like perfect green pools in the mid-day sun. They looked glassy – human.

Nalia wanted to fight, but something was strange. Something was different this time. Her mind told her this was only a dream, but she was unable to wake herself up. Her body was a prison. She wanted to scream. She wanted to breathe. She wanted to move. Nothing! Panic seared her brain as she realized she was paralyzed, completely captive to the terror before her. The belladonna was a ruthless jailor. Its hold on Nalia's body trapped her mind in the nightmare with no means of escape.

Nalia turned her head as the beast slid its tongue up the side of her neck and tightened its grip on her wrists. Across the room, a sliver of light spilled in through the open doorway, and Nalia could see the tall, dark figure watching over the beast. Its haughty glare burned Nalia's stomach. Its eyes were wide and vigilant, never blinking. As more light crept through the door, Nalia saw a face emerge on the head of the dark figure. It was a human face – the face of a woman.

The beast tightened its grip again and let out a raspy howl. Pain like Nalia had never known tore through her body as the world faded away into a dizzying spiral of darkness.

CHAPTER TWENTY

Morning was a bitter old friend. Fatigue lingered heavily with Mama Lu as she put a pot of coffee on to brew. She spent much of her evening checking in on Nalia once the ritual was concluded. All night, Nalia was plagued with restlessness. She mumbled and stirred but never awakened. Mama Lu considered the possibilities for the drastic change. Either the nightmares had ceased, the magic had run its course, or the belladonna was more potent than anticipated.

There was also the possibility that the protections put in place by the elders were working so well, they had calmed Nalia's spirit into a sleep deep enough to fend off the nightmares. Had the older ways proven that much more effective? Mama Lu was doubtful. Confident as she was in the bond they shared, she knew the protections were as much for the elders as they were for Nalia; they guarded their own minds and memories from revealing the one secret Nalia must never know.

Regardless of the reason behind it, Nalia experienced a night of semi-restful sleep without waking in the throws of terror. Mama Lu hoped that was a good thing as she waited for the coffee to finish dripping. Johnny the Conqueror was tucked into the pocket of her silk robe getting an early morning rub-down.

Mama Lu leaned against the counter, breathing in the rich aroma of brewing coffee as it mixed with the humid morning air wafting through the screen door. The temperature was already rising, and soon the summer heat would blaze down upon the city. Mama Lu was not looking forward to it. It was not the heat that bothered her, it was the tension. Summers in the south always had a way of making people irritable and quick tempered. There was enough of that going around already.

As the coffee continued to drip, Mama Lu wondered about the belladonna. She questioned her hasty decision to mix it with Mr. John's potent herbs, worrying she might have done more harm than good.

She knew the nightmare would soon reveal its true nature, and Nalia would see it just the way she witnessed it as a child. If that transpired while Nalia was sedated by the belladonna, it was possible she could relive the traumatic events over and over. Mama Lu shuddered at the thought but knew she could not risk the alternative. She would not have Nalia going off high-strung in search of some fantasized family past that could lead her down the same road that captivated her mother. She must stay sedated until all of her memories returned.

At least with the belladonna relaxing her, Nalia would be safe from physically harming herself.

Hopefully the protections would guard her mind in the same manner.

Drip, drip, drip.

Mama Lu poured herself a cup of the freshly-brewed java and sat down in her usual seat at the kitchen table. As she sweetened the steaming beverage with honey from the glass jar, she heard the sluggish footsteps of Mr. John on the back porch. Right on cue, she thought, as he popped open the screen door and entered the kitchen without a word. His eyes were only half open as he headed for the coffee pot. On the counter, he found his favorite blue mug, set out for him just moments before. Without hesitation, he filled the mug and joined her at the table. The two sipped in silence for at least half a cup, staring at each other. Theirs was not an awkward silence, but a comfortable familiarity in which each tried to pry open their eyes. Quietly, they listened to the songbirds in the trees outside and waited for the caffeine to work.

When the fog finally lifted, Mr. John spoke first. "Well?" he asked.

Mama Lu dropped her head, resting her furrowed brow in the palm of her hand. She placed her thumb on one throbbing temple and the tip of her middle finger on the other while gently applying pressure. She closed her eyes tightly as she rubbed, trying to alleviate the mounting tension in her head.

"She alright fo' now," Mama Lu finally replied. "Rough night tho'. I looked in on her jus' 'bout every hour. She didn't wake up screamin' or havin' fits like befo', but she wasn't sleepin' good neither. She tossed and turned all night long, mumblin' the whole time. Looked like she was strugglin', but it was never enough to wake her up." Mama Lu stirred her coffee nervously. She was still weighing the outcome of her choice to use the belladonna, and did not want Mr. John to know. Carefully omitting that detail, she continued. "Dis one time I went in, 'bout 4:30, and she was sort of sittin' up. She looked dead at me, but she didn't see me. I waved my hand right in front of her face, but she couldn't see nothin'. She was still asleep. I didn't think much of it 'til I noticed she was cryin', then it scared me half to death. Reminded me of that night years ago when we found her cryin' on the floor and she'd done scratched herself to ribbons."

Mama Lu paused and stared blankly across the room, picturing the scene in her mind. Mr. John could see the conversation was upsetting her, but he let her finish.

"I can't tell how much of her memory's come back. She aint screamin', but she ain't talkin' either, so dat makes it hard to tell. All I know is what she told me last night, and dat's got me worried. She done been down to the library and pulled up everything she could find on her daddy. Came in with a real nasty attitude askin' a bunch of questions 'bout him and his money. I swear, John, I looked at her and I saw her momma standin' right in front of me. I spent mos' of the night tryin' to figure out how to keep her from goin' down dat road. We gon' need to wait 'til she wakes up and see what her mind is like, but I tell you, John, I don't want to go through another nasty confrontation like dat one."

Mr. John waited patiently for Mama Lu to finish. When she began to wring her hands, he rose from his chair. Without a word, he walked around the table. Mama Lu assumed he was returning to the coffee pot, and was surprised when he stopped behind her chair and wrapped his arms around her shoulders. Placing his cheek alongside hers, he squeezed her gently and held her for a long moment.

"I was gon' ask how *you* were holdin' up, Mama," he said, kissing her on the temple.

Mama Lu allowed all her guards to fall away as she melted into Mr. John's tender embrace. She cleared her mind and allowed herself this rare opportunity to be at peace, even if it was only for a moment.

176

Mr. John cherished encounters like this. He saw them as grand treasures, too few and far between. If it were up to him, their lives would be filled with a continuous stream of similar tender moments, but Mama Lu was a strong-willed woman. She was always quick to point out the fact that she lived her life without depending on any man. She was a proud woman – a little too proud, Mr. John would say. Despite her rabid independence, he loved her dearly. He always had.

As he released her from his embrace, he moved his hands to her shoulders and gently rubbed the tension from her neck. As the tightness reluctantly left her muscles, Mama Lu closed her eyes and placed her hand kindly on Mr. John's. At times like these, Mr. John felt most complete.

Mama Lu and Mr. John were so caught up in the tenderness of the moment, neither heard the footsteps on the porch until they were just beyond the back door. The morning sun beamed through the screen casting the shadow of an elegant, wide-brimmed hat onto the kitchen wall.

"Come on in, Madame T., its open," Mr. John called out, savoring the last few seconds of privacy.

The screen door opened, and a white, stiletto-heeled shoe hit the kitchen floor as the velvety voice of Madame Vivian Luciénne made known her arrival. "Well, I guess I'm not exactly who you were expectin' but I appreciate the invitation, John."

Mama Lu jumped up from her chair as Madame Luciénne strode boldly into the kitchen and walked right up to the table. Mr. John quickly stepped around and across Mama Lu, planting his foot firmly in front of her. He held up an arm, not so much to protect Mama Lu as to hold her back. He was enjoying the morning and did not want to see it marred by watching Mama Lu strangle someone in her own kitchen.

"I was hopin' I could find you here," Madame Luciénne continued. "I went by the shop earlier, but it was closed," she purred with a sinister grin. "Strange too, I saw one of the windows was all boarded up. Dreadful sight. Did y'all have a break-in?"

Mama Lu could not contain her rage. "You wicked, evil cockroach," she spat as Mr. John asserted a bit more force on the arm holding her back. "How dare you have the nerve to set foot in my home?"

Madame Luciénne looked behind her as if expecting to see the person Mama Lu must be talking to. She held a hand gently to her chest and raised her eyebrows with an inquisitive expression. She had chosen a white dress for the occasion, playing her innocent role to the hilt.

"I beg yo' pardon, Lucia, but John just invited me in. I must say, you sho' have a funny way of treating yo' guests."

Mr. John continued to push Mama Lu backward as she rifled off angry comments.

"Guest?" she yelled. "Vivian, you ain't, and never will be, a guest in my home."

Madame Luciénne dropped her jaw. "Now, Lucia," she said, "There was a time when I practically lived here. You and I were like family. I jus' can't imagine wha's brought on all dis hostility."

Mama Lu lunged, but Mr. John's arm was strong.

"You know good and well what dis is 'bout," shouted Mama Lu. "I knew you was behind dis. You and Tony Leonetti. I knew dis wasn't no coincidence." She pushed Mr. John away and stepped backward toward the stove. Mama Lu breathed deeply, trying to calm herself to a state of reason. When Mr. John stepped toward her, she gave him a strong glare, warning him to keep his distance.

Madame Luciénne maintained her shocked expression as she tried to be convincing. "I don't know what you're drivin' at, Lucia, but if you think I spend my time associating with the likes of Tony Leonetti..."

"You 'spect me to believe he busted up my store on his own?" Mama Lu interrupted. "Dat snivelin' lil' piece of trash ain't got the guts to cross me without somebody pullin' his strings."

"Are you sayin' Tony Leonetti broke into yo' store?" asked Luciénne, with a less-than-believable gasp. "My goodness, Lucia, I had no idea, but I'm simply appalled that you think I had something to do with it."

"You must have somethin' powerful good on Tony to convince him to cross me," insisted Mama Lu. "I ain't had reason to do it in a long time, but I ain't forgot how to 'fix' somebody when they need it. Dat goes fo' the ones who put 'em up to it, too."

"Now, Lucia," said Madame Luciénne, lowering her gaze into a grave expression. "That is a very strong accusation, indeed. Now unless you've got some kind of proof to back it up, I would caution you against makin' such remarks, from a legal standpoint, you understand? My name is my business, Lucia, and I can't have somebody slandering my good name. Let me just say for the record that I have absolutely no affiliation with Tony Leonetti and no knowledge of the unfortunate break-in at your store. I find it most disturbing that you would attack an old friend, in such a manner, when I merely stopped in to see if you had reconsidered my invitation to attend the ritual we gon' be reinstituting on St. John's Eve." Madame Luciénne finished with an upturned nose and a 'how dare you' stare as she awaited Mama Lu's response. She was pulling this performance off better than expected.

Knowing rage was consuming her, Mr. John was surprised to see tears pooling in Mama Lu's eyes. He couldn't tell if it was anger, frustration, or reflection. Mama Lu was not sure either. Her eyes were alight with a flame of fury, but her heart was steadily breaking. She recounted all the years Vivian Luciénne spent under her instruction: the secrets divulged, the traditions passed on, the knowledge imparted. What a waste, she thought, to have a pupil show such promise, only to sacrifice it on the altar of pride. This was the woman she once entrusted with the secrets of her craft, the apprentice she groomed to take over and carry on the faith of her ancestors. She had even trusted Vivian with the care of Nalia on many occasions.

Now that trust was shattered like the doll of Marie Laveau that had so long been a part of Mama Lu's religion. Just like the doll, Mama Lu's trust for Madame Luciénne was broken beyond hope of repair. Luciénne was twisted now, consumed by greed just like Margaret Barronne. It was that fate from which she hoped to rescue Nalia, and the thought of having to do so infuriated her all the more.

Mama Lu stared at Madame Luciénne with all the anger of a raging sea swirling in her tear-threatened eyes. "Invitation?" she asked, folding her arms across her chest and leaning her head to one side. "Is dat what you call yo' insistence dat I attend yo' lil' make-believe ritual? The one where you gon' try and fool folks into believin' you the almighty Voodoo Queen o' New Orleans?" Her tone became calm, but her tongue was like acid. "You really think people gon' put their faith in some poor, pathetic piece of two-bit trash like yo'self? You really believe dat they can't smell dat cheap perfume, see dem knock-off designer clothes, and know you jus' as big a fake as they are? You think you got everybody fooled into thinkin' you something you ain't jus' 'cause you half-way look the part? You jus' foolin' yo'self, Vivian."

Mama Lu leaned comfortably against the stove. She raised a single finger in front of her face and pointed it straight at Madame Luciénne. "You nothin' but a fraud," she continued. "Everybody knows dat, so no matter what happens at dat ritual, people ain't gon' see you no different. If you think I'm gon' jump up and try to change their minds with some public rite of passage, well then, you jus' sadly mistaken."

Madame Luciénne clicked her tongue against the roof of her mouth, then tucked it inside her cheek. The ever-present voices were screaming inside her head, taunting her like schoolyard bullies, scolding her like the mother she loathed. She struggled hard to keep her rage in check so she could further coddle the drama. She was not finished yet, by any means. She harnessed her anger, locked her eyes on Mama Lu, and pulled out a chair with a swift, hateful motion. Never breaking her gaze, she boldly tossed her white, satin clutch onto the table and gracefully took a seat. "Sit down, Lucia," she said with a sinister sneer and an inflection that announced her sense of superiority. "Listen good while I tell you how dis is gon' go down." She could not believe the words had come from her own lips. Her heart pounded nervously in her chest.

Mama Lu was furious, but she had figured out the game Madame Luciénne was playing. The more rage Mama Lu allowed to show, the more Madame Luciénne enjoyed watching. Luciénne was trying to control Mama Lu's emotions, thinking if she could keep her on edge, she could wear her down. Mama Lu refused to play along. She decided she would no longer give Madame Luciénne the satisfaction of seeing her react in anger, but she was not about to take orders or sit down in a bargaining posture.

It took all she had to hold back her rage, but when Mama Lu spoke, her tone was calm and pointed. "I'm fine standing, thanks," she said. "Say what you came here to say. Yo' welcome is wearing thin, and so is my patience."

Mr. John did a double-take when he heard her passive, almost business-like tone. He stared at Mama Lu, amazed at how well she was controlling her fury.

Madame Luciénne was caught off guard by her adversary's lack of aggression. She felt nervous tension building inside her, but she did not dare let it show. She caught herself tapping her nails and searching for words. She spoke quickly, trying to regain her composure before its absence became noticeable. "Lucia, you know dis ritual is gon' happen," she said, matter-of-factly. "The transference of power is gon' take place. It's just a matter of how much more *convincin'* you gon' need."

Madame Luciénne looked up at Mama Lu, studying her eyes for a reaction, but Mama Lu stood steady as a statue. Though her knuckles turned white under her folded elbows, she did not allow her expression to waver.

"Now you can call it coincidence or karma that the break-in at your store happened to coincide with your refusal to cooperate," Madame Luciénne went on. "How you choose to label it is not my concern, but I would certainly hate to see any more *misfortune* befall you before St. John's Eve. Such a terrible shame about your shop," she said shaking her head. "I hope nothing valuable or…sentimental was damaged."

The steam was rising, and Mama Lu was about to boil over. Finally she could keep quiet no longer, but she held her tone to a slow burn. "You know very well what was damaged, Vivian. You also know what kind of repercussions follow dem folks who cross me. You ought to remember dat well."

"I recall witnessing your wrath on several occasions," said Madame Luciénne, swallowing hard. Her voice cracked, and she silently cursed herself for allowing fear to surface above the façade. She certainly remembered what Mama Lu was capable of and it terrified her, but she could not allow her weakness to show. She had to remain calm. "On the other hand," she continued, removing a cigarette from her bag and holding it to her lips, "You have just scratched the surface of *my* wrath." She took out her lighter and gestured with it as she spoke. "You were quite fortunate no one was at the store when it was burglarized. Someone could have been injured. Just think if the burglar had been an arsonist."

As she flicked the lighter, Mr. John stepped to the table, snatched the cigarette from her mouth, and snapped it in two. Madame Luciénne looked up at him with disgust, but the look in his eyes said she was way over the line. She knew enough about Mr. John to heed his warning. Still, she thought, she was only going to get this chance once. It was time to play her biggest role yet, and she was ready for her close-up.

She looked back at Mama Lu, straightened her back, flared her nostrils and donned her best tough-as-nails face. "You've got three days, Lucia," she said, surprised her voice was not shaking. "Three days to change your mind, or I'll be forced to change it for you," said Madame Luciénne, jutting out her chin. She was quite pleased with her performance.

Mama Lu simply stared at Madame Luciénne with her eyebrows raised. She had done such a good job of managing her anger, it was now well under control and could be honed to her advantage. Reining in her emotions allowed Mama Lu to clear her mind and see Madame Luciénne for the insignificant speck she was. She actually found the ultimatum amusing.

Mama Lu refrained from laughing in order to make her point well understood. "Are you finished?" she asked after a brief silence, unfolding her arms and dropping them casually into the pockets of her robe.

Madame Luciénne did not speak but sat back in her chair smugly, awaiting Mama Lu's response and desperately trying to calm her racing heart.

"Good," said Mama Lu. "Now you listen up, 'cause I'm jus' gon' say dis once. You can make all the threats you want, and you can lay down ultimatums if dat makes you feel better. It don't bother me none 'cause here's the truth." Mama Lu pushed off the stove and walked slowly toward the table. "Truth is, darlin', dat the only reason you able

182

to speak such things, the only reason you still sittin' here in my kitchen, is 'cause I allow it."

Madame Luciénne shifted nervously in her seat. It became increasingly difficult for her to look Mama Lu in the eyes.

"Every aspect of yo' life is lived 'cause I allow it, chil', and don't you ever think no dif'rent, 'cause I can change dat wit' a snap of my fingers. Dat's what real power can do."

When Madame Luciénne's wandering eyes finally met Mama Lu's again, her anxiety jumped to a new level of intensity. It had been years since she saw such a wild look in Mama Lu's eyes – since before reason and logic ruled her practice, since before Nalia. Despite her best efforts to contain it, Madame Luciénne became visibly frightened. She tucked her clutch underneath her arm and rose to stand behind her chair.

"Now let me tell you somethin' 'bout dat ritual," continued Mama Lu, still advancing. "If I was you, I'd stop makin' all dem plans fo' St. John's Eve, 'cause it's likely you ain't gon' be around to carry 'em out."

With her eyes locked on Luciénne, Mama Lu slipped her hand inside the pocket of her robe and produced a blood-stained scrap of denim. With a snap of her fingers, she thrust an open palm toward Mr. John who recognized her need immediately. Raising a hand to his neck, Mr. John tightened his fingers around the bone pendant of his necklace and pulled, snapping the leather cord with a swift, powerful motion. Pocketing the pendant, he placed the broken strip of leather into Mama Lu's waiting hand. With a stern look of righteous emotion, she folded the denim swatch twice over and began to bind it methodically with the leather cord.

Madame Luciénne's eyes grew wide as dinner plates. She held a hand to her chest as her breathing quickened.

"Right now, *yo'* friend Tony Leonetti is still in a holdin' cell down at the police station bein' watched over by some friends of my own," said Mama Lu holding up the denim so Luciénne could get a good look as she wrapped the cord tighter. "You see, he left dis behind at my shop, and dat makes fo' some powerful gris-gris gon' fix him up right."

Mama Lu chanted low and quick in a tongue Madame Luciénne recognized, but could not remember how to interpret. Her eyes danced wildly with fire as she spun the swatch over and over in her hands. Her chanting grew louder and faster, then suddenly came to an abrupt stop. Mama Lu looked up from the fabric and straight at Madame Luciénne with a disturbing grin.

"If you innocent like you claim, then you gots nothin' to worry 'bout," said Mama Lu as Madame Luciénne inched her way toward the door. "But if I'm right, and I know I am, then you lyin' to me. Dat means you and Tony Leonetti 'bout to meet the same fate."

Mama Lu's face seemed to change appearance as she finally released all the fury she had kept in check. In a rage, she spat violently onto the bound, blood-stained fabric and threw it at Madame Luciénne, hitting her firmly in the neck.

Barely able to breathe, Madame Luciénne said nothing, but turned quickly and fled through the door, allowing the screen to bang shut as she strode swiftly down the walk like a dog with its tail tucked between its legs.

Mr. John wanted to laugh at her reaction, but he knew the spell was real. He had seen Mama Lu cast it before and knew this was no laughing matter. The hex would follow the guilty as Mama Lu indicated, but it would also follow the blood it bound. Unless Madame Luciénne's blood was somehow on the fabric as well, the spell would never reach her, but she didn't know that.

It would, however, reach Tony Leonetti. Mr. John had a brief moment of sadness for the son of his dear, departed friend. Then again, he thought, Tony Leonetti sealed his own fate years ago, and time had finally caught up with him.

Mama Lu and Mr. John stared out the window as Madame Luciénne's car raced away. They did not have time to speak before a shrill scream from the room upstairs pierced the silence.

CHAPTER TWENTY-ONE

Mama Lu rushed up the stairs with Mr. John at her heels. The staircase seemed to stretch for miles, and Mama Lu felt she would never reach her screaming daughter. Arriving at the top, they sprinted down the hall, and Mama Lu burst into the bedroom to find Nalia sitting up in bed with her knees pulled to her chest and her arms wrapped around her folded legs. Her chin was tucked tightly between her knees, and she rocked violently back and forth. Her eyes were wide, and she stared blankly across the room, entirely unaffected by the opening door or the entry of Mama Lu and Mr. John.

The morning sun lit the room through the window, casting shadows deep across the floor and up the opposite wall. For a moment, Mama Lu thought she saw shadows circling Nalia's head, but by the time she reached her side, they were gone. When she sat down on the edge of the bed, Nalia flinched, but her demeanor did not change; her eyes stayed fixed across the room. Nalia was breathing so rapidly Mama Lu feared she would hyperventilate. Tears flowed in a steady stream down Nalia's cheeks, and her tee-shirt was soaked around the neck where the flood was settling. Her eyes were bloodshot and her pupils dilated. Her hair was matted and tangled, and she had scratch marks on her neck and legs. Though none of them were deep enough to break the skin, the scratches were numerous, like she had been steadily clawing at herself for hours.

Mama Lu softly whispered her name, but Nalia did not respond. She called a second time, louder, but again got no response. The same happened when she waved a hand in front of Nalia's face. Frustrated and worried, Mama Lu looked at Mr. John and shrugged her shoulders. She could see the sadness welling in his eyes and knew his heart was breaking for his baby girl. She could feel his pain in her own breaking heart. As Mama Lu turned her eyes back toward Nalia, she was overcome with a feeling of helplessness. She wanted to break Nalia out of this fugue state, hold her, and make it all go away.

Desperate, Mama Lu gently raised her hand to stroke Nalia's hair. The instant she touched her daughter's head, Nalia's eyes grew unnaturally wide, and she stared at Mama Lu as if she were seeing a stranger. She opened her mouth and let loose the piercing scream of a six-year-old girl. Her head began to shake from side to side. She kicked her legs and flailed her arms like she was fighting off a swarm of bees. Mama Lu jumped to her feet quickly as Nalia continued to shudder uncontrollably. Finally her thrashing feet found the bedding, and she pushed hard with her heels, propelling her body backward to the head of the bed. Nalia's eyes rolled into her skull as she leaned forward, then thrust her body hard into the headboard. She slammed her arms down and gripped the sheets tightly, as if trying to claw through the mattress. With her hands and feet rigidly locked into place, Nalia began throwing her head violently into the dark, carved cherry wood.

Mama Lu cringed with fright. Afraid Nalia would crack her skull, she yelled at Mr. John. "Hold her!" she screamed. "Grab her legs!"

Mr. John lunged forward and tackled Nalia around the knees. He pulled her legs straight, taking away her leverage, but Nalia continued to slam her head backward as blood began to trickle onto the rough edges of the circus train. Mama Lu jumped into the bed and managed to position herself between Nalia and the headboard. Over and over Nalia continued to throw herself back, pummeling Mama Lu between her body and the hard wood.

Finally, Mama Lu secured her arms around Nalia's torso and held her fast. The blood from Nalia's head wound smeared onto Mama Lu's face and into her eyes, but she held on tightly, lessening the force of the convulsive thrusting. Despite the tumultuous struggle and her hindered vision, Mama Lu noticed the cup on the bedside table, still half full of the belladonna-laced tea.

"Help me!" she cried to Mr. John as she reached for the cup. Mr. John sat on Nalia's legs, holding them down. He helped to restrain her arms as Mama Lu forced the cup to Nalia's lips and pulled back hard on her forehead. Nalia resisted, but Mama Lu managed to pour the tea into her mouth. She choked and spit, but Mama Lu was determined; she had no choice. Again she poured the liquid. Nalia continued to resist, struggling and fighting as the tea dripped onto her chin and down her neck. Finally Nalia gasped, then swallowed hard and Mama Lu was able to get the last of the tea down her throat.

After a few short moments of residual struggling, Nalia's body began to relax. Soon her eyes glazed over, and her muscles released the stiffening tension. When Nalia's breathing returned to normal, Mama Lu relinquished her grip. Mr. John helped lift Nalia's body enough to release Mama Lu from behind her. Together they helped Nalia lie flat, tucked a pillow under her head, and covered her sleeping body.

Mama Lu was exhausted and sore. Mr. John was not much better off. He reflected briefly on his age as his muscles began to cramp and spasm. Mama Lu left the room in search of bandages, but Mr. John lingered, sitting beside Nalia on the duvet. He gently stroked her hair with the back of his fingers. Tears filled his eyes as he watched Nalia sleep. Quietly, he hummed the old Creole songs he had sung to her so many times when she was a child.

––––––––––––

Darkness flooded in like water topping a levee and soon Nalia felt her body floating, numb to the searing pain in her muscles and her head. She could not tell if her eyes were open or closed, if she were awake or asleep. Her body floated peacefully on the current of darkness until finally, she felt the bump of solid ground beneath her, like a rowboat gently run aground by the lapping waves of a placid lake.

Nalia stood up, surprised to find her body completely dry. She opened her eyes wide and held her hands in front of her face, but could see nothing. The combination of darkness and disorientation pushed Nalia to the edge of panic. She was afraid to move, but anxiety would not allow her to stand still. Nervously, she managed small steps while stretching out her arms for anything she could take hold of. Her desperation produced nothing but open air; the soggy ground was her only point of reference. As she walked, Nalia felt the earthy sensation of twigs and wet leaves under her bare feet. The ground seemed to slope, giving her the indication she might be walking along a riverbank. As she made her way up the shallow grade, Nalia noticed the ground's moisture decreasing, and soon the damp terrain yielded to the cool softness of dry dirt. Shaking with apprehension, Nalia continued to take careful steps across the dark, open area. She knew it must be vast, judging by the empty, hollow sounds and the fact she had not come into contact with a single thing except the earth. The air was warm and humid, but an occasional cold wind gusted out of the darkness, like someone was opening and closing the door of a large freezer.

Soon the ground hardened, and the coarse soil become like dust as Nalia felt the rough texture of wooden boards beneath her feet. The pungent smell of mold filled the air, giving her the impression she was walking into a large basement or dungeon. She could hear the sound of her rapid breathing and the shuffling of her feet reverberating off distant, hard surfaces she could only imagine were stone walls. Nalia began to shiver as the frequency of the icy winds increased. Her tee-shirt was hardly ample covering for the chilly gusts.

Still groping aimlessly in the dark, Nalia was about to give up hope on ever seeing daylight again, when a thin shaft of sunlight extended from far above her head. As her eyes adjusted, Nalia could make out a wide, concrete staircase. If the darkness had lingered a second longer, she would have run straight into it. The steps ascended all of seven feet to a large landing, then continued up and to the right. The bright beam of light shone down at an angle such that both sets of steps were illuminated. An assembly of gold bars was bolted onto each side with a railing that was smooth and flared. A gnawing feeling told Nalia she should see Queen Marie, but the doll was nowhere in sight.

The sunlight was warm and tranquil, compelling Nalia's anxiety to flee. Led by the inviting beam, she placed a hand on the shining rail and started up the stairs. The concrete was ice-cold on her bare feet but grew warmer as she climbed. When she reached the landing, Nalia noticed the second set of steps led to a small balcony. At the edge of the balcony was a tall vertical ladder made of iron. It stretched to a small, open hole in what Nalia assumed was the ceiling of the colossal, darkened structure. Just beyond the edge of the hole, she could make out a tiny glint of gold and the hem of a flowing blue garment.

"There you are," Nalia said quietly, to herself. As she started up the steps toward the balcony, Nalia detected the faint smell of automobile exhaust and heard the sounds of traffic coming from the hole in the ceiling. As she approached the foot of the vertical ladder, she gazed straight up through the opening, relieved to see the clear, blue sky beyond. It was a welcome sight after walking so long in the dark, musty cellar. A quick glance back into the blackness below solidified her decision to ascend.

Nalia placed her hands on the ladder's rungs and began to climb skyward. The iron was rough and rusty, hardly a stable structure, but she pressed on despite the unsettling amount of give and sway. Halfway up, the ladder shook violently, as a large, black shadow covered the hole, then passed. Nearly loosing her footing, Nalia gasped and hugged the ladder tightly, fearful of going any further. She stayed there for a long moment, trying to catch her breath and build courage, her body pressed tightly against the rusty iron rungs. It was a long way down, but it was also a long way up. Curiosity and desperation finally overcame fear and she continued to climb, hand over hand, cautiously watching the hole for movement.

When she reached the top, Nalia breathed a deep sigh of relief and locked her arms over the top rung. She carefully peered through the hole and examined as much of the world above as she could see. The smell of exhaust lingered, but the clamor of traffic grew distant. Judging all was safe, Nalia popped her head through the opening, and found herself in the middle of a street. To her right, she could see the cover for the manhole from which her head protruded. Though she could not tell what street she was under, she knew it was in the Quarter. She tried to make out landmarks, but found it surprisingly difficult from the perspective of the pavement.

Noting the bright red streetcar and the palm trees at the nearby intersection, Nalia determined she must be just off Canal Street. With a better sense of her whereabouts, she began to climb from the hole, when out of nowhere, the blaring sound of a car horn ripped through the air.

Startled, Nalia turned her head to see a large, silver Cadillac speeding toward her. She closed her eyes and ducked back into the hole just before her head contacted the massive chrome bumper. Air rushed down the manhole, shaking the ladder once again as Nalia hung on for dear life.

When all was finally still, Nalia opened her eyes to find herself sitting in the back of a moving car. The world was strangely blurry, like looking through a smeared window. Confused, she found it difficult to focus or make out the particulars of the car's interior. The only detail she distinctly recognized was the smell of Margaret Barronne's perfume. Clarity struck and Nalia realized she was sitting in the back of her mother's Cadillac. She could hear Margaret's voice. It sounded agitated, and it did not take long for Nalia to figure out why. In between her mother's frustrated outbursts, Nalia heard an angry male voice.

The man spoke with a commanding tone, in short bursts of sarcastic loathing. Looking up, Nalia could make out the indistinct image of her mother and the ill-tempered man beside her, Michael Barronne. Nalia tried her best to sharpen her vision. She wanted desperately to see her living, breathing father. She tried rubbing her eyes and squinting, but nothing helped. Frustrated and helpless, she sat listening to the conversation. Michael verbally attacked his wife and complained vehemently, while Margaret defended her position. The tension was painful for Nalia, and she found herself wanting to cover her ears.

It was not until she instinctively squeezed her that Nalia realized she was holding Queen Marie. Strangely, the doll was the only image that came into focus. She sat comfortably on Nalia's lap with her gold hoop earrings swaying to the rhythm of the bumpy road. Her blue dress was nearly the same color as Nalia's. "This is strange," she thought, surprised at the absence of her familiar sleep shirt. Although Nalia could not see with clarity, she appeared to be wearing a plaid school jumper.

The bizarre change caught Nalia off guard and prompted her to look for other divergences. She noticed she was wearing long, white sleeves – a turtleneck. Holding her palms to her face, Nalia was shocked to see the hands of a little girl. "Oh my gosh," she thought, "Am I a child?" The question in her mind was overshadowed by the throbbing pain emanating from the side of her face. Lifting her tiny hand to her cheek, she found it was swollen and puffy. She could feel a small bandage just under her eye.

Before Nalia had the chance to thoroughly examine her wound, the car slowed to a stop and she saw a familiar storefront. She did not need clear vision to recognize it as Mama Lu's shop. She pressed her tiny palms against the window and looked out to see the fuzzy image of Mr. John sitting at his shoe-shine stand, smoking his pipe and tying knots in a length of hemp cord. He smiled and waved when he saw Nalia through the car window.

"Don't be long," said the male voice from across the back seat. "We're already late." He was thumbing through a stack of papers, shaking his head and twitching angrily.

"I just need to pick up my purchase for the foyer," said Margaret, reaching over Nalia to open the car door. Nalia bounded out onto the sidewalk.

Remembering the visible bruises on her daughter's face, Margaret worried about what people would think. "Not today, Nalia," she said. "You wait here in the car."

"Take her with you," said Michael Barronne curtly. He never looked up from his papers.

Reluctantly, Margaret took Nalia by the hand and yanked her toward the doorway. Nalia felt a painful twinge in her wrist as Margaret tugged her along. It took several moments for her to realize… she felt Margaret's hand. She was holding her mother's hand, and she could actually *feel* it for the first time she could ever remember. Nalia was ecstatic, but only for a moment. She spent so many years of her life envisioning her mother's touch as warm and nurturing. Now the painful grip of a cold, indifferent charade of a parent turned her stomach.

Mr. John tipped his hat to Margaret as she passed, but she did not notice. He smiled at Nalia as she realized he could see her. She was actually interacting with the dream, the memory, she thought.

As Margaret pushed the brass handle of *The Doll Maker*, a familiar, dazzling light burst through the crack, blinding Nalia for a brief moment. During the few seconds of her disoriented confusion, Nalia felt a vicious tug at her rib cage, like something inside was trying to break free.

When her sight returned, it was crystal clear, and she saw the image of a young girl – a young her, walk right out of her body and into the shop behind her mother. Nalia could not believe it. She looked over at

Mr. John for affirmation, but he no longer seemed able to see her. Nalia suddenly felt cold, abandoned, and empty.

When she heard the tinkling of the bells above the shop door, she decided to hurry inside after Margaret and the little girl. She swore she felt the door pass right through her shoulder as it closed. Nalia stood just inside the entryway, once again dressed in her oversized sleep shirt. She watched as Margaret and the child walked around the display trees. The girl appeared withdrawn and afraid. She kept her head down and walked slowly, without speaking. Vivian was seated on her stool at the register behind the counter, looking nervous. The shop was devoid of customers, save for Margaret and her daughter, with Mama Lu nowhere in sight.

Margaret Barronne gave strict instructions to the scared little girl. "Wait there, by the door." She inhaled deeply, straightened her posture, turned and walked toward the counter. Vivian trembled with anxiety as she approached.

"I'm here to pick up my doll from yesterday," said Margaret, darting her eyes around the shop. "Was Lucia able to finish it?"

"I believe so," answered Vivian, clearing her throat. "She's in the back. I'll go and get her."

Margaret was unsure if Vivian was referring to Mama Lu or to the doll. She hoped it was the latter. She did not want Mama Lu getting a look at Nalia's eye. Margaret walked back over to the display to wait, shielding Nalia from sight. The bells above the door startled her as Mr. John entered the shop. Margaret thought it was strange he did not speak or even smile. Mr. John simply stepped inside the doorway and stood there, still, as if guarding the exit. Margaret grew nervous. She began to get the odd feeling she was a pawn in someone else's hidden agenda.

The door to the sewing room swung open wide, and Mama Lu emerged from the back with Vivian in tow. She was carrying the doll and a stern look.

Eager to do business and leave, Margaret hurried to the counter with a bright but awkward smile. "Oh, there she is, all fixed up," she said, gushing over the extravagant doll. "She's simply beautiful."

"Where's my girl?" asked Mama Lu.

Hearing her, Nalia timidly peeked out from behind the display and began walking quietly to the counter. Her mother cringed as she approached Mama Lu.

"Nalia!" Margaret exclaimed in haste, trying to stop her, but it was too late. Nalia walked right up to Mama Lu and hugged her around the waist. Mama Lu knelt down beside the little girl, immediately noticing the wound under her eye. Nalia was trembling, on the verge of tears. Mama Lu put a hand up to Nalia's chin and gently turned her face to the side to get a better look. Her cheek was red and swollen, and the skin was beginning to bruise around the eye. Mama Lu lifted the bandage to reveal a small cut, scabbed over where the skin was torn.

"Oh, baby," said Mama Lu with all the compassion in her breaking heart. "Does it hurt?"

Nalia nodded, fighting back as many tears as her little eyes would hold. Despite her best effort, a few spilled over onto her cheeks. Mama Lu pulled Nalia in and held her close as she cut a scathing look at her mother. Margaret kept silent, running through a thousand different excuses and false scenarios in her mind.

Releasing her embrace, Mama Lu held Nalia at arms length. The little girl held Queen Marie close to her chest and twisted nervously from side to side. Mama Lu smiled at her with understanding eyes. "Why don't you go in the back wit' Ms. Vivian, chil'?" she said. "I got some cookies and juice set out fo' you. I'll be there in jus' a minute."

"Oh, I'm afraid we don't have time for that today," said Margaret, sounding a bit more like she was asking a question than making a statement.

Mama Lu put her hand gently on Nalia's back and led her away from her mother, toward Vivian. She stood and stepped uncomfortably close to Margaret, speaking right into her face. "I don't remember askin' you," she said without blinking.

Margaret looked shocked and frightened. She took a step back and stood with her jaw slacked open, watching while Vivian led Nalia into the sewing room. Vivian had been given strict instructions to hide Nalia away in the back and keep her occupied. She was to show Nalia how the sewing machines worked, generating enough noise to drown out any conversation that might be audible from the front room.

"We gots a few things to discuss," said Mama Lu, pointing an accusatory finger at Margaret.

Margaret swallowed hard. She gave a quick glance through the window to the car outside as her pulse quickened. Mr. John was leaning against the door jamb with his arms folded, like a nightclub bouncer.

"You want to tell me wha's goin' on?" asked Mama Lu in a pointed tone.

Margaret stammered and fruitlessly tried to play innocent, claiming no knowledge of anything unusual. Mama Lu became furious. Her eyes narrowed, and she paused briefly to keep from cursing.

"Don't you play games wit' me, Margaret. You think I'm stupid? You think I can't see wha's goin' on? I know yo' husband is abusin' dat chil', an' I ain't 'bout to let it continue."

Margaret felt threatened by the mention of her husband and became defensive. "I don't think this matter is any of your concern," she said looking down her nose, with a newfound sense of superiority.

"Oh, yo' damn right it's my concern," said Mama Lu, putting Margaret back in her place with a superior look of her own. "And it ought to be yo's too, but fo' some reason it ain't. I want to help, Margaret, but you gots to talk to me. Is he beatin' you, too? Dat wha's goin' on? Do we need to get y'all to a safe place?"

Unsure of what to say, Margaret silenced herself. She couldn't look Mama Lu in the eyes. She looked nervously around at everything else in the store, avoiding eye contact. She even shot a few desperate glances at the car outside. Tears began to pool in the corners of her eyes, and her chin quivered as the rest of her body began to tremble. Margaret's mouth was dry, with a lump in her throat the size of a grapefruit. As she tried to speak, she noticed Mama Lu's expression change from anger to concern. She wrung her hands together and hung her head in shame. "You're right," she finally managed. "It is him. He beats her when he's frustrated, and lately that's been a lot."

Mama Lu put a hand on Margaret's shoulder. "And you too?" she asked.

"No," replied Margaret, "No, not yet."

194

"Well, we gots to get you out," said Mama Lu. "We gots to get Nalia out. Y'all gots to leave dat man."

"We can't," said Margaret, her voice trembling. "If I try to leave or take her away, he'll cut me off."

Mama Lu removed her hand. Her expression changed from compassion to confusion, then back to anger as she realized what Margaret was saying. "You talkin' 'bout money?" she exclaimed as Margaret nodded. "Are you actually tellin' me you won't leave him 'cause o' his money? Dis is yo' daughter we talkin' 'bout! There ain't no amount of money in the world dat's worth dat lil' girl gettin' beat every night."

Margaret sobbed and stammered as her makeup began to run. Guilt was firing arrow after arrow at her heart, but greed had shielded it well over time. She pulled herself together enough to defend her position.

"I came from nothing, Lucia!" she shouted with a spark of fury in her eyes. "When I met Michael, I was working as a waitress in a roadside diner, just trying to keep the lights on in a run-down, one room shack outside of Atlanta. Dirt poor and no hope! Nothing going for me but decent looks, a little charm, and just enough self-respect to keep me one step up from prostitution." She paused to catch her breath before continuing, as a stern expression blanketed her face. "Well, I used what I had. Fate smiled on me, and I hooked myself the wealthiest man that ever set foot in that little hole-in-the-wall café. I charmed my way out of that situation into a better one where I don't ever have to worry about money again. One where I don't have to worry about where I'm going to sleep, or if I'll have enough to eat." Margaret straightened her back and launched her chin high into the air, looking down at Mama Lu as if she were a dirty dishrag. "I will never go back to living in poverty, Lucia. Do you understand? I don't care what he does with her."

An icy cold sensation shot through Mama Lu's spine when she heard the words "what he does with her". Remembering the bruises around Nalia's wrists, Mama Lu finally realized the man was doing much more than just beating her. She recalled the words of Old Man Leonetti when he discussed Michael's deal with the Verellis. Mama Lu almost vomited when she thought of the possibilities. Rage consumed her like a wildfire and Mama Lu held nothing back. "Do you know who I am?" she yelled as Margaret winced. "Do you know who dat is?" she continued, pointing a rigid finger at Mr. John. "You realize you standin' between two of the mos' powerful Voodoos dis city ever seen? Woman, you know I could snuff yo' life wit' a snap o' my fingers?"

Fear was building inside Margaret as she began to realize the stories she'd heard about Mama Lu and Mr. John were quite possibly more credible than she originally deemed them. Friends warned her about doing business with Mama Lu, saying she was "some type of Voodoo witch". If all the rumors were true, she knew this was no bluff. She had been told Mama Lu could make people disappear in the blink of an eye and no one ever asked questions.

"Dis is yo' own flesh and blood," Mama Lu continued. "Yo' own innocent chil'. Don't dat mean anythin' to you? You can't put material things befo' her." Mama Lu snatched the lavishly dressed doll off the counter. A sick feeling settled in her stomach as she surveyed its statuesque form, over-indulgent fashion, and sparkling jewels – all things Margaret prized far above her daughter's innocence. She stared at the doll, shaking her head. "Dis?" she asked Margaret, "You sellin' yo' chil' out fo' dis? Dis don't mean nothin' compared to the safety of dat lil' girl. Dis is nothin'!" With all the fury in her body, Mama Lu lifted the doll over her head and brought it down swiftly onto the hard, pointed corner of the cash register. The doll cracked and shattered, sending jagged bits of porcelain flying like shrapnel. The doll's wide necklace broke and its diamonds spilled and scattered onto the floor. Margaret was speechless and frightened, but could not keep her eyes from following the gems as they bounced and danced around her feet. She felt a nearly irresistible longing to gather them up, but the fear gripping her body kept her from doing so. Margaret knew Mama Lu was serious.

"Now you 'bout to be dirt po' again, one way or the other," said Mama Lu in a controlled and authoritative voice. "'Cause either you gon' handle dis, or I am! And trust me, honey, you don't want me to get involved. But make no mistake, dis ends now."

Margaret was terrified. Her mind went into overdrive as she realized she had to play this right. She needed to work out a way to keep Mama Lu at bay, her husband out of the fray, and her riches intact. Never once did she think of Nalia.

196

From the corner of her eye, Margaret saw the car door open outside. An incredibly agitated Michael Barronne stepped out and stormed up the sidewalk to the entrance. Margaret gasped as her husband flung the door open and placed his foot inside. He looked over at Mr. John like he stank of rotten waste but did not consider him worthy of addressing. Instead, he made eye contact with Margaret and spoke commandingly. "What's the holdup?" he asked curtly.

Mama Lu made a move for the door and opened her mouth to speak, but Margaret stepped in front of her, holding up her hand and gesturing for her to stop. She looked at Mama Lu with reassuring eyes and silently mouthed the words "I'll do it."

Mama Lu was hesitant, not entirely trusting. She shifted her head to one side with an inquisitive stare, considering Margaret's credibility. Margaret's eyes pleaded with Mama Lu to keep quiet.

"I don't have time to wait out here while you gossip with the rabble," said Michael from the doorway. Mr. John gave him a severe look of disapproval, but nothing fazed the greasy-haired businessman in the designer suit.

"Two minutes, almost done," Margaret called back, mouthing her silent claim to Mama Lu again.

"Now!" said Michael as he turned back toward the car and let the door close behind him.

Margaret repeated her statement to Mama Lu, audibly this time, and thanked her for not addressing the situation with Michael. "If he thinks you know about what's going on, he'll kill both of us and Nalia too. I'll take care of it. I'll get her out safely."

Mama Lu continued to study her eyes, but Margaret was very convincing. "If you lyin' to me, I'm gon' come after you," she said. "Then you gon' wish you'd died and gone to hell."

Margaret swallowed hard and breathed an abbreviated sigh of relief as Mama Lu turned and walked to the sewing room door. Mama Lu held Nalia in a long embrace before sending the little girl to her mother. She looked at Nalia with tear-filled eyes and assured her everything would be alright; her Mama Lu was going to make sure of it. The child nodded trustingly, holding tightly to Queen Marie. Mama Lu felt as if her heart would rip into pieces as she watched Nalia and

Margaret walk out of the store. She felt helpless and weak, berated by the notion she was making a terrible mistake. "Tonight!" she called after Margaret.

Margaret turned and gave a quick, silent nod through the window as a single silent tear fell from Mama Lu's eye.

Watching from the corner of the shop, still standing there in her oversized tee-shirt, Nalia felt nothing. Her body and her mind were completely numb, but one thought pummeled her brain over and over – the more answers she got, the more questions she had. She turned her head away. She did not want to see any more. She wanted to leave, but she did not want to move. She could not even find the strength to walk to the door. After all, she thought, if this were truly just a vision, why couldn't she just walk through the wall?

As she tried, the blinding light consumed her once again, and searing pain shot through her wrists. Nalia could feel pressure pulling her hands above her head and as the blinding light succumbed to the darkness of the all-too-familiar bedroom, she could hear the beast's menacing laughter. This time, Nalia was not afraid. Not even the familiar smell of gasoline could frighten her. She transported her mind to a place where she could feel no pain. The voices in her head returned and instructed her not to fight, but there was no fight left in her. She was empty and numb. She closed her eyes, turned her head, and flew to a distant place in her mind, far away from pain, fear, and even love.

The beast continued to laugh as it ripped and tore at Nalia's body. Soon the sinister snickering multiplied. Two distinct cackles filled the air, then a third. The strange sounds pulled Nalia's mind back from its astral travel. She opened her eyes to see not one beast, but three. Razor sharp claws tore at her flesh as the beasts laughed and talked among themselves. Two of the beasts passed a large glass container of gasoline back and forth, drinking from it heartily and pouring it onto Nalia's body.

"My turn," snarled one of them, shoving the other two out of the way for his turn to tear at Nalia's flesh. A sudden impulse told Nalia to

198

struggle, but the beast made a fist and struck her hard on the side of her face. Stale sweat dripped from the beast's head, stinging and burning Nalia's eyes as all the pain slowly returned. Her wrists, her stomach, her thighs, and her midsection all burned with agony.

As panic swelled in her throat like vomit, Nalia turned her head to see the dark, looming shadow standing across the room. Tonight, she could not see its eyes. Its head was turned, staring out of the doorway. As light flooded in from the hall, Nalia could easily make out the feminine profile of the dark figure. It was the unconcerned face of her mother, Margaret Barronne. She was staring casually into the hallway, absentmindedly fondling her large diamond necklace.

CHAPTER TWENTY-TWO

"Belladona?" Mr. John exclaimed with a worried look in his eyes. "Woman, is you crazy? What makes you think you can jus' go addin' ingredients to my gris-gris all willy nilly? Why don't you give her a handful o' vicodin to go wit' it?"

"You got any?" asked Mama Lu, thinking of relief for her throbbing head.

"I'm serious, Lu!" Mr. John went on. "Dem herbs I gave you already *got* nightshade blended in. You puttin' sedative on top o' sedative. It's a wonder she woke up at all! Too much of dat stuff is lethal."

Their conversation was interrupted by the melodic chimes of a jazzy ring tone. It took a moment for Mr. John to realize it was his. The cell phone Mr. John carried rarely rang, and when it did, it usually startled him. He said he kept it for emergency calls only, but more often than not, his emergency calls closely resembled the same type of gossip one could overhear at his shoe-shine stand.

While Mr. John took the call, Mama Lu sat with her aching head in her hands. The pounding was nearly unbearable. She found it increasingly difficult to concentrate but listened to the one sided conversation as Mr. John's voice became very serious. He did not say much, but repeatedly acknowledged the information being conveyed. When the conversation was over, Mr. John snapped his phone shut and returned it to his pocket. He did not look up. Mama Lu knew what he was going to say. She had already felt it.

"It's done," said Mr. John in a grave spirit. "Tony Leonetti is dead."

Mama Lu rubbed her temples with excessive pressure. Her headache was getting worse. She wondered if the battle with Nalia or the spell had caused it. She never reacted this way to a hex before, but it had been a long time since she cast one of this magnitude.

"They say early dis' mornin' he got dis wild look in his eyes and started mumblin' to hisself," Mr. John went on. "Kept sayin' dat voices was talkin' to him inside his head. Dem guards thought he was just comin' down off the smack. Anyhow, next time they looked in on him, he'd done hung hisself wit' a leather belt."

Through the throbbing pain, Mama Lu recalled the feeling of satisfaction that used to engulf her when a "fix" came to fruition, a sweet portion of justice served to those who deserved it. She did not feel it today. She no longer felt the desire to celebrate the fulfillment of a curse when a human life was the cost. She was not saddened by the loss of Tony Leonetti, and she felt no remorse, but neither was she spirited. Justice had been served, and that was that. She was simply satisfied.

Mr. John sat quietly taking in the gravity of the situation. After what he felt was a sufficient moment of silence, he returned to the conversation. "Dis don't change nothin', Lu. We still got to think about dat baby girl. She layin' up there trapped by dem drugs we slipped her, and dem nightmares is havin' they way with her. We got to put an end to dis. We got to move it along."

Mama Lu looked up, her eyes sunken with fatigue and pain. "John, we doin' all we can do. The magic gon' have to run its course. You think dat if I knew a way to do it any quicker and not bring no harm, I wouldn't have already done it by now?"

"We need to come together," said Mr. John. "Me, you, and Madame T., all in the same place wit' Nalia. We gots to try, Lu. Together, I think we can finish dis. We can make the strongest bond we done ever made, get dem memories back and dem nightmares gone. We gots to try."

Mama Lu could only nod in agreement. Her head was pounding like a drum. She covered her eyes and held her forehead.

"I'm gon' take the truck and go fetch Madame T.," continued Mr. John. "I want you to go upstairs, take you some aspirin." He reached for his wallet and removed a small piece of white paper folded like a dollar bill. He lifted one side and retrieved a sprig of lemongrass that was flattened inside. "Here," he said, handing the herb to Mama Lu.

"Bite down on dat a few times after you take dem aspirin and lie down fo' a spell. Dat'll help."

———————

Four blocks away, the black Lincoln of Madame Vivian Luciénne pulled into the shell-scattered drive and parked, slightly askew, along the fence. Her house projected a foreboding air of mystery. It was a two-story, wood-frame structure, dark grey with ivory and chocolate trim, with a small porch on the front. On either side were large windows covered with decorative, wrought-iron burglar bars. The bars were much wider than the windows they covered, and stretched nearly to the second floor, creating the appearance of a prison. They were tall, strong, and alive with ivy.

The small porch was flanked by two massive columns that consumed its outer corners. Smooth and rounded, the columns were fat at the bottom but gradually slimmed in a tear-drop curve as they rose. The column on the right was painted flat black, while the left one was chalky white. Madame Luciénne had them done this way to resemble the High Priestess tarot card, but their odd shape made them look more like oversized chess pieces. The porch featured a low overhang, and its sides were covered with latticework also overgrown with ivy, creating a dark, cave-like entryway. The house was secluded from the neighborhood by a high fence all around, except for one opening for the driveway at the corner of the lot. The fence was thick with shrubbery, further sheltering the property from the outside world.

Madame Luciénne nervously turned the key and killed the engine. She was driving herself today, which she hated. Times were not as easy as they once were, and she could no longer afford to keep her driver on a steady schedule. That would all change soon, after the ceremony. Voodoo could be a lucrative business in the underworld of New Orleans. Not the kind of product-based dealings common to Mr. John's trade, but more along the lines of what Madame Luciénne liked to call "professional services." There were more secrets in New Orleans than most people cared to imagine, and though the well-to-do did not discuss it in their social circles, nearly all of them needed someone to perform a hex now and then. Desperate times meant desperate measures, and the wealthy of New Orleans were known in the underworld for being desperate.

Madame Luciénne threw her cell phone into the passenger's seat and began to look in her white satin clutch for the last cigarette she knew was in there. She had just fielded the fourth in a series of calls from a grapevine alive with news of Tony Leonetti, and she was terrified.

Just as she found the cigarette and her lighter, she was startled by a heavy thud on her windshield. Madame Luciénne looked up to find her windshield cracked and a dead crow lying just on top of the wiper blades. Knowing this was an omen, she began to tremble. Mama Lu's hex was working.

She pulled the key quickly from the ignition and stepped from the car to find a far more frightening sight awaiting her. Hundreds of black crows sat anywhere and everywhere they could perch, ruffling their feathers and watching Madame Luciénne's every move.

Petrified, she pressed her back against the vehicle and stood stone-still. Birds continued to gather, swooping down and finding perches along the roofline and utility cables. Thinking her safest move would be to get back in the car and drive away, Madame Luciénne turned quickly and reached for the handle. Before she could pull, a group of seven crows landed, nearly all at once, on the roof of the car. The one closest to the driver's door hopped forward and cawed threateningly in Madame Luciénne's face. The panicked "priestess" stepped back and soon found herself surrounded by crows gathering around her feet, their shining black feathers contrasting her stark-white shoes.

She had to get inside the house. She shooed the birds and nervously kicked at them, but they were resilient, ruffling their feathers and flapping their wings. The more Madame Luciénne moved, the more angry the crows became. Cautiously, she made guarded moves toward the porch, gingerly stepping between the birds, careful not to disturb them. By the time she reached the steps, she was trembling so wildly she could hardly stand. Her keys shook nervously in her hand as she passed underneath the watchful row of birds lining the low roof at the edge of the porch, just inches from her head.

Madame Luciénne kept her eyes straight ahead as she inched her way past the fat, black and white columns and through the mass of birds gathered on the porch beside the door. She did not dare turn around. In her mind she saw a scenario where all the crows followed her, creating a massive black wall trapping her in the small, lattice-lined enclosure.

Madame Luciénne managed to fit her key into the lock on the first attempt, despite the fact her hands were trembling like the last autumn leaf. With one fluid motion, she threw open the door and rushed inside. Eager to the keep the birds at bay, she turned quickly to slam the door behind her. As she did, her terrified eyes caught a glimpse of the scene outside. The lawn was empty; there was not a crow in sight.

CHAPTER TWENTY-THREE

Mama Lu stood in the open doorway of Nalia's bedroom, watching her for signs of movement. Nalia's restlessness seemed to have faded. In fact, she exhibited hardly any signs of activity at all. Belladonna was a tricky substance, one Mama Lu did not at all like dealing with. In the right dose it could be a suitable sleep aid or stomach soother, but when used improperly, or when necessary, it was also an effective poison. If Mama Lu had only known Mr. John's blend of herbs was already laced with belladonna, what he called nightshade, she would have never considered adding more. Uncertain of the dosage Nalia had ingested, Mama Lu was fearful.

Finally, she saw the gentle rise and fall of Nalia's bedding. Satisfied that her baby was breathing comfortably, Mama Lu sighed with relief and leaned her aching head against the door facing with the markings from Nalia's many birthdays. She wondered just how much of her life had been spent standing in this doorway. In her younger years, countless hours were logged looking in on Nalia night after night. More recently, with Nalia away at college, Mama Lu found she could hardly pass the doorway without stopping to reflect on the markings. A different memory came to mind each time, and Mama Lu could not help but smile as she ran her fingers along the door. She was thankful for the hand dealt by fate, when Nalia was placed in her care. She thought of how much growth had occurred over the years: not how much the broken little girl had grown, but how much she had grown because of the broken little girl. Mama Lu was grateful for the opportunity to have, hold, and love the child that now lay sleeping, all grown up and ever so troubled.

Mama Lu closed the door as slowly and silently as she could until she heard the latch click in the jamb. The afternoon sun lit the hallway with a vibrant amber glow through the single window at the end of the corridor. The house was oddly silent as Mama Lu shuffled off to her bedroom to rest her aching head.

For the first time in days, Nalia's eyes popped open. She did not awaken screaming in terror from visions of a nightmare clawing its way toward reality; she simply woke up.

Though her eyes opened as if she were awakening from a long, peaceful slumber, Nalia's spirit was far from rested. Over the past several days, her soul experienced a train wreck of emotions: sadness, anger, depravity, guilt, fear, pain, and scorn. Now Nalia was numb, stripped bare of emotion and driven by a raw sense of self-entitlement. The more memories she witnessed, the more she realized how much was taken from her and how much she wanted it back. So far she had learned of a father who beat her, a mother who did not care, and a trail of lies that threw Mama Lu's credibility into question.

A quick inventory of her faculties told Nalia her body had undergone a great deal of trauma. All her muscles ached, and she felt like her head was in a vice. She reached up to find a blood-soaked bandage covering the cut on the back of her head. It was a matted and tangled mess.

Nalia eased herself out of bed, though her muscles screamed in opposition. Slowly and painfully, she made her way to the vanity. "What have they done to you?" she asked the reflection in the mirror. Her dark, sunken eyes and her shallow cheeks more closely resembled a corpse than the vibrant young woman who graced her college campus just days before. "And where do you go from here?" she continued. She could not help but think they had turned her into a monster. They took a happy young woman and stripped her of everything she knew. How could she not be jaded? She had every right to be, and they were all to blame: her parents, Mama Lu, Mr. John, even Madame Toulouse seemed to be hiding something. None of them could be trusted.

Nalia picked up the polished silver brush and began the process of straightening her matted hair. She gingerly removed the bandage from her scalp. The cut was no longer bleeding but still tender with a good-sized knot marking its location. Nalia did not recall how it got there, but not even that surprised her now.

She gently brushed through the tangled mess of hair, wincing each time the brush pulled at the scabbed-over sore and wondering how she would untangle the sordid mess her life had become over the last few days. The best way, she thought, was to find out what was left of her family's fortune and initiate a plan to get her hands on it. She needed to do some digging, but it would have to be done in secret. Surely there had to be a way to get back the inheritance that was stripped away from her. The thought burned inside Nalia like salt in an open wound. All her life, she felt abandoned. Now she felt betrayed and cheated to boot. Knowing the truth about her disgraceful parents fueled her desire all the more; she wanted to take what was theirs, what should be hers. But where would she begin?

Nalia needed help, and she was not going to get it from Mama Lu, Mr. John, or Madame T. She could think of only one person with the kind of connections she was going to need and the ability to keep her plans hidden from Mama Lu. Nalia's mind drifted to the memory of Vivian Luciénne ushering her off to the sewing room to watch over her while Mama Lu confronted Margaret. Despite the sleaze Madame Luciénne had become, she had ties to many influential people who might be persuaded to lend a hand in the search for her father's lost estate. Nalia did not like Madame Luciénne at all, but she was not above using her to get what she wanted. After all, it was rightfully hers. A sly smile slithered across her face as she set the silver brush back on the vanity.

Nalia turned and looked around the sun-drenched room. Such a simple upbringing for someone of her stature, she thought. Her eyes were drawn to the hutch where her collection of porcelain figurines was displayed. Nalia grimaced as she rose from her chair and walked over to the wood and glass cabinet. She noted the details in the silk dresses and shining jewels worn by the dolls. "That should be me," Nalia thought.

She turned a disgusted eye toward the simple burlap poppets stationed on top of the hutch. Made to bridge the gap to the spirit world, to commune with her ancestors, she thought. Who was she kidding? These were not even her ancestors, no real relation, yet she had been taught to honor them as such. Lies.

Nalia turned her back on the hutch and walked to the dresser where she stood before Mary, the striking resemblance of her mother. The doll looked older now and rightfully so, thought Nalia. It turned her stomach to think of how Mary stood there for all those years just as Margaret stood in the doorway in her nightmare. Tears of anger threatened her eyes. She wanted to snatch the doll off the dresser and smash it into a thousand shards, but for some reason could not bring herself to do it. Perhaps when she regained her family's fortune, she would destroy the doll out of spite. Yes, that would do, Nalia thought. She would destroy the image of her mother after possessing the wealth Margaret so destructively coveted, and Madame Vivian Luciénne would help make it happen.

Nalia retrieved a pair of denim shorts and a plain, white V-neck tee from her duffle bag. She was sure there had to be an old baseball cap in her closet somewhere. She got dressed, pulled back her hair, and headed for the stairs.

The silence was unusual. As Nalia left the amber hallway and took the stairs down to the kitchen, she was struck by such a sense of déjà vu that she watched the clock on the stove for a full minute, just to make sure she saw it change. She definitely remembered leaving Queen Marie upstairs, so any appearance of the doll would alert Nalia to the possibility she might not be awake. She wondered just how blurred the line between dreams and reality could get as she looked around for determining factors. She saw no sign of Queen Marie or Mama Lu.

Nalia quietly made her way to the window near the back door and gently pushed the curtain aside. Looking across the street, she noted that Mr. John's truck was gone, but just in case, she decided to leave the house by the front door.

As she closed it quietly behind her and stepped onto the front porch, she pulled the ball cap down tightly and checked the neighborhood for prying eyes. Seeing no cause for concern, she made her way quickly down the oak-lined sidewalk. Taking her car was not an option. Madame Luciénne lived too close for Nalia to take a chance on her vehicle being seen. Despite adamant protest from her screaming muscles, Nalia walked swiftly with her head down and her hands tucked deep into her pockets. She turned the corner at the end of the street and headed west toward the setting sun.

Before long, she found herself standing at the edge of the overgrown fence, staring at the house with the black and white columns, a menacing sight in the light of early evening. She walked quickly up the shell-covered drive, past the black Lincoln and onto the cave-like porch.

Driven by her secret purpose for four blocks, Nalia never looked back. Now, however, for a reason she could not explain, anxiety would not allow her to ring the bell. Once she touched that dimly-lit button, there was no turning back. She dried her sweating palms on the front of her shorts and tried to summon the courage. Nalia's conscience made one final attempt to stop her, but it was conquered by greed as she reached out her hand. As the low chimes echoed through the old house, Nalia's heart raced like a steam engine. She shifted her weight nervously from one foot to the other and stood close to the latticework so as not to be seen.

Finally, the door opened, only as wide as its taut chain would allow, and the face of Madame Luciénne appeared in the gap, confused and apprehensive.

"I need to talk to you," Nalia blurted out in a trembling voice.

Madame Luciénne raised an eyebrow, wondering if this could be another hallucination. The surprising look of desperation in Nalia's eyes told her otherwise.

"You need to talk to me?" Madame Luciénne asked, looking around to make sure Nalia was alone. "Wha's dis about, darlin'?" she asked, leery of Nalia's motives.

"It's about my father," said Nalia nervously. "But Mama Lu can't know I'm here."

Madame Luciénne's curiosity overcame her apprehension. She smiled modestly and closed the door. Nalia heard the chain slide across the latch, and then the door reopened wide. Madame Luciénne stood in its berth with her head held high. She was still wearing her innocent, white dress and her wide-brimmed hat, a daunting image for Nalia's anxious eyes. "Com' on in, darlin'," she said, "I'll put some tea on."

Madame Luciénne studied Nalia's apprehensive mannerisms as she entered the house. Could this be one of Mama Lu's tricks, or had the lamb really just walked into the lion's den?

Nalia was shown to a small chair in a large parlor where she waited until the aroma of lavender tea overcame the stale smell of dust. The room was dark, lit only by a pair of cheap wall sconces and an antique lamp. Several of the small chairs were arranged around a petite coffee table, with a taller high-back, Victorian style chair at the end. The floor was done in hardwood with a large, Persian rug gracing the sitting area. The walls were adorned with thick, red drapes that oddly did not appear to be covering windows.

Madame Luciénne liked to keep her guests waiting, even if it was only long enough to steep tea. It helped add to her air of superiority. It told her guests they would be seen in her time, on her terms. When she finally entered the parlor, she would carry a large silver tea tray with a polished pot and porcelain cups. This would allow her guests to share in her obvious affluence. It was important for her guests to feel included. She would then take a pretentious posture in her high-back chair to silently announce she was in charge; the illusion would then be complete. Madame Luciénne treated Nalia to this familiar routine, and it worked like a charm. Nalia felt comfortable enough to speak openly, but uneasy enough to wait for permission.

The tea was good. It was not Mama Lu's, by any means, but it was good. Nalia sipped hesitantly as Madame Luciénne sat back in her chair and crossed her legs. The only item missing from her modern-day throne room was a jeweled crown for her head, but Madame Luciénne did an excellent job of making sure one was implied. "Now then," she said with a cat-like grin. "What is it I can help you wit'?"

Nalia was all too forthcoming with information about her father. She told all about her research and about discovering her father's business records. Conveniently omitting the details about the mob, she told of his death and how Mama Lu kept *her* identity a secret for years through lies and manipulation. Nalia enthusiastically shared her plan to learn more about her father's wealth and eventually reclaim as much of it as she could.

Of course, Madame Luciénne already knew nearly everything Nalia told her as she was still apprenticed to Mama Lu when Nalia was taken in. She knew about Michael Barronne and his notoriously materialistic wife. She knew about Nalia's tortured family life, the nightmares, and even the magic that stole her memory. Madame Luciénne actually knew far more than Nalia did, but she listened intently, expressing concern and gaining her trust. She was interested in how Nalia's memories had returned and what else she knew. Surely, Mama Lu had not revealed everything. A bit of prying could yield enough information to provide just the leverage she needed with Mama Lu. Better yet, a well-planted seed could lead to a profitable bit of blackmail.

Madame Luciénne waited for Nalia to finish, then chose her words carefully. "So why dis sudden interest in yo' father, darlin'?"

"Because up until a few days ago, I didn't know who he was," replied Nalia. "Mama Lu didn't just keep me a secret, she kept him a secret from me. I grew up thinking my father left my mother before I was born."

"You poor dear," Madame Luciénne sympathized. "I'm sure yo' Mama Lu had good reason to let you believe that story for all them years." She was careful not to join in Nalia's attack on Mama Lu. She thought it better to stay neutral and allow Nalia to rage on, unabated. Madame Luciénne knew when family ties were involved, it was easy for the complainant to switch and begin defending the subject when an outside party became overzealous. She had seen it many times. It was better to play the innocent, and let Nalia do all the badmouthing.

"She's lied to me my whole life!" shouted Nalia, her anger mounting just as Madame Luciénne expected. "I don't even know who I am anymore."

Madame Luciénne remained calm; she was leading the lamb to the slaughter. "What prompted her to finally tell you?" she asked.

"That's just it, she didn't," Nalia tried to explain. "I'm having these dreams, only the dreams are really my memories. It's hard to understand. She took my memories away from me when I was little, through Voodoo."

"Ah," said Madame Luciénne, mocking surprise, "She hid them from you. I 'spect she thought they was too painful for you to deal wit' as a chil'."

"But who was she to make that decision?" Nalia complained. "It's my life, not hers!"

Perfect, thought Madame Luciénne. "But now she's returnin' them to you. I've heard about this," she said, sitting up and looking intrigued. "Tell me, did she use somethin' to induce the dream? An object, perhaps, to help guide you?"

"Yes!" replied Nalia enthusiastically. "My doll, Queen Marie."

"Interesting," said Madame Luciénne calmly, though she was about to burst with excitement. This was vital information. "I believe I remember that doll," she said. "Blue dress?"

"That's right," said Nalia. "She looks just like the big one that's in Mama Lu's shop"

Not anymore, thought Madame Luciénne.

"In the first dream," Nalia continued, "The first... vision, I guess you could call it, Queen Marie led me to Mama Lu. She wasn't really Mama Lu; she was just in the dream. It's confusing, but that's when she told me about the memories and how I would see them. Not just my memories, but hers, Mr. John's, and Madame Toulouse's as well."

"They are all connected through the doll," explained Madame Luciénne. "They form a bond with their Voodoo, then they connect to you through Queen Marie." Madame Luciénne could hardly contain herself. This was like knowing the winning numbers before playing the lottery. She hid her excitement by channeling it into an inquisitive expression.

"What is it?" asked Nalia.

"I was just wonderin' somethin'," replied Madame Luciénne, playing up the drama. "Wonderin' if it might help you, but it's probably nothin'."

Nalia took the bait. The look on her face told Madame Luciénne it was time for the pitch. "Tell me," Nalia insisted. "If it could help, I want to hear."

Madame Luciénne hesitated for effect. "I knew yo' father," she finally said with a sigh. "Yo' mother, too. Not well, but I dealt with 'em on several occasions. It was so long ago, there ain't much I remember, but I was wonderin', if I was to somehow join their bond..." She let the thought linger while Nalia's ears perked up. "If I was able to show you my memories, too, I wonder if it might help you find out more about yo' father. You know, from someone outside yo' family."

Nalia's mouth fell open wide. "Can you do that?" she asked with all the naivety of a school girl.

Don't want to seem too eager, thought Madame Luciénne. "Well, for the right price, of course," she said. "Anything for the right price." *Now for the clincher.* "After all, dis could open the floodgate for a fortune that is rightfully yours. Just think of how profitable dis information could be."

Madame Luciénne leaned forward and placed her teacup back on the tray. She could see the dollar signs twinkling in Nalia's eyes. She took great pleasure in how easily she could toy with the daughter of her nemesis. *Time to seal the deal.* "Tell you what," she said. "I could be persuaded to forego any initial payment in exchange for a small compensation on the back end – say twenty percent?"

Nalia considered the offer. Madame Luciénne was dangling the potential for recovering her family's fortune in front of her face like she was teasing a cat with a feather. She could almost reach out and touch it, but twenty percent was a big cut. "Ten sounds more like a 'small compensation' to me," she finally replied, attempting to negotiate.

Madame Luciénne's expression soured. She stiffened her posture and sat back in her chair with her nose turned up over an offended scowl. "I ain't jus' talkin' 'bout the dream, sweetheart," she said, her anger bringing out the Creole accent she tried so hard to keep in check. "I'm talkin' 'bout helpin' you get hold of dis money however I can. I'm talkin' 'bout research work, legal advisors, connections to people, and access to records you ain't even thought of yet. Not to mention a little bribery and blackmail, should such actions become necessary. Ain't no secrets 'round dis town that I don't know 'bout, and that goes a long way when people need to be persuaded to cooperate. Ain't nothin' fo' free 'round here, sweetheart, but I tell you what I'll do."

Nalia placed her teacup on the tray next to Madame Luciénne's and slid up to the edge of her seat.

"I'll take fifteen if the dreams turn up nothin'," continued Madame Luciénne. "But if they lead to some vital information, I get the whole twenty."

"Alright," said Nalia, reluctant to give up any of the riches she had yet to obtain. "I can do that."

Madame Luciénne smiled with sinister satisfaction as she and Nalia both leaned in close.

"How do we do it?" Nalia asked.

"First of all, we agree on yo' initial request, and that is yo' Mama Lu can't never know you was here," explained Madame Luciénne as Nalia nodded in agreement. "Then you got to let me into the dream." Madame Luciénne reached up into the band of her wide-brimmed hat and removed a long, straight hat pin. Raising a thin finger, she pricked the tip and rolled the pin through the emerging drop of blood. "When you go to sleep tonight," she said, her eyes dancing with excitement, "You take dis pin and stick it in yo' doll, Queen Marie. Jab it right into her neck and shove it all the way down inside. If the doll is yo' guide, it might just be that simple."

Nalia took the pin and stared, like it was the key to a lost treasure chest. "Do you really think it will be that easy?" she asked.

"The strength of their bond depends on the purity of their ritual. If we poison the purity, we break the bond," said Madame Luciénne with an eyebrow raised in confidence.

Nalia slipped the pin into the brim of her cap and rose to leave with a great sense of accomplishment and anticipation.

"One more thing, darlin'," said Madame Luciénne, walking Nalia to the door. She retrieved her satin clutch from the table in the entry hall and pulled a tiny, oval-shaped, white tablet from inside. "Take dis fifteen minutes before you go to sleep," she said, handing the pill to Nalia. "It'll help you drift off and sleep soundly, so you can see everything you need to see."

Nalia thanked Madame Luciénne and left with a gleam in her eye, believing she just made the deal of a lifetime and a windfall of riches lay just over the horizon. Madame Luciénne watched her leave from the seclusion of her darkened porch. She could not help being pleased with her performance. She knew there was little chance of any of Michael Barronne's estate ever being recovered; that money was long gone. Madame Luciénne had her eye on a different prize. She was about to breach the bond of three Voodoo elders with a simple hat pin.

CHAPTER TWENTY-FOUR

Johnny the Conqueror was raw. Mama Lu had not stopped rubbing the twisted little root since she awakened and found Nalia's empty bed. She paced back and forth from the stove to the kitchen window while Mr. John and Madame Toulouse sat at the table, arms folded, staring at each other.

"I don't know which one you gon' rub a hole in first," said Madame Toulouse, "Ol' Johnny or yo' kitchen floor. Pacin' back and forth ain't gon' bring her back no quicker, Lu."

"It's gettin' dark," Mama Lu replied. "We need to go and look fo' her."

"I'm ready," said Mr. John producing his keys.

"How many times am I gon' have to tell y'all?" insisted Madame Toulouse, "She gon' be back soon enough. That girl's up to somethin' secret, and she don't want to be found. That's why the vision is cloudy. Otherwise, I'd be able to see her, crystal clear. She don't want nobody knowin' what she's up to. That's all the more reason we got to stay one step ahead of her. We can't do that if we go looking for her. If she suspects we're watchin', then we fall one step behind."

Mr. John swung his keys around his index finger and smacked them into the palm of his hand. His furrowed brow reflected his impatience.

"Trust me, John," said Madame Toulouse reassuringly, "This ain't my first go 'round, by any means."

Mama Lu continued to pace. "Why wouldn't she take her car?"

"I'm tellin' you Lu, she's plottin' somethin'," repeated Madame Toulouse. "That girl was hopin' nobody would notice she was gone. She got that money on her mind, I can smell it like yesterday's trash."

"She's confused," said Mama Lu, "She's hurt, and lost. She ain't thinkin' straight."

"Stop makin' excuses for her, Lu, and call it what it is," Madame Toulouse went on. "Them dollar signs got hold of her and won't let go. How else you explain this notion she got to get back her family fortune? Nonsense! That money's long gone. Even if there was a way for her to claim it, do you realize who she would have to take on to get hold of it? Any reasonable person would know they better off wit' what they got instead of chasin' after what they never had. Open yo' eyes, Lu. This is her momma talkin'."

"*I'm* her mama," snapped Mama Lu as the trio heard the distinctive creaking of the front door.

"Well now, *Mama*," said Madame Toulouse with a raised brow, "Yo' daughter is back." Madame Toulouse did not like having to be the voice of reason when reason was unpleasant, but she had never been one to mince words or dwell in denial. She understood Mama Lu's defense of the girl she raised as her own, but refusal to face reality would only lead to destruction. The first step to a cure was proper diagnosis. Without it, you could spit into the wind all day long, never accomplishing a thing.

"Nalia?" called out Mama Lu.

Nalia did not audibly answer, but responded by peeking around the door facing in the hallway. She still wore the ball cap pulled down tightly over her eyes, and her body language was guarded.

"Oh, thank goodness yo' home safe," said Mama Lu. "We was worried."

"*You* was worried," corrected Madame Toulouse. "I told her you'd be back soon, baby, but you know how she gets."

"Well, it's jus' dat yo' car was still here, and..." stammered Mama Lu.

"I went for a walk," replied Nalia. "It's better not to drive when you go for a walk."

"You see, Lucia," continued Madame Toulouse, "I told you there was nothin' to worry 'bout. She's a grown woman after all." Madame Toulouse shot a cautionary look at Mr. John and Mama Lu, warning them to play along.

"I just needed some time to think," said Nalia. "I've had a lot on my plate the last few days. I just needed to sort some things out."

"How's yo' head, baby girl?" asked Mr. John. "You sure knocked a right good-sized knot on it."

"I'm fine," Nalia responded in an uncharacteristically curt tone. "Listen, can we not talk about that? I'm tired, and I just want to go upstairs and soak in a hot bath."

Mama Lu was stunned at the way Nalia dismissively addressed Mr. John. She looked over to gauge his reaction. He was hurt and disappointed. He could forgive Nalia's tone, but it pained him to realize that Madame Toulouse was right about her behavior.

With the three elders left staring at each other in confusion, Nalia ducked her head and walked up the stairs. The trio held their tongues until they were sure she was out of earshot.

"I don't like it," said Madame Toulouse, slapping her hand down on the table and pointing a thin finger at Mr. John and Mama Lu. "I don't like it one bit."

"Dat's why we gots to end dis tonight," said Mr. John. "We got to form the bond together. I'm gon' fire up the pit soon as she's off to sleep, and we gon' do dis right, 'round the fire like the ol' days."

"I ain't leavin' dis house, John," retorted Mama Lu. "I ain't leavin' her side."

"You will if you want to help her," said Madame Toulouse leaning across the table. "It's not like we gon' be across town, Lu. You ain't gon' be out of sight of her window. This has to be done and done right. Who knows what that girl got up her sleeve, and we might not get another chance. It's tonight, Lu, in the tradition of the elders 'round the bonfire, jus' like Marie Laveau used to do down by Lake Pontchartrain on the sacred grounds."

A chill went through Mama Lu's body when she recalled memories of the sacred grounds. Not only had Marie Laveau performed her rituals there, but Madame Toulouse and Mama Lu had officiated many ceremonies in that consecrated place. Powerful mojo inhabited the hallowed ground where the water met the earth. The magic was especially strong when offerings were burned, drawing together the elements of earth, air, fire, water, and spirit. It was this sacred ground Madame Luciénne intended to defile with her theatrical production. Mama Lu would not allow that to happen, and she could not let Nalia suffer any longer. Reluctantly, she agreed for the ritual to take place around Mr. John's fire pit, just beyond his workshop and concealed by the high fence bordering his small back yard.

"Trust me, Lu," consoled Mr. John. "She gon' be fine. If she's in trouble, you gon' know. I done watched dat window many a night, and I tell you, sometime I know wha's goin' on befo' you do."

Johnny the Conqueror was smooth as glass.

Four blocks away, Madame Vivian Luciénne prepared her altar. Though her craft had become mostly theatrical to the outside world, a trendy and profitable blend of cultures that capitalized on the glamorization of Paganism, Madame Luciénne had not forgotten everything she learned under Mama Lu's instruction. Her private practice was just as impure in its tradition, a twisted mixture of Voodoo and Wicca. Nevertheless, Madame Luciénne was confident if her instructions were followed, she would be able to feel the rhythm of the sacred drum and enter the elder's bond. Once she was in, she had a direct line to Queen Marie – to the guide.

She entered her candle-lit altar room like a geisha, wearing a black, silk robe with the traditional red sash binding her waist. She walked barefoot across the hardwood floor, carefully carrying a glass jar filled with salt. The altar was made of a small table draped in black velvet with a short, wooden stool set before it. Two large pillar candles stood against the back edge of the table, each on its own wide-based, wooden candle stand: one black to draw in energy, the other white to send it out. Between them, on a thin wire frame, stood a diamond-shaped piece of coal-black glass with a unicursal hexagram etched in the top corner and an upright pentacle at the bottom. A solid silver plate lay flat on the table in front of the diamond-shaped scrying mirror and beside it, a long double-edged dagger. On the left, near the black candle, stood traditional elements of Voodoo in the form of cubed

218

sugar, two dark vials of oil, a length of black silk ribbon, and a small burlap poppet, wet and stained with the remnants of tea leaves from Nalia's cup.

Madame Luciénne approached the altar with her jar of salt and tipped it over, carefully spilling its contents in a thin line to form a circle around the altar and the stool. It had been a long time since Madame Luciénne performed any real magic, but she was confident she could still pull it off. It was like riding a bike, she thought.

When the circle was complete, Madame Luciénne placed the empty jar on the altar and sat down on the wooden stool. After several deep, cleansing breaths, she picked up two of the sugar cubes and held them between her palms over the silver plate. Applying firm pressure she rubbed her hands back and forth vigorously, grinding the sugar into a fine powder and letting it fall onto the plate. When she was finished, she lowered her head and blew a gentle breath over the surface of the plate, scattering the sugar to its edges. Placing the tip of her index finger to her tongue, she moistened it and carefully drew the triple-spiraled symbol of the triskele into the sugar. When the Celtic symbol was completed, Madame Luciénne picked up the tea-stained poppet, bound it tightly with the black ribbon, and placed it in the center of the plate of sugar. She then anointed it with oil from both of the dark vials.

After several more cleansing breaths, Madame Luciénne removed the red, silk sash from her waist and laid it flat across her knees. Placing her fingers inside the collar of her robe, she slipped it off her bare shoulders and let it fall to the floor around the stool. Bathed in candlelight, she wrapped the red sash back around her waist and tied the required seven knots.

Madame Luciénne focused her mind on Nalia and Mama Lu. She was going to enjoy this. She smiled balefully as she lifted the dual-edged athemé skyward. Her menacing reflection stared back at her from the scrying mirror. Their eyes locked over the poppet as Madame Luciénne silently awaited the call of the drum.

———————

The hot soak had relieved much of the soreness in Nalia's muscles. The lavender bath salts she used helped sooth her mind, enabling her to focus on the task at hand. Until now, the visions, memories, and nightmares had control, coming and going through her slumber uninvited. Tonight, Nalia would willfully seek them out. She planned to welcome the dreams, take control of them, and use them for her own gain.

Mama Lu left a cup of tea on her bedside table, as usual. She would need it to help wash down the small, oval pill she turned over in her hand. She assumed it was some type of sleep aid. She did not trust Madame Luciénne, but she knew they both stood to make a great deal of money from their secret arrangement. If Nalia could trust anything, it was Madame Luciénne's love of money. Armed with confidence of her associate's greed, she placed the tablet on the back of her tongue and swallowed it with the lukewarm tea.

Queen Marie lay on the pillow beside her. Eagerly, she picked up the doll and searched for a soft spot in the back of the neck where the porcelain pieces were joined with cloth and batting. Locating an appropriate place for the hat pin, Nalia took a deep breath and pricked the fabric. As the pin pierced the cloth, Nalia flinched as if expecting something to happen. It did not. There were no flashes of light, sudden gusts of wind, or drastic changes in temperature. Nothing supernatural or even theatrical happened when she plunged the length of the pin into the body of the doll. She was slightly disappointed. Nalia did not understand that despite its simple appearance, the insertion of another practitioner's hat pin into a ritual object would have a critical impact on the energy flowing through it. Brick dust, gris-gris, incantations, and all the protective mojo that could be conjured was all useless if the enemy had a foothold on the inside. Nalia was at risk. Everyone was at risk.

Holding Queen Marie tightly to her chest, Nalia turned off the bedside lamp and pillowed her head. For the first time since the nightmares began, she did not feel like a frightened child. She had a plan and a purpose, and she was not afraid.

Across the narrow street, Mr. John stood inside a large circle of brick dust and struck a wooden match against the side of its box. His solemn face reflected the glow of the flickering flame as he cupped his hand and lit his pipe. Mr. John drew several quick puffs as the tobacco began to burn cherry red in the bitter blackness of the night.

He held the match steady, ensuring the integrity of the flame before tossing it into the large metal pit of accelerant-soaked wood. With a single, loud *whoof* the night was alight with the glow of the bonfire. The trio looked on in tethered anticipation. Each elder was anxious, in their own way, to get the ritual started and finished, to build the strongest bond yet and draw out the hidden memories once and for all. They were all eager put an end to Nalia's private hell as well as their own.

Mr. John studied the fire carefully. He watched for patterns of light and shadow, reading them like a novel and waiting for the proper time to begin the cadence. The earth's balance of light and dark was like a vigorous dance between good and evil. The two adversaries twirled together inharmoniously, each struggling to take the lead. At times, light conquered darkness. At others, darkness overshadowed light, but overall, balance prevailed as a result of the perpetual battle.

The spirit world was no different, and in the flame, Mr. John could interpret its balance of good and evil. The flame was heavy with shadow tonight. Mr. John watched and waited for the light to prevail, but that time did not come. Hiding his apprehension, Mr. John reluctantly began the cadence on the ancient drum, hoping the elders' bond would be strong enough to overcome the shadow in the spirit world.

Mama Lu and Madame Toulouse stood before the flame, draped in ceremonial robes with arms raised toward the sky. In his nearby box, Draco stirred as the women began to chant:

Loa… Loa… come b'tween. Sing you to Bondye. Sing you of me.

Mama Lu began an old Creole dance, one like Marie Laveau would have led in Congo Square or down at the sacred grounds. As she danced, a warm gust of wind blew in from the south and whipped around the bonfire, sending embers spiraling skyward. Mama Lu twirled and chanted, her mind heavy in the spirit world, calling out to the Saints on Nalia's behalf. With every fiber of her body and soul, she petitioned for the deed to be completed. Around the fire she danced, throwing her head back and forth to the rhythm of the drum, taking in the energy of the gathering spirits. Faster and faster she whirled in a dizzying circle until she collapsed upon the large wooden box. She felt the energy of the bond pulsing through the ground, the box, the snake, the air, and her spirit. It surged stronger with every resounding beat of the droning drum.

Mama Lu removed the rosary from the silver latch and placed it around her neck. Boldly, she flung open the lid of the box to find Draco coiled and raised as if to strike, but his head submissively bowed. Mama Lu reached in and picked up the great snake, lifting him high above her head as she stood and continued her Creole dance. Round and round she turned with the serpent as her eyes rolled into a hypnotic trance.

Madame Toulouse could also feel the resonance of the drum pulsing through her blood as she stood chanting beneath the cloudless night sky. Embers from the fire continued to circle upwards like tiny shooting stars. She could feel the energy swelling in the ground beneath her, moving through her bare feet and into her body. She watched Mama Lu and Mr. John, their images distorted by the rising heat and smoke as they continued to channel the energy of the drum through their veins.

Then she felt it. The drumbeat was off. No, the pulsing was off. Madame Toulouse lowered her hands and directed her attention to the drum. She watched as Mr. John struck its taut leather head with the palms of his hands and noted the energy flow was not in sync with the rhythm. Something was terribly wrong. Madame Toulouse felt a prickling sensation in her muscles, like thorns tearing at her flesh. In the midst of the ceremony she screamed, "Stop!"

Mama Lu and Mr. John looked up, pulled from their trance by the cry. Madame Toulouse was shaking with panic. "Something ain't right," she said, her eyes wide with fright. "I can feel it. There's somethin' here. Somethin' from the outside. There's dark magic here, I tell you."

The shaking turned to convulsions as Madame Toulouse's body grew weak. Mr. John reacted, rushing to her side just before she collapsed. As he caught her in his arms, Madame Toulouse's eyes rolled back into her head, and her arms began to twitch uncontrollably. Mama Lu returned Draco to his box and hurried over to find her mentor incoherent and sucking down ragged breaths. Though she moved her head toward their voices, Madame Toulouse was unable to make eye contact or focus at all. Her mouth hung open lazily, and her head bobbed as she lost control of the muscles in her neck. Mr. John cradled the feeble woman in his arms, allowing her head to fall into the bend of his elbow. The heat radiating from her neck nearly burned his skin.

"Lu, feel dis!" he said with surprise.

Mama Lu slipped her hand under Madame Toulouse's neck and felt the heat from the blistering sore forming there. She cut her fearful eyes to Mr. John.

"What is it, Lu?" he asked.

"I don't know, but it sho ain't good," responded Mama Lu. "We gots to get her inside."

Mama Lu gave a quick glance to Nalia's window before attempting to move the debilitated woman. The room was still dark, and there was no sign of trouble.

———————

As Nalia slept, the pill took her down into a deep, comatose state. Her heartbeat and breathing slowed to levels of mere survival. Though her body's systems barely clung to life, Nalia's mind waited with anticipation in a darkened void, ready for the dreams to come.

Soon a fragrant floral scent stirred her senses. She felt the damp sensation of soft, dewy grass beneath her body, and though her eyes remained closed, she could feel the sun shining down on her face. Stretching out her hands, she felt an abundance of velvety flowers and clover. She opened her eyes to see the bright blue, cloudless sky above as tiny insects danced merrily around her head.

Nalia sat up to find herself in the middle of a vast meadow, stretching as far as she could see, thick with wildflowers and shade trees. She sat in the middle of a narrow path that divided the field in two. On the left, the flowers were all bright blue and on the right, a brilliant gold. A gentle breeze touched her face as she offered it to the summer sun. Nalia breathed deeply, filling her lungs with the clean, fragrant air. She felt she could stay in this place for all eternity.

Folding her arms around her knees, she watched the breeze toy with the wildflowers. The blue flora resembled an ocean with gentle waves lapping their way toward the shore. The field of gold called to mind images of the wind whipping through wheat fields. For what seemed like hours, Nalia watched the flower's hypnotic dance, while bathing in the tranquility of the meadow. She wished it would last, but when she saw a familiar glimmer of light in the distance, Nalia knew it was time to go.

She stood slowly, dusted herself off, and stared down the path. The light flashed again, a reflection of the sun. Nalia knew, without a doubt, it was Queen Marie waiting to show her the next vision. As she contemplated the call of the dream, Nalia felt her soul sigh. While part of her did not want to leave the field, she was eager to learn more about her father and her past. Driven by curiosity, Nalia took a deep breath and started down the path. The further she walked, the less her heart wanted to stay. It was as if the notion gave up hope and let go.

As Nalia followed the glinting light down the pathway, the sky above grew dark and storm clouds threatened the horizon. The gentle breeze that so softly caressed her skin strengthened to a brisk wind as Nalia reached the path's end. On the ground before her, Queen Marie stood just on the edge of a large, rectangular opening that resembled a freshly dug grave. The hole sloped downward into a wide, dark tunnel. The wind whipped over the opening, generating a hollow howl that echoed across the vast field. An unexpected chill swept through Nalia's body as the faint smell of gasoline wafted from the gaping hole.

She looked past Queen Marie into the blackness. She could see nothing, but she knew what was waiting for her down there. The nightmare had been fighting its way to reality for some time, and Nalia knew what to expect. The horrific images her child's mind turned into monsters long ago were gradually becoming clearer. She knew what the images were, and she knew the monstrous substitutions her mind had created would soon be stripped away leaving her to fully remember the horror she experienced at the hand of her father, with the apparent blessing of her mother.

Queen Marie stood still at the edge of the opening. She did not lead Nalia onward, nor did she hold her back. Nalia knew this had to be her decision. Her mind rushed back and forth from peace to pressure. She heard voices calling out in her mind. A gentle one told her it was perfectly alright to stay here in the meadow, at peace. Another one stung her brain and urged her to witness the vision, to find out more about her past. "Secrets will be revealed," the voice promised, "All things can be known."

Nalia could smell the rain, but the storm clouds kept their distance on the horizon, as if waiting for a cue. Nalia was torn. The decision was painful. The call of the meadow was comforting and restful, but the enticement of knowledge and revelation was overwhelming. Nalia's curiosity could not be satiated. The promising voice gnawed at her brain like a starving rodent, and try as she might, Nalia could not silence it. She had to see; she had to know.

As Nalia picked up Queen Marie, the dark clouds began to roll in from the distance, casting a shadow over the field and bringing with them an icy wind. Nalia recognized the warning, but her mind was made up. As the cold rain began to fall, Nalia clutched Queen Marie tightly to her chest and stepped down into the opening. Lightning danced across the clouds as the sky continued to weep.

Just before Nalia's head cleared the opening of the grave, she looked back one last time into the meadow. In the distance she saw a young girl, no more than six, dressed in a navy school jumper and holding a small doll. The child was wearing a melancholy expression and waving goodbye.

Before Nalia could wave back, the loud rumbling sound of shifting soil overtook her. She ducked down just in time as the earth around her snapped shut violently, plunging her into total darkness.

CHAPTER TWENTY-FIVE

Nalia could not see a thing. She felt the solid ground drop from beneath her feet, leaving her body to float in space and time. She sensed a presence, but it was not human. Silently, a disembodied force wound itself around her ankles like a snake. It tugged forcefully, pulling Nalia horizontally down the wide tunnel. She could feel her body moving faster and faster. Nalia knew the vision was inevitable and thought she was prepared, but the terror gripping her body told her otherwise. Her mind cried out in protest as her muscles clinched in fear.

Abruptly, her body lurched to a halt, as if the force dragging it hit a brick wall. Nalia dropped quickly, onto what felt like the springy surface of a dusty mattress. Her vision still dark, Nalia's nose filled with the gasoline-like smell of rotgut whiskey. As she attempted to open her swollen eyes, she realized a glass bottle was being waved under her nose like smelling salts, rousing her from an unconscious state. Her head was sore and pounding, as if it had been struck by something heavy.

Nalia managed to gradually open her eyes into narrow slits, revealing the monstrous face of her father. His bright green eyes were glazed over by the alcohol. He was so close Nalia could feel his weight upon her. His breath was hot against her skin as he dragged his lips the length of her neck.

Nalia's breathing quickened and her heart raced. Her instincts wanted to fight him off, but a voice inside her head pleaded with her to stay still. *Don't fight him. It only gets worse when you fight.*

Michael Barronne held Nalia's wrists tightly above her head with one hand as he passed off the bottle with the other. Two other monstrous faces of Italian descent appeared beside him, snickering and drinking from the glass container.

Pain shot through Nalia's body as her thighs were forced apart. She pushed back with all she had, but one of the Italian men struck her hard in the side of the face. *Don't fight! For God's sake don't fight!*

Nalia's ears began to ring as if she was inside a large bell, and her vision blurred as her sense of orientation spiraled.

"My turn," she heard a muffled Italian voice say, her ears still ringing from the blow. She felt the cold sting of whiskey being spilled onto her scraped and beaten body.

Nalia turned her head and closed her eyes. Her mouth began to utter words on its own. *No. Don't please, don't. Not again. Please, don't. No.* She forced her mind to drift into a dimension where she could not feel anything at all. Her body grew numb as her mind flew out beyond the stars.

The three men continued to violate Nalia's body until each one ran out of strength. All the while, the dark figure of Margaret Barronne stood watching from the doorway, never moving, never protesting, and never ceasing to lovingly fondle her wide, diamond necklace.

A blinding flash of light jarred Nalia's mind back from its travel. Still groggy and incoherent, she could barely make out voices.

"I tell you, John, I jus' can't stand it," said a voice Nalia finally recognized as Mama Lu's. "I don't trust her. I can't believe I let dat baby go back wit' dat woman. I gots a bad feelin', John, you hear me? A bad feelin'."

Nalia opened her eyes to find herself standing in the corner of the parlor in Mama Lu's house still dressed in the familiar, oversized tee she wore to bed. Mama Lu was pacing back and forth across the room. Mr. John sat hunched over on the divan, forcefully rubbing the back of his neck, worry weighing heavily on his brow. Across the room was a young Vivian Luciénne. She sat sideways in Mama Lu's high-back chair with her legs thrown over one arm.

"So what do you think we should do, just go on over to the man's house and yank the lil' girl out of there?" Vivian asked.

"Dat's exactly what I think we ought to do," replied Mama Lu passionately.

"We can't do dat, Lu," said Mr. John.

"I bet ain't nobody gon' stop me," interrupted Mama Lu. "I put a *fix* on 'em good if they try."

"You do dat and the police gon' hand her right back over to 'em. Then you gon' get yo' behind thrown in jail, and dat lil' girl gon' be worse off than she is now," said Mr. John. "I tell ya, Lu, you don't know who dis man is."

"Dat man don't know who I am, John," replied Mama Lu, stiffening her back. She began to chant under her breath as she paced and wrung her hands together. Vivian and Mr. John exchanged looks of desperation.

Suddenly, Mama Lu stopped pacing and looked at Mr. John gasping in a panic.

"What is it, Lu?" he asked.

"They here!" said Mama Lu, bolting for the front door. Vivian and Mr. John followed her into the entry hall. The chimes barely had a chance to ring before Mama Lu threw the door open. Nalia could hear the hysterical cries of Margaret Barronne from the parlor. She stepped into the hall but did not have a clear view of the front door. She could barely see Margaret standing on the porch, crying uncontrollably.

"Let us in, please!" she screamed as Mama Lu stepped aside.

Though Nalia's view was still blocked by Vivian and Mr. John, Mama Lu's reaction told her to expect the worst.

"Oh my God!" cried Mama Lu, "What happened to dis chil'? Did her daddy do dis?"

Nalia craned her neck for a better view but Vivian and Mr. John were huddled in close.

"No," cried Margaret, "It wasn't him. It was his partners, the Verelli brothers. They did this, then took Michael. They're going to kill him, and they're after us too."

"Get 'em inside," shouted Mama Lu.

Mr. John and Vivian flanked the little girl, ushering her down the hallway and into the parlor. When the child finally came into view, Nalia grew sick to her stomach. The little girl was virtually unrecognizable. Her bottom lip was cut and bleeding. Her face was bruised and swollen with one eye completely closed up. Dried blood covered her right cheek, and her nightgown was torn to rags. She wore no shoes, no coat, and had no belongings, save one – a tattered doll with a bloodstained, blue dress. She clutched it tightly against her body as she walked slowly, taking small steps. Her eyes were fixed straight ahead, oblivious to what was happening around her.

Margaret trailed behind the child, trembling. She still wore her wide, diamond necklace and a silk evening dress with a fur wrap. Were it not for her panicked expression and her running mascara, she would be ready for the ballet.

Nalia watched from the end of the corridor as Mama Lu followed everyone down the hall and into the parlor. She had never seen such intensity in Mama Lu's eyes before – a mixture of guilt, sadness, and pure rage threatening to erupt. Ducking into the room behind Mama Lu, Nalia found Mr. John and Vivian tending to the little girl. The child sat on the floor in the corner, behind a small end table, with her knees pulled up to her chest and her arms locked firmly around them. She held Queen Marie tightly between her knees and chin as she rocked back and forth gently bumping herself against the wall. Large spots of smeared, dried blood covered the child's legs. Her haunted eyes reflected no emotion whatsoever; they were cold and lifeless.

When Vivian and Mr. John attempted to approach her, the little girl recoiled like a frightened animal. She displayed no signs of normal human behavior, no indication of anything beyond mere survival instincts.

Margaret sat on one end of the divan, turning her hands over in her lap as Mama Lu stood over her firing off questions.

"You tellin' me the Verelli brothers did *dat* to her and left you lookin' like a ripe Georgia peach? Yo' story ain't addin' up. You better start speakin' some truth 'round here, befo' I have to teach you how," she said in the most commanding tone Nalia ever heard.

"They took Michael, I…I…couldn't get to Nalia," stammered Margaret.

Mama Lu leaned into the lying woman's face and looked her straight in the eyes. Margaret jumped with fright as Mama Lu's eyes began to burn with fire.

"You tell me what happened to dat lil' girl," demanded Mama Lu, mumbling hexes in a low voice.

Margaret went silent. Her body grew still, and her hysterics ceased. Her breathing returned to normal, and her eyes drifted slightly out of focus as she sat up straight and answered Mama Lu in a calm, clear voice.

"The Verelli brothers showed up, and Michael took them upstairs to Nalia's bedroom like before. He owes them, see? Michael had his turn with Nalia like always, then he gave them each a turn. They've done this before, but tonight was different. Things got rougher than usual – really violent. I thought it was just because they were drinking so much, so I didn't mind at first."

Mr. John and Vivian listened intently to the story as they sat with the child and tried to remain calm. The tension in the room climbed to its boiling point. Mama Lu was bursting with fury. She could hardly keep her body from shaking as she continued to stare Margaret down while listening to her sickening tale.

Still under the influence of the spell, Margaret continued. "This time when they finished with Nalia, they turned on Michael. They told him they knew he'd been talking. Said some old man had been running his mouth down by the docks, asking too many questions. Leonetti, I think his name was. They said they needed to tie up all the loose ends. Then one of them pulled out a knife and cut Michael, right across his gut. There was so much blood. He couldn't even stand up. They had to carry him out when they took him. One of them told me to stay put. He said they'd be back for me. While they were on their way out, I heard them telling Michael they had killed the old man and made it look like a robbery. They're going to kill him too."

Everyone in the room was stone-still in shock. Mama Lu could not believe what she heard. She did not care at all what happened to

Michael Barronne so long as he did not live through it – her focus was Nalia, and there was one question still unanswered.

"Where was you when they was goin' at yo' baby girl?" Mama Lu fumed, afraid she already knew the answer.

"I was there in the doorway," replied Margaret without batting an eye. "Michael likes for me to be there. He says it keeps Nalia from putting up too much of a fight."

Mama Lu lost all control and backhanded Margaret brutally across the face, releasing her from the trance. Margaret collapsed onto the divan as Mama Lu turned to Mr. John.

"Go!" she said, "And get it ready!"

"Now?" Mr. John asked, puzzled.

"Now!" Mama Lu replied with vigor, "She needs to be split."

Mr. John nodded nervously in agreement, exchanged a stern look with Vivian, and left quickly by the back door.

Margaret stirred and came to, looking around in a daze. She did not remember relating the events of the evening or being hit by Mama Lu. She had no recollection of anything that transpired since being told to explain herself.

"Can you hide us until I can get my precious baby out of town?" she asked, intense fear returning to her eyes.

Mama Lu's stomach turned, but she controlled her anger. She needed to remain calm in order to orchestrate her newly-hatched plan accurately. Mama Lu shared understanding eye contact with Vivian before responding to Margaret.

"The first thing we gots to do is get dem Verelli brothers off yo' trail," she said. "How'd you know where to find me?"

"I got friends who told me," Margaret replied. "Same ones that warned me not to be dealing with you. It ain't exactly a secret where Mama Lu lives, you know?"

"Then the Verellis gon' know where to come lookin' fo' you," said Mama Lu. "We got to get yo' car out of here, and get you and Nalia separated. Dat way, y'all ain't easy to find."

Margaret nodded in agreement as Mama Lu turned to Vivian who was still on the floor with the child. "Vivian, take the keys to the shop," instructed Mama Lu. "Take Margaret and show her to the upper room. She gon' be safe there 'til we can get her out of town."

Vivian's eyes grew wide as saucers, but she did not question Mama Lu. She rose and went to the kitchen for the keys as instructed. When she re-entered the parlor, she received an affirming nod from Mama Lu, whose eyes were alive with a disturbing, but necessary purpose. Vivian understood what had to be done.

Mama Lu extended her hands to Margaret and helped her up. She placed an arm around the trembling woman and walked her to the door. "Vivian's gon' take you up to the shop. I got a room upstairs where you can hide out fo' a while," Mama Lu told her. "Leave Nalia here wit' me. She gon' be safe here. Dem Verelli boys ain't gon dare come lookin' fo' her here. They know better than to fool wit' Mama Lu."

Margaret's eye widened with wonder. Her running makeup gave her the look of a frightened raccoon.

"All those stories I've heard about you?" Margaret asked, "They're true, aren't they?"

"You have no idea," Mama Lu responded, looking her straight in the eye without the slightest smile.

Margaret was trembling. Her whole world was collapsing around her and she was helpless. A fitting state, thought Mama Lu, considering Margaret's refusal to defend the helpless child hiding in the corner.

From the opposite side of the parlor, arms folded in disgust and mouth agape in disbelief, Nalia watched as Vivian led Margaret cautiously from the house to her vehicle. Tears streaking her cheeks, she watched as Mama Lu sat on the floor near the bloodied and beaten little girl. She kept a fair distance, not attempting to approach young Nalia. Mama Lu did not try to talk with the child. She simply sat with her, matching her posture. Her tranquil demeanor assured the child there was no threat. They rocked together on the floor for a long time until Mama Lu decided the time was right to speak. Though she addressed the child, Nalia got the impression Mama Lu was reassuring herself.

"You safe now chil'," she said, "Ain't nothin' bad gon' happen to you here. Mama Lu gon' see to it." Nalia listened as Mama Lu whispered the words over and over until they became a soothing mantra. Then Mama Lu sang softly to the child in an old Creole dialect,

Peace gon' come. Peace gon' come.

Darkness flee and peace gon' come.

The incandescent bulbs of the antique lamp grew brighter until Nalia's eyes were blinded by brilliant light and she soon felt the familiar comfort of her warm, ivory duvet. Nalia wrapped herself in its softness, knowing she was back at home and the vision was over. There was no smell of gasoline or whiskey, no snarling voices, and no pain from the sharp claws of monstrous beasts intent on devouring her flesh. Nalia sensed only tranquility as she breathed in the fresh smell of her clean linens. She held Queen Marie tightly as she sank into the pillowy warmth of her bedding. Finally, she thought, she was free of the nightmares.

Then the irksome thought plagued her brain once again – she was no closer to learning anything useful about her father. The vision taught her nothing aside from the fact that Michael Barronne was a diabolically sick individual who prostituted his six-year-old daughter to settle his gambling debts. If the Verelli brothers were running the Italian mob in New Orleans back then, Mama Lu was right about her father's murder. At least she had been truthful about that.

Nalia's mind was suddenly abuzz with questions. Try as she might, she found herself unable to relax. When Nalia opened her eyes, it surprised her to find the bedside lamp on, and the clock beside it showing 12:01. Nalia felt a sudden stiffening of her muscles as she realized she was not alone.

Across the room, standing in the open doorway was Madame Vivian Luciénne wearing a flame-red dress and matching hat. A devilish grin stretched across her face as she greeted Nalia with dripping, sweet sarcasm.

"Hello, darlin'," she purred, raising her eyebrows into a scheming expression.

Nalia looked back at the clock – 12:01.

"Am I still dreaming?" she asked.

Madame Luciénne leaned against the door frame, folded her arms and crossed her ankles.

"I wouldn't exactly call it dreaming," she said with a smile, "But yo' definitely not awake."

"So, this isn't real?" Nalia asked, confused and growing frustrated.

"Oh, it's real," replied Madame Luciénne, "All too real. We're just on a different plane, chil'. I'm sure your guide explained how that works." Madame Luciénne smirked deviously as if keeping a secret she was dying to tell. Her astral projection was in her element. "Yo' body is still lying right there in yo' bed, and if you took that sleepin' pill I gave you, it will be for quite some time."

Nalia grew worried. Madame Luciénne did not seem nearly as benign as she had earlier in the day. There was an intimidating edge to her tone. It frightened Nalia, causing her to question the integrity of the deal to which she had agreed.

"If I'm not awake, then how are you here?" Nalia asked, still trying to make sense of what was happening. "How are we having this conversation?"

"Our minds are linked together through that doll," explained Madame Luciénne, "Through Voodoo."

Nalia's eyes widened; she was stunned and afraid. The thought of her mind being linked to this threatening, slimy side of Madame Luciénne made her skin crawl and her stomach turn. Luciénne used the brief moment of silence to creep closer to the bed. She sat down right next to Nalia and raised her hands to her eyes. "Boo!" she said abruptly, stretching out her fingers in an exploding motion and cackling loudly. When Nalia jumped, Madame Luciénne placed a patronizing hand on her leg and patted it gently.

"It's alright, darlin', there ain't nothing to be afraid of. It's the same way Mama Lu and her bunch have been talkin' to you through these dreams, showing you all the things they remember 'bout yo' past."

"Are you here to help me find out about my father?" Nalia asked, apprehensively. "Are you going to show me what you remember?"

"About that," said Madame Luciénne, biting her bottom lip, "We need to have a little chat."

Nalia's expression soured to a reflection of unsettling anger. She pulled her leg away from Madame Luciénne and absentmindedly squeezed Queen Marie up to her chin.

"You need to give up on finding yo' family's fortune, darlin'," Madame Luciénne went on. "Yo' daddy was so far in debt when the Verelli brothers got hold of him there wasn't enough coin left to fill a piggy bank. So even if you do track down the *inheritance* that you think you're entitled to, you ain't gon' find nothing but a stack of loans that never got paid back." Madame Luciénne pursed her lips, "There ain't no money left, sweetheart."

Nalia was devastated and embarrassed. As she pondered the shocking truth, fear caused her body to tremble. If Madame Luciénne had no financial interest in being here, then what was she up to?

"Oh don't worry, darlin'," Madame Luciénne reassured her, aware of the distressed look in Nalia's eyes, "I told you I was gon' help you, and I am. There's still a whole truckload of money to be made here, just not the way you expected."

Nalia recoiled and straightened her back against the headboard. She looked at Madame Luciénne with growing suspicion.

"How do I know I can trust you?" she asked.

The snakelike grin slithered across Madame Luciénne's face once again as she batted her lashes.

"Why, my darlin'," she said, mocking offense, "I'm about to prove I'm the only one you *can* trust. All dis time," she went on, peaking Nalia's interest, "All these visions you've seen, all these 'answers' you've been spoon-fed – there's still one question burning a hole in yo' brain, isn't there? There's still one little thing that no one will tell you."

"My mother," Nalia whispered, almost inaudibly.

"That's right," Madame Luciénne taunted, "Why did she leave? Where did go? Why did she leave you behind?" Madame Luciénne let the questions marinate for a moment. She could see Nalia's mind working overtime, racing from one thought to the next, from one question to another.

"Forget about yo' father, sweetheart," Madame Luciénne continued. "The big question you've wanted answered all these years is – what happened to yo' mother?"

Nalia looked like a lost puppy. Even though she now knew her mother's nasty, evil nature, her spirit reverted to that of a six-year-old girl longing to be loved.

"C'mon chil', surely by now you've seen enough know the story yo' Mama Lu's been trying to sell you ain't *entirely* true."

Nalia stared silently into Madame Luciénne's eyes, resembling more and more the broken child who sat in the corner of Mama Lu's parlor so many years ago.

"Do you want to know what really happened to yo' momma?" Madame Luciénne asked leaning into Nalia's face with a sinister satisfaction dancing wildly in her eyes. All Nalia could manage was a bashful nod. "Well then, let me show you."

CHAPTER TWENTY-SIX

Madame Luciénne extended her hand and offered her open palm to Nalia. With one arm still clinging tightly to Queen Marie, Nalia hesitantly stretched out the other until her hand hovered over Madame Luciénne's. Uncertain, she allowed her outstretched fingers to linger in mid-air for what seemed like a lifetime before dropping them into Madame Luciénne's waiting hand.

When their fingers finally touched, Madame Luciénne released a resounding cackle as a brilliant flash of light shot forth from their clasped hands. Once again, Nalia found herself surrounded by darkness, listening to the thump of her rapidly beating heart.

Before she could see, Nalia smelled the unmistakable scent of Margaret Barronne's perfume and heard the low hum of an automobile, coupled with the faint noises of passing traffic. She could feel the gentle vibration of the car's movement as a tiny pinhole of light pierced the horizon of her darkened vision. The image gave Nalia the illusion she was traveling inside a long tunnel, but as her vision grew clearer, she recognized the light as the low-beams of an automobile in the opposing lane. As the oncoming car approached, its headlights illuminated the interior of the car in which Nalia rode. She was alone in the back seat, sitting behind the sobbing silhouette of her mother, with Vivian at the wheel.

Nalia's mind immediately drifted to scenes from gangster movies, where the unknown assailant strangles the passenger from behind with a piano wire. She felt around in the back of the vehicle, but found no wire or other available weapon of strangulation. It was just as well, she supposed. After all, this was only a vision.

Vivian seemed uncomfortable operating the large vehicle as she sat hunched over the steering wheel with her knuckles growing white. The two ladies in the front seat did not speak. They kept an awkward distance between them, each huddled against their respective car doors.

Margaret continued to whimper as she had when seated on Mama Lu's divan. She seemed nervous and fearful, but noticeably devoid of grief. Nalia was not surprised at Margaret's lack of visible distress over the imminent demise of her husband or the forced separation from her injured child. If she had to guess, she would say Margaret was too busy worrying about how to secure her husband's assets to be bothered by such trivial matters as her daughter's well-being.

The car slowed, and Nalia saw the familiar sights of Decatur Street. She recognized Mama Lu's building, even in the dark. Vivian did not stop, but instead drove the car to the corner and made a right, eventually pulling behind the building. A single streetlamp illuminated the narrow alleyway where Vivian pulled the Cadillac to the back entrance of the shop. The rear of the building was quiet and deserted except for what Nalia thought might be a pick-up truck parked in the shadows at the far end of the alley. The two ladies exited the vehicle into the brisk, night air. They hurried to the door as Vivian fumbled with the keys in the darkness.

"You gon' be safe here," said Vivian. "Nobody ever goes up to dis room. You can stay here 'til you get things sorted out."

Margaret nodded and continued to sob, daubing her nose with a mangled scrap of tissue.

The door opened into the workroom, and Vivian reached for the light switch. To her surprise, the room remained shrouded in darkness. She flipped the switch again, up and down several times, but got the same result. "Breaker must be tripped," she said. "Can't be all of 'em though. I noticed the display lights were still on when we passed in front. Wait here," she said, motioning for Margaret to step inside.

As Vivian allowed the heavy door to close, it passed right through Nalia, who had followed the ladies over the darkened threshold. The slamming noise echoed eerily through the empty workroom.

Margaret waited by the door and listened as Vivian's footsteps got farther and farther away. Soon a thin beam of light slipped through the shadows from the far end of the room as Vivian propped open the door to the storefront.

"Now at least we can see to walk," said Vivian, returning to the back door and motioning for Margaret to follow, "This way."

The sobbing woman walked cautiously through the dimly-lit workroom, following the outline of her guide around the tables to the staircase. Looking down at her footsteps, Margaret bumped into Vivian, who stopped at the foot of the stairs to look for the proper key before ascending the darkened steps. After a brief apology and a successful search, Vivian led Margaret up the staircase. Cautiously, they braved the shadowy steps together, gliding their fingertips along the papered walls for added peace of mind. When they reached the top, Vivian felt for the deadbolt locks and made surprisingly quick work of them in the blackness.

The door creaked as Vivian pushed it open and turned on the light. The single bulb dangling from the wire in the center of the room sparked to life, spilling a soft glow into the stairwell. As her eyes adjusted to the light, Vivian saw the terrified, makeup-streaked face of Margaret, huddled just inches behind her and trembling like a wet cat.

"I know yo' scared right now," Vivian tried to reassure her, "But go 'head on in. This will all be over soon."

Margaret stepped carefully around Vivian and entered the upper room. She was only just inside when she noticed the markings on the walls – strange symbols and ancient runes covering every visible surface. Margaret stood slack-jawed as she beheld the large painting that hung on the wall above the rudimentary altar. She could just make out the image of the woman dancing with the snake around the bonfire. Her pulse quickened as all the stories and warnings she dismissed about Mama Lu pushed through to stark reality.

The commotion of rustling feathers caught her attention as she looked beyond the large, round table to the wooden crates underneath the altar. The light was dim and the shadows were heavy, but Margaret was sure she saw several chickens, scratching at the straw-covered bottoms of their cages.

Just as she thought she was going to hyperventilate, Margaret felt intense pain at the base of her skull as a loud *clang* echoed through her brain. In an instant, she felt the blood rushing to her head as her body grew weak and her vision faded to black from the outside in. Her body hit the floor with a thud. She rolled onto her back, staring at the rune-covered ceiling. The last image she saw before the world went dark was the muscular figure of Mr. John standing over her, holding a length of half-inch galvanized pipe.

————————

Madame Toulouse had to be carried inside. As much as Mr. John hated to admit it, he had not retained the strength that once defined his youthful body. He was able to manage her through the shop well enough, but when he reached the steps to the kitchen, Madame Toulouse came to, long enough to struggle. Afraid he would drop the elderly woman, he set her down on the steps until she finally calmed down.

Madame Toulouse was a pitiful sight. She appeared to have lost all her mental faculties. Her eyes were glassy, her mouth was drooping, and her muscles were weakened to the point of immobility. The only indications of life were the shallow rise and fall of her feeble chest, and the occasional tracking of her eyes toward sound.

Mama Lu was in a frightened panic. She tried in vain to rouse Madame Toulouse from her incoherent state. She held her hands, called her name, and asked her questions, but got little response. "Stay with me!" she instructed as they attempted to move her again.

Eventually, Mr. John was able to lift Madame Toulouse under her arms while Mama Lu helped by grabbing her around the knees. Together, they moved the frail woman through Mr. John's kitchen into a small sitting area. There, they laid her on the loveseat, propped up her feet, and placed a small cushion under her head. Mama Lu pulled up a nearby chair while Mr. John retreated to the kitchen for a cold compress.

"She's burnin' up," Mama Lu called out. "She done come down wit' a fever."

"Dat ain't no normal fever," Mr. John shouted back. "You heard what she said."

"I know," replied Mama Lu as Mr. John returned with a damp towel, "Dark magic." She wiped Madame Toulouse's forehead and

240

neck gently with the cool rag and continued to speak encouraging words as a lump of worry gathered in her throat.

Mr. John slipped his hand underneath Madame Toulouse's neck. The sore was still there and searing hot. The dark magic was physically manifesting itself through the eldest member of their bond.

"I'm gon' get an ice pack," said Mr. John, showing Mama Lu the redness left on his hand where he touched the burning sore.

As he left the room, Madame Toulouse opened her eyes wide. Though she still lacked the ability to focus, she responded when Mama Lu called her name. Madame Toulouse made a feeble, wasted effort to sit up. Her mouth was dry, but her lips were moving, trying to form words. Mama Lu called out for Mr. John to bring water as Madame Toulouse spoke in a raspy voice.

"Lu," she said.

"I'm here," responded Mama Lu.

Madame Toulouse shook her head, "Luci…"

"I'm here," repeated Mama Lu, "What is it?"

Mr. John returned with an ice pack and a small glass of water just in time to see Madame Toulouse managing to pull up on Mama Lu's hand. She struggled with every ounce of energy she could stir and finally focused on Mama Lu's frightened face. She shook her head from side to side in a wide, sweeping motion as her voice broke through in a hoarse warning.

"Luciénne!" she said, just as her eyes glazed over and she collapsed onto the loveseat once again.

———————

From a darkened corner of the ritual room, Nalia watched as the horrific vision continued to unfold.

Margaret stirred. Her head was pounding, and her vision was hazy. She struggled to focus her eyes, only to wish she had not. She found herself stripped to her undergarments and chained to the center of the large, oak table, her limbs stretched in every direction. The single light bulb swayed gently from side to side on the wire above her head. She was flat on her back, staring at the rune-covered ceiling. Lifting her head, Margaret saw her body was marked with similar runes and symbols.

She tried to move her arms and legs, but the chains pulled them so tightly she could barely flex her muscles. The most she could manage was the frantic thrashing of her hands and feet where cold, iron shackles secured her wrists and ankles.

Panic, like Margaret had never known, surged through her body as she tried desperately to break free from the chains that held her. Sweat poured like water from her brow, stinging her eyes as she struggled to slip out of the shackles.

Though the room was quiet, Margaret could tell she was not alone. She opened her throat to scream, but no sound came forth. She felt only a violent burning, like fire in her esophagus. Again she tried, and again the searing pain ripped through her throat, but the only sound she heard was the low, belly laugh of Mama Lu steadily growing louder. Margaret's heart raced like a rabbit as she intensified her efforts to escape.

Soon the smiling, upside-down face of Mama Lu entered Margaret's field of vision from above her head as she continued her painful attempts to scream.

"Scream all you want," said Mama Lu, her smile fading to a sneer. "Dem vocal chords ain't never gon' work again." Standing over her, Mama Lu placed her hands on either side of Margaret's head. She squeezed tightly, forcing Margaret to gaze up into her upside-down eyes. "You feel dat burnin' in the back of yo' throat? Dat's Mr. John's seven-pepper sauce. Oh, I know it might sound tasty, but I assure you it ain' fo' cookin'. Jus' one swig of dat stuff and folks can't speak fo' a week. 'Cept in yo' case, it's gon' be a lil' longer." She lifted Margaret's head slightly by the ears and slammed it down hard against the table. Margaret's vision went blurry once again. "You see," Mama Lu continued, "You had plenty of chances to speak up when yo' lil' girl was bein' raped and beaten every night, but you kept yo' mouth shut didn't you? Well, now you gon' keep it shut fo' a good long time."

242

Mama Lu grabbed Margaret by the hair with both hands, twisting it around her fingers as she made fists for a firm grip. She pulled so hard, Margaret's neck stretched to the point of agony. Margaret grimaced as Mama Lu bent low over her captive. Bringing her lips to Margaret's ear, she whispered, "You see, the only thing worse than someone who abuses a child is someone who stands by and lets it happen."

With a quick jerk, Mama Lu released the tension on Margaret's neck by ripping out the handfuls of hair by its roots. Margaret screamed in silent, burning pain. "So now you gots to learn yo' lesson," said Mama Lu, tossing the bloodied wads of hair and bits of scalp onto Margaret's near-naked body.

Tears flowed from Margaret's eyes, down the sides of her face and into her ears. The moisture muffled the sound of the congas as Mr. John began to thump a low, steady rhythm. Mama Lu circled the table while her apprentice, Vivian, watched from the doorway. This would be her first time to witness a split. She was nervous and yet excited.

The rhythm of the drums filled the room as Mama Lu began to chant in an ancient, tribal language. Her tone was crystal clear and pointed as if this were her native tongue. Methodically, she moved around the table in a hypnotic, dance-like fashion, flailing her arms in a serpentine rhythm.

Margaret continued to sob as Mama Lu made the full circle around the ceremonial table and once again approached her head. "Oh you feel like cryin' now?" asked Mama Lu. "I see. All dis time you ain't shed one tear fo' yo' baby girl, but now you wants to cry. Do you even care where yo' chil' is right now?" Mama Lu paused and stared vehemently at her mute captive, as if expecting her to answer. "She at the hospital, where you shoulda sent yo' devil of a husband the firs' time he laid a hand on her." Margaret tried to speak, but could not make a sound; the burning was unbearable. "What's dat?" taunted Mama Lu, leaning her ear toward Margaret's mouth, "Speak up, darlin', I can't her ya."

Mama Lu laughed and sauntered toward the altar against the wall. It was a rustic assembly of boards stretched across the top of several wooden crates. On the boards were many candles arranged in an arc around various ritual objects. Mama Lu took a deep breath and waved her hand over the candles in a large circular motion. The candles burst to life with flame all at once, casting a loving glow on the painting above them.

Vivian was fascinated. She desperately wanted to learn that trick. She watched as the bonfire in the painting seemed to come alive in the glow of the candles. If she did not know better, she would swear she saw the silhouetted figure of the woman move with the snake to the beat of the drum. Vivian's blood was pumping fast and strong.

When Mama Lu whirled around, she was holding a slim, double-edged knife. It gleamed in the candlelight as she carried it toward the table where Margaret lay, still squirming.

"I find it ironic dat you is so fascinated wit' my dolls," she said, approaching Margaret's right side. "You 'bout to find out why they call me the doll maker." Mama Lu touched the cold blade to Margaret's neck. "You 'bout to find out how it feels to be split." She trailed the knife down Margaret's heaving chest and stabbed its point into her flesh just below her right breast. Mama Lu cut just deep enough for blood to flow freely as she dragged the blade down Margaret's rib cage. Margaret threw her head from side to side in pain. She tried to move, but the chains held her flat against the table, at the mercy of her captor.

"In Haiti, they have an ancient tradition – an art form, really," explained Mama Lu. "They call it the art of the split. It's known by few and practiced by even fewer. They pass dis knowledge down from mother to daughter, only one in each generation. It's been 'round so long dat no one can recall its origin. It's so respected and so feared dat there is only one doll maker in any village at any one time. It's a secret well kept and well protected."

Fire danced in Mama Lu's eyes as she lifted and repositioned the blade to start a second incision while the first poured blood onto the table. Mama Lu made the second cut a few inches down from the first, pulling the blade parallel as she continued to enlighten Margaret on the ancient art of doll making.

She explained that in some parts of Haiti and in the remote tribes of Africa there has, for centuries, existed a practice of splitting a person's soul away from their body. Not entirely, as in death, but in such a way as to leave just enough of the soul for the body's tissue to cling to life. Tales evolved from this practice that told of the "walking dead" or the "undead". Once stories of the walking dead of Haiti reached the United States, Hollywood and other entertainment media seized a lucrative claim to the notion of "zombies". As eager audience's comical fascination grew, the true and ancient art of doll making was pushed further into obscurity, where its practitioners were content for it to dwell in secrecy.

Mama Lu made four identical cuts into Margaret's flesh, allowing the blood to flow out to the edge of the table where it gathered and dripped onto the floor. She then moved around to Margaret's left side and began repeating the process. With each cut, Margaret became weaker, putting up less of a struggle. She felt the sharp pain of the blade each time it entered her body, but she lay motionless wishing she could scream, wishing she could die.

In the purest form of doll making, there was no such thing as the "walking dead". Reality had been twisted into legend, and legend into grandiose tales, but the truth was much less glamorous. The doll maker, through ritual, would split the soul from the body and store it separately, usually in a sealed jar. The body, with its tiny bit of the severed soul intact would then be wrapped and buried by a witch doctor in a hallowed place, where earth and water became one, for a period of seven days. During that time, the body's tissue would wither and shrink to one third its normal size, while the magic of the earth and water would keep it hydrated and youthful. When the body was retrieved on the seventh day, it was brought to the doll maker to be painted and adorned. It was said that the "dolls" could see and hear everything around them. Some say they could even feel, but remained unable to move or speak. They were imprisoned inside their own disfigured bodies, sentenced to silently observe the world around them until the doll maker released their souls to the hand of death.

Three incisions were made on Margaret's left side for a total of seven. The blood loss would keep her weak but would not be enough to kill her. As Mr. John increased the intensity of his pounding on the congas, Mama Lu retrieved vials of oil from the altar and poured them into Margaret's wounds. The fragrant oils stung and burned Margaret's raw flesh, causing her to writhe in pain, even in her weakened state.

The drum became louder as Mama Lu reached into one of the crates under the altar and produced a live rooster. Holding it aloft by the throat, she danced around the table chanting as Margaret wept and bled. Vivian watched in nervous anticipation as the rooster flailed about and the dance became more vigorous. When the cadence reached its culmination, Mama Lu gripped the rooster with both hands and wrung its neck. With one swift motion, she pulled the animal's head clean off and spilled its blood over Margaret's writhing form. Mama Lu's voice grew louder, and her chanting swelled with intensity, echoing with the pounding of the drum.

Vivian grew sick to her stomach. She covered her mouth and slid down the door facing to the floor. She sat with her knees at her chin, breathing deeply and trying not to vomit, but never looking away from the captivating ritual.

Mama Lu let the rooster go under the table where its struggling, headless body continued to flap and flail wildly. With a disturbing grin, she placed her hands, palms down, in the blood on the table and smeared it around her neck to bind the spell. She cackled loudly, watching Margaret drift in and out of consciousness.

Dancing back around the table, Mama Lu made her way to the altar where she retrieved the final ritual object – a small teardrop-shaped jar made of glass. She removed its stopper and carried it to the table. The blood from her hands smeared over the surface of the glass giving it the appearance of a beating heart. She held it under the swaying light bulb, over Margaret's body. "Now, sleep," she said as she watched Margaret's eyes close.

Soon, tiny rays of light began to break forth from the seven cuts in Margaret's torso. They drifted upward, like glowing smoke, gathering above and dripping into the glass jar. The hazy streams of light flowed like water into the container until the bleeding cuts finally grew dark.

Mama Lu carefully stoppered the jar, and with wide eyes, carried it back to the altar. Setting it down near the candles, she picked up the bloody knife and held it to her palm. With a deep breath she closed her fingers and drew the edge of the blade across her hand. Squeezing her bleeding fist over the flame of a large candle in the center of the altar, she allowed her blood to drip into the pooling wax. She watched as the blood streaked a swirling pattern around the flaming wick; all the while she chanted softly in a sinister whisper. Retrieving the glowing jar, she turned it upside down and plunged it into the bloody wax, snuffing the candle in the process. Then, Mama Lu lifted the jar to let it cool and repeated the action, allowing a thick seal of blood and wax to form around the stopper.

When she was satisfied with the seal's integrity, she carried the jar containing all but a fragment of Margaret's soul, back to the table and held it proudly over her sleeping victim's head. The wax from the seal dripped in thin streaks down the side of the glass like veins on the heart-like jar.

"Yo' soul is sealed wit' my blood," Mama Lu whispered with a menacing grin, "And so long as I'm alive, dis seal will never be broken. Death will never claim you, no matter how much you beg."

A final tear spilled from Margaret's eye and fell onto the table as Mama Lu smiled and motioned for Mr. John to silence the drums. "Take her body to the sacred grounds," she instructed. "Bury it in the marshy soil where the water meets the earth, for seven days time. Then bring her back to me, so her punishment can begin."

Mr. John nodded in agreement as Mama Lu left the room. With the help of an eager, but still queasy Vivian, he wrapped Margaret's body in oil-anointed gauze and a pure white sheet, bound it with hemp cord, and carried it to his truck.

From the corner of the darkened room, Nalia stood sickened and terrified. The only image she could call to mind was that of the doll, Mary, who had stood watching her from the top of her dresser for as long as she could remember.

CHAPTER TWENTY-SEVEN

The light bulb swinging above the table flickered and died, leaving the upper room wrapped snugly in a blanket of darkness. The silence was thick enough for Nalia to hear her own heartbeat, pounding in her chest like the cadence of the drum. She stood alone in the corner of the room, rubbing her arms with the palms of her hands in an attempt to stop shivering.

Nalia wondered if her mind could ever be rescued from the realm of the surreal. At present, she could envision no possible scenario where returning to a normal life would be the eventual outcome. This must be how it feels to have a breakdown, she thought.

The buzz of the light bulb caught her attention as it began to burn once again. A tiny spark of life ignited the filament like an ember until it resembled a cherry-red silkworm hovering in mid air. Slowly the light intensified, eventually glowing just enough for Nalia to make out the grisly details of the empty room. The blood-soaked table was jet black in the faint luminescence. Nalia watched it turn red as the light burned brighter. Soon, the room was fully alight with the glow from the single bulb. The intensity continued to grow until the details of the room washed out, surrendering to the blinding radiance. Nalia was forced to shield her eyes as the brilliant, white light consumed the world around her. She wondered if it would be like this when they locked her in the asylum.

In the stark-white luster, dark shapes began to form, blurred and distorted by the glare. Shadows moved in and out of the glow, like children peeking through a frosted window. Nalia squinted, trying to make them out, but the light was overpowering. She could hear noises and muffled voices but could not discern their words.

In the pit of her stomach, a sickening feeling grew and Nalia's numb body slowly began to take on a feeling of tangibility. Warmth radiated outward from her gut as her spirit settled into the vision. Nalia's stomach churned with trepidation when the light began to fade.

As the brightness dimmed, the images before her became clear, and Nalia could see distinct movement. There were people working diligently, like surgeons over an operating table. As the voices became less garbled, Nalia could make out conversation.

"Slowly Vivian, careful wit' dat wrap. It's gon' try and pull a little. You gots to be ready," echoed the muffled voice of Mama Lu.

Nalia could see the shadows of three figures working feverishly over what looked like a pile of dirty rags. Carefully, they pulled long strips of cloth from the bundle. The distorted image resembled a large spider, spinning and binding its catch.

As the figures came into focus, Nalia identified Mama Lu, Vivian, and Mr. John removing large strips of slimy, wet gauze from a miniature mummified form. The earthy stench of mildew hung thick in the stagnant air.

"Careful now, John," said Mama Lu, "You down to the tissue."

Nalia felt the urge to vomit. She took deep breaths through her nose, expelling them quickly through her mouth in an attempt to assuage the nausea. As the queasiness subsided, Nalia could not help looking back at the body. It drew her eyes the way roadside carnage draws the attention of passing motorists after a collision.

"Lift her gently," said Mama Lu, "While I unwrap the face."

Nalia watched as roll after roll of gauze was removed from what was left of her mother's head. The flesh underneath retained a reddish hue, like that of a newborn baby, but it was wrinkled and withered like an aged woman.

"There you are," said Mama Lu, looking into Margaret's glass-like eyes. "I hope you enjoyed yo' time wit' the earth. Lots o' critters down there dat likes to gnaw at yo' flesh, ain't they? I told you once, you was gon' wish you'd died and gon' to hell, didn't I? Dat's 'cause hell ain't got nothin' on Mama Lu."

While Mr. John collected the wrappings and stuffed them in a large trash bag, Vivian helped Mama Lu prepare the powder. Finely ground porcelain, the consistency of dust, was held in a large, ceramic jar on the table near the body. At Mama Lu's instruction, Vivian shook the jar vigorously, agitating the powder. She then opened the lid and handed the jar to Mama Lu along with a wide, cosmetic brush.

Mama Lu studied Margaret's face, observing it from all sides. She looked at the color and surface variations. Holding the jar against Margaret's cheek, she asked Vivian for the dye and the beads, then continued her study of the face. Coming to a final conclusion, Mama Lu opened the bottle of dye and drew its dark liquid into the dropper. She held it over the jar and squeezed until one delicate drop slipped from the tip and landed in the powder with a tiny puff.

Mama Lu then took a small aspirin bottle from Vivian. She shook it in a circular manner, listening to its contents rattle like a desert snake. Popping its lid, she poured the contents of copper-plated, buckshot beads into the jar and secured the top. Grasping the jar tightly between her palms, Mama Lu agitated the powder, allowing the dye to darken its color while the beads prevented clumping and caking. It was important for the texture to be as perfect as the color. If the powder was not just right it could ruin the finish.

After several minutes of loud, vigorous shaking, Mama Lu opened the jar and examined the color by pinching a small amount of powder between her thumb and index finger and rubbing gently until it smoothed into a fine coat. "Perfect," she said, holding her fingers up to the withered body of Nalia's mother.

Reaching for an alcohol swab, Mama Lu cleaned the powder from her fingers thoroughly. "Can't leave it on too long," she said to Margaret, coldly. "Burns like hellfire after a while." She looked at Vivian with a knowing smirk. Vivian returned the acknowledgement with her own sly grin as they both donned a pair of surgical gloves.

In the ancient tradition, the shrunken body was simply treated with oils and spices for preservation, but Mama Lu had developed a better method. By using layers of porcelain powder cured with UV-lighting, Mama Lu was able to preserve the body for much longer and even slow down the aging process of the tissue, keeping the "dolls" looking young for very long periods of time.

The process of replication was tedious. It would take Mama Lu nearly nine hours to cover the body with the powder, layer after layer, until it resembled one of her porcelain dolls. When the process was complete, special precautions would be taken to protect Margaret's eyes and hair before a quick round in the kiln formed the final seal. A dusting of paint, with Mama Lu's impeccable attention to detail, would ensure the doll's perfection. It would then be dressed and accessorized to mirror Margaret Barronne's living image. It would become the beautiful and macabre likeness of the woman who lay imprisoned underneath in her very own private hell.

Nalia watched as the women and Mr. John worked on the body. She endured the process for a long time while the withered and shrunken remains of her mother were transformed into a beautiful work of art. Mama Lu took great care in covering up every unpleasant detail, erasing as much of Margaret Barronne as she could. Nalia's memory needed to be purged of the wickedness that once dominated her life, leaving beauty and love to steer its new path.

When the process was complete, Mama Lu made sure to replicate the tear in Margaret's eye – a symbol of the compassion that would have saved both her and Nalia from their respective fates, if she had ever possessed it. Mama Lu clothed the doll in a finely tailored red dress and a red velvet hat with white lace. She adorned her ears and hands with gold jewelry similar to the treasures that captivated Margaret to her demise. Around the doll's neck, Mama Lu hung a tiny, heart-shaped locket containing a small picture of Nalia. She felt it was a fitting substitute for the wide, diamond necklace which no longer rested there. The necklace had been removed and sold for a healthy amount, which Mama Lu put into a savings account for Nalia's education.

As the scene before her faded once again into a blinding white void, Nalia felt nothing but cold indifference. Soon, she found herself back in her bedroom. She was growing accustomed to the changes of scenery as she traveled in and out of the visions, and wondered how all this insanity came to feel so normal. The room was bright, lit by the overhead light and the morning sun shining through the window where Benjamin was noticeably absent. It took only seconds for Nalia to realize all of her dolls were missing. The hutch was gone, and in its place was a small table with a sewing machine. Nalia noticed the bed on which she sat was different as well – a small metal-frame toddler's bed, well worn with scratches and dents. It was the type of used children's furniture often found at garage sales. The rest of Nalia's furniture was gone, too. Her large dresser was replaced by a small chest of drawers, and the vanity was missing altogether. Everything about the room was different, like it was not hers at all.

Rising from the small bed, Nalia walked to the open doorway. Her heart sank when she saw fresh paint on the door frame and the markings that tracked her height over the years were gone. She noticed the house even smelled different, more like the workroom at the shop.

From behind, Nalia heard footsteps and turned to see Mama Lu ascending the staircase carrying the transfigured body of Margaret Barronne. It looked just like a freshly-fired china doll, dressed up and ready for sale. The doll was impeccably made and lavishly dressed, a perfect likeness of Nalia's mother before the split. As Mama Lu passed through the hallway, Nalia noticed the humanness captured in the doll's eyes – the tiny piece of Margaret's soul peering out of its prison. The nausea returned, and Nalia had the sudden urge to walk across the hallway to the bathroom. She leaned against the door frame, taking deep breaths until the sick feeling subsided.

From the bedroom, Nalia could hear Mama Lu talking to the doll. She looked around the door to find her placing the doll on top of the small chest of drawers opposite the tiny bed.

"Welcome to yo' new home," Mama Lu said, straightening the doll's dress and smoothing her hair. "Dis where you gon' stay from now on. Dis gon' be Nalia's room now. She comin' home from the hospital today, to her *new* home. A home where she ain't got to worry 'bout no one harmin' her. You gon' have a front row seat. You see, all dem years you spent turnin' yo' back on what was goin' on, gon' be made up fo', right here. All dem years you refused to watch over yo' lil' girl done come back to haunt you. It's time you paid the price fo' yo' neglect. Mama Lu gon' make sure you witness everything now."

Nalia saw tears begin to well up in the great Mambo's eyes. The vengeful fire that consumed them during the ritual seemed to be fading, replaced by pain and pity.

"All dat money you had," Mama Lu continued quietly, "All the many things you coulda gave to dat chil', all dat opportunity fo' a good life, wasted. Wha's really sad is, not one of yo' possessions mattered one lil' bit to her. All dat chil' ever needed from you was love and attention, and you couldn't even manage dat."

Mama Lu stopped as if having difficulty breathing. She placed her hands, palms down, on the chest of drawers and stared at the floor. She took several deep breaths, trying to regain her composure. Nalia could see she was struggling to fend off the tears. Finally, with a deep breath and a renewed resolve, Mama Lu straightened herself and looked into the doll's eyes once again.

"Now you gon' stand here and watch," she said. "You gon' watch while somebody else gives yo' lil' girl the love and attention she deserves. I may not know nothin' 'bout raisin' no chil', but I'll figure dat out along the way. I know the main thing, and dat's how to love somebody and treat dem wit' the respect they deserve, even if they is only a chil'. I'm gon' do everything I can to make sure dat baby grows up knowin' dat she's loved. She gon' get treated like the precious lil' angel she is, and you gon' watch it all from right here."

Mama Lu took another deep breath and steeled herself before turning to leave the room. Just before she reached the doorway, she looked back at the doll, reached into the pocket of her dress and pulled out a glowing, teardrop-shaped, glass jar sealed with hardened, blood-stained wax. Mama Lu stared at the jar, examining its swirling, smoky content. The soul seemed to glow brighter in the presence of its former body. Looking back at the doll, Mama Lu spoke with rejuvenated animosity.

"You told me befo' to call you Mary," she said. "Well, dat's what yo' lil' girl gon' call you from now on. You don't deserve to be called momma no mo'. You never did."

With that, she pocketed the jar and headed for the stairs. Despite Mama Lu's callous outer appearance, Nalia saw her wipe a tear from her eye as she passed.

Curious, Nalia followed Mama Lu down the stairs and into the hallway just off the kitchen. The house was empty and quiet, yet Mama Lu walked softly, as if conducting her affairs in secret. Nalia followed her down the corridor where she stopped just short of the front door, outside the entry hall closet.

Nalia wondered where she was going. She watched as Mama Lu stepped into the closet and closed the door behind her. Confused and intrigued by the odd behavior, Nalia followed. She leaned close to the folding doors and allowed her astral body to pierce the surface. Although the sensation was strange, she walked freely through the closed doors and the hanging clothes. Nalia was surprised to see the back wall of the closet opened up like a doorway and Mama Lu standing in a hidden room on the other side. The room was small and dark, but soon candles sparked to life, revealing an altar on a large desk with many small drawers. Above the altar hung a large painting of a woman Nalia recognized as Marie Laveau. She was depicted wearing a blue dress and large hoop earrings, just like Queen Marie. The walls around the painting were covered with small drawings and runes, reminding Nalia of the shop's upper room. On the desk beside the candles were several ritual tools. One in particular caught Nalia's eye – a double edged knife similar to the one Mama Lu used to perform the split.

Mama Lu stood before the altar and removed the small, glass jar from the pocket of her dress. After observing the contents of the teardrop container one last time, she opened the top, right-hand drawer of the desk and placed the jar inside. The fact that the jar seemed to fit just right into the unusually small drawer gave Nalia cause to question if the desk had been crafted specifically for this purpose. She wondered how many other souls were imprisoned here inside Mama Lu's altar.

As Mama Lu closed the drawer, the flames of the altar candles flickered and died, leaving Nalia once again in the familiar shroud of darkness.

"Creepy, ain't it?"

Before Nalia's vision returned she could hear the shrill voice of Madame Vivian Luciénne. A cold hand touched her leg, and Nalia was

254

startled back to lucidity. She jerked away quickly as her vision slowly cleared. She found herself back in the familiar surroundings of her room, sitting on her four-poster bed, with Madame Luciénne perched uncomfortably close. The clock on the bedside table still read 12:01.

Nalia's attention immediately shifted to the doll atop the dresser as Madame Luciénne forced a wicked chuckle.

"Yeah, yo' Mama Lu was a real nasty piece of work back then," she gloated. "She calmed down as the years went on. You know, after you came to live wit' her. She all but gave up her practice after a while – turned it over to me." A toothy grin crept across Madame Luciénne's face as she slid even closer to Nalia.

Nalia did not notice. Her eyes were still fixed on Mary.

"How many has she split?" she asked in a bashful whisper.

Attenuating to Nalia's fixation, Madame Luciénne turned to look at the doll.

"Hard to say, really." she replied. "But I've heard that upper room saw plenty of action long before I ever knew about it, and I would bet there's at least a dozen souls hidden away in yo' Mama Lu's secret closet."

Nalia cringed at the word "souls". It was hard to imagine a desk full of human immortality tucked away in a room downstairs.

"I will give yo' Mama Lu credit fo' one thing," Madame Luciénne went on, "She never split nobody that didn't deserve it. At least as far as I know, she didn't."

Nalia finally broke her gaze with Mary and stared at Madame Luciénne with wild confusion. She could make no argument that Margaret Barronne had not earned the hell in which she currently existed, but she wondered what action would cause someone to *deserve* being split. Did someone have to commit a heinous, unforgivable act against an innocent party, or did they simply have to cut the wrong person off in traffic? Where was the line? Who made the rules?

"What I mean by that is," continued Madame Luciénne, as if reading her mind, "She always knew who she was splittin' and why, or so I'm told. She never split nobody fo' money, like I've heard they do in the old world. As for how she determined who got split, I can't tell you. That's always up to the doll maker."

"In the vision, I saw her teaching you," said Nalia, her lips pursed in suspicion. "How many have you split?"

Madame Luciénne paused and pondered the question. She consciously tried to keep her expression from revealing her dilemma. Normally, in a situation such as this, she could use deception to her advantage by instilling fear in the mind of her client. However, there was a greater manipulation at stake, for which she needed to gain Nalia's trust.

"I never split nobody," she finally answered, truthfully. "In fact, I only witnessed one other split beside yo' mother's. Well, two others depending on how you look at it."

"What do you mean?" asked Nalia.

"Well, yo' Mama Lu underestimated the Verelli brothers when she thought they wouldn't come lookin' for you," said Madame Luciénne, eager to disclose more juicy tidbits of Mama Lu's nefarious past. "Turns out they did, or at least they tried. Mr. John caught wind of it before they got the chance."

Madame Luciénne sat up straight and smirked as if sharing gossip in a beauty parlor. "You got to understand something about Mr. John," she went on. "He's content to let everyone believe how simple-minded he is. Truth be known, the man's a genius, and he knows everybody from here to Baton Rouge. He'd never tell you, but the man's got a network of intelligence that covers the whole city of New Orleans and then some."

Nalia was intrigued. She always suspected that Mr. John and his clientele were up to more than just simple shoe-shine chit-chat.

"Now, after things went south wit' yo' father," Madame Luciénne continued, "The Verelli's went on a killin' spree – cleanin' house, so to speak. They was offin' everybody they thought was connected. Turns out their chauffer was one of the talkers who got whacked, so when they picked up a new driver, he jus' happened to be in Mr. John's circle. That's how Mr. John found out they was plannin' on goin' after you, Mama Lu, and him too, if they had to. Well, between the chauffer, the cook, the fella who kept the grounds, and God knows who else Mr.

John had involved, the right gris-gris got slipped in the right place at the right time. Those big, bad Verelli brothers got themselves delivered, curbside, to *The Doll Maker* in the trunk of their own car. That's when yo' Mama Lu got the idea she could split them boys together."

Madame Luciénne's voice became softer, and her expression changed from passion to ponderance. "We chained 'em up on that table side-by-side, head to toe. Mama Lu tried to do the ritual for both of 'em at the same time. It worked for one, but the second one didn't take."

Madame Luciénne swallowed hard as she called to mind images that were forever burned into her memory. "When he saw the first one split, that other boy started thrashin' around like some kind of animal. He nearly got free, too, only his soul was already splittin'. Mr. John had to stop the drum and lay on top to hold him down." Madame Luciénne stared at the floor as she recalled the memory of blood covered bodies, lashing about in a violent struggle for freedom and control. "From what yo' Mama Lu says, by the time a person's soul splits, they done lost so much blood they never feel it slip away. But dis guy was strong, and he fought it tooth and nail. In the end, instead of splittin' like it was s'posed to, his soul more like… ripped into pieces. We never did figure out if more of it left or stayed behind. I know one thing for sure, though – he felt every second of it. I'll never forget the sound of that man screamin'."

Madame Luciénne became silent in her reflection. When she finally realized she had stopped speaking, she silently applauded herself for unintentionally creating such a dramatic pause.

"Anyway, I'm pretty sure yo' Mama Lu didn't do no more splits after that," Madame Luciénne continued. "She says she keeps the twins in her workshop to remind her of what can happen when a ritual goes wrong." *Sort of like tonight*, she thought.

Nalia sat quietly, staring at Mary and thinking of the twins – the two, well-dressed, Italian-looking dolls on the upper shelf in Mama Lu's workroom. The image of the one brother's grotesque and disfigured face was haunting. It was hard for Nalia to believe Mama Lu kept this underworld of dark dealings hidden under her nose for so many years.

Though she could see the convincing evidence in Mary's eyes and in Madame Luciénne's expression, Nalia still questioned the validity of the story. She had to.

"How am I supposed to just accept that all this is true?" she asked. "Who's to say this isn't just some elaborate lie to get me to go along with you?"

Madame Luciénne was offended. She did not like being questioned when she was manipulating the truth, let alone when she was upholding it.

"First of all," she responded with a sneer, "You need to realize I didn't have to tell you the truth about yo' father's money. I could have just led you along, letting you believe I was gon' help you recover some lost family fortune worth millions. Secondly, if I hadn't shown you any of dis, you'd still be just as confused and in the dark as you've always been. Given that, I believe I'm owed a bit more respect." Madame Luciénne stood swiftly and elevated her chin in a confident pose. "Now I've made it no secret I can use yo' help, and I'm willing to help you in return. There's still a bundle of money to be made if you cooperate and help me convince yo' Mama Lu to turn over her power to me at my ritual. But, if you need some kind of proof to believe what I'm telling you is real, then just go downstairs and take a look beyond that closet in the hall and see what you find. I'd be willing to bet that little glass jar is still right there in the same drawer where it's always been."

Madame Luciénne turned and walked to the door. Before exiting, she gripped the glass doorknob and swung around to Nalia. "The choice is yours, sweetheart," she said, with thick sarcasm and a dismissive stare. "I'm gon' have my way wit' or wit'out you. So come along, or sit and rot!" she finished, giving a cursory nod to Mary. With a dramatic spin, Madame Luciénne departed, slamming the door behind her.

The noise jarred Nalia to her senses, and she awakened sitting straight up in a cold sweat. Frightened, she looked around the darkened room. There was no sound and no movement, only the macabre figure of Mary staring back at her from the dresser. The clock read 12:02.

CHAPTER TWENTY-EIGHT

The darkened room was suddenly alight with a fiery glow as Nalia heard the distant *whoof* of Mr. John's bonfire roaring to life. The firelight bounced along the walls of the bedroom, sending eerie shadows dancing like a demented ballet. As the shadows leapt around her, Nalia sat fixated on Mary. The doll was watching her; it had always been watching her, its glassy eyes taking in every moment of her turbulent life.

Nalia's mind filled with images from her childhood, cherished times spent with Mama Lu in this very room. She remembered tea parties, bedtime stories, and dress-up. Nalia was sickened by the realization that the memories she so fondly treasured were really a twisted form of torture. She felt like a puppet, dangling on a string for the watchful eyes of her mother, a tormented soul imprisoned in a body which could not die. Her mother was still in there somewhere, behind those eyes.

Or was she? Nalia could not dismiss the notion this could all be an elaborate lie, orchestrated by Madame Luciénne for the purpose of turning her against Mama Lu – not that she needed a great deal of persuasion, at present. Still, was it not possible Madame Luciénne constructed the vision from her own imagination?

Nalia tried to set her mind right by analyzing the motive. She knew Madame Luciénne needed Mama Lu to relinquish power, whether real or imaginary, in front of a crowd. If Nalia were to side with Madame Luciénne, it would be much easier to convince Mama Lu to cooperate. If she did not, Madame Luciénne would have to get forceful.

Maybe that was it, Nalia thought. Perhaps Madame Luciénne was bluffing and did not really have the means of successfully coercing Mama Lu, as she claimed. Maybe she needed Nalia's cooperation more than she let on. Either way, Nalia could not think of a reason for Madame Luciénne to fabricate such a ridiculous story, unless there was a grand satisfaction for her in the successful execution of such a twisted mind game.

"Why bother debating?" Nalia thought, "Just go downstairs and see for yourself." A thick lump gathered in her throat as she entertained the thought of unearthing the truth, while she stared into the eyes of the doll possibly containing a piece of her mother's split soul.

Nalia knew the truth. She had stared into the life-like eyes of the doll too many times to deny it. She realized now why the doll appeared older than it had in her childhood. All the evidence added up, and two plus two was never three. Still, she needed to see proof for herself. Nalia's thirst for the truth would not be quenched until the voice in her head was silenced.

"Go downstairs and take a look," she heard the voice say in Madame Luciénne's taunting tone. She had to go.

Just as she made up her mind, Nalia's attention was pulled away from her task by the rhythmic beating of a drum in the distance. The sound made her skin crawl. Visions of the ritual flashed through her head like lightning as the thundering cadence grew strong and steady. She rose from her bed and walked to the window. The glow of the fire was intense. Staring across the street, Nalia could see the blaze topping the fence, just beyond Mr. John's workshop. She picked up Benjamin from the windowsill and instinctively held him tight as she studied the figures around the fire. She felt the sudden, and strange sensation she was intruding. Although the ritual was clearly visible to anyone in the general vicinity peering out of an upstairs window, Nalia could not help but feel she was witnessing something that was supposed to be secret and sacred. She saw Madame Toulouse in her ceremonial robes with her hands raised to the sky and watched as Mama Lu held the snake aloft, twirling in her ritualistic dance. Though Mr. John's body was blocked by the fence line, Nalia could see his head bobbing up and down. She recognized the unmistakable motions of his neck and shoulders as he beat out his tribal rhythm on the drum.

Nalia wondered what the ritual's purpose could be. She witnessed a number of ceremonies over the years, mostly on holidays and especially on the Day of the Dead. She knew each ritual had a meaning and a specific goal, but she never saw one like this. Nalia wondered if its purpose was to protect their secret.

Regardless of the ritual's intent, the fact it was being conducted across the street meant the house was empty. If Nalia was going to investigate the secrets revealed by Madame Luciénne in the vision, now was the perfect time.

As Nalia turned away from the window, she heard the drumbeat stop and knew she had to hurry. If the ritual was concluded, Mama Lu could be back soon. Avoiding eye contact with Mary, Nalia made her way to the door, depositing Benjamin on the vanity in her haste. By the time she reached the doorway, the ritual across the street had been violently interrupted with Madame Toulouse collapsing into Mr. John's arms.

Nalia raced down the darkened stairs. She did not dare turn on any lights for fear someone across the street would see. She rounded the corner in the blackness and headed for the entry hall. The porch light spilled through the glass in the front door, making the hallway easy to navigate. Nalia pulled open the closet's folding doors, took a deep breath, and stepped inside between the hanging clothes. She closed the doors behind her and reached up for the string attached to the light socket in the ceiling. More visions of the bloody ritual ripped through Nalia's mind as the single light bulb came to life above her head. Her heart raced as she felt along the back wall of the closet. The surface was smooth, but pliable. Unlike a fixed wall, it gave a bit when she pushed. Nalia's body tensed with anxiety when her hands found the two small knobs in the center of the wall. Between them was a small metal latch. Flipping it, Nalia was able to push open the second set of folding doors. Her heart beat with such force she thought it would jump right out of her chest.

As Nalia stepped into the hidden alter room, all hope that Madame Luciénne was lying came crashing down; against the wall before her stood the desk with tiny drawers just like in the vision. For a reason she could not explain, Nalia wanted to cry. The truth materializing before her eyes was too much for her. The nightmares, the visions, the secrets, the lies, her mother – how much was one person expected to take before they went mad? Despite the anxiety, Nalia could not bring herself to stop after coming so far. She had to open the drawers; she had to see it for herself.

The room was small, just big enough for the desk with the altar on top and a small stool. There was no light in the room itself, only what spilled in from the bulb in the closet. It was just enough for Nalia to identify several ritual tools and half-spent candles on top of the desk. The painting of Marie Laveau hanging on the wall above the altar seemed to stare at Nalia through the darkness as she stepped up to the desk. Trying to breathe, Nalia fixed her eyes on the drawer in the upper right corner. If Madame Luciénne was right, Margaret Barronne's soul was still sealed in a glass jar inside.

Nalia had to know, but she could not muster the courage to open the drawer in question. Instead, she placed her hand on a drawer in the center of the desk and talked herself into pulling it open. Slowly, she slid it from its socket and peered inside.

Nothing. The drawer was empty.

Nalia breathed a short-lived sigh of relief as her anxiety swelled again and she moved on to the next drawer, one up and to the right. She slid it open, a little quicker this time, to reveal two vials of dark-colored oil and a tarnished silver rosary with black beads.

Nalia began to breathe easier. Perhaps the story was a farce after all, she thought. She opened another drawer, one over to the right, to reveal a bit of parchment with scribbled writing in a language she did not recognize. Relieved, Nalia tried another, then another, uncovering only ritual items and empty drawers. Either the vision was false or the captured souls were no longer here. Nalia nearly chuckled. How could she buy into such a far-fetched tale? Then again, there were still two drawers left unopened.

The lump returned to her throat as once again Nalia focused her attention to the upper right drawer. She reached out her hand for the tiny handle, but still found herself unable to pull it as scenes from the vision flashed in her mind again. Reluctantly, she moved her hand to the drawer beside it and slowly slid it open. Her heart sank at the sight of the small glass jar inside. Still skeptical, Nalia removed the tiny, round orb and held it to the light. Her mouth dropped open as she realized the jar contained a faint smoky substance that seemed to glow dimly in the darkness. The jar was sealed with blood-red wax all around the stopper, with a large letter V etched into the top.

Nalia was devastated and fascinated all at once. She held the jar close to her face and studied it as the smoky substance began to slowly swirl inside the glass. Was she actually looking at a human soul imprisoned in this round container? Could this be the soul of the first Verelli brother? Nalia shivered at the thought as her eyes shifted to the upper right drawer. It was true, she thought. It was all true, and her mother's separated soul was sealed in the desk before her.

Nalia set the jar down on the altar and tucked her hand under the handle of the upper right drawer. With a quick tug she pulled it from its socket and was briefly blinding by the glowing, white light emanating from the glass jar inside. Just as she feared, it was a teardrop-shaped container, sealed with wax dripping down the side, like the veins of a beating heart. The smoky substance inside gleamed and swirled swiftly, like a gathering storm.

Nalia did not realize she was holding her breath until she heard the pounding of her heart. It echoed in her ears, steadily growing louder and faster. Then she heard a voice, soft as a whisper, calling her name.

"Nalia," it said as the jar grew brighter. The voice was faint, but it echoed inside her head like a shout in a canyon. Gently, Nalia reached inside the drawer and picked up the small jar. When her fingers touched the glass, the smoke inside the sealed container grew more vibrant, as if feeding on her mortality. It spiraled faster, like a tornado, as the voice whispered again.

"Flesh and bone," it echoed in Nalia's mind like a craving. Nalia could not stop staring at the swirling smoke. Images from the vision raced through her mind once again: Mr. John beating the drum, Mama Lu smiling balefully over her mother, the blood of the rooster spilling over the body, the final tear falling down Margaret's cheek.

"Flesh and bone."

The cloudy substance swelled as it coiled into a frenzy. The jar began to shake in Nalia's fingers. She loosened her grip and allowed the jar to dance across the palm of her hand, as if it had a mind of its own. The smoky matter inside wanted free of its prison. Jerkily, the jar moved with a final liberating lurch and jumped from Nalia's hand. She watched, wide-eyed, as the jar fell. Time seemed to stand still as it plummeted toward the floor. Nalia grabbed at the air, trying desperately to recover the glass container, but it was too late. The jar hit the floor hard, and though its wax seal proved strong, the bottom of the tear-shaped glass shattered on the wood floor.

In an instant, the gleaming haze escaped, floating upward just as it had in the vision. It flowed like water toward Nalia's face and turned blood-red, glowing with radiant energy. Nalia was frightened. She did not know what to expect as the glowing, red vapor circled her head like a swarm of angry fireflies. She stood petrified, afraid to move, afraid to breathe.

Finally, the glowing substance gathered like a cloud in front of her face. For a split second, Nalia swore she saw a pair of eyes staring back at her from the haze. As she drew a ragged breath, the smoky light moved swiftly toward her nostrils and entered her body. Nalia had no choice but to inhale as the smoke forced its way violently into her nose. Her lungs began to burn with a new-found intensity, and soon she felt her whole body boiling and shaking like a pressure cooker.

Nalia felt a presence swelling inside her as intense stinging struck her abdomen. She doubled over in agony as a wave of sharp, knife-like pains ripped through her body. She felt as though someone was trying to tear her organs out through her flesh.

Nalia sensed a separate consciousness taking control of her mind, blanketing it with anger and despair. She felt as though her head was going to explode. She heard her mouth make a noise that was not hers – the distinctive cackle of Margaret Barronne. An intense, burning sensation shot straight up Nalia's spine like wildfire and settled at the base of her skull. As her eyes rolled deep into her head, Nalia's soul slipped away, displaced to the spirit world.

––––––––––

When Mama Lu heard the name "Luciénne", she knew immediately what Madame Toulouse meant. She remembered Madame Toulouse exclaiming, "There's somethin' here. Somethin' from the outside." Mama Lu knew Luciénne was in the dream. She did not know how, but she was sure Luciénne had managed to break their bond and step into the vision.

Instructing Mr. John to look after their elder, Mama Lu raced out of the kitchen door, through the workshop and across the street. Nalia's window was still dark. With any luck, thought Mama Lu, she could get there before any damage was done, before any secrets were revealed, before any harm befell her daughter.

She sprinted up the walk as fast as her aging legs would allow and scrambled across the back porch. Nearly tearing the screen from its hinges, Mama Lu ran through the kitchen and up the stairs to Nalia's bedroom. The hallway was quiet, but Nalia's door was cracked open. Fearing the worst, Mama Lu pushed open the door and turned on the light.

The scene inside was devastating. Nalia's bed was empty except for a daunting display of ripped pillows and broken dolls. The hutch was shattered and its figurines emptied onto the floor where they lay in pieces amid a war zone of broken wood and glass. The burlap poppets that once sat on top were torn open and their sawdust innards strewn about the room. The high shelves lining the walls were ripped down, their display of dolls cracked into heaps of porcelain shards and torn fabric.

Benjamin, the wooden puppet, lay on top of the vanity, snapped in two amongst fragments of broken mirror. At the foot of Nalia's bed, Myra, the likeness of Nalia, lay cut open down the middle with her insides turned out and her porcelain pieces scattered and broken.

The only doll in the room that seemed to have been spared from ruin was Queen Marie. She was proudly displayed in the center of Nalia's bed, face down, with a long hat pin jutting from her neck.

Mama Lu was nearly too weak to stand. She braced herself against the door frame, gasping for air as if she had found her child lying dead on the floor. Anguish pained her heart as her hand slid down the markings that reflected Nalia's life, and she began to weep uncontrollably. So many years spent loving and nurturing a broken child into a healthy young woman, only to have the effort backfire in a violent act of rebellion. Mama Lu held her chest as she questioned every decision she had made since taking Nalia away from Michael and Margaret Barronne.

Still gasping and barely able to walk, Mama Lu stepped into the room and managed her way to the bed. She picked up Queen Marie, removed the vile pin, and threw it onto the floor. "Luciénne," she said, turning the doll over, "What have you done?"

As she turned to leave the room, Mama Lu cast her tear-filled eyes toward the dresser, searching for the root of her daughter's torment, but Mary was missing. She looked around the room, but found no trace of the doll. Wherever Nalia was, Mary was with her.

Still sobbing, Mama Lu walked into the hallway calling out for Nalia. She was almost scared to hear a response, but even more afraid not to. To her disappointment, silence filled the house. Mama Lu never felt so helpless. Her heart ached for her daughter and for the pain Nalia must be feeling. Who knew what kind of images, whether real or imaginary, were planted in her mind by Madame Luciénne? How deeply would she be cut by the truth?

Mama Lu managed to make it down the steps, out of breath and overcome with sorrow. She continued to call Nalia's name but was answered only by the echo of the empty house. Mama Lu stumbled through the kitchen and was approaching the parlor when she felt a draft wafting down the hallway. The front door was ajar, revealing the moon-bathed front lawn. As she made her way to the entry hall, Mama Lu found the shocking sight of the closet's open doors. The hanging clothes were pushed aside and the doorway to her altar room was open wide. In a panic, Mama Lu stepped inside to find the drawers of her desk opened, their contents exposed. Worst of all, the upper right compartment was pulled completely from its socket and was lying on top of the altar where her ritual knife should be. Mama Lu dropped to her knees among broken pieces of the teardrop-shaped jar, weeping bitterly for the sins of her past.

CHAPTER TWENTY-NINE

Under the still, dark sky of the witching hour, the black column on the left side of Madame Vivian Luciénne's wide porch was nearly invisible. The result was an optical illusion of the overhanging structure supported solely by the white column on the right – an unsettling, asymmetrical scene. The high-fenced yard was drenched in the bluish glow of the full moon as Margaret Barronne, occupying the body of her daughter, approached the ivy-covered house.

Fourteen years had passed since Margaret's soul became disembodied – fourteen long, grueling years. Every moment was spent in agony, trapped in a withered, shrunken form that was once young and vibrant; each minute, she stared at the same walls of the same room. She watched, taunted and tormented, as that evil sorceress raised her daughter for fourteen excruciating years.

Margaret liked her new body. It was young and athletic, even better than the one before. It came with its fair share of aches and pains from the trauma she watched it endure over the past several days, but it was fit and would recover in time. Having admired her new body in the mirror of the vanity, while helping herself to Nalia's clothes, she was satisfied with everything but the eyes. Nalia's eyes were always a beautiful caramel brown, crystal clear and perfect. That changed when Margaret's twisted soul took over; the irises swirled into a clouded, smoky haze – the reflection of a soul not quite complete. It was this hazy imperfection that earned the mirror its shattered fate.

Margaret was fascinated by the separation of consciousness from the body. While she still retained her prior knowledge and memories, Nalia's body had memories of its own. It remembered pain, it remembered the nightmares, and most importantly for now, it remembered where to find Madame Vivian Luciénne. As she walked across the dew-soaked lawn, Margaret breathed deeply, filling her lungs with the warm, damp air. It felt good to breathe again. Air meant life, and life meant purpose. Margaret's purpose was well defined by fourteen long years of loathing. Under the cover of darkness, she stepped onto the cave-like porch.

Inside the house, Madame Luciénne draped her black, silk robe back over her shoulders as she listened to the chimes echo through the hallway. Who on earth could be ringing her bell at this hour? She expected a visit from Mama Lu if her plan was discovered, but surely Nalia had not turned on her so quickly. She kicked a line through the ring of salt on the floor to break the circle and made her way to the door in the candlelight.

With the door cracked wide enough for the chain to catch, Madame Luciénne peered into the darkness. She was surprised to see the shadowy figure of Nalia, wearing jeans and a silk shirt, with a large doll tucked under her arm. Recognizing the doll immediately, Madame Luciénne knew the vision had been fruitful.

"So now you know the truth," she said.

Margaret nodded.

Madame Luciénne smiled with sinister satisfaction as she closed the door and released the chain. When she opened it again, Margaret violently forced her way inside and kicked the door shut behind her. With all the rage of fourteen years, she slammed Madame Luciénne against the wall, shoving the doll into her face.

"Remember me?" she asked, pinning the doll tightly against Madame Luciénne's turned cheek.

Madame Luciénne was terrified. It took a moment for the reality of the situation to unfold in her mind. Though the woman before her looked like Nalia, one glance into the swirling smoky eyes told her she was dealing with something bizarre and unnatural. If Nalia had explored the hidden room as advised, it was likely the soul had been discovered. However, this new development was entirely unexpected.

"Margaret?" grunted Madame Luciénne, barely able to speak. Her head was pinned hard against the wall by the force Margaret was exerting on the doll. Realizing what had transpired, Madame Luciénne released a demented chuckle as she stared, from the corner of her eye, into the churning, smoky haze of Margaret's soul. Her twisted amusement was short-lived as she felt the force of the doll lessen, only to be replaced by the cold sensation of a steel blade against her neck.

268

Margaret held the stolen ritual knife firmly to Madame Luciénne's pulsing veins as she leaned in close, sizing her up.

"The years have been kind to you, Vivian," she said, watching the veins throb as Madame Luciénne's sweat began to drip down the blade. She could feel her victim's body shaking against hers. "Your skin has retained its youthful glow, unlike mine that still rots away underneath the porcelain shell you helped provide."

Margaret threw the doll onto the floor and pushed the knife upward, forcing the elevation of Madame Luciénne's chin. Grabbing her by the throat, Margaret pressed hard, restricting the woman's airway and causing her to gasp for oxygen. Slowly, Margaret trailed the blade down her captive's neck to the collarbone where she jabbed the point in just enough to pierce the skin. As Madame Luciénne winced and struggled for air, Margaret leaned in closer, until their faces nearly touched. She could smell the fear rising from Madame Luciénne's sweating body.

A thin line of blood began to trickle slowly from the puncture wound. It ran down Madame Luciénne's collarbone, over her heaving bosom, and dipped into the V of her black, silk robe. Margaret's mouth hung open in anticipation as she watched the blood run and followed it with the point of the blade. Using the knife to push aside the flaps of the ceremonial garment, Margaret exposed Madame Luciénne's chest to the sharp edge. She drew an excited breath as she placed the point of the knife over her prey's pounding heart and gripped the handle forcefully. She twisted it slightly, reminding Madame Luciénne how easily the blade could penetrate her flesh.

"Tell me, Vivian," she said in a taunting timbre, "Tell me why I shouldn't cut out your beating heart where you stand." She could feel Madame Luciénne's neck swell under her grip as she swallowed hard, still fighting for air. Luciénne's struggle to live excited Margaret even more. She tightened her grip, pressing the trembling woman's neck harder against the wall until her airway was completely closed.

"Do you know how it feels to suffocate?" she asked, mere millimeters from Madame Luciénne's terrified face. "Ever been held underwater until your lungs burned, feeling the need to breathe but unable to open your mouth for fear you'd drown? Ever feel your lungs screaming out for air until you panic because you know even if you try, you can't give it to them?"

Madame Luciénne's eyes began to bulge, and her face turned red as Margaret pushed the blade in a little harder. Panic raced between her throat and her heart.

"That's how it feels to be split!" said Margaret. "That's how it feels when the tissue of your body is still somehow clinging to life, but there's no air to fill your lungs. That's how it feels day after day, night after night, year after tortured year – a constant state of suffocation! Like being buried alive and unable to die!"

Madame Luciénne became weak. Her lungs began to burn as her mouth made the gasping motions of a beached fish.

"Oh, don't worry," whispered Margaret, her lips brushing against Madame Luciénne's cheek, "I'm going to let you live." Just as Madame Luciénne's eyes began to roll back into her head, Margaret released her grip.

Madame Luciénne slid down the wall breathing as deeply as she could. As she collapsed, Margaret retracted the blade from her chest. With one fluid motion, she swung the blade upward catching Madame Luciénne's chin on the way and slicing it to the bone.

"I didn't say you'd be unharmed," she chuckled, "I said you'd live."

Luciénne continued to fill her lungs with generous breaths as she clasped a hand to her bleeding chin and held it tightly. As she watched Margaret turn toward the parlor, Madame Luciénne was overcome with rage, looking around for any object heavy enough to wield and strike down her adversary.

"Don't even think about it," said Margaret, calmly, "I can still see through those eyes." It was only then Madame Luciénne noticed the doll lying on the floor, staring up at her. "Get up," Margaret continued. "Bring the doll. We've got business to discuss."

_____

The throbbing sore on the back of Madame Toulouse's neck was shrinking. Her temperature began to drop as soon as Mama Lu removed the hat pin from Queen Marie. She was lucid, and her strength was returning. She sat on the small sofa, sipping cool water and trying to comfort Mama Lu, who was still weeping hysterically. She knew what happened to Nalia; her inner sight was crystal clear and she could already feel Nalia's presence in the spirit world.

Though Mama Lu's sight was clouded by her overwhelming grief, she knew it too. However, she was not ready to admit or accept it. In her mind, it was not possible for Nalia to be gone.

Mr. John had tried to embrace Mama Lu, if for no other reason than to keep her from pacing, but she would not allow it. He sat across the room with his head in his hands, trying to make sense of the world around them. On the table before him were broken shards of the teardrop-shaped bottle. He stared at the shattered pieces as he attempted to wrap his mind around what happened.

Madame Toulouse explained the unusual phenomenon that took place when the jar broke. She told them when a split soul with that much vengeance contacts its own flesh and bone, it can overpower the resident spirit and take over the body, leaving the other soul displaced, just as in death. Madame Toulouse hated to be the bearer of the news of Nalia's death. Even worse, she hated trying to explain how her spirit passed on to the next world while her body remained alive in this one. But passed on it had, and the news was not easy for any of them to accept, least of all Mama Lu. She had not stopped crying since she returned to Mr. John's with the shards of broken glass and Nalia's oversized tee-shirt, now soaked with tears.

Mama Lu paced back and forth across the room with the anxiety of a high-strung drug addict. Her heart raced out of control and her breathing was short and quick. She seemed unable to sit down or be still. Her steady stream of tears was rivaled only by her constant chattering.

"She ain't gone. She can't be gone," she insisted over and over. "We can bring her back. Her body is still here, we can fix dis. I can fix dis." On and on she muttered the same phrases, drowning herself in denial.

"Lucia, I want her back jus' as much as you do," said Madame Toulouse in a comforting tone. "But you know ain't nothin' we can do gon' bring her back. Her spirit done crossed over to the other side, Lu. I can feel her there, and I know you can too." Her voice shook as tears welled up in her eyes. "She's gone, Lu."

"No!" cried Mama Lu, collapsing onto the floor and wringing Nalia's tee-shirt around her hands. "She was just here. She had come so far. She was so young. My baby!"

Her sobbing continued for a long time, while Mr. John and Madame Toulouse sat silently fighting back tears of their own. Mr. John was eventually able to sit down on the floor beside Mama Lu and place his arm around her shoulder. Mr. John was always strong in a crisis. Though his heart was breaking, he needed to be there for Mama Lu. There would be time to fall apart later, in his own time and in his own way. For now, he would be her rock, and though she would never admit it, she needed that rock more than ever. She laid her head gently on his shoulder and allowed him to hold her close as she rocked back and forth, crying into the tear-soaked tee.

Soon, Mama Lu's denial turned to blame, and Mr. John could feel the tension building in her body. "Luciénne is responsible fo' dis," she said, "Luciénne and Margaret Barronne."

Mr. John could see schemes of vengeance forming in Mama Lu's eyes, a torrent of emotion turning into a diabolical plan.

"They ain't gon' get away wit' dis," said Mama Lu through clenched teeth as she unconsciously began to tear at Nalia's shirt. "They gon' get wha's comin' to 'em. They done had it comin' fo' a long time." Rage was swelling inside her. Mr. John could feel it like heat from a blazing fire. She repeated the same hushed phrases over and over, grinding her teeth harder each time. Her knuckles whitened with tension as she ripped and tore at the fabric, her mind a world away.

Then suddenly, all her muttering came to a halt and Mama Lu was silent and still, except for her cheeks. While her uncontrollable tears continued to flow, she gently pushed Mr. John away and stood up, leaving the tee-shirt on the floor in tattered strips. "I needs to get on home," she said heading for the door with an absent look on her face. "I gots work to do."

"Hold on jus' a minute," said Mr. John rising to follow, "I'll go wit' you. You don't need to be by yo'self."

"No," she replied, "I *gots* to be by myself. I gots to do dis alone."

Madame Toulouse shook her head as Mama Lu headed for home, leaving Mr. John standing alone in the middle of the room.

"It ain't you, John," she assured him. "You know she thinks she got to do everythin' by herself. Thinks she don't need nobody, that she's strong enough on her own. One o' these days she gon' realize no matter how strong we are, we still need each other."

Mr. John fought back tears as he picked up the damp scraps of Nalia's tee-shirt, torn fragments of a life ripped away. He held them between his fingers and felt their soft texture, wishing he had spent more time holding the young lady he would forever call his baby girl. Everything that transpired was built upon the past, he thought. He could not help but entertain the notion his involvement somehow led to this ultimate end.

Mr. John found a nearly square strip of the tattered fabric, folded it neatly like a handkerchief, and tucked it into the pocket of his shirt. There he would keep it, close to his heart.

"Lu's gon' be alright, John," said Madame Toulouse. "She jus' gon' need some time. Right now she's cookin' up some big plan to get back at Luciénne, but when she stops long enough to look at the bigger picture, she gon' realize she's jus' as much to blame. All them splits she done years ago is finally catchin' up to her. When she sees that for what it is, that's when she really gon' need you."

"But she let all dem souls go," replied Mr. John. "When she took Nalia in, she released all dem souls to death so they could be at peace. Only ones she ever held on to was Nalia's momma and dem Verelli boys."

"It ain't 'bout how many she kept and how many she released," Madame Toulouse explained. "It's just like a spinning wheel, everything you do gon' come back around to you. Death is an unforgiving adversary. Lucia toyed with death for far too long, and now death has required a sacrifice."

CHAPTER THIRTY

Nalia's body, possessed by the angry spirit of her scorned mother, sat poised like a queen in the high-backed chair at the end of Madame Luciénne's parlor. The sight made the pretentious charlatan boil with rage as she sat submissively, holding pressure on her chin to stop the bleeding. It infuriated Madame Luciénne to have Margaret sitting before her in a place of power, a makeshift throne designed for *her* to lord over her clientele. To Madame Luciénne, presentation was everything. She liked to keep her patrons in a lower position, gazing up at their obvious superior. She loathed looking up to Margaret Barronne from the smaller chair beside the coffee table. It was even more disturbing to see her restored soul occupying Nalia's body.

Except for the eyes, Nalia's body still looked the same, but its demeanor was altered. The habitation of Margaret's spirit gave Nalia's form a sinister and sleazy appearance. She sat cross-legged in the high-backed chair with the doll, Mary, lying in her lap. Methodically, she toyed with the ritual knife stolen from Mama Lu's altar. She placed the point of the blade on the edge of the doll's left eye and held the knife upright while she fondled the handle.

"Fourteen years I watched my daughter through these eyes," she said, staring hatefully at the glass-like orbs. "Fourteen years I spent imprisoned behind them, looking through them like the tiny windows of a basement cell. Every day, I stared at the same walls of the same room."

She slipped the knife into the soft edge of the eye and drew a quick breath of anticipation as the point nicked the tissue. She savored the moment, closing her eyes and allowing her neck to relax in satisfaction as waves of pleasure coursed through her new, young body. She held the knife's handle with her fingertips and twirled it slowly, allowing the weight of the steel to push the point deeper into the doll's eye. She cackled softly as she looked up at Madame Luciénne over the handle.

"Never again will I look through these wicked little windows," she said with a sneer, plunging the blade into the doll's eye, twisting it viciously and wallowing out the socket. Margaret exhaled deeply as the tension of fourteen years of captivity was released in a single, satisfying explosion of emotion.

Madame Luciénne was frightened. She had dealt with spirits in the past, even witnessed cases of possession during rituals, but this was exponentially different. During certain Voodoo ceremonies, spirits from beyond the grave were apt to share a living body for a time, but Madame Luciénne never heard of one essentially evicting the body's resident soul and moving in. Never in the farthest reaches of her imagination had she foreseen encountering a tortured soul, returned from the spirit world, commandeering the body of someone she knew. She was especially distressed to be hunted down by one with a fourteen year vendetta and a wicked disposition.

Madame Luciénne had all but given up on any real dealings with the spirit world years ago, in favor of the over-dramatized charade that proved so lucrative. Truth be told, the splitting of the Verelli brothers was enough to scare her into abandoning the practice, or at least pursuing a much more benign path than the one taken by Mama Lu.

Madame Luciénne cringed as she watched Margaret reposition the knife over the doll's other eye, jabbing, twisting, and gouging as she released a chilling torrent of depraved laughter.

"Never again!" said Margaret with a genuinely psychotic look in her smoky eyes. "Never again."

Deciding the mutilation was sufficient, Margaret flopped the doll onto the arm of the chair and rested her elbow on it as she twirled the knife over in her hands watching it shimmer in the reflected lamp-light. "Now," she said, "Let's discuss the terms of my abundant generosity that allows you to continue living."

Madame Luciénne swallowed hard. Not wanting her fear to show, she quickly cleared her throat and listened attentively.

"You're still alive for one reason," Margaret went on, "Because I need your help."

Madame Luciénne's ears perked up. She liked it when the playing field was level. She took even greater pleasure when she could gain the upper hand. If there was something Margaret needed from her, perhaps she could work it to her advantage. She allowed a slight grin to break through her apprehension.

"What is it you could possibly need from me?" she asked.

"I need your help in arranging a very special get-together, a ceremony of sorts," said Margaret, heaving the doll onto the floor and sliding to the edge of her seat. She propped her elbows on her knees and flattened the blade against her forearm. "You see," she went on, "Fourteen years is a very long time to think about revenge." Margaret's eyes began to swirl faster as her head listed lazily in solemn reflection of her years of entrapment. "When you're imprisoned, you can go crazy dreaming up schemes to get back at those responsible for putting you there." She lifted the knife, absentmindedly tapping the flat edge of the blade against her skull as she pulled her gaze back to Madame Luciénne's eyes. "But what will really drive you insane is the incessant longing to carry them out." Margaret flipped the knife over in her hand and pointed the blade casually at Madame Luciénne. "Well, I'm not going to waste the chance I've been given," she said tenaciously. "I'm going to do what I've waited fourteen years for, and if you're fond of breathing, you're going to help me. We're going to split Mama Lucia Deminy."

Madame Luciénne's face turned to an ashen scowl. The very thought of Margaret's plan terrified her, but she was adamantly determined not to show weakness. She convinced herself she was in control. If Margaret needed her to perform the split, then she had more bargaining power than previously anticipated.

Margaret could see the scheming wheels of Madame Luciénne's mind begin to turn. She sat back nonchalantly in the chair and ran her fingertip across the razor sharp ritual blade, cutting herself just enough for blood to flow. "Of course, if you're feeling uncooperative," she said, placing the finger to her tongue and savoring the blood, "We can simply end it right here." Her menacing stare never strayed from Madame Luciénne's eyes.

The drama did little to assuage Madame Luciénne's thought process. Theatrics were a tactic with which she was well acquainted, and she knew it meant there was some degree of bluffing involved.

Madame Luciénne's confidence was rising. Convinced Margaret needed her, she was ready to negotiate.

"There ain't nothin' in dis world I would delight in more than splittin' Mama Lu," she said with a bittersweet sense of sarcasm, watching for a reaction. "Only trouble is, I need her alive and well fo' a ritual I'm planning on St. John's Eve. You see, I need her around for wha's called a transference…"

"Transference of power," interrupted Margaret, "Yes, yes, I know all about your stupid ritual and your grand plans. With all the pointless mutterings I've heard, I know a lot more than you could imagine. Mama Lu talks to herself, especially when she's cleaning. She's been so nervous the past few weeks, she must've dusted Nalia's bedroom a hundred times, all the while rambling on and on. God, it's going to be nice when I finally silence that relentless chattering. So yes, I know all about your little plans for St. John's Eve."

Madame Luciénne was caught off guard, but regained her composure quickly and resumed her bargaining posture.

"Well, then you can understand how splittin' Mama Lu would not be in my best interest jus' now."

"Is breathing in your best interest *just now*?" snapped Margaret, leaning forward and stabbing the knife aggressively into the arm of the chair.

Madame Luciénne was alarmed, but she knew she had Margaret in a quandary. If Margaret really aimed to kill her, surely she would have done it already. Madame Luciénne resolved if she could be bold enough, she could play Margaret's bluff to her advantage.

"Do it!" she said, audaciously rising from her small chair.

Startled, Margaret pried out the knife and held it rigidly toward her advancing captive. She was shocked when Madame Luciénne stopped at arms length and pressed her supple neck against the outstretched blade.

"Go ahead and do it," said Madame Luciénne, trembling on the inside but outwardly steady as a rock. "Slit my throat right now and you'll never be able to split Mama Lu on yo' own."

"I'll kill you right here!" said Margaret, rising to her feet and pressing the blade firmly against Madame Luciénne's neck. She drew her body close and her face within inches. "I might not be able to perform a split, but there's nothing keeping me from cutting you up, and doing the same to her."

"Then what?" asked Madame Luciénne with a light chuckle. "What you gon' do after that? Fourteen years of vengeance boiling inside you, and you tell me you gon' end it all with the quick flash of a blade? I don't think so. You'd get no satisfaction from that."

Madame Luciénne felt the pressure of the blade lessen as Margaret allowed her arm to relax. She sensed the tide turning and decided to dive a little deeper. "No, I don't think you want it to end that way at all," she continued with a teasing tone. "You planned dis out all too well; you waited far too long. You want to show that woman jus' as much pain as she showed you all those years. A quick and easy death jus' wouldn't be justice, would it? Hell, it almost sounds merciful." She donned a sly grin of satisfaction as Margaret took a small step backward and dropped the knife to her side. "Then what you gon' do? Fourteen years spent tryin' to cross back through the veil, only to fire all yo' guns at once? With Mama Lu dead, you got nothin'."

Pausing, Madame Luciénne allowed Margaret to consider the possibility of dissatisfaction before proposing an alternative solution. "Keep me around, and I'll do the split after the ritual. That way you get the trophy you've wanted so badly. Then, you can keep Mama Lu captive for as long as you want, watchin' her suffer every day, just like she did to you. Now, that's the kind of revenge worth stickin' around fo'."

Margaret sat back down in the high-backed chair, assuming a defeated and aggravated posture. She craved control, but she knew Luciénne was right. Her bluff was called. She did not make the journey back to the world of the living to compromise her plan. The split must happen, and as much as she loathed the idea, she needed Luciénne to do it.

"St. John's Eve is close," Madame Luciénne went on. "Once we convince Mama Lu to transfer power over to me for everyone to see, then I'll perform the split."

Fourteen years of tortured exile did nothing for Margaret's patience. Waiting for St. John's Eve to enact her revenge on Mama Lu was simply not an option. "There must be another way," she thought. As she stared into the reflection of Nalia's face in the luster of the ritual blade, Margaret's smoky eyes began to swirl with renewed intensity. Her mouth dropped open, and her head tilted as she considered a fresh possibility. She sat up and straightened her back, staring right into Madame Luciénne's eyes.

"What if we didn't need to convince Mama Lu at all?" she asked, as if struck by brilliance.

Madame Luciénne was puzzled. Did Margaret think they could just ask Mama Lu nicely and she would waltz into the ceremony to hand over her power?

"All you need is for people to witness the rite and believe," Margaret explained, standing and slithering toward Madame Luciénne with a scheming smirk. "If Mama Lu were to meet an unfortunate and untimely demise, the power would then naturally transfer to her daughter, right? Isn't that how the traditions of Voodoo are handed down in your culture, mother to daughter, generation to generation?"

Madame Luciénne's familiar, sly smile stretched across her face as she began to understand what Margaret was proposing.

"Mama Lu's beloved daughter, Nalia, would then willfully participate in the transference of power ritual for all to witness," Margaret continued, gesturing toward her new body with the ritual knife. "You help me split Mama Lu tonight, and I'll make sure your St. John's Eve ceremony goes off without a hitch."

Madame Luciénne placed a hand on the hilt of the ritual knife next to Margaret's. They held the blade tightly between them as they shared a sinister smile of agreement.

———————

Mama Lu walked back and forth across the floor of Nalia's bedroom. She rummaged through the wreckage gathering bits of burlap and other cloth, collecting remnants of the poppets that once sat on top of Nalia's hutch in the corner of the room. Each time she found a recognizable scrap, she would place it in the pocket of her dress. The poppets were the most treasured items in the room, not because of their monetary value, which was next to nothing, but because of what they stood for and their function. Each one represented a different ancestor, someone related by blood or by religious practice, who had passed on to the spirit world. The poppets allowed for communion with the spirits during rituals through prayer and offerings; they served as messengers between the worlds. The poppets in the bedroom were mostly representations of Mama Lu's friends and family that passed on when Nalia was a child, most of which Nalia had only a vague recollection. Only one poppet was younger. It was made to honor a classmate whose life was tragically taken in an automobile accident just before Halloween in Nalia's junior year of high school. Nalia was moved to make the poppet herself, and place it on the altar for the Day of the Dead. It was the last time she celebrated the holiday.

Mama Lu had collected identifiable bits of fabric from all the poppets but one, and so she continued to search. Her purpose was well defined. She would gather what was left of the poppets and place them on her altar for a special ritual. She would arrange them among cubes of sugar and bowls of water in a grand petition to the spirits on the other side. She would hold Guinea peppers in her mouth, just like Marie Laveau, to gain sympathy from the spirits. The spirits of Voodoo were always kind to those who endured suffering and sacrifice. Her petition would be simple. She would ask the souls in the spirit world to find her daughter and keep her close until a way could be found to draw her back through the veil.

As Mama Lu continued to hunt for the last poppet, anxiety caused her mind to wander and she found herself pacing and plotting. She contemplated the most effective way to get back at Margaret Barronne and Vivian Luciénne. A fix to end all fixes was what those two needed. She would require Mr. John's assistance for a powerful gris-gris, and then she would weave a spell like no one had ever known. Excruciating pain and torment would follow the two women like a shadow until their slow and agonizing deaths. By the time Mama Lu finished with them, they would gladly greet death with open arms.

Snapping to her senses and scolding herself for allowing her mind to stray to vengeance above her daughter's welfare, Mama Lu refocused her efforts on the quest for the final poppet.

Overturning a tattered pillowcase, she finally found it – a length of red ribbon pinned to a torn bit of burlap. As she bent to retrieve the final scrap, Mama Lu was startled by the sound of the doorbell.

Instantly she felt trepidation. A burning sensation in the pit of her stomach indicated something was not right. She sensed a malicious spirit.

Cautiously, she leaned into the hallway as if expecting to find someone there, but the corridor was empty. The doorbell chimed again as Mama Lu made her way toward the stairs. Her mind raced with questions of insecurity. Who could be on the doorstep? Had she locked the front door? She was relatively sure, but at the moment she could not be certain. Why did she have such feelings of intrusion and darkness?

Mama Lu moved quietly through the dimly lit kitchen and peeked into the front hallway. She could see the front door and noted the chain was secure. The glass panel was illuminated from the other side by the porch light, and a blurry figure moved slightly in the glow.

Mama Lu felt drawn to the doorway. As she inched closer, her apprehension waned. The figure beyond the glass grew clearer and more familiar – a young lady with almond skin and dark brown hair. At first, Mama Lu was certain her mind was playing tricks on her. Nalia could not possibly have returned. Though the figure outside bore a striking resemblance, it was surely an illusion.

The closer Mama Lu got to the front door, the more clouded her mind became. Abandoning Madame Toulouse's notion that Nalia's body was possessed by the spirit of Margaret Barronne, Mama Lu could think of nothing but her daughter's face, smiling in the mid-day sunshine on a bright autumn day. Other memories played like movies in Mama Lu's mind producing similar feelings of euphoria as she reached for the chain. Memory changed to fantasy, and then to expectation as Mama Lu slid the chain from its socket. She imagined opening the door to find her baby girl, returning home, safe from whatever misfortune had befallen her. She was there with open arms and an open heart, waiting to be welcomed inside. She was hurt and broken, just the same as when she was a child. She needed help; she needed her Mama Lu.

With a motherly desire to make it all better, Mama Lu turned the knob. Her heart lept as she opened the door slowly to reveal exactly what she had envisioned. A tear of joy spilled onto her cheek as she beheld the beautiful caramel eyes of her daughter. Mama Lu stretched out her arms to embrace Nalia and stepped out onto the porch. As she crossed the threshold, her foot came to rest on a velvet bag. Mama Lu felt the crunch of dried herbs and the snap of tiny animal bones as she realized she had been hoodooed.

Looking up, she saw Nalia's face change from vibrant and youthful to slightly ashen with swirling, smoky eyes. By the time Mama Lu came to her senses, it was too late; the cold, steel blade of her own ritual knife was at her throat, and the devilish voice of Madame Vivian Luciénne was in her ear. In a whisper from behind, Madame Luciénne boldly issued her instructions.

"We gon' walk back in, real slow. We gon' get the keys to yo' shop, then you gon' come wit' us. Otherwise, dis blade gon' cut clean through yo' neck."

Mama Lu could do nothing but comply. As she stared into the hazy eyes of Margaret Barronne, all she could see was the face of her daughter, held captive by a demon from beyond this world.

CHAPTER THIRTY-ONE

The bindings were exceptionally tight, Margaret's rage made sure of it. Stinging pain from the stiff, dry ropes surged through Mama Lu's wrists as she breathed in dust from the rear seat cushion of Madame Luciénne's black Lincoln. Her throat was dry. A rag was shoved into her mouth and secured with a length of the same rope that bound her wrists. It was scratchy and carried the faintest trace of solvent. Sweat poured down Mama Lu's forehead, stinging her eyes and pooling in her ears as she lay motionless on the jostling seat of the speeding car. Her pulse raced and her mind scrambled to focus on a means of escape as she scolded herself for succumbing to the effects of such a rudimentary gris-gris as the one left on her doorstep. Avoiding the influence of such an amateur effort was child's play for the strong willed and clear minded. Unfortunately, Mama Lu had been neither when she saw Nalia standing at her front door, and the momentary lack of clarity garnered her an up-close and personal audience with the stench of stale cigarette smoke on the vehicle's upholstery. Not to mention one monster of a headache.

Her face was swollen and sore where Margaret had been obliged to unleash some aggression while tying her up. Mama Lu could not help but think of the first time she found Nalia swollen and bruised. Her heart ached all over again for the little girl who lived a life of torture at the hand of the Barronnes. She remembered dressing similar wounds with Mr. John's peppermint and lavender beeswax salve on the night Madame Toulouse took Nalia to the hospital. It was the night she split Margaret's soul. Mama Lu remembered the blank expression haunting the little girl's eyes that night. She recalled telling her everything was going to be alright, that Mama Lu would see to it. It took a long time for the little girl to learn to smile again, but she had. Mama Lu missed that little girl – the one whose grown-up body just gave her the swollen eye currently throbbing in her skull like a bass drum.

Margaret stopped the beating there, but Mama Lu wished she hadn't. She noticed how Margaret managed to handle herself with great restraint, keeping her pent-up rage in check. Mama Lu knew all that aggression was being saved for a more sinister purpose, and she had already figured out the plan; she knew Margaret would try to split her soul. Why else would she be going to the shop, with Madame Luciénne along for the trip? She wanted revenge, and she was going to have Vivian attempt the ritual. What concerned Mama Lu the most was her lack of faith in Vivian to recall and perform the ritual properly, and she knew what happened when a split went wrong.

Margaret was silent in the front seat except for an occasional snicker of anticipation. Madame Luciénne sat white-knuckled over the steering wheel with an eerie sense of déjà vu. Heavy drops of rain fell against the windshield as steam began to rise from the gutters along Decatur Street. The road was dark with minimal traffic and only a few, scattered pedestrians. Madame Luciénne noticed the storefront of *The Doll Maker* was still boarded up as she drove past and made the turn into the alleyway along the back.

The narrow lane of dirt and shell was still draped in the darkness of the broken streetlights. A memory of Tony Leonetti flashed through Madame Luciénne's mind as she realized her part in the orchestration of this grand design.

With the headlights doused, the car crept along the alley until pulling to a stop just outside the back door of the store. The rain poured heavier, shining like amber waterfalls in the glow of the Lincoln's running-lights. The heavy doors swung open as Margaret and Madame Luciénne exited the vehicle and dragged Mama Lu from the back seat.

"Get the keys," Margaret snapped, "Unlock the door."

Madame Luciénne fumbled in the darkness and the escalating downpour for the key to the building. By the time she gained entry, the three women were soaked to the bone. Madame Luciénne flipped on the lights of the workroom and led the others inside.

As Mama Lu crossed the threshold, she lost her footing on the wet floor. Still bound and gagged she was unable to break her fall. She went down hard, hitting her head flat against the concrete. Her mind went fuzzy, and her eyes rolled as she blacked out momentarily.

"Get up!" yelled Margaret, pulling Mama Lu by the shoulder. "You're not getting out of this that easily. I want you fully awake for this. Every minute!"

Mama Lu came to, still groggy but able to walk as Margaret shoved her through the workroom, prodding her with the ritual blade. Her head throbbed with the intensity of a jackhammer.

Anxiety grabbed hold of Madame Luciénne's gut as she made her way through the workroom. The smell of porcelain powder and paint opened a floodgate of nauseating memories. She shivered as she caught sight of the twins on the high shelf above the painting table. The grotesque face and mangled body of the second Verelli brother seemed to be sending her a message of warning as she heard his piercing screams play over and over in her head like a broken record.

Turning her eyes away, she led the others toward the stairs. Her heart raced wildly as she flipped the light switch. Madame Luciénne was not surprised when the narrow stairwell remained dark. She could not recall ever seeing that particular light bulb burn, but it did not matter; she remembered which keys fit the locks upstairs like she was there yesterday.

With a deep breath, Madame Luciénne nudged the door and stood back. A low, creak echoed through the silence, as the door to the upper room swung slowly open. The smell of dust and stale herbs rushed out onto the small landing where the trio huddled together. Madame Luciénne stared at Margaret, afraid to cross the threshold. Anxiety rose to her throat as she pressed her back against the wall, just outside the door.

"Get in there," insisted Margaret.

"You first," replied Madame Luciénne, holding her ground.

The two women were locked in a standoff. Margaret raised her eyebrows and set her jaw. Her posture became rigid, and her patience grew thin. Without breaking her stare, Margaret shoved Mama Lu through the doorway. Throwing a patronizing look over her shoulder, she entered the room behind her victim, leaving Madame Luciénne panting heavily outside, as a clap of thunder rattled the sky.

By the time Madame Luciénne gathered the courage to enter the ritual room, Mama Lu lay bent over on the thick, round table with her hands still bound tightly behind her back. The single light bulb swayed gently back and forth from the old wire above.

Margaret loomed over Mama Lu like a vulture, with a look of pure, unadulterated evil swirling in her smoky eyes. Viciously, she grabbed a handful of Mama Lu's hair and jerked her head to one side. Mama Lu stared up in disgust, biting down hard on the foul rag in her mouth. Her nostrils flared as the swelling in her face made it increasingly difficult to breathe. Margaret noticed her struggling for air and smiled.

"That's it," she said, "Fight for it. Fight hard for these last few breaths. I want you to feel your lungs burn and know that it's just the beginning."

Mama Lu grunted a muffled message and struggled against the ropes that bound her wrists.

"What's that?" asked Margaret, leaning in low. "Speak up *darlin'*, I can't hear ya!" She cackled loudly as she slammed Mama Lu's head back down.

Bending low, Margaret grabbed hold of Mama Lu's legs and heaved them up. With a satisfied grin, she stretched her victim out, face down, on the same table where her soul was split. Holding Mama Lu's feet firmly, Margaret yelled to her assistant, "Get the chain!"

Madame Luciénne retrieved a length of old, rusted chain from the floor in the corner of the room. The two assailants crossed Mama Lu's ankles and wrapped her feet together with the heavy binding. When convinced their work would hold, they fastened the chain to one leg of the table.

Weary, Madame Luciénne wiped the sweat from her brow and leaned against the wall. Mama Lu put up more of a fight than they expected for a woman of her years.

"Don't get comfortable," snapped Margaret. "We're just getting started."

Margaret shouted instructions to untie the length of rope that held the rag in Mama Lu's mouth and secure it around one of her still-bound wrists, forming a tether with which they could lash her to the table. As Madame Luciénne struggled with the knot, Margaret crossed the room to the rustic, wooden altar and laid the ritual knife down among the large display of spent candles. She stared up at the painting above the altar and the drawings of the Catholic saints surrounding it. Her eyes were drawn to the smaller painting of the woman in blue holding the peppers and the rosary, praying for the demon-oppressed man in the jail cell. The image confused her. Fourteen years spent among people and symbolism deeply rooted in this bizarre religion, and she was no closer to understanding it now than she had been years ago. Like the runes and phrases written in the ancient language on the walls all around her – the entire history of a culture lay spelled out before her eyes, but she could not read a word of it. The only thing Margaret understood from this world was the suffering it caused her and the desire for revenge it sowed inside her.

When Madame Luciénne finally conquered the knot, releasing the ropes and the rag, Mama Lu gasped frantically, filling her burning lungs with life-sustaining oxygen. As her head began to clear she exhaled a barrage of threats.

"Vivian, you twisted witch!" she shouted in a strained voice, "You gon' pay fo' dis. Jus' you wait!"

"You don't seem to be in the position to threaten anyone," laughed Margaret turning back toward the table. Approaching her prone captive, she grabbed her by the hair once again and yanked her head to the other side. Bending low, she stared into Mama Lu's eyes and puffed her bottom lip, mocking sympathy. "In fact," she continued, "You look rather helpless to me. Pathetic, really."

Mama Lu tensed her neck and snapped her teeth like a biting animal, causing Margaret to jump back, startled. She chuckled as Margaret fumed with embarrassment.

"You seem mighty frightened of dis *helpless* ol' woman," Mama Lu taunted as Margaret's face turned blood red. "And you gon' call me pathetic?"

Angry at herself and the situation, Margaret retrieved the knife from the altar. Straightening her back and strengthening her resolve, she slid the blade underneath her victim's throat. Mama Lu arched her back and strained to keep her neck above the razor sharp edge. Sweat poured down her face as her tense muscles fought to hold their position.

"I no longer know fear," steamed Margaret. "For what is left for me to fear – death? I've already seen the other side, and I've known a fate worse than death. I've longed for death, and it would not have me! The only thing keeping me on this side of the veil is the thought of watching you suffer the same fate. Fear is nothing to me."

Margaret removed the knife, allowing Mama Lu to relax the cramping muscles in her back and neck. Walking slowly and methodically around the table she pointed the blade at Madame Luciénne.

"Finish what you started!" she ordered.

Madame Luciénne's angst was waning. The prideful display of control and Margaret's commanding tone helped squelch her apprehension about the ritual room, giving rise to anger and throwing their partnership into question. Margaret seemed to have forgotten she was in need of her assistance, and without it, she was nothing.

"You ain't gon' forget our agreement, now are you?" she asked in a tone intended to remind Margaret of her place. "You ain't gon' back out on me after I do dis fo' you, right?"

"No," Margaret replied, understanding the implication. "Neither will I forget what happens if you don't cooperate," she added in an attempt to keep the upper hand.

"You both gon' burn fo' dis!" shouted Mama Lu from the table. "I'll see to it! I'll stick you both on my shelf and watch you rot!" If she could not break free of her binding to bring vengeance upon her attackers, at least she might be able to push Margaret's buttons. Mama Lu knew agitating her could create the potential for an outburst of violence that would bring a quick death and spare her the torture of a split gone wrong. With Nalia's soul already given over to the other side, what reason did she have for staying in this world anyway? Surely Mr. John and Madame Toulouse would understand.

Snapping to her senses, Mama Lu scolded herself for entertaining the thought of giving up – for the thought of letting Margaret Barronne win. She struggled against her bindings with renewed vigor. She twisted and turned, causing Madame Luciénne tremendous grief in securing the end of the rope around her wrist. When the struggle and the knots were finally complete, both women were exhausted.

Margaret took advantage of Mama Lu's weakness to untie the original lashes that bound her wrists together. With one wrist secured by Madame Luciénne's rope, Margaret tied hers around the other, allowing them to stretch their captive's arms out to the edge of the table.

On Margaret's instruction, Madame Luciénne joined in helping her pull Mama Lu's arms up over her head and painfully flip the woman onto her back. Once Mama Lu was in the appropriate ritual position, they secured the ropes to the wide legs of the table. Mama Lu spent the last of her fleeting energy struggling in vain to pull free.

As thunder once again shook the building, Margaret positioned herself menacingly above Mama Lu's head. Her swirling, smoky eyes stared upside-down into those of her fatigued prey. Sweet satisfaction graced her face as she lowered it within inches of Mama Lu's.

"Fourteen years I've waited for this," she said in a slithery whisper. "Fourteen long, tortured years I've craved this moment like a drug, every second of every day hell-bent on making you pay for what you did to me. You took everything from me. Do you realize I could have left this city and started over in a life of luxury? You ruined it all. You robbed me!"

"Even now, you jus' don't get it do you?" said Mama Lu, between labored breaths. "Listen to yo'self. Did you ever care about yo' daughter at all?"

Margaret did not respond, nor did she need to. Mama Lu knew there was nothing in her soul but pure, selfish evil – a bastardization of humanity leeching off those around her. What could she expect from an entity that pushed the soul of her own daughter into the spirit world in order to occupy her body for a well-seasoned vendetta?

"Vivian," said Margaret, "Take the knife. Start the ritual."

Madame Luciénne did as she was told. Taking the knife from Margaret's hand, she placed the blade inside the neck of Mama Lu's dress. Avoiding eye contact, she sliced the fabric until Mama Lu's rib cage was exposed. Thunder rocked the building once more as the rain pounded on the roof like a barrage of tiny bombs.

Madame Luciénne tried desperately to remember the ancient language she knew must be chanted for the ritual. The eyes of the paintings around the room seemed to watch her, mockingly – like they knew what she needed but were unwilling to help. She stared at the runes and symbols covering the walls and ceiling, trying to recall their meanings. Sweat began to drip from her brow as she realized what the consequence would likely be for botching the ritual. Should she take the knife and strike Margaret down now? The thought taunted her as she realized she did not have the strength to overpower Margaret's new, younger body. Even if she could, the result would mean the total loss of her St. John's Eve ceremony and the resulting gain it would provide. She had to remember.

"It must be done to the rhythm of the drum," she said finally, thankful the recollection of that detail would buy her more time.

Margaret was confused, but driven by desire for vengeance she stepped to the corner of the room and brushed the dust off the heads of the old set of congas.

"What do I play?" she asked, staring at Madame Luciénne in frustration.

"It's not what you play that matters," she replied, "But it's important the ritual is timed to the drum, so each step in the sequence falls in harmony wit' the next."

Mama Lu cringed. Madame Luciénne could not be more wrong. Every detail of the ritual was important and deeply rooted in the ancient traditions of Voodoo. Performing a split properly was like a planetary alignment; all the elements had to be perfect. Everything had meaning: the drums, the cadence, the candles, the knife, the oils, the blood sacrifice – even such minor details as the talismans worn by the participants had a significant impact on the outcome of the ritual. This is why the doll maker was so revered by the all the tribes of ancients in Haiti and as far back as Africa. This was powerful, complex magic – strong Voodoo.

Margaret timidly struck the palm of her hand against the tight head of the larger drum and gave a questioning look to Madame Luciénne, seeking approval. After receiving a nod of acknowledgement, she struck the head again, firmer, and listened to the hollow resonance of the ancient wood as its reverberating drone filled the room. Margaret smiled as the sky outside echoed its own thundering cadence. The light bulb over the table flickered as lightning charged the air with static electricity.

"Get on with it!" shouted Margaret as she beat out an awkwardly unsteady rhythm on the drums.

Madame Luciénne focused her mind on memories of the splits she observed in the past. Raising the knife toward the ceiling, she threw her head back and relaxed her body. She allowed her mind to lull into a shallow trance as she prayed for her subconscious to take over and recall the ancient language required for the split.

As Margaret became more comfortable with the drum, the rhythm grew steadier, aiding Madame Luciénne's recall. To the droning of the congas she stepped, in time, up to the table and placed the point of the blade over Mama Lu's heart.

Mama Lu noticed her trembling hand, and her breathing quickened with fear. She felt the blade trail down her chest, coming to rest between her ribs on the right side. She closed her eyes and prepared for the worst. Wincing, Mama Lu felt the blade pierce her skin just enough to draw blood. Pain surged through her abdomen as she felt the knife slice through the flesh along her side.

The angry sky cried out in protest with a deafening clap of thunder. As lighting ripped the night in two, the light bulb above the ritual table flickered and died, plunging the room into total darkness. Margaret stopped the drum. Mama Lu's labored breathing was the only sound in the resulting silence. "The power is out!" Margaret yelled, "Don't let it stop you."

"But I can't see," replied Madame Luciénne. "I need to see to make the cuts."

Mama Lu was in pain. She could feel blood flowing from the open wound in her side as it ran down and pooled into the torn fabric of her dress. The power outage had startled Luciénne into cutting too deep. She wondered how long it would take to loose consciousness from the loss of blood.

Madame Luciénne stood stone-still, holding the ritual blade aloft, afraid to move in the blackness. She reached out for the table in an attempt to orient herself as she heard Margaret shout.

"Light the candles, you fool!" she cried from her own petrified position behind the drums.

Cautiously, Madame Luciénne turned toward the altar as another tumultuous round of thunder rumbled across the sky. The sound of rain on the roof grew louder, like an army marching to war above her head.

Unable to see a thing, Madame Luciénne's journey across the room seemed to last a lifetime. Taking one step too many, she bumped into the altar and nearly fell over. Still gripping the knife tightly in one hand, she felt among the candles with the other. Clumsily, she ran her hand the length of the table, searching for matches. The tinkling sound of tipped-over glass vials echoed through the room as Madame Luciénne's fingers fumbled over the wax-covered altar. Her breathing quickened with desperation. Frustrated with her futile efforts, she flailed faster, knocking down candle stands in her panic.

As the clatter of her search cut through the silence of the pitch-black room Madame Luciénne felt a presence next to her. Stunned, she stopped, afraid to budge. A chill ran through her blood as she felt the hair-raising sensation of hot breath on the back of her neck. All at once, the darkness of the room fled as all the candles on the altar spontaneously burst to flaming life. Madame Luciénne screamed in panic as she turned to behold a large, shadowy figure, just inches away. It was Mr. John, soaking wet from the rain, holding a live rooster.

CHAPTER THIRTY-TWO

With one continuous motion, and with the speed of his youth, Mr. John snatched the ritual blade from Madame Luciénne's hand and caught her in the temple with the blunt end of the handle. The wicked woman dropped like a stone. As she fell, Mr. John let the rooster loose in Margaret's direction. The large bird flapped and flailed toward the startled woman, threatening her face with its feet and beak. As Margaret tried desperately to fight off the thrashing bird, she became enveloped by a large cloud of white powder. Her eyes began to burn in the noxious fog as her vision faded. The last image her smoky eyes beheld as the cloud dissipated was the face of Madame Toulouse, lips pursed, still blowing the white powder from her outstretched palm. The next sensation the blinded woman felt was the strong arm of Mr. John holding her from behind and the cold ritual blade against her neck.

As Madame Toulouse freed Mama Lu, Margaret kicked and fought against Mr. John to no avail. He strengthened his grip and pressed the blade firmly against her throat.

"Do it, old man!" she mocked, struggling to escape his grip. "Slit the throat of your precious, baby girl!"

"No!" screamed Mama Lu, as if Mr. John could ever actually bring himself to do it.

"Don't listen to her!" Margaret went on as she continued to fight. "Do it! End it!"

Mr. John's nerves could hold out no longer than his muscles. His will was strong, but his patience and his body grew weak. Realizing his grip would soon fade, he pressed the hilt of the knife firmly into the carotid artery on the side of Margaret's neck. With his thumb on the opposite side, just under her chin, Mr. John squeezed tightly. After a few short moments, Margaret became dizzy. Her face turned red and began to tingle as the body she stole from her daughter grew heavy in Mr. John's arms. Moments later, Margaret passed out from lack of oxygen to her brain. She slid silently to the floor and collapsed near the limp body of Madame Luciénne.

Indistinct voices scrolled through the silence like stations on a radio dial. Bits of whispering, protesting, crying, and stern instruction collected in Margaret's brain like a scrambled puzzle. She heard the shackles snap closed before she felt them – before she realized they were closing on her own wrists. The metallic clanks echoed through her throbbing head, first one then another. Her consciousness drifted back as her limbs were stretched tight against the table.

Snapping back to coherence with horrifying memories, Margaret cried out in protest as she fought to break free of the bonds that held her. Her efforts were strong, fueled by rage and violence, but they were ultimately useless. The iron was cold and unyieldingly tight against her wrists and ankles. A warm draft over her borrowed body told her she had been stripped to her undergarments. Though she could not see them, heavy cloths had been lovingly draped over her breasts and hip region for the sake of modesty.

The voices continued. Margaret shifted her head from side to side toward the chatter, but could see nothing. Darkness held a death-grip on her vision, and her eyes stung like hellfire. Blinding dust was as old as Voodoo itself. Mild forms of it had been used for centuries in less-than-noble hoodoo cultures. It could easily be tossed into the eyes of an unsuspecting adversary when passing on the street, causing temporary blindness. A day or two of darkness was typically all it took to have the victim believing he or she was cursed or *fixed*, and willing to do, or pay, anything to have the "spell" removed. The powder used by Madame Toulouse, however, was no mere novelty or bit of hoodoo trickery. It was specially mixed for her by Mr. John, and was nothing short of a chemical weapon that would blind someone for months at a time and cause severe burns to the skin. Margaret could feel the burns around her eyes as her salty sweat caused them to sting profoundly.

The crying became louder as Margaret identified the sobbing, distressed voice of Mama Lu.

"I can't do it," she wailed, her voice shaking through the heavy tears. "I can't split my baby."

"That ain't yo' baby," answered Madame Toulouse, sternly. "You know it Lu. Look into her eyes. That's a demon, come back from the other side."

From her captive position on the table, Margaret could not help but laugh. If she was a demon, then it was Mama Lu who made her one. Her sinister cackle echoed loudly through the room.

The three elders turned their attention to the laughing, shackled victim.

"You see how she mocks you, Lu?" Madame Toulouse went on. "Yo' baby ain't in there. That ain't nothin' but a parasite, infestin' Nalia's body."

Mr. John turned his head. He could no more bear to see what looked like Nalia strapped to the ritual table than Mama Lu could. It was Mr. John who covered her body with the cloths, leaving only the necessary flesh showing. As far as his eyes could tell, that was still his baby girl chained to the table, and regardless of what had to be done, he would not have her exposed.

"I jus' can't do it," Mama Lu repeated over and over, "I can't cut my daughter."

"You've got to!" shouted Madame Toulouse, taking Mama Lu by the shoulders and shaking her vigorously. "Don't you see, Lu? Until you flush that wicked, twisted soul from her body, Nalia's spirit will never be at peace." Madame Toulouse's eyes softened as she pleaded with Mama Lu, while the shackled prisoner continued to laugh. "Fight through the tears, Lu. Yo' grief is cloudin' yo' inner eye. If you could see into the spirit world right now, you'd see Nalia beggin' us to let her go. She wants to be at peace."

Mama Lu moaned, doubling over in anguish. She was still not ready to admit that Nalia was gone, let alone seal it by taking the last bit of life from her body. Mama Lu knew a soul could not be split twice. If the ritual was performed, Margaret's soul would pass on to the next world, leaving Nalia's body devoid of a spirit, just as in death.

Madame Toulouse bent low, huddling with Mama Lu who was holding her stomach and dry heaving. The pain in her heart was greater than the wounds on her head and face or the cut in her side.

"Lu, it has to be done," said Madame Toulouse, placing her forehead against Mama Lu's. "You know that I can't see the outcome of any situation. I only see possibilities, and this is the only way I see any possibilities at all."

"What do you mean, possibilities?" asked Mr. John. "Possibilities fo' what?"

"Fo' anything remotely resemblin' humanity to be salvaged," Madame Toulouse retorted. "She's sufferin' John."

"We all sufferin'!" Mr. John snapped back, placing one hand over his heart and gesturing toward Mama Lu with the other. "Can't you see dis is tearin' her apart?"

"You think it ain't tearin' me up too, John?" Madame Toulouse asked. "But we got to think about Nalia. It's the only way she gon' be at peace. It's the only way peace gon' come to any of us." Madame Toulouse placed the ritual knife in Mama Lu's shaking hands and spoke with the compassion of her whole heart. "Don't let yo' baby suffer in this life *and* the next, Lu. Set her free. It's the only way."

Mama Lu's body trembled with angst. Her eyes reflected the numbness of her soul as she stared up at Madame Toulouse. She could not bear the thought of performing the ritual on the only daughter she had ever known, but she no longer had a choice. She promised Nalia long ago the pain was over, that "Mama Lu would see to it". Now was the time to make good on that promise, once and for all.

Mama Lu stood up straight and stared into the eyes of Mr. John. He wanted to look away, but could only stare. He knew breaking eye contact with Mama Lu would open a window for doubt. He had to be strong for her, and for Nalia. So with a breaking heart, he stared at Mama Lu in support and stepped backward toward the congas.

Madame Toulouse grabbed Mama Lu tightly by the wrists and steadied her trembling hands.

"She's suffered long enough, Lu. It's time."

Mama Lu nodded in agreement as the drums began to echo the familiar cadence of the ritual. The sound filled the room, reverberating off the walls as if the room and the drums were one. The heavens answered in harmony as a loud clap of thunder rolled across the sky outside.

The noise roused Madame Vivian Luciénne from unconsciousness. With blurred vision and a spinning head, she found herself sitting in the doorway. Her wrists and ankles were bound with the same rope she used to immobilize Mama Lu. From the floor, her view of the ritual room was all too familiar. She knew what was about to happen, and could only wonder if she was next.

As Mr. John pounded away on the drums, Mama Lu began to circle the table with tears streaming down her face onto her bloody, tattered dress. With a shaking voice and a weakened body, she began to chant in the ancient language Madame Luciénne had tried so desperately to recall. The language was like a native tongue for Mama Lu, flowing and eloquent. It calmed her mind and soothed her spirit into a more relaxed and focused state. It even reduced her heart rate, slowing the flow of blood from her wounded side.

On the table, Margaret struggled with the strength of a caged gorilla. She screamed insults at Mama Lu, trying to break her concentration. She pulled at the chains with her arms and legs, exhausting her muscles and causing the shackles to cut into her flesh.

As Mama Lu continued around the table, she raised her arms in a serpentine dance. She felt a commanding sting of pain as she lifted her hands above her head. The cut in her side was tearing. Blood once again began to flow heavily down her hip. Fighting through the pain, she continued the dance, focusing her mind on Nalia.

When she reached Margaret's right side, Mama Lu lowered the blade to her victim's rib cage and started the shallow incision. Looking away as much as possible, and avoiding eye contact altogether, Mama Lu slowly dragged the blade down the side of the body, cutting steadily.

Margaret, exhausted from the struggle, managed a faint scream of protest. "No!" she shouted, reduced to pleading, "No."

With heavy tears and an even heavier heart, Mama Lu moved the blade and made three other identical incisions before staggering to the other side of the table. The pain in her side was growing, making it harder to stand, much less focus, but Mama Lu thought of Nalia. She called to mind visions of a young child's smile – a genuine smile that had not been found easily, the kind that comes from truly knowing you are loved. The image gave her the strength to keep going.

The left side of the body would see the last three cuts. Fighting back the emotions of a life spent protecting her baby, Mama Lu lowered the knife and began the incisions. Margaret's breathing was reduced to shallow gasps as Mama Lu made the first two left-side cuts.

With only one incision left, Mama Lu fought to keep control of the blade and her emotions. Her mind and her body were numb. She positioned the blade properly and closed her eyes, unable to watch. As she prepared to make the final cut, Margaret cried out in a tiny, sobbing voice that sounded like Nalia.

"Mama," she said with the shaking tone of a whimpering child, "Please don't cut me anymore, Mama. It hurts."

Mama Lu was so taken aback she nearly dropped the knife. She opened her eyes and stared at the bloody mess of her daughter's body on the table before her.

"Please, Mama," Margaret continued. "Stop hurting me."

Mama Lu looked up at Nalia's face. She could see only a frightened little girl with beautiful caramel eyes full of hurt, sadness, and confusion. A lump the size of a grapefruit gathered in the back of Mama Lu's throat. She could not speak, let alone chant.

Hearing the voice, Mr. John looked up in suspicion and slowed the rhythm of the drum. Madame Toulouse shouted out to Mama Lu.

"It's a trick, Lu! Don't let that evil woman fool you!"

But Mama Lu was convinced. Her mind saw nothing but her helpless baby girl, lying on the table, crying and bleeding.

"Take me home, Mama," Margaret continued. "Please?"

"Of course, baby," said Mama Lu, laying the knife on the table. "Let's get you out o' here."

Madame Toulouse and Mr. John looked on in horror, mouths agape and speechless, as Mama Lu reached for the shackles. Margaret's twisted soul could not help but laugh in satisfaction. When the sinister cackle became audible, Mama Lu snapped to her senses and picked up the blade, infuriated.

"Almost had you," laughed Margaret with a diabolical grin.

Driven by rage, Mama Lu had to restrain her hand in order to make the final cut with precision. As she inserted the blade for the last time, Mama Lu tried to refocus her mind on Nalia and the peace she needed to achieve.

Margaret's muscles were exhausted, and so was her spirit. As blood continued to pool onto the ritual table, her body went limp in surrender.

Mama Lu walked around the table to the altar as Mr. John picked up the tempo. She laid the knife down among the candles, retrieved two vials of oil and emptied them into the incisions before returning for the rooster. The drum grew louder as Mama Lu reached down and grabbed the bird by the neck. Holding it aloft, she returned to the table and closed her eyes. As she prepared to wring the rooster's neck, she heard Madame Toulouse shout.

"It's happening!"

Mama Lu opened her eyes to see tiny rays of light breaking forth from the wounds in Nalia's body. Like glowing smoke, the rays drifted toward the ceiling, flowing steadily, like an overturned waterfall. The glowing haze gathered and swirled slowly above the table like a storm cloud.

"Dis ain't supposed to happen yet," thought Mama Lu, "The blood sacrifice ain't been made yet." Her side seared with pain causing her to drop the rooster. Placing her hand to the wound on her ribs, Mama Lu realized blood had already been shed. She looked across the room at Madame Toulouse with the expression of a lost child.

"The soul is leaving!" cried Madame Toulouse, observing the gathering cloud churning over the body. "Hurry, to the altar! There might still be time!"

CHAPTER THIRTY-THREE

The three elders converged on the altar as Vivian watched from the doorway, confused and frightened. In a quick display of extraordinary foresight, Madame Toulouse produced several packets of sugar from her handbag.

"We've got to call Nalia's spirit," she said, scattering the sugar across the altar. "We've got to summon the aid of the ancestors."

Mama Lu could not stand. The pain in her side was becoming unbearable and increasingly crippling. With Mr. John's help, she knelt before the altar and retrieved several bits of burlap from the pockets of her slashed dress – pieces of the poppets from Nalia's bedroom. Quickly and lovingly they lined the bits and pieces along the arc of candles at the back of the altar, bringing to mind the loved ones each scrap represented.

Without delay, Madame Toulouse began to chant, invoking the spirits of the elders and drawing them near the veil. Gradually Mr. John and Mama Lu joined in.

Loa... Loa... come b'tween.

Sing you to Bondye. Sing you of me.

Guide now the spirit, taken too soon.

Return her to us, lest darkness consume.

The flames of the candles grew to resemble tall spires rising from the tiny stumps of wax. They burned brighter as the cloud above the table rolled faster. The streams of glowing smoke emanating from the wounds on Nalia's torso grew faint and wispy as the cloud increased in size.

Mama Lu turned her eyes back to the table. Staring into the churning cloud, she saw Margaret's face taking shape in the smoke, writhing in torment and fighting to stay in the body.

Mama Lu became weak and fell over into Mr. John, holding her side.

"We gots to get dis bandaged up 'fore you bleed to death," he said in a panic, placing his hand over the cut.

"No," said Mama Lu, struggling to sit up, "The spirits of Voodoo are kind to those who endure suffering." She sat back up to her knees, applying pressure to the wound. Taking the deepest breath she could manage, Mama Lu continued to chant.

"We've got to get her spirit back before that cloud scatters," said Madame Toulouse, noticing it had already started to dissipate. "She's close. I can feel it. If only we had something of hers to help guide her over."

Mr. John's eyes grew as big as saucers. He reached into his shirt pocket and pulled out the small, folded square of tear-soaked tee-shirt Nalia slept in. With tears of roiling emotion streaming down his face, he placed it at the center of the altar and flattened his hand on top of it. Mama Lu placed her hand on top of his, and Madame Toulouse followed suit as they began the chant once more.

The energy was strong, and Mama Lu could feel the veil between the worlds growing thin. She could feel the strength of the ancestors guiding Nalia's soul toward them. Her heart leapt as she sensed her daughter's spirit drawing near.

Overjoyed and anxious, Mama Lu turned to see the cloud growing dark and breaking up. The swirling mass grew faint and took on the appearance of powder floating in the air. The fog became thin and translucent as it continued to disperse and vanish. Finally, with one last spiraling motion and a faint, high-pitched scream, the cloud and the soul of Margaret Barronne were no more.

Mama Lu broke the bond, pulling her hand from the others. With all the strength she could manage, she staggered to the table. Leaning against its edge, she grabbed Nalia's wrist, released the shackle that held it, and squeezed tightly. An eternity passed as Mama Lu waited to feel even the faintest pulse. Panic rose like acid in her throat as she squeezed harder, whispering words of desperation.

"C'mon baby, c'mon. Come back to Mama Lu."

Nothing.

Mama Lu pulled herself up and laid her head across Nalia's chest as the tears fell like rain. She listened intently, begging the spirits for the sound of a single heartbeat, but silence was her only answer. Her soul cried out as she frantically moved her head toward Nalia's and placed an ear directly over her lips. She would gladly give her whole world, her whole life, if she could only hear the faintest breath of air being drawn into her daughter's lungs.

Nothing.

Shaken to her very core, Mama Lu felt the pain of losing her daughter all over again. Her heart burned with anguish. She felt as if her own soul was being ripped from its body as she began to wail loudly.

Madame Toulouse joined her at the table. Mama Lu felt her presence but did not have the strength to look up.

"We did all we could," said Madame Toulouse in a labored voice. "Death is an unforgiving adversary. You toyed with death for far too long, Lu. Now death has required a sacrifice."

Mama Lu felt the strange sensation of warm liquid falling in drops onto her feet. Lifting herself from the table, she stood and stared into the compassionate eyes of her mentor, as Madame Toulouse drew a ragged breath. Dropping her gaze to the elderly woman's abdomen, Mama Lu saw the hilt and handle of her ritual knife surrounded by a growing blood-red stain.

"I've lived my life without regret, Lucia," said Madame Toulouse, pulling the blade from her gut and dropping it to the floor. "Now you look after my gran'baby."

With a final breath, Madame Toulouse collapsed, caught from behind by Mr. John. Mama Lu fell to her knees. She placed both hands on her mentors wound and applied pressure, but it was too late. Blood and tears continued to flow and sorrow hung thick over the room.

Through the silent sobbing, Mama Lu heard a faint gasp of air and a forceful cough. Riveting her attention to the table, she saw Nalia's chest rise and fall with life.

In the doorway of the ritual room, Madame Vivian Luciénne sat with bound wrists and ankles as tears flowed down her cheeks like a river. She had just witnessed a power greater than any magic ever known – the ever-prevailing power of love.

CHAPTER THIRTY-FOUR

The late-afternoon sun glimmered off the gold trim of the emerald green casket as a warm, gentle breeze weaved its way through St. Louis Cemetery No. 3. From the far end of the north section, a lone trumpet could be heard blowing a solemn arrangement of "When the Saints Go Marchin' In".

The casket rested on a stand covered in green velvet, in front of a faded grey family tomb marked "TOULOUSE". A small crowd gathered around the coffin, each person holding a long-stemmed white rose. As the director concluded the service, Mr. John pulled a damp, white handkerchief from the pocket of his suit-coat, and wiped the tears from his eyes. Mama Lu did the same with the mangled bits of tissue she had used throughout the service.

She was dressed all in black, wearing a small pillbox hat with a tulle veil. The wound in her side was bandaged tightly under her dress and was healing nicely. However, the wound in her heart remained open. Time would heal the brokenness, but nothing would ever fill the void created by the loss of her mentor. Though overjoyed by the return of her daughter, Mama Lu's elation was bitter-sweet. Madame Toulouse was like a mother to her. The loss was great, and the emptiness would linger for a lifetime. As tears streaked her face, Mama Lu wondered if she would ever know another day without them.

On her arm, wearing a knee-length white dress with a jet-black stole, stood Nalia. Stiff and sore from her well-bandaged wounds, Nalia stood straight and tall, wearing a fanciful white hat with a black veil. On her arms were white theatre-length opera gloves, worn to honor her grandmother, and to help hide the cuts and bruises left by the shackles. The burns around her eyes were hidden by large, round sunglasses. Most of the guests presumed they were worn to hide her crying, but Nalia would shed no tears for Madame Toulouse. Though saddened by her loss, Nalia had seen the other side of the veil stretched between the spirit world and the world of the living. Having sampled a brief taste of the joy and peace that lay waiting on the other side, Nalia would never again weep for those who crossed over. Her heart and her spirit would miss Madame Toulouse, but her eyes remained dry in quiet reflection behind her dark glasses.

Nalia's vision would return in time, but her nightmares would not. Neither would her desire to investigate her biological history. She would call herself Nalia Deminy, and would never again question who her *real* family was.

On the cemetery road, in the distance, Madame Vivian Luciénne leaned against the front quarter-panel of her large, black Lincoln with her head bowed in respect. Her chin was bandaged and hidden under the thick black veil that flowed from her wide-brimmed hat. From beneath her Lennon-style, mirrored sunglasses, a single tear dropped onto her cheek and glistened through the veil in the light of the sun. As the service concluded, Madame Luciénne reflected on her own mortality. Mama Lu could have easily taken her life a few nights ago as she sat helplessly bound in the doorway of the upper room. Perhaps she should have. But Mama Lu stayed her hand, remembering the words of her fallen mentor, "Just like a spinning wheel, everything you do gon' come back around to you." Madame Luciénne was grateful for that wisdom.

One by one, the guests made their way to the casket and laid their roses among an enormous spray of peace lilies that graced the lid. Gently positioning his rose, Mr. John paused for a moment and placed his hand on top of the casket, whispering words that would be heard by no one else – a private, parting message to the woman for which he held a world of respect.

As he brought his tear-filled goodbye to a close, Mama Lu led Nalia by the hand to the side of the gleaming, green coffin. After laying her rose among the others, Nalia removed her gloves and arranged them gingerly in the center of the spray. With Mama Lu's help, she placed her hands on the lid of the casket and felt its warm, smooth surface. She lingered a while, touching the spray of lilies, feeling the softness of the leaves and the petals. She breathed in the fragrant aroma of the roses and called to mind cherished memories of the woman she would forever call grandmother. In the absence of her sight, Nalia continued to survey the casket with her hands. She traced her fingers around the trim and onto a shining gold plate on the side, just below the lid. Mama

Lu placed a trembling hand to her lips, kissed her fingertips, and pressed them to the plate which bore the inscription – NO GREATER LOVE.

With sadness closing their throats, making it difficult to breathe and impossible to speak, Mama Lu led Nalia away from the casket and together with Mr. John, they turned to leave. As the small crowd dispersed, the trumpeter in the distance increased the tempo and the energy of the tune so that many were shuffling and smiling as they left. After all, Madame Toulouse would have wanted nothing less.

On the night of St. John's Eve, a private memorial was held in Mama Lu's parlor. On the far wall, an altar was erected in honor of Madame Toulouse. At its center was an antique brass picture frame with flourishing detail etched into the edges. The frame contained a photograph of the elderly woman some eight years younger. It was taken at Nalia's twelfth birthday party, snapped as the child opened a beautifully wrapped box containing a silver hairbrush. On Madame Toulouse's face was a smile that reflected the joy of a life well-lived.

The photo was surrounded by a large display of candles arranged in a wide, sweeping arc. Among them lay Madame Toulouse's tortoise-shell cigarette holder, resting on a bed of sugar. In front, were two small bowls used for summoning spirits: one contained clear water, the other a sweetened mixture of black-eyed peas and rice.

Leaned against the brass picture frame was a small burlap poppet with strips of emerald green fabric pinned to its chest. On its head, Mama Lu fashioned a tiny hat with a small clipping of peacock feather to complete the loving depiction of her long-time mentor and friend.

Mama Lu, Mr. John, and Nalia sat on the floor in the middle of the room surrounded by tall lamp stands. There were at least a dozen, all topped with one of Madame Toulouse's elegant hats. The trio laughed among the memories, telling stories and singing old Creole songs while Mr. John played his guitar. Sudden outbursts of tears were frequent, but whether of joy or sadness, they all contributed to a memorable occasion – a time to reflect, reminisce, and commune with the spirits.

306

Toward the end of the evening, Mama Lu began to chant a familiar old recitation of an ancient verse used to call spirits from the other side. The ancient language took Nalia back to her childhood when the elders would celebrate Voodoo holidays in much the same way. Sometimes, when the spirits joined them, their energy would be manifested at the altar, in the form of ripples on the surface of the water in the bowl. Tonight, Mama Lu and Mr. John watched the bowl vigilantly for any such sign from the spirit of their departed loved one.

Nalia desperately wished she could see. Her vision was slowly progressing, which is to say she could distinguish light from shadow, but it would be months before her sight fully returned. The thought saddened her, especially tonight. She longed to witness the tiniest ripple in the water, should one appear – to feel the spirit of her grandmother.

As the trio continued to chant among the lamp stands, a phenomenon, like none they had ever witnessed before, took place. The energy of the spirit world rushed into the room like a wind, forming a union between them stronger than any bond the elders ever created. As they felt it rising among them, the hats on the lamp stands began to twirl. All at once, in perfect synchronization, the hats danced round and round. Mr. John and Mama Lu stood to their feet, slack-jawed. Their eyes darted from one lamp stand to the next in disbelief. It was like being on stage in the midst of a grand ballet, watching the dancers whirl around them to the slow rhythm of the orchestra.

"She's here," said Nalia, still seated and smiling the most genuine smile that had graced her face in a decade. "I can feel her," she continued. "I can see her face in my mind, clear as day. I see her walking among the lamp stands, spinning the hats and smiling. She's letting us know she is with us."

Mama Lu and Mr. John looked at each other in amazement, then back at Nalia as she began to giggle.

"What is it, chil'?" asked Mama Lu. "Wha's funny?"

"It's Madame T.," she answered. "She says the hats are to remind us that life is like a spinning wheel."

Mama Lu and Mr. John smiled as they each placed a hand on Nalia's shoulders. With a loving look, they joined their other hands together. They stood in the candle light among the spinning wheels and lifted their voices in the old Creole chant sung for so many years, now appropriate to wash away their sorrow.

Peace gon' come. Peace gon' come. Darkness flee and peace gon' come.

\- The End -

About the author –

L. E. Gay is a recreational author from Southeast Texas where he lives, works, plays, and writes. He is blessed to be supported by his wife and children. He is currently working on the next chapter of Nalia's life with Mama Lu and Mr. John.

Visit L. E. Gay online at www.legayauthor.com for additional works and news about upcoming projects. Thank you for your support!